Ghost Key

TOR BOOKS BY TRISH J. MacGREGOR

Esperanza
Ghost Key

TRISH J. MacGREGOR

Ghost Key

Book Two of The Hungry Ghosts

A Tom Doherty Associates Book

New York

GHOST KEY

Copyright © 2012 by Trish J. MacGregor

All rights reserved.

A Tor Book
Published by Tom Doherty Associates, LLC
175 Fifth Avenue
New York, NY 10010

www.tor-forge.com

Tor® is a registered trademark of Tom Doherty Associates, LLC.

ISBN 978-0-7653-2603-4 (hardcover)
ISBN 978-1-4299-4817-3 (e-book)

First Edition: August 2012

Printed in the United States of America

0 9 8 7 6 5 4 3 2 1

This one is for
Rob and Megan, again and always.

I'd also like to thank:
my sister, Mary Anderson,
Nancy Pickard and Jenean Gilstrap,
my agent, Al Zuckerman, and my editor, Beth Meacham,
for their insights and suggestions about the story.

Invasion

. . . .

Cedar Key and Homestead, Florida

Collective they stream
down the road like a swarm,
seeking ruin, with cries in the air.
Harm and destruction
secreting a chill
that swells to a violent cold dare.

. . . . . . fragile the silence
they leave in their wake
'mongst litter that blows in the breeze,
dark'ning the day
with destructive intent,
when hatred to ruin carries.

Verena Scott
http://gsp-shadow.blogspot.com

Behind every man now alive stand thirty ghosts, for that is the ratio by which the dead outnumber the living.

—Arthur C. Clarke, *2001: A Space Odyssey*

One

A small detail, something only a bartender would notice, triggered Kate's first suspicion that nothing on Cedar Key was what it appeared to be.

It was a chilly night on the island, temps hovering in the mid-thirties. The weather boys predicted frost in Gainesville fifty miles inland, with a promise of snow flurries by Sunday. No snow out here, not on this punctuation point surrounded on three sides by the Gulf of Mexico and connected to the mainland by four bridges. But a heavy fog blanketed the island, great, swelling banks of the stuff, the likes of which Kate Davis had never seen in her forty years here.

The fog pressed up against the windows of the hotel bar with the persistence of a living thing. It eddied, flowed, constantly moved. Through the glass, she could see it drifting across the weathered brick in the courtyard, wisps of it caressing the leaves of the potted plants, and wrapping around the trunks of trees like strings of pale Christmas lights.

The strange fog looked dirty, greasy as kitchen smoke.

It gave her the creeps, even though she'd always been somebody who loved cozy days or romantic nights of fog. But this fog wasn't cozy; it wasn't sexy. The thought of entering into it when she left work made her stomach clutch, got her imagination working overtime, as if something malevolent might grab her from out of this nasty gray weather.

But that was ridiculous. This was an island of sunshine and benign, lazy days. There was nothing threatening about it, or hadn't been until recently, and she hoped she was only imagining those changes in people she thought she knew.

Kate took a breath, braced her palms on the bar, and looked around to steady herself with what was bright, clear, and familiar.

The Island Hotel had stood on Second Street since it was built in 1859. It was small, like the town—something she loved about both of them—just three stories of wood and glass, thirteen guest rooms, the bar tucked like a postscript behind the lobby. The floor sloped in here and the ceiling sagged enough so that most people instinctively ducked when they walked in—and then laughed and looked around to see if anyone had noticed them doing it, embarrassed that they'd let the illusion fool them. It made them feel like old-timers when they spotted the next tourist doing it, too. The space between tables in the back room was barely wide enough to squeeze through. Kate had worked here for five years and had never been able to shake the claustrophobic feeling of these two cramped rooms. Tonight it was worse because the place was crowded. And because of the fog. The bar seemed more closed in—isolated—than she'd ever experienced before.

"Stop that," she chided herself.

Locals filled the stools along the bar, the six tiny round tables that lined the walls, and occupied the larger tables in the back room. During the winter, the island's population usually swelled from seven hundred and fifty to several thousand, but the season had been slow this year. It surprised and pleased her to see half a dozen tourists, folks in shorts, sandals, and lightweight sweaters who probably hailed from some Scandinavian country and thought this weather was balmy. Tourists tipped well, locals did not. Maybe tonight would be a prosperous night after all.

She hoped so. Her son, Rocky, wanted to take advanced placement courses in Gainesville this summer, as soon as he turned sixteen, so he could get into college earlier. He would need some sort of car or motorcycle to get to and from Gainesville. It didn't have to be a new car, just something reliable that wouldn't break down on that lonely fifty-mile stretch of road that ran from here to Gainesville.

Her old VW might work for a while, but it had more than a hundred thousand miles on it and the local mechanic had told her already that it was going to need new tires and a new clutch soon. She had a college fund for Rocky, but didn't want to dip into it for a vehicle. So for the last several months, most of her tips had been going into his car fund. With what Rocky had saved from his job at the animal rescue center, the fund now had about $1,500. She hoped for another thousand before summer.

Her boss, Bean, had offered to loan her the difference she needed. Kate loved Bean like an older brother, appreciated his offer, but considered it a last resort. Bean told her she had too much pride; Kate preferred to call it self-reliance. All she had was herself and Rocky; they needed to be able to make it on their own; she wanted to set a good example for him.

Now and then, music blasted from the jukebox, an old Wurlitzer Bean had restored to pristine condition. Banjos twanged, fiddles screeched, country tunes that made her smile at their lyrics—"Baby, come back to me, or I'll come back to haunt you, baby!" In between, the constant murmur of voices washed over her; she was used to it. She didn't need to hear these voices to know the alcoholic preferences of her customers. She knew the regulars well enough to worry about them.

For instance, Marion the librarian—not her real name, but what people called her—loved her Skip and Go Naked, a wicked mixture of ice, lime-ade, lemonade, Sprite, vodka, and beer. By the end of the night, with a few more of those in her skinny little body, she would be doing the cha-cha without music or a partner. In the past few weeks, she'd been in here every night, hitting on any man alone at the bar. Kate thought it was sad, but she also thought it was odd, because Marion hadn't behaved like that until lately. Usually, she was nice, kind of shy.

Kate wondered if it was only the alcohol, or if Marion's past had finally worn her down. She had been the librarian for only six or seven months. She was in her fifties, attractive except for the tragedy in her eyes. Kate had heard that her husband and two kids had died in a car accident in Gainesville a few years ago.

Maybe she had simply succumbed to the same thing that ailed so many of the locals: alcohol as a way of life. A lot of them drank too much, Kate thought, while she scooped their tips. They claimed at one point or another that they were on the wagon, and promptly fell off that elusive wagon five minutes later.

The fact that she cared about all of that—about all of them—meant she was getting strongly attached to the place again. She'd been born here, then left for thirteen years, and now was back again. She'd never intended to stay, but more and more, it felt like *home* to Rocky, as it did to her.

She wasn't sure if that was a good thing or not.

She didn't have time to puzzle through it. She was alone at the bar tonight, one of the waitresses had called in sick, and Richard, her lover and the other bartender, was visiting friends in Gainesville. Since the hotel kitchen had closed hours ago, the only available food was from the bar menu, sandwiches and soups, mostly, that she prepared in between making drinks.

Kate finished an order for a table in the back room, put everything on a tray, and set it down in front of her boss, Bean.

Ted "Bean" Dillon was a scarecrow of a man who owned the hotel, had renovated it and put it back on the tourist map. He was sixty years old, divorced, a teetotaler who took no guff from drunks.

She gave him an affectionate and tired smile.

"Hey, boss," she said over the blare of conversation and music. "Can you give me a hand here and take this to table three?"

Bean was sitting on a stool at the bar next to Marion, the two of them howling with laughter. He didn't acknowledge Kate's presence, much less answer her question, so she slapped her hand on the bar, playfully, to get his attention. He stopped laughing and looked at her, bushy brows rising into little peaks.

"What?" he said irritably.

Kate pulled her chin in, not liking his tone, but then she realized that he was undoubtedly tired, too.

"I've got four more drinks to make, Bean. Could you deliver this to table three?"

"Oh, really," Marion said with a roll of her pretty brown eyes. "That's what he pays *you* to do, Kate."

Taken aback by the patronizing tone, Kate still managed to joke about it. "And not nearly enough, right, Bean?"

"More like too fucking much," he shot back at her, and it didn't sound like a joke.

"What?"

"Get us another round, Kate," he ordered, in a most un-Bean-like way. "Make it a pitcher of Skip and Go Naked for both of us, and more tequila for me."

He leaned in to whisper something in Marion's ear, and whatever it was made her laugh raucously again.

Kate stepped back, confused by this change in both of them. But the bigger surprise was that Bean clearly meant for her to bring him a drink, too. It was then she noticed that he had an empty shot glass in front of him, the kind they served to the straight tequila drinkers.

"You're drinking?" she asked him, dumbfounded.

Bean didn't drink. Ever. He was nearly religious about it, having been raised by drunks. And then something strange happened to her boss's face, something that made her draw in her breath and back off another step, so she felt as if she were about to fall off something high and deep. It was a little thing, subtle, and she might not have noticed it if Bean hadn't leaned forward at that moment and glared right at her. She was accustomed to looking into drunks' eyes to see if they were tracking, to check if they could still drive home. Bean's eyes looked like nobody's eyes she'd ever seen before, just as the fog was like no other: his eyes, his kind and sea-blue eyes, had turned cruel black and shiny, like smooth, damp stones.

A chill washed through her.

He gave her a hateful look that shocked her more than his drinking did.

He snorted. "You're such a prude. I don't know how Rich stands it."

Her mouth dropped open.

"Our *drinks,* Kate?" he reminded her, with a mean sarcasm that made the librarian laugh again.

She turned her back on him, on them, hurt and angry, and a little scared, and glanced at the wall clock. Just past eleven.

She tried to convince herself that she hadn't seen what she'd thought she'd seen.

That was the answer: it hadn't happened.

Eyes couldn't do that. Bean *wouldn't* do that.

Could she make it for another two hours? If she left now, Bean might fire her, given the strange and awful mood he was in, and in spite of their long family history. She couldn't afford to lose this job. Even though she worked at Annie's Café three days a week, she doubted she would get more hours there. Business was too slow. The terrible truth was that she needed both jobs to support herself and Rocky. Without this job, there'd be no gas for her own car, much less wheels for him.

She'd been born and raised on Cedar Key. The island was in her blood, just as it had been for both of her parents. She'd left here once before, to attend Florida State in Tallahassee, but returned two years ago when her relationship with her son's father fell apart. She was qualified to teach high school English, had applied for teaching jobs on the island and in Gainesville, but neither school system was hiring. She would make some calls tomorrow, she decided, get her name on the substitute list. She needed a backup plan. The fact that it made her heart hurt to think of leaving the island was going to have to be irrelevant.

Suddenly, Bean stood beside her, shoulders twitching as though his pullover sweater were too small for him. She nearly said, "What's *wrong* with you?" But before she could, he set a bottle of tequila down hard on the counter. "I delivered the meal, now you make Marion and me another round of drinks." He leaned toward her, his gaunt face so close to hers that she smelled his reeking breath. Air hissed out through his clenched teeth. "We clear, hon?"

WTF? Hon? What was *that* about? Before she could think of a snappy reply, he winked at her, patted her cheek as though she were a young child, and swung around the corner of the bar. He settled again on his stool, head tilted toward Marion, who giggled like an infatuated teen.

The jukebox came on again, and someone shouted, "Hey, Kate, where're our drinks?"

The temptation to water down Bean's order quickly gave way to making a pitcher of Skip and Go Naked. Kate set it and the bottle of tequila in front of them, without a word, and hoped they wouldn't notice her hands trembling. *It's just the booze,* she told herself. Bean wasn't used to it; as for the librarian, Kate didn't know what her excuse was for acting like a bitch.

Still feeling stung, she turned back to the blender to add more ice. It churned constantly for the next half hour. The music and noise got louder, the room grew warmer, her feet ached from standing so long.

Her cell vibrated and beeped, and she slipped it out of the back pocket of her jeans. A text message from Rocky read: *Mom, you getting off at 1?*

That's the plan.

You need a ride home? I'm over at Jeff's, got the cart. I can pick u up if u need a ride.

Kate had forgotten he was spending the night out. His friend lived on the other side of the island. Even though Cedar Key had practically no crime to speak of, she felt uneasy about Rocky being out and about by himself at one in the morning, driving the electric golf cart. *It's a short walk 2 the houseboat, I'll be fine. Luv u*

Text if u change yr mind. We'll be up late ☺. *Luv u 2!*

Her heart swelled at the affection in his text. "Love u 2!" That was pretty good for a fifteen-year-old boy, wasn't it? He wouldn't be caught dead saying it to her face or in public, but he could safely say it in a text.

Kate smiled down at her cell phone.

She wondered if his girlfriend, Amy, was part of the staying-up-late equation. Kate liked Amy, but worried about her and Rocky's raging hormones. From the time her son was old enough to understand what sex was, Kate had been utterly frank about safe sex. He knew enough to use condoms. *But. What if. Maybe.*

As Kate slipped the cell back into her pocket, she caught sight of herself in the window, the pallor of her skin, the circles under her eyes. Strands of her blond hair had worked loose from the large clip that held it off her neck and clung to her damp cheeks. This job, she thought, was aging her quickly. She cracked open the window for some fresh air. Ribbons of fog slipped through the screen and curled quickly around her wrist and forearm like a snake seeking warmth. It felt damp, slimy, cold, deeply unpleasant. She shuddered at its touch and then frantically slapped at it. She was startled to see the ribbons break apart, like the mercury in a thermometer had done one time when she accidentally dropped it.

"That's weird!"

She knew it was an understatement even as she said it.

It wasn't just weird. It was impossible.

Kate looked up, afraid of what she might see the fog do next.

Bits of the fog hung in the air the way smoke does on a windless night, and finally dissipated. Kate slammed the window down, disturbed that she could still feel the slimy cold on her skin. But when she looked out again, she saw the fog was back, pressing against the glass, looking as if it were trying to get in, to get at her.

Bean's nuts, and now you're losing it, too, she thought. She loaded a tray with drinks and sandwiches and carried it into the back room, to a table of four boisterous tourists, and looked at the clock again. Just an hour and fifteen minutes before she could close up. *And go out in that horrible fog,* her spooked mind said to her. *Oh, shut up,* she snapped back at it. Fog was fog. She was just nervous about losing her job and it was making her jumpy.

As she headed back into the main room, she had an unobstructed view of Bean and Marion. He was cupping her face in his hands, kissing her passionately, then his fingers roamed across her throat and breasts and slid through her hair. Marion responded like a young woman of twenty, head thrown back, exposing her throat, where Bean planted his mouth and sucked at her skin like a mosquito.

As Bean succumbed to whatever urge this was, his stool tipped back and he crashed to the floor and lay there, laughing. Marion got down on her hands and knees and leaned over him, kissing his cheeks, eyelids, nose, his mouth. His arms wrapped around her, their bodies pressed so closely together that his arms looked as if they were growing out of her back. Customers kept glancing at them; some laughed nervously, one of the locals called, "Hey, get a room, dude."

"Bean," Kate said, feeling deeply disturbed.

Her boss—her "older brother"—was making a fool of himself. She hurried over to see if she could distract him enough to get him outside and then get him home. He'd feel mortified in the morning, on top of being hungover.

But before she reached them, Bean ripped open Marion's blouse. The buttons popped off one after another, his hands slipped over her breasts as she reared back, her face seized with ecstasy, her eyes rolling back in their sockets. She unzipped his jeans and fell on him again, both of them now grunting, groping, moaning, rolling. Most of their clothes vanished with their decorum, his butt the color of a full moon, her pendulous breasts bouncing, dancing.

It happened so fast that for an instant, Kate just stood there, gaping along with nearly everybody else in the bar.

It was like watching a porn movie come to life.

Bean thrust himself into Marion and they rolled across the sagging floor, faster and faster, crashing into tables and chairs. People shouted, scrambled out of their way, tried to get past them to the door. They were oblivious. Kate ran toward them, shouting at Bean to knock it off, and someone else hollered to call the cops. Bottles and glasses tumbled off the tables, shattered against the floor. Kate grabbed Bean's shoulder, he shoved her away, and she stumbled back into the jukebox. The needle tore across the record, the old Wurlitzer went silent.

In desperation, Kate picked up the pitcher of Skip and Go Naked and hurled what remained of it over Bean and Marion. She squealed, he yelped, they fell away from each other. Kate snatched her bag off the counter, ushered the last two customers, inebriated locals, out of the bar. She killed the lights and slammed the door. Let Bean clean up the place. Let him sweep up the glass, clean the grill, restock the shelves, load and run the dishwasher. Let him explain to the cops what the hell happened and what had come over him.

All she wanted to be was out of there.

No one was at the front desk, but some of the customers milled around the small lobby. As soon as they saw her, they crowded around her, demanding refunds for the drinks they hadn't finished. Some of them twitched and jerked, just as Bean had, and had eyes like Bean's, dark and shiny. She fled from them.

"Talk to the management!" she yelled.

If you can get him off the customers . . .

As she burst from the hotel into the open air, she felt tears on her cheeks, tears of anger, confusion, and shock.

What a nightmare . . .

The chilly night air bit at her. She'd left her jacket in the bar, but wasn't about to go back inside to get it. She wished she had ridden her bike or driven to work. It was a mile to the houseboat and the prospect of walking through the fog didn't appeal to her in the least. But she heard the cop siren now and didn't want to be here when the chief or one of his lackeys arrived. She loved Bean, and was sorry he'd fallen off the wagon, but she refused to run interference for him on this one.

A tendril of fog slipped around her shoulders.

"Leave me alone!" she shouted at it, and then stood in the street, feeling absurd. Yelling at fog? Throwing drinks on her boss? What would she do next, scream at the rain? Kick her lover out of her life?

Maybe she was the crazy one.

The fog seemed to back off from her, like something almost human.

Kate walked briskly, shoulders hunched, past gift shops, a restaurant, the town's only bookstore, a consignment shop, all closed down for the night. Even on Friday nights, the town turned in early, except at the hotel and over on Dock Street where most of the restaurants and bars were. But tonight the emptiness was eerie, the silence pervasive, the fog snaking across the ground, creeping in between houses and trees, rolling steadily inland from the gulf. She felt as if she moved through a black-and-white photograph, everything frozen in time, even the echo of the siren.

At the intersection, the fog caught the glow of the blinking caution light and turned it a sickly yellow. She headed right onto the shoulder of State Road 24, the only route on and off the island, in the hopes that she would see cars, people. But it was devoid of humanity. Even Island Market was locked up for the night. She felt a sudden, ridiculous urge to just keep walking, to cross the four bridges that connected Cedar Key to the mainland, and to keep right on going all the way to Gainesville.

Is that idea really so ridiculous . . . ?

Sure. Like she would do that and leave Rocky behind. Like she would walk fifty miles through a dense pine forest by herself at night.

Take him with you, go get Rocky, and run . . .

She texted him that she had closed up early and was on her way home. It was one of their oldest traditions, texting each other when they were en route to and from anywhere. She had bought him his first cell phone six years ago, when he was just nine, so they could always be in touch. For a single mother who worked erratic hours, the arrangement worked well.

Kate felt anxious until he texted a reply moments later: *You ok? I heard something went down at the bar.*

News on the island grapevine traveled at the speed of light. *I'm fine. Ignore whatever u hear.*

You sure? Jeff and I can hop in the cart and pick u up. We were listening to the police radio, mom.

Thanks, but stay put. Nearly home. Call me in the morning. Luv u

Ditto ☺

You sweetie, Kate thought. *You're a good son.*

No need to worry him. But was it a mistake not to take him up on his offer to come get her, so she wouldn't have to walk this isolated route by herself? No, she decided, if there was risk, she certainly wasn't involving Rocky or his friends in it.

Almost there. Almost home.

Kate picked up her pace, anxious to get inside her houseboat, turn on the lights, and lock the doors.

Just before the first bridge, she turned right off SR 24, the road that shot straight toward Gainesville. Richard's place stood at the end of the street, with the back bayou stretching out behind it, nearly invisible in the fog. The stuff was thicker and higher here, but thanks to the starlight, she could see the corner of the house. One bedroom, one bath, tiny kitchen. She and Rocky had lived there with Richard for a while, until the cramped quarters had gotten on everyone's nerves. Their present arrangement worked better, the houseboat tied up at the dock behind Rich's house. The three of them often had dinner together, but they had their respective privacy; she didn't have to pay tie-up fees, and she and Richard split utilities.

Kate knew Rich wasn't the love of her life—or vice versa—but she liked him. Appreciated him. And he got along well with Rocky. Buddies, not father-son.

Her cell vibrated and buzzed. She slipped it from her jacket pocket, glanced at the ID window. Bean. Was he calling to fire her? If she didn't answer, he couldn't fire her. She was grateful that Rocky wasn't home, that she could just crawl into bed and listen to the soft caress of the water against the houseboat.

Images of Bean and Marion replayed in her head. She didn't understand any of what had happened tonight. But in her gut, she knew something was seriously wrong on the island and had been for weeks. If she were honest with herself—and how could she lie to herself any more after the scene in the bar tonight?—it wasn't just what happened there.

In late January, two bodies had washed in with the tide and been discovered under a pier on Dock Street. Both victims had died of massive loss of blood. *Total* loss was more like it. She'd heard it called "bleed-out," because that was literally what had happened to them—all the blood in their bodies had rushed from every orifice.

Kate shuddered to think of it.

"Murder, right here in River City," some wag had joked, but it wasn't funny.

The newspaper barely covered the mysterious deaths; it might be bad for tourism. The police department hadn't investigated too deeply, either, at least not that she'd heard, and she wasn't sure what had happened to the bodies. Were they still in the coroner's office in Gainesville? Had they been identified?

Then there were the rumors whispered in the bar at night, locals remarking on the changes in their partners, neighbors. She hadn't thought much about that until tonight. Or about how more and more homes were for sale. Even a lot of the weekender places on the salt marsh off Gulf Boulevard were for sale. She'd blamed the economy. Now she wasn't at all sure.

The familiar cry of the hawk echoed through the air. Liberty swept down until she was just above Kate's head, her wings flapping softly. Rocky had rescued the hawk last year, when he'd found her on the beach, a hook caught in her wing. Now she practically lived with them, perched either on the roof or the balcony railing. She flew with Rocky to school, to the animal rescue facility where he worked, and rarely strayed too far from them. She knew not to touch down on Kate's shoulder unless it was padded but stayed close all the way to the houseboat.

As she was unlocking the door, Liberty screeched and shot away from her, flying fast at a tall man hurrying along the side of the house, through the low fog, toward her. Liberty dived at him, the man threw his arms up to cover his head, but she drove him to his knees. He yelled, "Get this goddamn bird away from me."

Bean, it was Bean. Kate whistled for the hawk to back off and Liberty flew to the edge of the roof and perched there, ready to dive at Bean again.

He got to his feet, brushing off his jeans. "You didn't answer your cell, Kate."

"It's not on. I figured you'd be passed out on the floor in the bar, Bean." The starlight was bright enough for her to see his face, those dark, shiny eyes glaring at her. *You're not Bean.* She wanted to say it, but didn't. To voice such a thing out loud might make it true.

His frown thrust his eyes closer together. "What're you talking about?"

"Tequila straight up? Marion and her Skip and Go Nakeds?"

"I don't drink," he said. "You know that. You left me a big mess to clean up, Kate."

What the hell. Were they living in different realities? And given all that tequila he'd consumed, how could he even be standing, much less speaking? He appeared to be completely sober. Had she imagined everything? "You made the mess, you clean it up."

"I pay you to clean up."

"No, actually you pay me to tend bar and serve the customers, Bean."

He combed his fingers back through his thick gray hair. "You're putting me in an untenable position."

"*Me?*" Hysterical laughter bubbled up inside her. "*You're* the one who screwed the librarian on the barroom floor, in front of several dozen people."

Now he looked completely confused, like some little kid who had robbed a candy store but didn't remember doing it. Was that possible? That he didn't *remember*? As incredible as that seemed, it was the only explanation. He blinked and his eyes returned to their normal color, a soft blue. The transformation shocked her. Kate stepped back, fear shuddering through her, the skin at the back of her neck tightening. Bean squeezed the bridge of his nose, shoulders twitching.

"I . . . well, that was a big mistake."

A *mistake*. She could think of better words. Gross, disgusting, sordid.

"I suppose I, uh, have some apologies that are forthcoming for my behavior. You don't know how lonely I've been since the divorce."

Kate didn't know what to say. But she suddenly wanted to put her arms around him, to console him as she had the night his divorce had become final, when he'd knocked at the door of her houseboat, bereft and inconsolable.

Bean jammed his hands into the pockets of his jacket. A muscle ticked under his eye, and his mouth moved out of synch when he spoke again. "I came here to fire you, Kate. But I . . . can't do it." Those words came out as a gasp, almost a plea. "Too much history with our families."

Now he sounded like the Bean she'd known for years. "I'll come in early tomorrow and help you clean up. I'm going to bed, Bean. I suggest you do the same."

It seemed that his face collapsed, caved in, gave way to some sort of excessive gravity that caused the corners of his mouth to plunge, that made his eyes water. His arms jerked upward, as if to embrace her. The hawk didn't like it and dived at him, shrieking with alarm. But she didn't attack. She was just warning him. Bean's eyes held Kate's, and for the briefest moment, she slipped an arm around his shoulders and in a gentle voice said, "The loneliness gets easier to deal with as time goes on, Bean."

"I hope so."

Then he backed away, his head jerking to the right, the left, as though his neck were screwed crookedly on his shoulders and he was struggling to adjust it.

Kate watched him, shaken by the change in him, by what had happened, by what he'd said, the way his eyes changed colors, by all of it. Liberty pursued him back toward the front of the house and didn't return until he'd driven away. The hawk took up her position on the houseboat roof and Kate unlocked the door and slipped quickly inside.

She locked the door, leaned against it. Then she pressed the heels of her hands against her eyes and slid to the floor, a sob rising in her throat as she struggled against a terror she couldn't define.

March 10–14

. . . .

Two
HOMESTEAD, FLORIDA

Nick Sanchez had the uneasy feeling that his life was about to take a radical turn into unexplored country. The feeling wasn't specific, and given the nature of his work, every day was a trek into unexplored country. But it felt personal.

Even as he pounded out the last two miles of four along his jogging route, his golden retriever dashing along ahead of him, an eerie sensation spread across the pit of his stomach, as if he'd eaten something that disagreed with him. The scent of citrus from the grove of orange and grapefruit trees on his right, a fragrance he usually enjoyed, seemed cloying, excessive. He glanced at the canal on his left, the water level low because of the drought, and saw only peril. When Jessie bounded down the banks, he called her back. She gave him one of those dog looks that said, *Lighten up, dude,* but after that stayed close to his side.

The late afternoon sun spilled across the fields on the other side of the canal—tomatoes, strawberries, papayas, mango trees, everything transformed to a soft, shimmering gold. From here, it didn't look as if it were all withering in the unseasonal heat. But he could almost smell the parched plants screaming for rain, the dryness rising from the ground itself, almost smell it drifting in the air over Homestead and the surrounding countryside as though it were as permanent as the sky. The dryness reminded Sanchez of his childhood in Miami's Little Havana, the stink of scorched linen, burned *arepas,* black beans sucked dry and sticking to the bottom of a pan because his mother was too drunk to tend to anything.

His mother had died last year of liver and heart complications, a sixty-five-year-old gringa from North Carolina who never should have married his Cuban father. She had hated Little Havana, South Florida, and most everything in Cuban culture. Stranger in a strange land, that was his mother. Although she'd been emotionally absent for much of his childhood because of her alcoholism, they had been close.

Sanchez felt her around sometimes, heard her quick, impatient footsteps in his hallway, knew that she had fussed with stuff in his house. When he had mentioned this to his father, Emilio had gone ballistic, and accused Sanchez of subscribing to the same superstitious bullshit that afflicted so many Cubans, the belief that the dead could actually communicate with the living. Now he and his father rarely spoke.

His old man, pushing seventy-five, lived alone in the tiny house where Sanchez had been born. Sanchez's older sister, Nicole, a professor of cultural studies at the University of Miami, and her biologist husband, Carlos, lived eight miles from him and oversaw his care. Sanchez paid for the bulk of Emilio's expenses—a private nurse who came in three times a week to make sure he was taking his meds; a full-time housekeeper who purchased his groceries, cooked, and kept the house in order; a gardener; and a driver who took him to and from his domino games in a Little Havana park every afternoon. Sanchez's only condition was that he didn't have to see his father except for an obligatory weekly visit, when he basically made sure that everyone he paid was doing his or her job.

His old man knew that Sanchez worked for some ultrasecretive government agency that utilized his psychic ability and paid him enough that he could afford these expenses. But he'd never been able to reconcile the fact that Sanchez could see what he could not and had been able to do so since before he learned to walk. The one time Sanchez had tried to explain his job—that his mind reached out to view distant locations and people, usually based on geographic coordinates or random numbers—his father had exploded with laughter. *Eres un loco, Nico.*

You're a crazy, Nick.

Yeah. Bad memory, he thought, and stopped to gulp water from his aluminum bottle. He poured some into the plastic cup he carried for Jessie on his daily runs and she lapped it up. It apparently wasn't enough and she trotted down the bank to drink from the canal. Sanchez, still unable to shake his unease, hurried after her like a fretful parent.

The bank sloped steeply; the stones and dirt were loose, and he stumbled over something and lost his balance. Sanchez pitched forward, lost his grip on his water bottle, and landed hard on his hands and knees a foot behind Jessie, startling her. Her head turned and she didn't see what Sanchez did, a water moccasin whipping toward her through the water. Sanchez scrambled to his feet, threw his arms around her, and pulled her out of the way seconds before the snake struck the spot where she'd been standing. He grabbed hold of her collar and they ran back up the hill.

At the top, Sanchez dropped to his knees and doubled over, panting as hard as she was. She nudged him with her nose, then licked his face and hands until he slung an arm around her neck and pressed his forehead to hers. "You scared the shit outta me, girl."

She whined and pawed the ground.

"The run is over for the day, Jess." He pushed to his feet and walked over to the edge of the canal, Jessie trotting along behind him. He could see his bottle down there near the water, the aluminum glinting in the light. The snake wasn't in sight. "Stay, Jessie. Please. There's still water in that bottle and we've got a two-mile walk back to the car. Stay."

She sat down and didn't move as Sanchez started down the bank again, anxiously scanning the ground and the canal for the snake. He wondered if it was the cause of his earlier unease. The bite of a water moccasin could be fatal if not treated immediately. Losing Jessie, a stray he'd found two days after his mother's death, would definitely hurl him into an emotional tailspin, but he suspected it didn't qualify as a radical turn in life. He decided the snake was a warning. But about what?

He snatched up the water bottle and hurried back up the bank, where Jessie waited, tail wagging. They shared the remainder of the water and headed back toward the car. During the walk, Sanchez obsessed about the possible significance of the close call with the snake. He obsessed about every enigma he encountered, his brain chewing away at it until he found an answer. His mother used to comment on it, Nicole kidded him about it. But he couldn't help it. Some mysteries begged for answers.

The most obvious meaning was danger to someone he loved. Right now, his love life was a joke. The woman he'd been involved with during his first year of grad school at the University of Florida, the woman he'd thought he was going to marry, had walked out on him the same day his mother had died, February 13 of last year. He'd dated a few women since then, mostly women he met through his boss. But the moment they learned he was a remote viewer, they were only interested in getting readings from him. Sanchez invariably explained that he didn't give personal psychic readings, that his ability didn't work like that. But it didn't matter. These women hounded him until he simply stopped calling.

Family? Just his sister, brother-in-law, and his father. Maybe the snake portended danger to one of them? Or to Jessie? None of that felt right.

If he interpreted the incident like a dream, then in Jungian psychology, his major and grad school study, a snake represented both fertility and power, healing, spiritual activities, and what was hidden in the unconscious. Given the nature of remote viewing, which dealt with everything that was hidden, he supposed the snake incident could point to danger through his work. But in the sixteen months Sanchez had worked for ISIS, he'd never encountered physical danger, only psychic risk.

A few months after he'd been hired, Bob Delaney, his boss and monitor, gave him a target that turned out to be on the international space station. Sanchez remembered peering out a window and seeing the sunlit Earth swirling below him, its oceans and land masses crisply visible. Vertigo gripped him and he bolted from the viewing, puking. Maybe the snake portended something like that.

And maybe not. He didn't have a feel for this one way or another.

He and Jessie finally reached his lime-green VW convertible, the only car parked on the shoulder of a two-lane dirt road just outside town. He had bought it the day he landed the job at ISIS, and named her Gwen after Gwyneth Paltrow, with whom he had fallen in love after seeing *Sliding Doors*. The movie remained one of his all-time favorites, a portrayal of the probabilities his work entailed, a place his old man referred to as voodoo land, as though it were one of the Disney worlds.

Sanchez drove Gwen fast across town, Jessie riding in the passenger seat, her head hanging out the window. He pulled up in front of an old concrete barracks where he had spent eight to ten hours a day for the last sixteen months. ISIS headquarters, three connected concrete barracks that looked like neglected postscripts of another age, had survived Hurricane Andrew in 1992 when it had slammed into Homestead with winds in excess of 175 miles per hour. What a perfect metaphor for ISIS, he thought, the ugly Stargate stepsister that initially scrambled for funding, validation, oxygen.

Stargate's remnants had endured in a vastly different form and landed enough funding to pay eleven remote viewers and half a dozen monitors. Tighter protocols had been implemented and yet the information gleaned by individual viewers didn't always have to be verified by other viewers. At ISIS, the process was less of a team effort than it had been at Stargate or its earlier incarnation, Grill Flame. Monitors still assisted the individual viewers during sessions, provided feedback when necessary, recorded and videotaped the sessions, and trained neophyte viewers. Five of the viewers, including Sanchez, were well versed in extended remote viewing—ERV— which entailed venturing deeply into a target site and staying there for long periods of time. As a result of these changes, ISIS had a higher success rate than Stargate ever did—nearly 90 percent.

Sanchez nosed his VW into a parking space, grabbed his pack, and whistled for Jessie. She trotted alongside him, her reddish-gold fur shining in the last of the light, and they headed toward the building. Shower, clean clothes, a bite to eat, then on to the target that Delaney would have for him. Jessie would be there with him during the viewing. She usually was; Delaney allowed it. He considered the dog a stabilizing influence. Maybe she was.

The only thing Sanchez had ever picked up on her was that she had belonged to a large family that could barely feed themselves, much less a young dog. So one sunny day, they had dropped her off in downtown Homestead, to make her own way. When he'd found her outside ISIS headquarters, she was emaciated, covered with fleas, and he'd adopted her on the spot.

Sanchez slid his ID through the slot, and the door beeped as it opened. Jessie trotted over to the large bowl that bore her name, next to the water cooler, and lapped in her usual pristine way, not a drop of water splashed to the floor, no fuss, no mess.

The old barracks ceilings always prompted him to duck. Sanchez didn't really need to do it; he stood six feet and the ceiling was seven. But Bob Delaney, a former pro basketball player who lumbered in from another room, had barely two inches between his skull and the ceiling and had developed a permanent hunch in his shoulders.

"Hey, Sanchez, you're twenty minutes late."

"Had a run-in with a snake."

Delaney fixed his massive black hands to his hips. "A snake. Well, if you'd jog on the running track at the park, you wouldn't run into snakes. Ten minutes, downstairs."

"Fifteen, I need to shower and grab a snack."

Delaney slipped his hand in the pocket of his jeans, brought out a dog treat, and tossed it to Jessie. She caught it in midair and he grinned like a proud father, as though he had taught her how to do that. Sanchez suspected Delaney had picked up info about her that he hadn't shared. He could be like that at times, a hoarder who evaluated the treasure before he placed a value on it. He'd been a part of the remote viewing program for twenty years and undoubtedly knew tricks Sanchez had never imagined.

An injury on the basketball courts at age twenty-eight—Sanchez's age now—had apparently blown open some psychic center in Delaney. Besieged by visions that poured through him 24/7, Delaney ended up on a shrink's couch. Luckily for him, the shrink was a consultant to Stargate, and Delaney was eventually recruited.

"Fifteen, then," he said, and brought out another treat for Jessie and wagged it in the air. "So who's it going to be? Treatless man or me, Jess?"

Without any hesitation, she trotted after Delaney. But in the doorway, she paused, glanced back at Sanchez, and barked as if to reassure him it wasn't about affection. It was about these utterly incredible treats.

Sanchez joined Delaney and Jessie in pod three. It consisted of two windowless rooms—control room and viewing room—and the walls were painted in soft lavender and pale blues, colors deemed to be conducive to a meditative state. Sanchez settled into the comfortable chair against the north wall of the viewing room, clipped his mike to the collar of his shirt, and Delaney disappeared into the adjoining control room. They went through the usual tests with the mike and speakers, mounted on the walls to either side of his chair, and everything worked fine. Jessie sat to his right, attentive, ears twitching. On the table in front of him were a sketchpad and pencil.

"Okay, Sanchez, cool down and then let's get started."

Every remote viewer had his or her own techniques for sinking into the zone. Alternate-nostril breathing worked for Sanchez. He had learned it as a kid in yoga classes he had gone to with his mother when she was in a rehab phase. It brought the hemispheres of the brain into synch, right brain images flowing into left brain analysis, and vice versa. He spent several minutes counting himself deeper, deeper, into the place where there was no time, no space, just a seamless whole. He flashed a thumbs-up to Delaney.

"All right, Sanchez, our target is thirteen-thirteen."

The numbers immediately threw him. Delaney knew about his aversion to the number thirteen. Not only had the thirteenth day marked his mother's death and his lover walking out of his life, Nicole's birthday was on April 13, Emilio's fell on May 13, and his own birthday fell on November 13. He couldn't view thirteens. His superstition was simply too great.

"I can't do this target, not with all those thirteens, Delaney."

"Sure you can. Just focus."

"Assign something different to it."

"C'mon, Sanchez. You know I can't do that. We'd have to do an entirely different target."

The numbers didn't mean anything to anyone but Delaney, who assigned numbers to specific targets. His intention, focus, and ability to clearly visualize the targets in his own head as he assigned the numbers were paramount to the unit's success rate. Random numbers were Sanchez's favorite way to remote view. Numbers possessed a purity, a psychic resonance, that called to him, pulled him in. Even though he disliked the idea of double thirteen, of thirteen anything, even though he hesitated, fighting with himself, his curiosity and resolve won. It was time to shove past his stupid superstitions.

"Okay, okay. I'll try. Give me a few more minutes."

He moved himself into the zone again through breathing exercises, then said, "There."

And he *was* there, near or on an island, that's what it felt like. He appeared to be on a pier raised above the street level that afforded him a view of a vast expanse of water, with sailboats, speedboats, kayaks, fishing boats. There seemed to be twin columns of smoke wafting up through the haze in the distance, but he couldn't tell what generated them. Off to his left were colorful wooden buildings raised on wooden or concrete pilings above the water. He shifted his perceptions toward the street, so he could see the people, cars, shops. He tried to see the names of stores that he could Google later, but it was like trying to read a book in a dream. The signs blurred, the letters melted together like wax.

People, he thought, and felt himself attracted to the energy of a red-headed woman who walked quickly, with purpose and determination, along the sidewalk. He came up behind her. With his eyes still shut, he picked up the pencil and started sketching: her clothing, the loose flow of her shiny hair, the shape of her body. He sketched the cars parked on either side of the road, the shops, restaurants, pier. He kept hoping to glimpse a street sign, license plate, something that would help him pinpoint the location.

Delaney now fired questions at him. What was the temperature? What did the shadows tell him about the time of day? What did he smell, taste? And on it went like that, not a constant barrage of questions, but intermittent questions, to keep him on track, to remind him of the goal. *Explore the target in as much detail as possible and report back.*

He followed the redhead again, her flaming hair pulled back with a tortoiseshell clip, the ends bouncing against the collar of her sweater. She moved with the grace of a dancer, carried a large bag over her shoulder, red and brown, like her outfit, sweater, jeans, interesting brown shoes. *Alpargatas,* a Latino thing.

He jotted the word on his sketchpad because he didn't quite know how to draw them, sandals but not sandals in the traditional sense. Woven at the toes, open at the back, they could be worn with or without socks. His mother used to wear them, one of the few details of Cuban culture that she liked. The redhead wore socks. She looked like a latter-day hippie.

The sidewalk emptied into a large marina parking lot with trucks, boats. He heard the cries of gulls. He looked out over the water again and realized that what he'd thought was haze might actually be fog. He no longer saw the twin columns of smoke. He shifted his perception again so that he was in front of the woman now. Her wild red hair framed a lovely, pale face with a defiant mouth, parrot-green eyes, and freckles that crossed the bridge of her nose. Certain that she was integral to this target, Sanchez moved in closer to her. He immediately sensed something inside her, a raw, primal power, an evil so terrible that he nearly bolted out of the viewing.

Was *she* evil? Or did the evil control her, like a cult, a terrorist? He immediately wondered if *she* was a terrorist.

Then the evil seemed to become aware of him and whipped toward him, just as the water moccasin had whipped toward Jessie, and attacked with a fierce brutality. It *invaded* him, choked him. It wanted his body. He fled the viewing gasping for air, Jessie in his face, barking, licking his cheeks. Delaney rushed into the room. "Christ, Sanchez. What's going on? You okay?" Delaney grasped Sanchez's shoulders, shook him.

Sanchez threw his arms up, breaking Delaney's grasp on his shoulders. "Don't *do* that."

Delaney's arms fell to his sides. "Okay, man, whatever. Calm down, okay? Just calm down, breathe. Deep breaths." He patted the air, and talked to Sanchez as though he were a wild, intractable animal.

As his breathing evened out, Delaney passed him a bottle of water. "What happened?"

"What happened is that you shouldn't have assigned me a target with double thirteens," he snapped.

"It fit the target, Sanchez."

"I don't give a shit what it fits. Just don't use it again. It threw me. I could've gone in deeper with a different number."

"Maybe. But maybe you got exactly what we needed." He paged through the sketches Sanchez had made. "Who's the woman?"

He didn't know. He suspected she wasn't the evil he had sensed, but that she might be its ward, its slave, its indentured servant. He didn't have any idea what that meant. When he said as much, Delaney looked interested.

"How old is she?" he asked.

"Barely old enough to vote." But pretty. And intriguing. "I think she's part of a terrorist cell that steals bodies."

"Bodies?" Delaney lifted his eyebrows. "You mean, that steals identities."

"No, I mean bodies. This cell steals bodies."

"What the hell does that mean, Sanchez?"

"I don't know. It was choking me."

"It. What do you mean by *it*?"

He shook his head. "I don't have any idea what it means. It felt like . . ." Like *what*? He struggled to find the right words, a comparison, an analogy, and the full horror of it struck him, the way this thing, this *evil*, had slipped into his consciousness, tasting it, tasting him, as if the taste alone would lead it to what it coveted most—his body. When he said all this aloud, it sounded nuts.

"We'll come back to that. What about location?"

"It feels like a tourist place, maybe an island. So what's the target? I should at least be entitled to know what kind of target deserves a double thirteen."

"The FBI asked us for help," Delaney said.

"*What*? Why? They don't put any stock whatsoever in remote viewing."

"True. But they know we get results and that's what they want. Thirteen bodies have been discovered in two landfills—one north of Gainesville and another outside of Ocala."

Sanchez instantly felt superstitious again. More thirteens.

"Two of the bodies had been in the water for quite some time before they were taken to the landfill. They were too badly decomposed for the autopsies to turn up much of anything other than genders and approximate ages. But the autopsies on the other eleven bodies indicated that they'd died of the same thing, massive bleed-outs, possibly caused by an unknown virus. Two county coroners did the initial autopsies, the FBI confirmed their findings. Not all the victims have been identified yet, but so far, they come from various states and range in age from early twenties to late sixties. The bureau boys suspect it's a biological weapon and need to know where this terrorist cell is located."

"The best I can tell you now is that the cell is located on or near a tourist island."

"In Florida."

"That makes sense, given where these bodies were found, but I didn't pick up anything specific about a state."

"Okay, let's assume it's Florida." Delaney went through the sketches again and picked up the one that showed the twin columns of smoke. "What's this?"

"It was something I could see from the pier. But the air was hazy or foggy, so it might be an optical illusion."

Delaney put a question mark at the top of the page, set it aside, then went over to one of the wall cabinets and brought out a rolled-up map. He smoothed it open on Sanchez's desk, a huge map of Florida. So damn many islands, Sanchez thought. They ran up and down both coasts, dozens of tourist destinations. And at the foot of the peninsula lay the Florida Keys, with more than 1,700 islands.

"What we have to ask ourselves," Sanchez said, "is how distant from the cell location would the terrorists haul the bodies?"

"The logical answer is far, far away."

"Terrorists aren't necessarily logical."

"Unless this is how they spread the bacteria or virus."

"Shit," Sanchez muttered, and he and Delaney looked at each other. "This could take months."

"We don't have months, amigo. For all we know, the virus has contaminated anyone who has come into contact with those bodies and we've got an incipient epidemic. Let's work on it separately tonight, with maps."

"Dowsing? You're much better at it than I am."

"But you've got a connection with the redhead now." With that, Delaney returned to the cabinet, pulled out another map of Florida, and handed it to Sanchez. "I've got a folder of photos you can take with you."

"Photos of . . . ?"

"The bodies. See you back here in the morning."

Sanchez had bought his home shortly after he'd been recruited by ISIS. It was supposed to be where he and the love of his life were going to live after they got married. He had carefully refurbished the place, landscaped the acre with fruit trees and flowers, had fixed up the swimming pool, installed a hot tub, screened the patio. The three bedrooms that he'd furnished in rattan and pine now echoed with solitude and loneliness. So as soon as he and Jessie were inside, he popped an Esperanza Spalding CD into the player and cranked up the volume. Now that the rooms rocked, he could think.

He fed Jessie, gobbled down his Chinese takeout, fixed himself a *cortadito*—a Cuban espresso with a dollop of milk—and spread open the map. His eyes roamed from one Florida coast to the other, south to Key West, north again to Ocala and Gainesville. He briefly shut his eyes, conjuring the image of the redhead. "Where are you?" he whispered, and opened his eyes again.

He positioned his left hand about an inch above the map, then moved it slowly eastward, down along the coast, all the way to Miami. Not a single flare of warmth, no tingle, nothing. But as soon as he moved his hand over the Keys, the center of his palm started to itch, then burn. *You're hot, Nick. Which island?* Even though the map was large, a foot square, the Keys were smaller than the tip of his index finger. He couldn't get a fix this way. He rose quickly, scanned the lower part of the map, enlarged the Upper Keys, printed it.

When he passed his hand over Key Largo, he felt the itch, the burning again. He circled Key Largo, returned to the regular map, and moved his hand slowly up the west coast of Florida, into the Panhandle, then south again. He felt something around Sanibel Island, a popular tourist destination near Fort Myers, and around Captiva, where writer John D. MacDonald had lived for years. He circled these islands, too.

He opened the folder Delaney had given him, turned it upside down, and the photos of the bodies slipped out. The ghastly pictures had been taken wherever the bodies had been unearthed, and some were clearer and more detailed than others. He'd never really thought about what it meant to *bleed out,* but from the looks of these photos, the victims had bled from every orifice, even from the pores of their skin.

Sanchez taped the photos to the wall until he had a row of seven and another row of six. Each photograph was labeled by gender and approximate age. He stared at the first one, a woman between the ages of twenty-five and thirty-five. He placed his index finger inches above Gainesville and kept staring at the picture as he spoke. "I need the path you took from where you died to where you were found."

The CD finished. As silence settled through the rooms, he could hear the house breathing around him. Jessie had climbed onto the couch in the family room and fallen asleep. The AC clicked on. Minutes ticked by. A lot of minutes. Nothing happened. Frustrated, he gave up in favor of a shower, a short nap.

Sanchez fell asleep in a chair in front of the TV, and dreamed of the twin columns of smoke, of the redhead with her freckles and seductive mouth, of the evil that had *tasted* him. But it was Jessie's soft growls that woke him. The dog was sitting up on the couch, staring at the French doors that led out onto the porch. The TV was still on, muted, some rerun of Jon Stewart.

"What is it, girl?" he whispered.

She climbed off the couch, the fur along her back standing up, and moved slowly and quietly over to Sanchez's chair, and sat up against his legs, as if protecting him. Her gaze moved from the French doors to the bookcase, and he suddenly heard the soft sigh of footsteps, his mother's footsteps. But never had he heard them so clearly. The sound moved away from him toward the room he used as his office, then came back toward him. Jessie's eyes moved in the direction of the sounds, convincing Sanchez that the dog could see his mother's ghost.

Jenean didn't materialize, not in the way Sanchez had grown up believing that ghosts took shape. She seemed to grow out of the books on the shelves, like a fictional character suddenly given life through some strange alchemy. His dead mother, in brilliant color, looked as real and solid as the dog, and not much changed from his childhood memory of her, specifically during that single magnificent year when she hadn't been drinking.

Her thick, chestnut hair fell in shiny waves to just below her ears. Her hazel eyes smiled, thin lines bracketed her expressive mouth. She wore yoga clothes, black cotton pants and a royal blue tank top that showed off her beautiful shoulders. After so many months of hearing her footsteps, of sensing her presence, Sanchez was freaked that he actually could see her. He had been psychic all his life, but had never seen a ghost. Was there a protocol here? Could she hear him? See him as clearly as he saw her?

"Mom?" His voice ground out of him, as if he'd swallowed gravel.

"Nicole has your answer."

His sister? How could she have an answer to this? Sanchez finally moved, was able to manipulate his body enough so it sat forward. "You've got to be able to see things I can't, Mom. *You* tell me where this redhead is. What's going on?"

She turned her head, as if talking to someone Sanchez couldn't see, nodded, and looked at him again. "Nick, I'm . . . trying to move on here, where I am. But I can't do it without . . . making reparations for what I didn't do as your mother, for the ways in which I failed you. My friend Charlie says I have to follow certain rules, so that's what I'm trying to do."

Charlie? Who the hell was Charlie? "You don't have to make amends with me, okay? I came to terms with all of it before you died."

"You did, Nick, but I didn't. It's what we carry with us into death that holds us back. The issues, the guilt, the what-ifs . . ."

Sanchez, on his feet now, stabbed his finger at the air. "You tell this goddamn Charlie to butt out, Mom. It's between you and me, not you and me and some third party, okay?" He realized he was yelling at his mother's ghost, that he sounded like a candidate for a padded cell. His arm dropped to his side, his voice broke. When he spoke again, it was in a whisper. "Jesus, Mom, just give me a hint."

"Charlie says I'm not allowed to . . ." She cocked her head to the right, perhaps listening to this Charlie guy again, then made a dismissive gesture, and stepped toward Sanchez. "Nicole has the first piece of the puzzle. The redhead's name is Maddie. Charlie Livingston is her grandfather. He loves Esperanza Spalding, too, and says you should try some Google combos with all these words and that he'll probably be kicked out of the chasers because of what I'm saying."

She laughed then, a quick, almost musical sound, and faded into the bookshelf.

Sanchez collapsed into the chair, every light in the house flared, the CD came back on, by itself, and Esperanza Spalding sang as though her heart were breaking, "I Know You Know."

Three

Mile after mile, town after town, straight up through central Florida, Wayra pursued Dominica's scent and that peculiar vibrational frequency unique to her. He felt certain he was closing in on her, that his long, lonely journey was nearing an end. Then, outside of Ocala, he suddenly lost her trail.

It meant she had seized and killed someone in this area. But why here? Ocala struck him as atypical of the places where Dominica usually seized a host. It was too rural, all rolling emerald hills and exclusive horse farms that raised and sold Thoroughbreds. The pool of potential victims seemed too small. Gainesville, thirty-five miles north, impressed him as more her style. Home to the University of Florida, its population numbered over a hundred thousand, most of them students, young and healthy and, most importantly, probably sexually active.

He pulled his old pickup truck to the shoulder of the two-lane county road and got out. He inhaled the chilly air, drawing it deeply into his lungs. The powerful sweetness of pine mingled with the odor of horses from the surrounding farms. He didn't detect a hint of Dominica. Other aromas reached him, though, textured smells too subtle for his human senses to identify.

Wayra glanced to his right, into a thicket of pines so dense the sunlight barely penetrated. He couldn't even make out shadows pooled among the trees. Had she seized some hiker in there? He could almost see her, stalking some unsuspecting soul, moving along behind him, as subtle as a shadow, then slamming into him from behind, seizing him so completely he never had a chance to fight.

He moved closer to the edge of the trees and considered shifting. In his other form, his heightened senses might be able to pick up her trail. But it would mean abandoning his truck for a while, probably not a wise idea. Sporadic traffic sped along the road, and if a cop saw the empty truck, it could be impounded. Right now, he needed the vehicle. It moved faster than he could in either of his forms. He would have to find a safer place to shift, he thought, and thrust his hands into his jacket pockets and turned away from the trees.

It wasn't the first time in all these months that Dominica had eluded him. When she'd fled Esperanza, Ecuador, last October, she'd flown to Miami first, then had driven to Chicago, Santa Fe, Denver, Atlanta, using these large cities to confuse him, lose him, and conceal her activities. In each of these cities, she had killed someone—a victim here, two victims there, never enough of them in one place to prompt the local police to make inquiries in other states, for authorities to connect the dots. Each time she killed, he lost her trail. Then he would have to comb through local Web sites, searching for unexplained deaths in that particular area during the last few weeks or months. In most instances, Dominica's victims bled out, so that was the search term he used for the unexplained deaths.

But because bleed-outs could occur for a variety of reasons, this process initially had taken him in directions that wasted time. He now knew to discount bleed-outs that occurred in hospitals, since those deaths usually had a natural cause. Besides, Dominica disliked hospitals nearly as much as she did cemeteries; both reminded her of what she was, a hungry ghost desperately in need of a tribe of her own kind. Motels were Dominica's favorite location—the privacy, the element of the forbidden, the likelihood that the body wouldn't be found immediately. Her next favorite location was in or around upscale bars and restaurants because they provided her with such a variety of potential victims.

Wayra pulled back onto the road and continued north toward the town. The horse farms gave way to commercial areas—family-owned businesses, then the usual strip malls and small shopping centers. He passed a few bars, redneck hotspots, and several local restaurants that boasted cuisines of smoked ribs, steaks, and home fries. None of these places would interest Dominica. The best he could hope for right now was that a synchronicity would lead him to yet another location where one of her victims had bled out and died. Whenever these synchronicities happened, they told him he was on the right track, searching for her in the right way.

In Santa Fe, he had gone into a taco place for a bite to eat and just happened to pick up a free newspaper that featured a story about a missing man. His photo was included; he could have been Wayra's twin brother. Right then, he knew the man had been one of Dominica's victims, that she'd seized him because of the resemblance. In her twisted mind, it was her way of killing Wayra.

He had driven over to the man's house, picked up his scent, and tracked his body to a spot in the desert, where much of it had been consumed by predators. But there, he had found Dominica's scent again.

And so it had gone, city after city, state after state, for months.

How many times through the centuries had Dominica seized men who resembled him? Their history extended back so far in time that it horrified Wayra to even consider how many hundreds or thousands of men had been seized and bled out simply because they reminded Dominica of him. At times during this long journey, their mutual history and his lapse in judgment had haunted him. How had he *ever* loved her?

Yet, when they had been lovers in Spain in the fifteenth century, everything had been different. He had already been a shifter for more than two hundred years and she was a beautiful woman who had not yet been corrupted by the evil of hungry ghosts, *brujos*.

Before he entered the Ocala city limits, Wayra noticed a landfill where dozens of tractors were clearing trees and moving great mountains of earth and trash. Three state police cars and an ambulance blocked the entrance to the area. Unusual, but as far as he knew, Dominica hadn't ever killed anyone in a landfill. However, if she had a tribe already and if members of her tribe had seized humans, then a landfill was an ideal spot to get rid of a body. Was it worth a look?

In Atlanta when he had lost her trail, he had started his Google search with broad terms: *unsolved deaths southeast U.S. 2009.* This had yielded a ridiculous number of links, so he had whittled them down by narrowing the time frame to the last four months in the Atlanta area, and stipulating the cause of death. By checking each link, each story, he had found two possibilities that fit her MO: a convenience store parking lot north of Atlanta and a seedy motel in downtown Atlanta. The first location yielded nothing. But the motel surrendered its secrets—her distinctive echo, the imprint of her essence, her scent. He even found the room where the death had occurred, number 1313. Since thirteen was significant in the history of Esperanza, the room number had been confirmation. A Mexican cleaning woman he'd befriended had told him the death happened in late November, around the holidays.

Once he had found Dominica's imprint in Atlanta, he was able to track her southward to Florida and then across the state to Naples and northward along Florida's west coast. It seemed a long way for her to go without indulging her sexual needs, but perhaps she knew he was close. After all, the connection between them was not easily broken. It spanned centuries and worked in both directions.

He passed the landfill, intending to drive through downtown and wander around in some of the neighborhoods to see if he could get a fix on her. But the landfill nagged at him. A quick look, he thought, that was all he needed.

Wayra turned into a shopping center, nosed into a parking spot, and got out. His pickup wouldn't attract any attention here and he doubted it would be stolen. Ocala didn't impress him as a high-crime area. But in the event he was wrong, car thieves wouldn't find much. He traveled lightly—no laptop, a prepaid cell phone, a pack with three changes of clothes and shoes, a few toiletries. His money, a debit card, and passport were zipped inside a pocket in his jeans. He purchased anything else he needed.

He slipped his keys in another zippered pocket, then headed toward the thicket of trees between the shopping center and the landfill. His long, narrow shadow moved alongside him, a silent companion. His shadow profile looked crisp, long hair gathered in a ponytail that bounced against the collar of his jacket, his nose and long legs visible against the ground.

"You again," he murmured to his shadow.

The shadow didn't reply; it never did. At one point in this journey, his loneliness had been so profound that he'd started talking to his shadow, speculating about what Dominica was looking for, what he would do when he found her, how long this pursuit might last, and why the hell he was bothering. In voicing everything he'd been thinking, he realized he already had some of the answers.

Dominica wanted what she had always wanted—a city of ghosts, specifically those ghosts known as *brujos* that knew how to exert power over the living by seizing them, controlling their bodies, and living out their mortal lives. Dominica and her kind lusted for physical existence and all its sensual pleasures. In Esperanza, where her tribe of *brujos* had supposedly been the largest in the world, more than sixty thousand strong, she had nearly succeeded in creating such a city. But last June, on the summer solstice, she was defeated and most of her tribe had been annihilated or had fled Ecuador. Her arrogance had been so great that she'd never considered the possibility that the thousands of individuals who had lost loved ones to *brujos* would coalesce into an army of twenty thousand and fight her kind.

Her other desire was someone to love. Nearly anyone would do. For a hundred and thirty-seven years, that someone had been Wayra. Then there was Ben, a man she had seized at the turn of the twentieth century, bled out, and, when he had died, he and Dominica had spent more than a century together. He had been annihilated in a hotel room in Key Largo by Maddie's aunt.

Shortly after Dominica's defeat, in July or August, Dominica had seized Maddie Livingston as retribution against her aunt for obliterating Ben, for aiding in the liberation of Esperanza. Wayra hadn't sensed that Maddie had been seized and no one in her family had realized it, either. He guessed that Dominica had scattered her essence through the young woman's cells, tissue, and blood, and hidden like a dormant virus. She undoubtedly had spied on him, on all of them, biding her time until she could figure out what to do next.

Then in early October, Dominica forced Maddie to write her aunt Tess a note that she was going to Quito for a week and had left. Or, at any rate, that was how Wayra had pieced things together.

Several days had passed before Tess's suspicions had taken hold, and by then, Dominica had a significant head start. Tess, her lover, and her mother planned to team up with Wayra to search for Maddie, but they were so involved emotionally he felt they would only slow him down. So he'd decided to do it on his own. He'd left suddenly the second week in October and had been on the move ever since.

He reached the edge of the trees, mostly pines and oaks. A cool breeze strummed the branches, his shadow companion melted into the shade. He could hear the tractors now, growling beasts that churned through the landfill, stirring up dust, old smells. Vultures circled overhead, smaller birds cried out.

"You'll have to get right into where they're digging, Wayra." Charlie Livingston materialized beside him, decked out as usual in his white shirt, slacks, hat, and white shoes. His Ben Franklin glasses stuck up from his shirt pocket, a fat Cuban cigar was tucked behind his right ear, and he snapped his silver Zippo lighter constantly. "And you'll have to shift to really get a sense of it."

"I'd appreciate it, Charlie, if you would save me a whole bunch of time and just tell me where Dominica is."

"I don't know where she is. Just because I'm dead, it doesn't mean I know everything. Besides, even if I *did* know, I wouldn't be able to tell you. The chasers are threatening to kick me off the council. I'm on probation and now they're monitoring me."

"On *probation*?" Wayra laughed. "What's that mean?"

"Nothing good, I can tell you that."

Charlie, dead more than ten years, looked as solid and real as the trees. They'd traveled together intermittently since he'd left Esperanza, and Charlie often provided hints and clues about where to go, new insights into Dominica's agenda. As Maddie's grandfather, he had a vested interest in Wayra's search. But he was also a member of the light chasers, the consortium of evolved souls who had been fighting *brujos* for millennia. Charlie and the other chasers knew that unless Dominica was annihilated once and for all, she would surface elsewhere. She would organize hapless ghosts into a formidable force and the struggle between good and evil would continue ad nauseam.

Wayra often wondered what was more important to Charlie—finding his granddaughter or finding Dominica. "Why're you on probation?"

Charlie made an impatient gesture, slipped out the cigar, lit it with a flourish, and puffed. The smoke was real enough so that Wayra could smell it. "For meddling, that's what they called it. But honestly, Wayra, if I hadn't meddled, if the chasers hadn't opened Esperanza to transitional souls, where would we be?"

Maybe in a better place, Wayra thought, but didn't say it. For centuries, Esperanza had been a nonphysical location for transitionals, the souls of people at the brink of death. There, they decided if they wanted to return to their bodies or move on into the afterlife. *Brujos*, the ancient ones like Dominica and her former tribe, had preyed on these souls, seized them, and lived out their mortal lives. Five hundred years ago, the chasers had brought Esperanza into the physical world in the hopes this would end *brujo* domination. It had, for a while.

But in those intervening centuries, Dominica and the ancient ones had evolved, learned to seize humans, control them, had used them in despicable ways. They had built a virtual city outside of Esperanza, gained numbers and power, and a decade ago had begun preying on the people of Esperanza again. And last year, the chasers had opened the city to two transitional souls—Tess and the man who became her lover, both of whom were in comas. And that was the beginning of the end for Dominica's tribe.

"Don't the chasers want Dominica found?" Wayra asked.

"Of course they do. But the council has all these incredibly arcane rules about how things should be done. And, well, I'm sorry, but a lot of the council members haven't been physical for centuries. They don't understand what the physical world is now. I do."

True enough. But even ten years outside of physical existence was a long time in today's rapidly changing world. "Do you tweet, Charlie?"

"Shit, no. I don't see the point of a hundred-and-forty-character limit. But I taught them about the Internet, Wayra. I told them they'd better learn the technology if they wanted to keep pace with the twenty-first century. *I educated these council members on what social networking is.*" He threw his arms out to his sides. "And I learned what I know from my granddaughter *after I died*. Most of them lack curiosity, Wayra. It's their greatest failing. I mean, please, if you want to be in charge, you've got to be curious, right?"

"I hear you, Charlie. You're preaching to the choir."

"I'm the most recently dead on the chaser council and the only one who still has physical ties to the living. Ten years is a blink in the cosmic scheme of things. It's probably why they haven't already kicked me out."

They were now deep in the trees. The tractors sounded louder, more invasive. Beyond where he stood, Wayra could see a sparrow hawk circling the landfill. "So tell me, Charlie. How badly are chasers outnumbered by *brujos*?"

Charlie puffed deeply on his cigar, then lifted his foot, stubbed it out on the bottom of his shoe, and stuck it behind his ear again. "It's not like anyone has taken a census, okay? But the way I see it, the ones we call *brujos*, like Dominica, are either so ancient or so aware that they know how to manipulate energy in the afterworld, they use the energy to their own advantage. Since Dominica's tribe in Esperanza was annihilated, their numbers are far fewer than they used to be, but still formidable."

Wayra should have known that asking Charlie what seemed like a simple question would not render a simple answer. But this was the first time any chaser had attempted to explain the nuances to him. "Give me a number, Charlie."

"Call it eight to ten thousand of the truly ancient, evil ones, the hungry ghosts, the *brujos*." He whispered now, as though he thought one of the other chasers might be eavesdropping. "There are tens of millions of ghosts in the lower astrals who would just love to hook up with an ancient one like Dominica and join a tribe where they could learn what she knows. They hang around close to physical existence because of guilt, confusion, anger, hatred, revenge, lust. Here you find criminals, some suicides, religious, social, and political wackos who propagated hatred and intolerance when they were alive. *Brujos* recruit easily from this group and teach them what they know and turn them into hungry ghosts. But among the astrals you also find souls who are just lost. They might not have had any kind of spiritual beliefs when they were alive, so when they died, they had no idea what was supposed to happen. Some in this group have tremendous fears and issues to overcome. We've recruited among them. They usually need rehab, but turn out to be quite proficient."

Eight to ten thousand Dominicas running around in the afterlife was eight to ten thousand too many. And that other figure, *tens of millions* of ghosts from which *brujos* could recruit, whom they could convert, staggered the imagination. The odds against success suddenly seemed impossibly huge to Wayra and that terrified him. "No offense, but your descriptions resemble personality types in physical life."

Charlie looked disgusted. "There's not much difference. One group is alive, the other group is dead. Do you have any idea how many people live their lives without any thought whatsoever about their own mortality? Death is the shadow that drives physical life. Eventually, you all die. Even you, Wayra."

Maybe, Wayra thought. For centuries, he had wondered if his battle with Dominica was what kept him alive. Following this line of thinking, what would happen if he finally caught her and annihilated her so she was free to move on in the afterlife? Maybe, in the deepest recesses of his heart, he didn't want to find her for fear it would mean the end of his own life. He and Charlie had discussed this in depth before. He didn't feel any need to go into it again.

"It sounds like some of the dead can't move beyond a certain point in the afterlife anymore, Charlie."

"More and more of them are getting stuck and we're not sure why."

The implications of stuck souls troubled Wayra. It meant the *brujos* would have even more ghosts to recruit. "Any other groups of ghosts I should know about?"

"Hundreds of small, independent groups and unorganized loners. They often act as guides and helpers for the living. They aren't involved in the battle against *brujos*. Only the chasers do that. But the largest category of ghosts consists of mothers and fathers, children, sisters and brothers, lovers, friends, even animals who hang around close to physical life because of their love for the people they left. This category holds our best candidates for recruitment."

"You're avoiding my question, Charlie. What's the present number of chasers?"

He looked utterly miserable. "About four thousand."

"Christ. We're outnumbered two to one."

"Yeah, it sucks, doesn't it?"

"It means we've got to work that much harder."

It also meant they couldn't afford any snafus, Wayra thought, and dropped to his hands and knees on a bed of pine needles and leaves, and started to shift. His spine crackled and popped, bones shifting, strengthening, rearranging themselves. The first few dozen times this had happened, after he had been transformed at the tail end of the twelfth century, the agony had nearly driven him, howling, into death. Now that his threshold was higher, the pain didn't register. His human skin went next, rapidly replaced by fur. This part had never hurt, but it should have. The skin was the largest human organ and kept dermatologists and plastic surgeons rich even in tough economic times. He much preferred his animal fur, the color of coal and softer than an infant's skin.

Then his limbs transformed and this part was just strange, not painful except when his thumbs were *absorbed* into his paws. But at that very moment, his animal and shifter senses kicked in, as if to compensate for the loss of physical dexterity. And those senses could follow anything anywhere, backward and forward in time, and do it in such amazing detail that he never mourned the loss of his thumbs.

The most painful part of his transformation, even after all these centuries, was when his face, organs, blood, and consciousness changed all at once. It didn't always happen that way, sometimes these areas changed separately. But when he was in a hurry, as he was now, the pain briefly stole all his senses, human and animal, and he stood there blind, deaf, dumb, beyond redemption, a boy born in 1162 and turned into a shifter eighteen years later. Then, somehow, his transformation all came together and he was a dog/wolf hybrid, the last of his kind.

Wayra trotted through the trees, snout raised into the air, reading it, following Dominica's putrid stench straight into the landfill. He was aware of Charlie moving alongside him, and of the sparrow hawk he'd seen earlier now circling overhead, spiraling lower and lower. A tractor lumbered toward him and Wayra dashed left to get out of the way. The driver saw him, stopped, bolted upright and waved his arms, shouting, "Hey, someone get this goddamn dog outta here."

He kept moving toward the source of the stench, up a steep hill blanketed with birds—crows, gulls, blackbirds, vultures. As he neared them, the birds cried out, shrieked, and fluttered upward, a dark mass. At the top of the hill, he started digging, fast, wildly, down through layers of garbage, through a profusion of odors. Some odors held stories, others contained an entire history, all of them whispered, *Follow me, learn who and what I am.* But the overpowering stink of Dominica kept him focused.

Wayra dug deeper, deeper, Dominica's smell now mixed in with the fetid stink of decaying flesh. Some of the crows and blackbirds returned, settling around him and pecking at the garbage he'd uncovered. Charlie, crouched beside him, kept muttering, "Hurry up, Wayra, hurry up. A couple of tractor drivers are on their way up here."

Then he found it, about two feet down, a rotting hand protruding from a filthy, bloodstained sleeve. It smelled male, young, early twenties. Wayra grabbed hold of the sleeve and tried to pull the body out, but the weight of the dirt was too great. He moved to the left and dug fast to uncover the rest of the body.

"Scat!" shouted one of the men who appeared in front of him, waving his arms. "You can't go digging around up— Holy shit. Clem, take a look. The dog found a body."

Wayra uncovered the front of the young man's chest, his bloodied shirt. Maggots slithered out from between the buttons, emerged from his pocket, crawled from the dirt around the man's neck. Wayra knew he had bled out. Dominica's stink nearly overwhelmed him.

He leaned in closer, inhaling the man's scent, following it, trying to find the thread of his personal story. But too many smells were mixed in with it. Then Clem and Hank, his companion, dropped down next to the body and Wayra smelled them, too. But their scents were radically different; they smelled *alive* and Wayra was able to filter out their odors and concentrate on the young man.

"Shit, just like the other two," Hank muttered.

A cop reached the top of the hill, obviously winded from the exertion. "What've we got?"

"Another body," Clem replied, and he and Hank moved aside so the cop could see.

The cop pulled the edge of his jacket over his nose and mouth and peered down. "Jesus. Another bleed-out. I'm supposed to call this in to the feds. Did either of you touch the body?"

"Fuck, no," said Clem.

"Did the dog?"

"He just dug it up," Hank replied.

"You sure?"

"What difference does it make?" Clem asked.

"Because they don't yet know if the virus is host specific."

"What the hell does *that* mean?" Hank kept his arm across his nose and mouth, breathing into his elbow, muffling his voice. "Speak English."

The cop looked irritated. "It means they don't know if the virus is sticking just to humans. If it can leap between species, then the dog could be contaminated. Does he have a collar or anything you can grab?"

"No collar," said Hank. "And I'm not grabbing for the dog, Sergeant. I'm not getting bit. You want him, you grab for him."

Wayra started backing away from the body, the men. The cop said, "Nice doggie, nice doggie." He came toward Wayra, snapping his fingers, speaking softly, and Wayra kept backing away from him, growling, baring his teeth.

"C'mon now, doggie. I don't want to shoot you."

"For fuck's sake," Hank snapped. "Just let him go. You said yourself they don't know shit about this virus."

"Got my orders, Hank."

"This is such bullshit," Clem said angrily. "The point is the body, not the dog."

Wayra whirled around and raced down the other side of the mound, the men still shouting at each other. The hawk shrieked nearby, and when Wayra glanced back, he saw it diving toward the cop, who stumbled back, lost his balance, and tumbled out of sight, down the other side of the hill of garbage. Wayra raced on into the trees, Dominica's smell still so thick in his nostrils he continued to follow it through time.

She had seized the young man while he was snorkeling in the gulf with his girlfriend. It seemed that Dominica was instructing another *brujo* on how to seize and control humans. Once she had shown her new recruit how to do it, she'd leaped out of the man and into the girlfriend, and the other *brujo* had taken the young man. Neither human realized it until they were on one of the deserted islands and *brujo* lust had overpowered them. Both of them bled out within minutes. Later, the rising tide washed their bodies out into the gulf.

Even though Wayra's sense of smell provided an abundance of information, it didn't give him everything. Huge gaps existed in his knowledge. How did the man's body get to the landfill? What had happened to his girlfriend's body? Where had Dominica left Maddie's body while she'd been teaching her recruit how to seize humans? He needed to look at a map and find the quickest way to the gulf.

As he neared the end of the woods, he shifted into his human form again, grateful that the man who had transformed him so many centuries ago had done so while Wayra was clothed. It meant that whenever he moved back to his human form, he would still be dressed in whatever he was wearing when he had shifted. It meant that anything he was carrying in his pockets would still be there. He didn't know why this was so; it simply was. As he slapped his hands against his dusty jeans, he heard the squeal of a siren—distant, but headed this way.

"They'll be looking for a black dog, Wayra," said Charlie.

"Idiots. What'd you make of that hawk?"

"You owe her. She probably saved your ass from being shot."

"Have you ever seen a hawk do anything like that?"

"No. But hey, you're a hell of a lot older than I am. Have *you* ever seen a hawk do something like that?"

"Never."

Wayra emerged from the trees, slipped inside the truck, dug out his keys. He sat there, studying a map. Two cop cars raced past the shopping center, sirens wailing. *No black dog around here, boys.*

"So where to next?" Charlie asked, now occupying the passenger seat.

"Cedar Key. It's the closest island in the gulf."

"Onward, amigo."

Four

Dominica pedaled her bike through the dusk, the most magical time of day for her. As it settled across the island, it transformed the old buildings in downtown Cedar Key into a city of gold. She felt as if she were riding her bike through a land of legends and myths, of dragons and knights, kings and queens and princesses trapped in towers. She conjured just enough fog to create an atmosphere of mystery and danger, and imagined herself on horseback, racing toward Wayra in the days centuries ago when they had still loved each other.

But the memories of those days were open wounds. She shook them away and tried to find her way into a better story, one in which Wayra had joined her and they had taken over Esperanza and turned it into a city of *brujos*. That story fit the fantasy of myths and legends, but it wasn't how it had happened. That blow still plagued her and, in her darkest moments, brought back the bitterness and despair of everything that had gone so horribly wrong.

She stopped in front of the Island Hotel, her headquarters since her arrival in January, and unlocked the courtyard gate. She pushed her bike inside, set it against one of the palm trees. From the basket attached to the back of the bike, she carefully withdrew a small, rectangular wooden box. She held it tightly in both hands and hurried toward the building that formed the northern boundary of the courtyard. It resembled an old barracks and had once housed Civil War soldiers. The front porch sagged, some of the windows were cracked, and the place screamed for a fresh coat of paint.

Dominica sensed the barracks was at least twenty years older than the hotel, dating back to around 1839. In the cosmic scheme of things, 1839 was yesterday. What a difference from Ecuador, where many buildings and plazas dated back to before the time of the Incas. Yet it was one of the oldest spots on the island and she felt at home within the barracks' chipped, barren walls, surrounded by the smell of its dusty history.

She hoped to eventually spiff up all these old buildings around town, make them more appealing for both tourists and locals. Whit, her expert on American culture, advised her against doing anything until the town was truly a *brujo* enclave. He said that any such activity might attract attention from the county commissioners, who forbade renovations to historical buildings without all sorts of bureaucratic red tape. She knew that for her plan to succeed, she had to avoid scrutiny by authorities.

Dominica entered through the door on the far side, so that no one inside the hotel could see her—or rather, see her redheaded host, Maddie. Today, Dominica controlled Maddie completely—no resistance, no fights, no arguments, just a blissful silence from the young woman's essence. Today, the ease with which she used Maddie's body made her feel as if it actually belonged to her. Dominica prompted her to reach into her jacket pocket for a flashlight, turn it on, then directed her to the interior of the building, to what used to be the barracks kitchen. No reaction at all from Maddie. These days, the only times she resisted was when Dominica urged her to have sex with Whit's host. And then she fought violently for control of her own body.

The linoleum floor was scuffed and filthy, dust covered the counters, a scarred wooden table stood in the middle of the room. Four flickering candles provided enough illumination for her to see the two others seated at the table, waiting for her.

Whit, her second in command, eyed her with such naked desire she couldn't wrench her eyes away from him. In the lambent light, his host, the island mayor, Peter Stanton, looked like a middle-aged Olympian god. His thick white hair, those smoldering dark eyes, those beautiful hands that scoped out her deepest sexual desires: Dominica drank in the sight of him. A quick, sly smile reshaped his mouth as she set the box on the table. She shrugged off her pack, set it on the floor, and sat down.

"Where're the others?" she asked.

"Late," Whit said.

Late. Now *that* irritated her. How could the other members of the committee be late for the first judicial hearing in her new tribe? In the old days, in Esperanza, when she had given an order, it was carried out immediately. But those *brujos* had been older, many of them ancient; the members of her new tribe were, for the most part, young, naïve, recently dead. They didn't understand the rules yet.

"I'm sure they'll be along," said Liam, nudging his host's glasses farther up on the bridge of his nose. "All our hosts are on island time. You know . . . no clocks."

Or the ghosts themselves weren't entirely adjusted to a twenty-four-hour clock yet. Cedar Key's perfect isolation—the nearest city lay fifty miles inland—was both a blessing and a curse. The live-and-let-live attitude made the populace more passive, but they could also be fiercely independent.

Inside the wooden box, the imprisoned *brujo* screamed to be released, screams that Whit and Liam both heard. Liam's host, Sam Dorset, winced as though he found the screams physically painful. He reminded her of a bear or some other lumbering creature, but his haunted eyes peered out from behind his glasses like those of an anxious dog that feared it might not be fed. Sam was editor of the local newspaper and, so far, he and Liam had been a good fit. But when Liam was alive, he'd been a lost human with an alcohol problem and sometimes in the bar at night, he tipped a few too many. That worried her. On the other hand, Liam obviously enjoyed physical existence and maybe that alone would prevent him from blowing it.

"Liam, I thought you posted the time of the meeting on the newspaper Web site," she said.

"I did. I guess they forgot to check the Web site, Dominica."

"I can see we need to rectify *that*."

"Hey, it's not like this is corporate America, Dominica," Whit remarked, and opened his arms wide. "I mean, really." His gesture encompassed not only the old scarred table at which they sat, but the entire dilapidated barracks with the lack of electricity, the faint stink of mold, the filthy floors. "They need an incentive to attend."

Whit surprised her, as he often did. She liked that, the element of surprise and mystery. Whit had been executed seven months ago for rape and murder, and until he had answered her call, he had been stuck wandering around the lower astrals, wondering what the hell had happened to him.

"The incentive is the vision, Whit. A *brujo* enclave in the U.S. Here."

"A lot of them may not understand what that means," Liam remarked.

"Since your host is the editor of the newspaper, Liam, it's your job to explain it to them, which you apparently haven't done. An editorial might do the trick, okay? Are we clear, Liam?"

Liam looked conflicted. "I don't know if that's wise until more of us have hosts."

Whit nodded. "I agree, Nica. A lot of residents have already left the island. We don't want to do anything that frightens away more potential hosts."

"How many in our tribe have hosts right now?" she asked.

Whit didn't hesitate. "Two hundred and two." Whit, the numbers man. "At least half of them are couples." He grinned. "Easy access to sex."

Good, she thought. That minimized the possibility of bleed-outs that sometimes occurred when her ghosts engaged in sexual encounters so passionate and lustful that the host bodies were overtaxed and bled out. Couples tended to be less forceful with each other. Since her arrival, thirteen hosts had bled out. Those bodies had been disposed of expeditiously so the deaths hadn't attracted attention from outside authorities. She intended to keep it that way. Early on, she had forbidden the seizure of any child under sixteen. Nothing would bring outside scrutiny more rapidly than a bunch of dead kids. She had also forbidden any more bleed-outs. Any *brujo* who violated that law would end up in this wooden box for a hearing, just like Von.

But Von's offense was far more serious. "Let's get down to the unpleasant business that brought us here," she said.

"We're not going to wait for the others?" Liam asked.

"They'll hear it through the net," Dominica said. Everyone in her new tribe would hear the proceedings through the telepathic net that connected them. "And if the other members of the committee choose to grace us with their presence, they can vote. But they aren't necessary to these proceedings. As Whit so eloquently pointed out, we're not a corporation."

The door behind them creaked, the old wood groaning, the rusted hinges squeaking, and Gogh lumbered into the kitchen carrying a paper bag. "Sorry I'm late," he called out, as if they were all hard of hearing. "Had to stop by the market." He set his bag on the table and brought out a selection of bottled water, soda, juices. "Take your pick."

Gogh's peace offering, she thought. He had died in an L.A. gang war about a year ago and had been trapped in the lower astrals by rage and confusion. His host, Richard Pinella, was the head bartender at the hotel, a handsome man in his late thirties whose curly black hair always looked as if he had just rolled out of bed. Those Mediterranean-blue eyes of his had gone dark, indicating that Gogh was fully in control of him and peering out.

"Thanks for the drinks, Gogh," she said, and helped herself to a bottle of cold water. "Could you try to be on time from now on?"

"Sure thing. Where're Jill and Joe?"

"They're late, too. Let's get started." She brought her hands to the box she had set on the table. "As you know, Von is accused of violating our most sacred law. He allegedly helped his host escape and it resulted in the annihilation of two members of our tribe. There were witnesses and we heard their testimony yesterday. Von has a chance to tell his side of the story, which will be broadcast throughout the *brujo* net. Then we'll vote on guilt or innocence."

"Just the four of us are voting?" Liam asked.

"That's how it's done, Liam. The committee votes. If members of the committee don't show up, it means fewer votes. But every *brujo* who listens through the net is entitled to state an opinion and all of that is taken into consideration. Up until we vote, business can be conducted mind to mind or through the physical voices of our hosts or a combination."

I have a request, Von shouted.

The net shuddered and trembled.

"What is it, Von?"

Could you let me out of the box, please? I promise I won't try to escape.

Dominica looked at the three men and they all nodded. She touched the rectangular box and slid the button on the side to the off position. It extinguished the fluorescent light that generated a field of extremely low frequency waves, which inflicted excruciating agony on any *brujo* that tried to pass through it. Von drifted out, no more than a whiff of discolored smoke, the way most *brujos* looked in their natural form.

"What's to prevent Von from escaping?" Gogh asked. "We don't have any ELF fields in here."

"If he attempts to escape, he'll be pursued," Dominica said.

"Yeah? By whom?" Liam asked. "Us? Or do we have a posse of ghosts for this purpose?"

"Yeah." Whit snickered. "We've got John Wayne and some of his buddies in the back room."

I'm not going to try to escape, Von said. *Where the hell would I go?*

The plaintiveness in his words pleased Dominica. "So tell us what happened, Von. The tribe is listening."

Two days ago, my host and I were over on the pier. He lost his wife six months ago and was feeling really sad and depressed. I kept telling him she still existed somewhere, like I do. I explained how my death was really sudden—my heart just stopped beating one day when I was doing an emergency appendectomy. I pitched forward, right onto the patient. When I came to, I was conscious and in my own home, struggling to communicate with my wife and kids.

"Get to the point, Von," Dominica said.

I kept talking to him like this, describing my own experience. And then he asked me how . . . how I ended up with such an evil group. And I . . . I started thinking about that and I couldn't remember how I ended up here. I heard a voice, I guess it was your voice, Dominica, and I answered the call. I . . . I was grateful when I became physical again, but I suddenly understood what he meant. It's like I had forgotten who I was and now I remembered. We have no right to possess someone else's body, it's—

"For shit's sake," Whit burst out. "I've heard enough."

The net shook with gossip, chatter, turmoil. Dominica thought a moment, then said, "He's entitled to tell his side, Whit." It was good for the tribe to hear how twisted Von's thoughts and beliefs were. *Brujos* weren't evil. They only wanted to experience physical life. "Go on, Von."

He and I walked into a place on the water for a bite to eat. Three brujos *were at the next table. It was just the four of us in the pub . . . well, eight of us if you count the hosts, right? One of them, a woman, came over to us. She said she found me and my host attractive and wanted to have sex with us right there, in the restaurant. I . . . I can't begin to describe what I felt just then. I told my host to get up and walk out of the restaurant and he did. We did. We got into a car and I told him to keep driving until he was so far from Cedar Key he couldn't even remember the name of the place. And . . . and then I leaped out of him and returned to that pub.*

I leaped into that bruja's *host, so two of us shared the woman's body, and drove the ghost out. Then . . . then I leaped into one of the men and he fell back into the lantern that was on the table and . . . and it broke and . . . I guess the* brujo *inside of him shot out the top of his head and straight into the lantern's flame, and was obliterated.*

"Hold on a minute," Gogh said. "You're saying the *brujo* intentionally shot into that lantern flame?"

I don't know.

"No ghost would do that," Whit added. "It's suicide."

"Go on, Von," Dominica said. "What happened next?"

Von's essence swayed from side to side, like a curtain blowing in the wind.

I leaped into the second man and he was so freaked out with two ghosts inside of him that he ran . . . out onto the balcony and jumped over the railing and . . . and he drowned before the brujo *escaped and—*

"And Joe had just entered the pub and saw everything and brought you the fuck down."

They all turned to see Joe, hosted by Bean, the hotel owner. Tall, much too thin and lanky for her taste, he reminded Dominica of a disheveled scarecrow. Right now, he looked like a pissed-off scarecrow, his eyes obsidian black as Joe peered from them, his muscles tight, fists clenched. "That was my wife who came on to you, Von. Jill. Her name's Jill."

And her host's name is Marion, she's the island librarian, and your wife has no business inside her. And what do you care about your wife, Joe? When you two were alive, she was screwing some other guy and you shot her and killed him and then turned the gun on yourself. You're the fucks who should be on trial here. That night in February when you screwed your brains out in the hotel bar, you compromised your goddamn tribe. That's when people around here started realizing that something was really wrong on Cedar Key.

Jill's host, Marion, propped her hands on her narrow hips. "Are you kidding me, Von? You wanted me that night in the pub." She laughed, a quick, mocking laugh, then she marched right over to the whiff of discolored smoke that Von was and poked her finger into it, into him. "You. Wanted. Me. You're a hypocrite of the worst kind."

Von suddenly dived through Marion's skull, so that she was now possessed by both him and Jill. He somehow drove Jill out of Marion's body and then spun Marion around and raced for the door. Jill, reduced to nothing but a puff of smoke, shrieked and streaked after them. Dominica shot to her feet, her chair tipped over and crashed to the floor, and she raced after Marion.

The woman exploded through the side door and moved so fast it astonished Dominica. How had Von managed to exert such perfect control over Marion? Dominica was vaguely aware of the pandemonium in the barracks kitchen, of Jill's wails; her host was gone, stolen, and none of the *brujos* had any idea what to do. Even though Dominica's host, Maddie, had been a runner she couldn't close in on Von. Desperation fueled him, and the more desperate he became, the faster Marion ran. Now he tore through the courtyard, headed toward the gate that led to the main road through downtown.

Dominica knew she had just one choice. "Whit, cover me," she hollered, and leaped out of Maddie and into Marion the librarian.

Von leaped out of Marion and shot up into the sky and Dominica soared after him, hating him for reducing her to this ridiculous cat-and-mouse game, ghost chasing ghost. Von saw himself as morally superior to her and her tribe, and yet he had given his word he wouldn't attempt an escape. He had *lied*.

Dominica closed in on him, then propelled herself the final yards and crashed into him, her essence melting into his, and they plummeted into the hotel courtyard. She heard Whit shouting that he had Maddie restrained, and sensed Gogh nearby, with the box and its ELF field that would trap Von. She and Von tumbled, rolled, and suddenly she vaulted away from him and Gogh nabbed him like an insect to flypaper.

Dominica instantly sought Maddie, and found her inside the barracks kitchen, bound to a chair, gagged. She dived into her again, right down through the middle of her skull, and quickly fitted herself into the young woman's body.

"Nica?" Whit leaned over her, anxiously scanning her host's face. "If it's really you, what's our code word?"

"Pensacola." It was where she and Whit had gone recently in their natural forms and had seized a couple of tourists to enjoy sex and good wine and a fantastic sunset. He knew she had blocked these memories from Maddie, that their code was genuine.

He quickly untied her, removed her gag, and wrapped his arms around her. "We won this round."

This round, but how many more were there in the future that they wouldn't win?

Gogh barreled into the kitchen with the rectangular box clasped in his hands. Behind him were Jill, Joe, Liam. Jill was back inside Marion, who looked exhausted, her face shiny with perspiration in spite of the cool air.

"Now what?" Gogh asked anxiously.

"Disengage from the net."

They did so, their lights blinking out like stars at the edge of sunrise. The white noise she had grown accustomed to, the communal voices in the *brujo* net, went silent. "Make sure we have six votes cast," she said, and told him what they should say. "This is the official record. We'll enter it into the net later."

While Gogh scribbled frantically, Whit went over to the counter, opened the cabinet under the sink, and brought out lighter fluid, rags, a box of kitchen matches. He put everything into his pack, glanced at Dominica, and tilted his head toward the door. She nodded, walked to the pantry, and removed five kayak paddles. She handed them out and picked up the wooden box with despicable, twisted Von inside.

"What should I do with the votes?" Gogh asked.

"Just leave them on the table," Dominica said. "I'll take care of them later."

Jill blew out the candles and they all followed Whit out of the building.

Once they were outside the hotel, they took different routes to get to the same place—the prayer rug of a beach just beyond the city park, where their yellow and red kayaks were neatly lined up on the sand. Still silent, they got into the kayaks and set off, Dominica in the lead, headed for Atsena Otie Key, the original Cedar Key, now a deserted island with deserted beaches, its inland overgrown, infested with mosquitoes, and home to a graveyard that all *brujos* avoided.

The night was splendid, clear and cool, with a slice of moon just visible now above the horizon. They would start the fire on the far side of the island, so that no one on Cedar Key would see the glow. By morning, every member of her tribe would understand that when a *brujo* broke a law, there would be consequences.

Maddie felt Von's distress and terror and it tore at her. She reached out to him, one consciousness to another, and tried to comfort him. *You won't be annihilated, Von. You'll be freed and will be able to move on into the afterworld.*

They're . . . going to burn me, to—

Von, you died already. All they're doing is freeing you to move into the afterworld, to get to where you're supposed to be. Hold on to thoughts of love.

How . . . how can you stand it, Maddie? When . . . when she went after me, slammed into me, it . . . it was . . . horrifying, like being buried alive.

I've learned to do whatever I have to do to stay alive. She's not going to defeat me. And you won't be defeated, either. They're doing you a favor. Believe me. When the box begins to burn, Von, reach for all that's good and loving in the world. There'll be guides to help you.

She kept talking to him like this as the *brujos* paddled out across the dark waters of the gulf. When he was calmer, she explained that she had to check on something and would be back shortly. Then she reached out to the man who had touched her mind several days ago.

It was the only time in all these months of being imprisoned within her own body that anyone had found her. And this man had actually gotten so close to her that she had seen his face—dark, penetrating eyes, hair the color of rich chocolate, a square jaw. Yet he hadn't been physical. It was as if he were a holographic projection. She had no idea what that meant and didn't get a chance to find out because something had spooked him and he'd disappeared.

Maddie extended her consciousness, thrusting it out through time and space, searching for him. She had learned to do this in the early days of her imprisonment within her own body, when Dominica controlled her so completely Maddie couldn't even relieve her own aching bladder unless the bitch allowed her to do so.

In those early weeks, she had learned a great deal about consciousness in general and her consciousness in particular. By stretching her awareness, she had been able to search for Wayra, her aunt Tesso, her grandmother, anyone she loved. She had found her family a few times, but because she was only consciousness, they hadn't been aware of her. Once, when Wayra had been in his shifter form on a highway somewhere, it seemed that he sensed her. He had stopped, snout raised into the air, as if to catch her scent. Another time, she was sure she'd seen her grandfather, Charlie, dead more than a decade. It had startled her, seeing the dead when she was possessed by the dead, and her consciousness had snapped back into her body.

Now she reached and reached, stretching her awareness until it felt as though it might shred apart like a wet tissue in a high wind. Then it popped free of her body, and she could see brilliantly colored filaments of light with her inner eyes. They seemed to extend outward in all directions, gossamer threads in a giant spiderweb. Maddie thought these threads might be Indra's net, a metaphor used by ancient Hindu mystics and Buddhists to illustrate the spiritual net that connected everyone in the cosmos. She suspected that if she followed any single strand, she would eventually reach a living being, a soul.

But which strand belonged to the man whose awareness had touched hers?

She focused on him, on what she had sensed about him, and thought she brushed up against his essence. She struggled to focus her inner vision and suddenly saw him and a golden retriever hurrying up the sidewalk to a small house with a pretty yard illuminated by outside lights. The clarity with which she saw them, the man and the dog, astonished her. It was as if she watched them through a pane of utterly clean glass. She didn't have any idea how this was possible, but stopped questioning the process and absorbed as many details as she could.

The man wore jeans, a T-shirt with a peace sign on the front, a blue and light gray windbreaker, black running shoes with luminous orange laces. He looked Latino, late twenties, about six feet tall. The dog wasn't on a leash and stared directly at her and started barking.

"What is it, Jessie?" The man glanced around.

The retriever's tail wagged, and she barked again. The man stooped next to the dog, his fingers sliding through her fur, and briefly shut his eyes. Then, softly, he said, "It's you, the redhead with the parrot-green eyes. Maddie, your name's Maddie. Are you out of body? Dreaming? Is that it? Tell me about the evil that tasted me, Red. Is it inside of you?"

It wasn't as if she could answer his questions. She was only consciousness. No body, no vocal cords. She desperately longed to speak to him in her mind, but the risk of doing so terrified her. Talking to disembodied Von was one thing; talking to a live human was something else. If Dominica realized what she was doing, she might plunge Maddie into a deep sleep and that would be it for the next ten or twelve hours. But would she ever have a better opportunity than right now?

She moved closer to him and the dog, brushed up against them. She offered an image first, of Esperanza, then of the battle last summer that ended the decades of *brujo* terror. Finally, she spoke to him in her mind, conjured more images, and hoped that for him it would be like reading an illustrated book. *The evil inside me is distracted right now. I can speak to you when her attention is elsewhere. She's a hungry ghost, a* bruja, *dead but not dead, and she and her tribe seek to possess the living and live out their mortal lives. She's ancient. Her new tribe is reckless. She intends to set up a* brujo *enclave in the United States that—*

"Red, slow down," he said softly. "I'm getting some of this, but you have to slow down. *Bruja,* I clearly heard the word *bruja.* That means 'witch.' It—"

In mythology, a brujo *is many things. It's what these hungry ghosts are called. It's the—*

"More slowly. Please. This kind of thing is . . . new for me, the words, the stream of consciousness. Where are you?"

On an island beach. These ghosts are about to annihilate one of their own who saved his host and obliterated a couple of brujos. She showed him what she was seeing, the six hosts building a fire in a rock pit, the wooden box in the sand. *The ghost is kept in that box.*

"Give me your location, Red. I can help you. My name is Nick Sanchez. I'm a remote viewer for the government and the FBI has asked for our help in locating a terrorist cell. These . . . ghosts you're talking about, they're the terrorists, right?"

Astonished and excited that he could actually hear some of what she was saying, she rushed on. *The hosts who have died have been hauled off to landfills, Sanchez. Dominica's tribe has seized the cops, some of the town's power base, and—* She suddenly realized she had to give him something useful, something he could *experience.* She instructed him to go to Annie's Café on any evening. *The real terrorists sit on the right side of the café dining room. They're the boisterous gluttons. They're the* brujos—*hungry ghosts who seize humans for the pleasures of physical life. The one in me is the leader. She intends to take over Cedar Key and make it a* brujo *enclave. They're terrified of fire. If a host is killed and the* brujo *doesn't escape before the host dies, then the* brujo *is annihilated.*

"But ghosts are dead, right? How can the dead be annihilated?"

Maddie felt Dominica's attention turning back to her and quickly thought of her body and snapped back into it.

"Nica?" Whit looked at her. "You okay?"

Dominica tightened her control over Maddie. "Yes. For a moment there, I couldn't feel Maddie's essence."

"They do that sometimes," Whit said. "Leave, wander around. To preserve their sanity or something."

It was almost funny, hearing creepy Whit talk like he was some sort of expert. But he was the one Dominica loved now, so she didn't call him on it. Maddie crawled back into the virtual room she had created months ago, her little cave of imaginary stuff—a MacBook, a comfortable couch, a TV, books, things she had created from memory by using the raw materials of her imagination. It wasn't so different from what the *brujos* did in their natural forms. She put on *Four Winds,* a CD by Bright Eyes, then fell back on the couch, waiting for Dominica and her minions to reach the island, and struggled against surrendering to despair.

There and suddenly gone. Sanchez turned slowly in place, eyes sweeping through the starlight and shadows in his father's yard. He glanced at the dog, now busily sniffing through the bushes along the side fence. Jessie had seen her, Sanchez had sensed her nearby. It was as if *she* had been remote viewing *him.*

Red. Definitely gone now. He slipped a notepad from his shirt pocket and scribbled a few notes on what he'd learned. Hungry ghosts, bleed-outs, some gorgeous city high in the mountains where a battle against these *brujos* had taken place, a ghost named Dominica whose tribe stole bodies, just as he'd seen in his viewing. Other bits and pieces came to him— words, a phrase, images. A café on an island. Which café? Where was the island? "Shit," he murmured. He'd gotten some of what she'd said, but not enough of it to find her.

Sanchez glanced through his notes. It all sounded nuts. *Hey, Delaney, the terrorists are ghosts.* Yeah, that would be a quick route to a psychological evaluation or a pink slip.

But it thrilled him that they had communicated.

He whistled for Jessie and they headed up the sidewalk toward the house where Sanchez had been born. Little Havana had been his father's haven for decades. Back in the day, the house and the neighborhood had been upscale. But in recent years, the entire area had slipped into decay and neglect. Now Emilio's windows were covered with bars to prevent robberies, but the bars also made the place look like a prison. The house on the left was in foreclosure, the one on the right had been vacant for months. He wished his father would move.

Before he reached the front door, he heard the shouting match between Emilio and Nicole. Not surprising. She had called Sanchez late this afternoon, asking him to meet her at Emilio's place. That meant some sort of crisis had developed. Every week a crisis ensued. He briefly considered just turning around and driving home. But Nicole could use some support at the moment, so he opened the door without knocking or ringing the bell and entered the house. Jessie bounded past him, nose to the tile floor, and disappeared into the kitchen, the source of the racket.

Sudden silence. Then Emilio shouted in Spanish: *"Get that goddamn dog out of my house!"*

Sanchez hurried through the kitchen doorway and nearly burst out laughing. Jessie, sprawled next to Emilio's chair, covered her ears with her paws. Nicole's eyes, dancing with amusement, met his, and she pressed her hands to her mouth to stifle her laughter.

"That's not a very warm welcome, Emilio," Sanchez said.

"Dogs have fleas and bad breath," he grumbled. "And they fart. When did you get a dog, anyway?"

"Months ago."

"And you never brought her here before?"

"Why would I, with a reception like this? And she doesn't fart or have fleas and bad breath. Where's Carmen?"

"He fired her." Nicole tucked her long black hair behind her ears. "Carmen called me a few hours ago to tell me."

"She was the most abusive housekeeper yet," Emilio grumbled.

"It was probably the other way around, Emilio. She's the sixth housekeeper you've fired in as many months. I hope you can do your own shopping and cleaning, because I'm not looking for another housekeeper."

His old man frowned. "But . . . but how am I supposed to—"

"Shop and clean? Cook? Get over to the park for domino games?" Sanchez shrugged. "Beats me. You figure it out."

"But . . . I . . ." he stammered.

"Look, Dad, I found this great facility just five blocks from Carlos and me," Nicole said quickly. "You'd have your own room, TV, all the comforts of home. They have a full nursing staff, a beautiful dining room with—"

Emilio slammed his bony fists down against the table, rattling dishes and coffee mugs, and shot to his feet with shocking swiftness. "*No.* I've told you both over and over again, *no, no,* and *no.* I am *not* moving. Everyone I know who has ever moved to one of those places dies there." He flung out his skinny arms, a gesture that encompassed not just the kitchen, but the house, the entire neighborhood. "All my memories, my photos, my friends live in the neighborhood, my—" Then something tragic happened to his face. Wrinkles collapsed, as if pulled down by a terrible gravity, his dark eyes flooded with tears. He sank into the chair, shoulders hunched, everything about his body whispering defeat and surrender. He pressed his hands over his face and cried.

Nicole, ever the nurturer, the one who always addressed him as "Dad" rather than as "Emilio," as Sanchez had for years, moved forward to provide comfort and solace. But Jessie was already nudging Emilio's leg with her snout, whining softly, and one of Emilio's hands dropped gently to her head. His knobby fingers slipped through her silken fur and he looked down at her, regarding her with his rheumy eyes as though she were a curious object he didn't remember buying. When she licked the back of his hand, Sanchez thought, *Shit, he won't like that.* But Emilio started to laugh.

It stunned Sanchez. He couldn't remember the last time he'd heard his father laugh. He watched Emilio transform from a bitter old man to one who suddenly discovered he still had a capacity for enjoyment.

"You are one beautiful dog," Emilio said softly, and leaned forward and rubbed his face against her head. She licked his nose and barked. "You are welcome in my house any time, Jessie."

Nicole stepped in then, talking quickly, calmly, petting Jessie, encouraging Emilio to call Carmen, apologize, and hire her back. Emilio didn't look too happy about the prospect, but Sanchez suspected Carmen would acquiesce, especially when he told her he would be paying her more. With two kids in college, she needed the money.

When Sanchez finally left half an hour later, Nicole walked out to the car with him and Jessie. She was a couple of inches shorter than he was, about five foot nine, and although she was eight years older, she could pass for a woman in her early twenties, something she attributed to daily yoga. He suspected good genes and a healthy lifestyle had a lot to do with it, too.

"Your dog is a miracle worker, *hermano*. I've never seen Dad respond like that to any animal."

"It's just a temporary reprieve, Nicole. Sooner or later, it's going to get to the point where he'll have to move."

"I know. Later in the week, I'm going to take him out to lunch and then drive him over to the facility, just so he can see it. The place is great. They've got domino groups, chess groups, book groups, everything Dad enjoys."

"He probably won't like it, but maybe he'll surprise us."

"What's going on with your work?" she asked.

"The usual." It was easier to say that than to explain. Nicole was many things, but a true believer was not among them. It had taken her years to accept his ability as genuine. He handed her three hundred-dollar bills. "For Carmen, a bonus and a raise. I'll call and let her know."

As their hands brushed, an image exploded inside his head with such violence and color that he felt himself falling into it and grabbed onto her arm to steady himself. Bad move. The images became specific, detailed. He saw her confront Delaney outside the ISIS building, her face set with fierce determination as she demanded to know where her brother was and what the hell was going on. Delaney patted the air as though she were a wild animal he hoped to tame.

Don't patronize me, Delaney. Something's happened to him.

I don't know what you're talking about, Nicole. I swear. He's on Cedar Key, on official business, and I'll be flying up there to meet him. He's fine.

Fine? She whipped out her iPhone. *These text messages are scary, they're—*

The next thing Sanchez knew, he was on his ass in one of the bushes, striated leaves cool against the sides of his face. Nicole reached out to help him up, while Jessie barked from the other side of the gate.

"Shit." RV wasn't supposed to work like this, wasn't supposed to be personal. But then, what had just happened didn't have anything to do with remote viewing, he thought. It was what had been happening to him most of his life, abrupt, explosive psychic connections with people he touched. His RV training had helped to mitigate and structure it, but hadn't eradicated it completely.

He started to grasp his sister's extended hand, but thought better of it. "I'm okay." He got up, brushing off his jeans, irritated with himself. "Do me a favor, Nicole. Don't confront Delaney."

She frowned. "That's what you just saw? Why would I confront him?"

He told her the rest of it and her frown deepened. "An unknown virus. What the hell does that mean?"

"I don't know yet." He hesitated, then continued. "Mom dropped by my place the other night. She told me you had the answer about where the terrorist cell is located. She was right."

Her mouth pursed with disbelief. "Mom? C'mon, Nick. That's crazy."

"Now you sound like Dad."

She threw her arms out at her sides. "So now you not only *hear* the dead, you *see* them, too?"

He jammed his hands in the pockets of his windbreaker, wondering why he always ended up defending his ability. "I don't see and hear the generic dead, okay? But I've been hearing Mom for months around my place, and the other night I woke up and she walked out of the bookcase and looked as solid and real as you do."

Nicole looked as if she'd bitten into a lime, mouth pursed, eyes bulging in their sockets. "Walked out of the bookcase." She made a quick sign of the cross. "*Dios mío, hermano.* You know how that sounds?"

"I don't give a shit how it sounds. It's what happened."

"Shit. Okay, okay. How'd Mom look?"

"Young. Beautiful. Whole." He didn't tell her about the rest of what Jenean had said, about her friend Charlie.

Tears brimmed in Nicole's eyes. "Did she say anything else?"

"Not really. The visit seemed to be primarily to tell me you had the answer about where the terrorist cell is located."

"But why Cedar Key? Why would any terrorist cell be located there? It's an old fishing village, a tourist place."

He didn't say anything.

"Listen, *hermano*." Her hands touched his shoulders and Sanchez shut down completely so he wouldn't pick up anything else. "I don't doubt your ability, okay? It's just that you caught me by surprise. If you end up in Cedar Key, just keep me posted about what's going on. Text or otherwise. And I promise not to confront Delaney." Her fingers traced an X over her heart, a childhood thing between them.

Sanchez hugged her. "I'll be in touch."

The bonfire burned brightly now, the flames dancing in the breeze, the wood crackling, popping. Maddie reached out to Von again, comforting and encouraging him to hold loving thoughts.

It's hard to hold loving thoughts, Maddie, when I'm about to be burned at the stake.

You're already dead, she reminded him. *You got confused and lost your way and now you're going to find your way to where you're supposed to be.*

Just then, an odd-looking man appeared next to the box—bald, portly, with Oriental features. It took Maddie a moment to realize he was a ghost and that none of the *brujos* could see him.

I'll take care of things from here, Maddie.

Who're you?

Name's Victor. Charlie sends his regards.

You're a chaser?

But he was already gone. Maddie reached out to Von, calling his name. She felt his essence, but he didn't answer.

"I think the fire's hot enough now," Gogh said.

"What's going to happen to him when he's obliterated?" Jill asked. "Where's he going to end up?"

"Nowhere," Dominica replied. "Obliteration means destruction, Jill."

"We went somewhere when we died," Liam said.

"Exactly," Jill agreed.

Maddie sensed Dominica's confusion about this issue and her annoyance at Jill's question. The bottom line was that Dominica didn't have any answers to the ultimate question, but she realized the others were expecting something from her, so she bullshitted her way through it.

"Well, yes, technically, we did go somewhere when we died. And we found out that being dead just meant we don't have bodies and that we have a whole lot of power to draw upon from the world of the dead."

Jill frowned. "So where're heaven and hell?"

"There're no such places," Whit replied. "Believe me, if there was a hell, I'd be there."

Joe nodded. "Me, too."

"So Von will just cease to be?" Liam asked.

Gogh rolled his eyes. "Yeah, dude. That about sums it up. Look, can we just get on with it?"

"This is really wrong," Liam burst out. "Von died once, why should he have to die again?"

Maddie understood that Liam, like Von, was waking up to the truth about the *brujo* world and she wondered if and when others would, too.

"He broke a sacred law and attempted to escape," Dominica snapped, her voice razor sharp.

Liam's face turned apple red, a pulse beat hard at his temple. "Fuck this. I refuse to be a part of this." With that, Liam strode away from them, pushed his kayak into the water, got in, and paddled off into the darkness.

Defiance. Rebellion. Independent thinking. The seeds of destruction, Maddie thought, gleeful at the prospect of insurrection within Dominica's tribe.

"Liam just lost his position on the committee," Dominica announced, staring after him.

No one leaped to his defense.

Dominica picked up the box from the sand and held it a moment. "Does, uh, anyone want to say anything?" she asked.

"I understand that Von committed a heinous act," Jill said. "But we're obliterating one of our own."

Joe nodded his agreement.

"He broke the law." Dominica didn't want to discuss this anymore.

Jill's mouth tightened. "It's still wrong."

"Your objection is noted." Dominica looked pointedly at each of the others. "Anyone else?"

"Let's just get it the fuck over with," Gogh said. "Joe and I need to get back to the hotel."

"All right, engage with the net," Dominica said.

Maddie sensed that Dominica expected to hear Von's wild, frantic sobbing, his wails. It confused her when she heard only silence. She frowned and tapped her finger against the lid. "He should be shrieking," she said.

Gogh impatiently shifted his weight from one foot to the other. "C'mon, c'mon."

Dominica tossed the box into the flames, and as they stood there, quietly, watching it burn, Maddie suddenly saw Victor and another man standing on the other side of the fire pit. *Von*, she thought at him.

He looked the way he probably had in his life as a surgeon, a tall African-American with salt-and-pepper hair. He brought his hand to his heart and his consciousness pressed up against hers. *Thank you, Maddie, with all of my heart. Victor assures me he and Charlie are working to get you out of this. I'll hold them to it, you have my word.*

Then he and Victor faded into the darkness and Maddie was alone again with the *brujos,* on this deserted strip of sand, the flames in the rock pit leaping higher and higher. The rectangular box in which Von had been imprisoned was now little more than a mound of glowing embers.

Five

As the tide rose, the water slapped rhythmically against the sides of the houseboat, a sound that always soothed Kate. Fish jumped, their bodies shimmering in the light from the rising moon. The moon wasn't full, but the light was bright enough to transform the trees and brush in the back bayou to silhouettes. It highlighted the striated golds in Liberty's wings, turned her red tail feathers the color of fire, and limned her profile as she picked at the bowl of raw chicken Rocky had set on the railing for her.

He and Kate were eating dinner on the back balcony of the houseboat. They often ate dinner together out here, with Liberty somewhere nearby, the hawk an endless source of fascination for them both.

"Mom, you think it's okay for us to feed her? I don't want her to forget how to survive in the wild."

"We've been feeding her for months. But it doesn't seem to have affected her ability to hunt on her own. She's always catching fish."

Rocky had his father's high cheekbones, Kate's blond hair, and eyes the same unusual shade of blue that Kate's father had. Tall for his age, he had the kind of good looks that girls in his sophomore class found irresistible. They called him night and day, but the only girl who interested him was Amy, who worked at the animal rescue center with him.

"And yesterday, she flew in here with a live rat."

Liberty swiveled her head to look at them. Her dark, deeply set eyes caught the glint of the moonlight and turned them to amber. She fluttered her wings, stretched out the left one, and tilted it slightly toward them, like a hand waving hello or good-bye.

"Were you on the porch at the time?" Rocky asked.

"Sitting right here. I shot to my feet and scrambled inside."

Rocky laughed, a sound so pure and musical that it made Kate smile. He had his father's laugh, too, full, vibrant, and filled with that seductive joy that had captured Kate's heart the first time she heard it in a mythology class her senior year in college. She and Jake had spent five years together, most of them good years. But when Rocky was born, Jake had changed. He hadn't taken to parenthood as she had. He was jealous of the time Kate spent with their son rather than with him. He began to have affairs.

When Rocky was a year old, she and Jake split up. Kate stayed on in Gainesville for another year, juggling her job as an English teacher with her responsibilities as a single mom. She moved back to Cedar Key when Rocky was two, and never regretted it. The island was home.

"What did Liberty do when you freaked?" he asked.

"Killed the rat, ate it, then tapped at the door."

The hawk looked at them again, almost as if she knew they were talking about her. "Sometimes," Rocky went on, "I get this weird feeling that she sticks around because she thinks she owes me a favor or something for rescuing her."

Kate thought of the night that Liberty had dive-bombed Bean when he'd come here after the incident in the bar. "She's definitely protective."

"The other day when I was riding the scooter home from school, these rednecks in an electric cart tried to force me off the road. Liberty went after them, Mom. You should've seen her. She made that high-pitched shriek, that *kree-ee-ar,* and then dived at them again and again, until they swerved off the road and into a ditch."

She could barely speak around a terrible lump that formed in her throat. "Rednecks? Who were they? Where were you? Jesus, Rocky, I told you to tell me if anything weird like this happened."

"Hey, there was nothing weird about it. They'd probably had too much weed or beer or something. I was never in danger."

"Did you know these kids?"

"Adults, they were adults. I think they were part of Zee Small's group."

Zee Small was an island old-timer, a survivalist and fundamentalist whom Kate had known since she was a kid. He and her father used to fish together. Back then, he was just a humorous eccentric. But during the Y2K hoopla, Zee believed the end-time had arrived and he and some of his flock had moved into the woods on the farthest island that comprised Cedar Key.

Cedar Key actually consisted of four small islands connected by isthmuses. The largest island was where they were—the tourist and downtown areas that extended to the first bridge. The second island was where the wealthiest people lived, their homes lining the island's runway. The third part of the island was located on either side of Gulf Road, a working-class area, blue-collar, where zoning laws were nonexistent. Here, everything was mixed together: trailers, new homes on pilings, old homes flush to the ground. Yards often looked like used-car lots.

Then there was the fourth island, middle-class homes that were once a gated community and great, deep thickets of trees at the northern end. That was where Zee and his group lived, in the woods, on land that had been in his family for generations. His group was like a commune of gypsies, people coming and going all the time, some of them living in old rusted trailers, others living in tents, the women cooking outdoors, kids and dogs running wild around the camp. Zee's Camp. That was how it was known on the island.

"What did the guys in the cart do when Liberty attacked them?"

Rocky laughed. "Got out of there very fast."

"I'll talk to Zee about it."

"No, don't, Mom. It's no big deal."

"It's a big deal to me."

"This is exactly why I didn't want to tell you about it." He sounded pissed. "I knew it would make you all paranoid."

With that, he picked up his empty dishes and went inside. What the hell, she thought, and cleared the table and followed him into the kitchen. She set everything on the counter next to the sink. "You know what happened at the hotel that night, Rocky, with Bean and Marion. It was weird, okay? And there's other strange stuff going on around here. I'm just asking you to be careful."

"Yeah, whatever." He rinsed his plates, put it all in the dishwasher. "I'm going over to Amy's."

Amy lived in one of the large homes along the runway. Her grandfather had invented the seat belt and they owned a Learjet that flew her dad to Atlanta a few times a week. She lived in another world altogether. "Have you noticed anything odd with her or her family?"

Rocky rolled his eyes, grabbed his pack, and headed for the door. "Nope. Nothing. See you tomorrow."

"Hey, Rocky. Hold on a second."

Another roll of the eyes, a huge, exaggerated sigh. Teenage bullshit, she thought, and got right in his face. "I told you what to look for. The dark, shiny eyes, the—"

"Christ, I get it. Really. There's talk, Mom, a lot of talk about how . . .

well, paranoid you've gotten. I understand you witnessed something weird in the hotel bar. Fine. But weird shit happens daily around here. It's the nature of Cedar Key."

Where the hell was *this* coming from? "I don't know who you've been talking to, Rocky. But until a few months ago, the kind of weird shit *I'm* talking about *never* happened here." She dropped her hands to his shoulders. "Hey, look at me."

At fifteen, he was her height, five foot ten, and when he met her gaze, she experienced a maternal time slippage: *Where did the years go?* She could still remember holding Rocky in her arms, reading him to sleep at night, tucking him in, trying to answer his questions about his absent father. Now he stood head to head with her, already had an iPod bud in one ear to block her out. She flicked the bud from his ear. "Listen closely, Rocky. Nothing on this island is what it seems. If Amy or someone else you care for has dark, glossy eyes, exhibits jerky movements and twitches, if their mouths seem to move out of synch with what they're saying, then run fast in the opposite direction. Promise me you'll do that."

"Fuck." He jerked away from her, stuck the iPod bud in his ear again. "You sound nutty, Mom. Honestly, that's how you sound."

"Promise me," she snapped.

"Okay, okay, I promise. Are you closing up the bar tonight?"

"Yeah, I'll be home after one."

"I'll be here," he said, then moved swiftly past her, his body language screaming that he couldn't get away from her quickly enough.

When she heard the sputter and gasps of his scooter pulling away from the houseboat, she opened the French doors to the back balcony. Liberty fluttered her wings and hit the empty bowl with her beak. It clattered against the floor. Then she made that high-pitched keening sound and took off after Rocky.

When Kate stepped outside the houseboat at 8:20, a fog rolled off the back bayou, long, white ribbons of the stuff swirling across the surface of the water, making its way toward land. That was another thing that had changed on the island, she thought. Never, in all the years she'd lived here, had fog on Cedar Key been as frequent as it was now, coming in nearly every night, thick and strange, swelling like a tick until dawn. She decided to drive to work. The memory of walking home in the fog that night in February was much too vivid in her mind.

Kate walked briskly along the side of Richard Pinella's house and was surprised to see the lights on. He had gone into work at the hotel bar at one this afternoon and wasn't supposed to get off until she arrived. She rapped at his front door. "Hey, Rich," she called. "It's me."

"Hold on," he shouted.

Moments later, he opened the door, a towel wrapped around his waist, his curly black hair wet from the shower, water beaded on his muscular arms, his broad shoulders. He was a year older than she, and they had known each other since they were kids. He had gotten married right out of college, then divorced a few years later and returned to Cedar Key. His daughter, whom he rarely saw, lived in Boulder with her mother. Kate had never married Rocky's dad and had sole custody of Rocky, but otherwise their lives had followed parallel tracks until the tracks had intersected last year.

"I thought you were working," she said.

The flash of his smile, the way his hazel eyes undressed her in a single, swift glance, excited her. It had been weeks since they'd made love, weeks since they'd spent any quality time together. "I was. But late this afternoon, Bean asked me to help him move a boat to the marina on the other side of the island and the tide was out and we got stuck out there for a while." He opened the door wider. "C'mon in. It's chilly."

Kate entered the house, he shut the door, and without another word, he slipped his arms around her, holding her close. He was several inches taller than she and her face fit perfectly into the curve of his shoulders. She breathed in the scent of his skin, of the soap he'd used, something new she didn't recognize. It reminded her of autumn here on Cedar Key, when the wind brought in the salty odors of the marsh, of the mud flats that appeared at low tide, a masculine smell. His towel was new, too, fluffy and thick, a bold purple. Rich never bought new towels or new sheets. He prided himself on making do with what he had.

He slid his fingers through her hair, tilted her head back. "I've missed you, Katie-bird," he whispered, and kissed her so passionately that she felt as if she were falling and stumbled back against the wall.

Then her hands moved of their own volition, tugging on his towel until it dropped away. He unzipped her jeans, rolled them down over her hips, and kissed his way from her mouth to her thighs. She gasped at the exquisite sensations that coursed through her, her senses burned with desire.

She and Rich moved as though they were joined at the hips, lurching and stumbling until they fell onto the couch. When he slipped into her, her body arched, her nails sank into his back, her legs locked around him, and he thrust with a kind of fierceness that shocked her. In the time they had been lovers, he'd never made love to her like this, as though she were not only the focus of his intense desire, but his *only* desire.

At one point, Kate drew back, her hands at the sides of his face. "What?" she whispered. "What is it?"

His eyes seemed to darken and gloss over, as Bean's had that February night when he'd come to the houseboat. She pressed her hands against his shoulders, pushing him back slightly so that she could see him better, see him outside the thick shadows that fell over this part of the couch. His eyes looked fine. Of course they did. She had imagined it.

"I've just missed you," he said hoarsely, and brought his mouth to hers again and thrust on to his own completion.

Her desire turned to dust. She couldn't help it. She lay beneath him for a few moments, then said, "Listen, I need to get to work. Bean will have a fit if I'm late. I'm already treading on thin ice with him."

"I'll walk with you."

"I'm driving."

"Can I hitch a ride with you?"

His eyes looked as they always did, a pale, almost transparent blue, and she wondered what was wrong with her. Ever since that night in February, she'd been suspicious of everyone, even Rich. Maybe her son was right that she was overly paranoid. She resolved to be more trusting.

The two buses from Georgia pulled up to the hotel ten minutes after Kate and Rich arrived at work. The buses held several dozen tourists headed for Disney World tomorrow morning. Tourists meant business and business meant tips and tips meant she would be able to stash away more money toward Rocky's car.

The hotel courtyard overflowed with people, the dining room and bar were jammed. Bean took over the front desk and assigned Maddie to the courtyard with Kate and told Rich to cover the inside bar with one of the waitresses from the dining room. The place teemed with people, adults, kids of all ages, a madhouse.

The younger kids ran wild through the courtyard until Maddie herded them into the lobby, turned on the DVD player, and popped in a Harry Potter movie. They were short on chairs in the courtyard and Kate headed for the old barracks with a flashlight to look for additional chairs. She caught sight of a black dog slinking along the fence, where the shadows were deepest, but it fled before she could approach it. It must've gotten in through the open courtyard gate. Or by digging under one of the fences. Cedar Key had a lot of stray cats and dogs, drawn here for many of the same reasons that humans were—the isolation, the live-and-let-live attitude, and the fact that the residents fed the strays.

Kate opened the creaking door of the barracks and slipped inside. It was one of the creepiest spots, a kind of postscript tucked back at the edge of the property, shrouded on three sides by tall weeds. It supposedly had been a general store in the 1860s and had also housed both Confederate and Union soldiers. Now it just stank of mold and rotting wood, was infested with cockroaches and ants, and she wondered when Bean would get around to renovating it.

She found more chairs in what had been the kitchen and noticed candles and dried wax on the old wooden table. Weird. Who would bother coming in here with candles to sit around the table? Maybe some of the hotel employees came in after the bar closed to tip a few.

She carried two chairs out onto the porch, went back inside for more. This time, the beam of her flashlight caught a partially open cabinet door under the sink. She opened it all the way, expecting to see a trash bin filled with beer and wine bottles. Instead, she found rags that stank of lighter fluid or gasoline, a box of kitchen matches with spent matches inside, and a trash can jammed with all kinds of stuff—empty pizza boxes and Chinese takeout containers, empty soda cans, water and beer bottles, more rags, and wadded paper. She plucked out one piece of paper, smoothed it open against the counter. Just four words were printed on it: "Yes, annihilation by fire."

"What the hell," she murmured, and fished out the other wads of paper, six in all. As she smoothed open each one, she heard the door open.

"Kate? You in here?"

Maddie. Kate shoved the pieces of paper into her jacket pocket. "Yeah, back here, Maddie. I found another dozen chairs."

The pretty young woman hurried in with a dim flashlight, her wild red hair pulled back in a loose ponytail, strands curling at her temples. "It's crazy out there. The dining room is, like, totally jammed, so more people are coming into the courtyard to eat. And the kids are bored with Harry Potter."

"There're more movies in the storage room. Maybe *Lady and the Tramp* would suit them. Or *Narnia*. Or *The Golden Compass*."

"Wow. *The Golden Compass*. I mean, that movie blew me away, you know?"

Kate nodded. "I know people who wouldn't let their kids see that movie when they found out the author is an atheist."

"What?" Maddie squealed and wrinkled her nose. "Are you kidding me?" Then she rubbed her hands together and blew into them to warm them. "So what should I grab here?"

Kate gestured at the chairs. "They're dusty and rusted, but they'll have to do." She drew Maddie's attention to the candles. "You guys coming in here after hours to drink?"

"Me?" Maddie pressed her thumb to her chest. "When I leave here, I go home and crash. Maybe it's the kitchen help." She stacked several chairs and pulled them through the kitchen and out the door, holding it open with her foot. "We've got a dozen of these tourists staying here tonight and a few dozen more staying over on Dock Street at the B and Bs. But they all want to eat breakfast here in the morning and Bean says we're to be back here at six-thirty tomorrow morning."

"I'm a bartender," Kate remarked, following Maddie through the open door. "I'm not sure that even double time would get me back here at that hour."

Maddie laughed. "Yeah, I know what you mean."

They got the chairs outside and two of the waiters dispersed them among the tables. Kate eyed the crowd—large and loud, but not boisterous and rowdy like the customers in the bar that night in February. The difference was subtle, but she knew it was important. Wisps of fog swirled into the courtyard, but stayed low to the ground, twisting like pale vines across the tiles.

"Hey, Maddie, can I ask you something?"

"Sure."

"Have you noticed anything weird about the locals lately?"

The young woman looked at Kate, her expression a complete blank, her body utterly still, unmoving. It was as if she'd turned into a mannequin, eyes wide, unblinking, staring, limbs frozen. Kate couldn't even say for sure if she was breathing. Seconds later, she became animated again, mouth twitching into a half smile, hands fiddling with her ponytail. "I haven't really been here long enough to know what's weird and what isn't. Can you be more specific?"

It was as if she'd had a ministroke during that moment of utter stillness; that was how strikingly different she was right now. "You heard about the incident in the bar in February, didn't you?"

"Yeah." She laughed. "Who didn't? That was plenty weird." She tapped Kate's arm with the back of her hand. "We'd better get moving here, huh?" And she hurried down the old balcony steps and into the courtyard.

Kate stared after her, frowning, perplexed, uneasy.

Maddie knew she'd blanked out there for a moment and that Kate had noticed. It happened sometimes. Someone would say something that surprised or puzzled Dominica, and she would immobilize Maddie—freeze her limbs, vocal cords, eyes, mouth—until she could come up with the appropriate response. Worse, Kate was now front and center on the *bruja's* radar.

Maddie feared for her. Kate hadn't been seized yet; Dominica already knew the woman was suspicious about what was going on here, and now she'd come to the bitch's attention in a way that put her at risk. She might be able to warn Kate if Dominica were sufficiently distracted, but what the hell would she say? *The island is filled with hungry ghosts. Get the hell out while you can.*

It mystified her that Kate hadn't been seized yet. Nearly every other hotel employee had been. What protected Kate?

Maddie allowed herself to slip into Dominica's memories, a morass of nonsequential events, emotions, and relationships down through the centuries. As she sank into the sludge of Dominica's past, she felt soiled, corrupted. It was so easy to get lost in here, inside Dominica's alien psyche. Some memories dead-ended, others hopscotched around in no particular order for decades or centuries, and a few connected with her most ancient memories, when she was the only daughter of a Spanish nobleman.

In those years, she'd been in love with Wayra, but her father had married her off to another nobleman who ditched her when she couldn't have kids. Dominica had wandered through Spain, searching for Wayra, only to discover that her father had had him killed. She died at thirty-six from consumption and a broken heart and Wayra had been waiting for her when she crossed over.

But in Dominica's version of events, Wayra had swept her onto his horse and they had ridden off into the sunset. Unlikely. Wayra had never impressed Maddie as a hero in a romance novel. What seemed most probable was that Dominica selectively edited her memories, filtered them, chose this memory but not that one, and then spun it all to her satisfaction, creating a colorful fiction that suited her.

Maddie swam quickly out of these deeper memories, searching for the more recent stuff. It could be anywhere—at the very surface of her memories, down some shadowed side street, on a mountaintop, in a hotel, a bar, no telling. Then she stumbled over it, tucked away in a culvert near the surface of Dominica's memories.

Kate had a fifteen-year-old son with a pet hawk. Maddie already knew that. Rocky had dropped by the hotel bar a few times, the hawk always nearby. Was Dominica afraid of the *hawk*? And if so, why?

Maddie went back inside, into the kitchen, to pick up four more meals. Dominica was preoccupied with the *brujo* net, the ghost equivalent of the human grapevine. Even though she still controlled Maddie, still possessed her, even though Maddie's lungs still breathed for Dominica and her heart still beat for her, Dominica wasn't fully present. Even she couldn't be fully aware in two places simultaneously. So as Maddie slipped her order pad from the back pocket of her jeans and read off the order to the nearest cook, she also tore a sheet out of the pad and scribbled on the back of it.

The cook, a small Mexican man with beads of sweat rolling down the sides of his face, just snapped his fingers without looking up from the salad he was preparing. "Leave the order, okay? I can't keep track otherwise."

Maddie tore the order from the pad, clipped it on the wire above his head, loaded her tray with meals, and headed for the courtyard again. The note she'd scribbled was in her shirt pocket, and she tucked that little secret into a sealed metal room identical to the room where the *brujos* imprisoned the essences of their hosts when they misbehaved. Maddie knew all about that metal room.

As she passed Kate in the doorway, Maddie intentionally bumped into her, knocking a metal bowl that held packets of sugar to the floor. As they both murmured apologies and stooped over to pick up the packets, Maddie pressed the note into Kate's hand. She picked up the metal bowl, set it on Kate's tray, and kept on walking, her hands sweating, her heart slamming against her ribs, her mouth bone dry with fear.

* * *

Kate delivered the last of her meals and drinks in the courtyard, then went inside the hotel to use the restroom in the back room of the bar. She needed a few minutes alone to read the other notes she'd found in the barracks—and the slip of paper Maddie had pressed into her hand. But Rich motioned her over as soon as she entered the bar.

"What is it?" she asked.

"The waitress on duty is useless. Could you take this tray of drinks to table two?"

"Not a problem. It's on my way to the restroom."

He leaned forward, elbows resting against the edge of the bar. "Think we'll get outta here by one?"

"Fat chance." She tilted her head toward Sam Dorset, the editor of the local newspaper, who was six sheets to the wind. "You'd better cut him off, Rich. He's starting to act like Bean did back in February."

"Sam's harmless." He reached out, touched her chin, drew her face closer to his. "Hey," he whispered. "We have to finish what we started, Katie-bird."

Kate stepped back, picked up the tray of drinks. "We *did* finish it, Richie-bird."

She made her way into the back room. This silly nickname was something new, too. The first time he'd used it was in early March, when they'd gone fishing one Saturday afternoon and made love while anchored by one of the islands. She'd thought it was strange then, knew it was strange now. Until that day on the boat, they had always been just "*Kate*" and "*Rich*" to each other, one-syllable names, sharp, definitive.

Kate set down the tray of drinks at table two, just put them all in the middle, let them figure out what was what, and headed for the restroom. As soon as she was inside, she backed up to the sink and brought out all the slips of paper, puzzled over them. What did "annihilation by fire" mean? Why did one person vote no? What did "banishment" mean? What did "yes" mean? "Yes" to what?

She brought out Maddie's crumpled note. *You're in danger. Speak to no one, not even me. Move your houseboat to some other place on the island. Arm yourself. The hawk may be your greatest protection, but I don't know why.*

Maddie's note triggered a visceral urgency in Kate to—what? Run? Should she grab Rocky and the hawk and take off? But for where? Nothing good was happening on Cedar Key, of that much she felt certain. But she still couldn't define the malaise, the infection, the source of her unease. She was paranoid, yes, she couldn't deny it. She'd been paranoid when Jake was so often absent from home, paranoid that he was having affairs, and her paranoia had proven to be correct. But just because she was right back then didn't mean she was right now. Yet, deep down, she knew that what she felt surpassed mere paranoia.

Cedar Key was her home. She didn't intend to let anything or anyone chase her away.

The door to the restroom suddenly slammed open, banged into the wall, and the editor of the paper stumbled in. Sam Dorset stood for a drunken moment in the doorway, a large bear of a man, and peered at her as though she were a curious piece of furniture that had appeared out of nowhere.

"You've got the wrong restroom, Sam."

"Nope."

He hit the dead bolt, lurched toward her, threw his arms around her, and they fell back against the wall. Kate tried to shove him back, but Sam outweighed her by at least seventy-five pounds. He trapped her against the wall with his body, his hands groping at her breasts. When she struggled to knee him in the groin, he stepped on top of her feet, pinning them to the floor. She screamed and clawed at his face and skull, beat her fists against his shoulders, his temples. He slapped his hand over her mouth, his face so close to hers she nearly gagged on the reek of alcohol. "Don't scream, you can't scream, I can smell him on you, it excites me, it—"

Kate bit his hand hard, drawing blood. He jerked his arm away, his feet slipped off hers, and she kneed him in the groin. Sam fell back, gasping, clutching himself, and Kate lunged for the door.

Her hands shook so terribly she fumbled with the dead bolt, and before it clicked open, he slammed into her from behind, pinning her against the door. One hand gripped her hair, forcing her head back, and the other hand groped between her thighs. She kept shrieking, shouts erupted on the other side of the door, then someone crashed against it and the old wood splintered and the door flew open.

She and Sam fell back into one of the wooden stall doors; it flew open and they crashed into the toilet. Rich and Bean rushed in, but Sam was oblivious. He kept jerking on her hair, clutching the back of her sweater.

Kate jabbed her elbow into his stomach, slammed it into his chin. Rich and Bean, shouting and dancing around like boxers in the ring, kicked Sam in the side, and he finally released her. Rich grabbed Kate's forearms and heaved her to her feet.

She tore away from Rich and stumbled out of the stall, pushed her way through a clutch of men and women gathered around the outside of the restroom, and ran out of the bar. Adrenaline coursed through her, and she felt the lingering sensations of Sam's hands and mouth. Great heaving shudders of horror gripped her. She ducked behind the front desk, snatched her bag off a shelf, grabbed the receiver, and punched out 911.

It rang and rang and rang. She hit the disconnect button and called Chief Frank Cole's home phone.

As it rang, Rich hurried over to the desk. "Are you okay?"

"I . . . I think so . . . I . . ."

He pressed his finger over the disconnect button. "No need to call the cops, Kate. Bean and I will take care of it."

She dropped the receiver, so infuriated by what he'd just said that she could barely speak. "He nearly *raped* me. Don't tell me what the fuck I can or can't do, Rich. I'm filing assault charges against him."

He touched the back of her hand. "I'm trying to . . . protect you," he whispered. "Please don't make waves."

Kate jerked her hand away, slung her purse over her shoulder. *"Don't make waves?"* she hissed. "What the hell is *wrong* with you, Rich?" She spun around and dashed for the door, nearly barreling into Bean and another man as they hauled Sam between them, toward a back room employees used.

Some of the Georgia tourists had heard the commotion and stepped out of the dining room to see what was going on. Kate just kept on moving, fast, eyes on the front door, anxiety gnawing through her. All she wanted to do was get out of here.

"Kate!" Bean shouted at her from across the lobby.

She swung her arm into the air and shot him the bird. She never hesitated or stopped, but barreled on through the front door.

Six

The moment Wayra saw Maddie march toward the hotel, he knew Dominica had full control of her. He didn't need to stick around. Maddie was here, Dominica had a new tribe of misfits—it was all he needed to know.

He slipped under a back fence where he'd dug a sizable hole, and trotted through an alley and then under another fence on the eastern side of the courtyard. He moved swiftly through the overgrown yard of a house that smelled abandoned and came out at the front of the hotel. The tantalizing aroma of food nearly drew him back onto the property through the open courtyard gate. But he wanted to peer into the front windows of the hotel to find out what had happened inside. Wayra had heard a woman shrieking—not a drunken shriek, but one of terror.

He climbed under the balcony railing and plopped down in front of one of the lobby's floor-to-ceiling windows. Other people apparently had heard the woman's screams. Employees emerged from the kitchen, customers hurried out of the dining room, the bar, even a couple on the staircase paused and glanced back to see what was going on.

One man shouted at a woman hurrying away from him and she flung her arm into the air, middle finger extended. She burst through the front door barely stifling a sob, whipped out her cell phone, and punched out a three-digit number. Nine-one-one? Was she the woman who had shrieked? Had she been seized by one of Dominica's *brujos*?

Wayra sniffed deeply. *Brujo* stink permeated the air here, but it wasn't *inside* this woman.

"Shit," she murmured, moving swiftly down the steps. "I should've parked closer." She paused. "Talking to self, Kate. None of that. Shut up, just shut up and keep walking."

She punched out a number on her cell. Wayra, trotting after her, heard her say, "Frank, it's Kate Davis. I want you to know I'm filing a complaint against Sam Dorset for assault and attempted sexual battery. He nearly raped me tonight in the hotel restroom. I'll drop by the station tomorrow and make a formal complaint."

Brujo sexual aggression. He decided to stay close to this woman. She seemed to be some sort of *brujo* focal point.

Kate snapped the cell shut, knuckled her eyes, and finally noticed him. Her eyes were lovely, but red from crying. "Don't go in there, dog. They might eat you for dinner."

Wayra wagged his tail and kept pace with her as she hurried up the street. He had checked into a motel early this afternoon and sooner or later would have to return for his belongings. But for now, this woman was the person to follow. He could smell her rage and horror at what had happened and, beneath this, smelled her worry about fog. Yet, no fog had risen yet, at least not here in the downtown area. He caught another odor, too. Kate recently had had sex with someone who had been seized, a man with whom she worked.

It was difficult to read the man's scent through Kate. But the *brujo* stink was like no other and he was able to follow it back to an event earlier in the evening, when the man had been with Dominica and several other *brujos*, on a beach somewhere. That event smelled of smoke and fire, destruction and death, Dominica's calling card. He kept trying to untangle the rest of the story, but couldn't.

Kate stayed on Second Street, where there were pedestrians, electric carts, a few cars. At the intersection, she turned right onto State Road 24 and walked fast. He stayed close to her side. When her cell rang, she glanced at the ID then took the call. "Hi, Frank. I assume you got my message?"

Wayra didn't have to strain to hear the man's response. His hearing, like his shifter sense of smell, was greatly heightened and it helped that the night was quiet.

"I did," Frank said. "I also spoke to Bean. He says Sam was six sheets to the wind, and right now, he's out cold in the office."

"And your point?"

"I'm not doing squat tonight. Let him sleep it off. Come by the station tomorrow to file your complaint."

"Excuse me, Frank. The fucker tried to rape me, okay? I don't care if he's in a *coma*. You need to take him in."

"If you're taking issue with my authority as chief of police, Kate, then I suggest you speak to the mayor, my boss." His voice bristled with anger. "See you tomorrow." He disconnected.

"Christ," she whispered, and her voice broke.

Wayra whined, and Kate ran her fingers over his head. "This picture is fucked up big-time, dog. *I'm* the one who got assaulted, but *Sam* is the victim."

Behind the Island Market, the fog had rolled in already and it was half a foot high and still coming in off the water. But it stopped within a foot of him and the woman. The ghosts who traveled within it probably sensed something unknown and deeply strange about him and wouldn't make any aggressive move until they understood what he was.

Kate paused at an older-model VW Bug, opened the door, glanced at him. Wayra sat back, mustering his best forlorn expression. "I must have rocks in my head," she said, and gestured at the open door. "Go on. Get in. I can't just leave you out here."

Wayra leaped into the VW and settled in the passenger seat. So many odors in here—of the man with whom she'd had sex, of a younger, hormonal man—her son?—and then the smells of her various moods, thoughts, suspicions. A complex woman, he thought, and what a bonus that she had a soft spot for animals.

As soon as they were on the move, Kate started patting her pockets, looking for something. She pulled pieces of paper out of a zippered pocket in her jacket, turned on the inside light, and read each note aloud as she drove. "'Yes, annihilation.' 'Yes, banishment.'" There were more, but based on just these two he knew they were connected to some rule or law that Dominica had established in her new tribe. She had tried this before when Esperanza was young and her tribe was relatively new. Back then, she'd failed to enforce her rules.

The last note Kate read aloud alarmed him. He felt sure that Maddie had written it. If so, it meant she had learned enough about *brujo* consciousness to communicate without Dominica being aware of it. Unless it was a *brujo* trick.

Kate punched out another number on her cell phone. He smelled her annoyance that the person on the other end didn't pick up. She left a message: "Rocky, I'm moving the houseboat over to the Island Marina in about five minutes. Give me a call. You'll need to drive the car over there while I'm moving the houseboat."

Wayra stuck his head out the window, dismayed to see the fog moving along with them, hanging back slightly from the car. Long tendrils of the stuff snaked between houses, through weeds, and slithered across blades of grass. He could just make out the *brujo* litany, that singsong refrain that Dominica had taught them. *Find the body, fuel the body, fill the body, be the body.* She apparently was trying hard to duplicate her tribe of ancient *brujos* in Esperanza, but he sensed that most of these ghosts were young, recently dead, naïve, reckless. They were like planets revolving around the sun, Dominica. Without her, the tribe would fall apart.

He smelled Kate's fear again, a different sort of fear, about traveling within the fog to move her houseboat through the back bayou to a marina. He wished she would wait until morning, when even *brujo* fog usually burned off, but he didn't have a say in any of it. The most he could do to repay this woman for her kindness and the inadvertent insights he'd gained was to stay with her until she made this dangerous move.

She hung a right down a narrow street shrouded by huge trees. The fog here remained low to the ground, but there was so much of it he feared it might already be too late for Kate. Once Dominica had someone in her sights, she brought the full force and power of the dead to bear against the person. Few survived such an experience. Those who did were permanently changed. Many were irreparably damaged.

The headlights impaled a tall, slender man in the distance, at the end of the street, waving his arms. He stood next to a scooter with a hawk perched on its handlebars. *"The hawk may be your greatest protection, but I don't know why,"* Maddie had written Kate. Was this the hawk?

The bird suddenly lifted into the air and flew toward them, its high-pitched keening both a greeting and a cry of alarm. Wayra drew its scent into his lungs, but couldn't read it. And yet, it was a sparrow hawk, just like that hawk in the landfill near Ocala. But was it the same hawk? Was this the synchronicity he'd hoped for?

Kate stopped alongside the scooter, got out, and the young man threw his arms around her. "Jesus, Mom. One of Amy's neighbors was at the hotel and told us you got raped."

"Nearly. It's okay, Rocky. I'm okay."

"I . . . I was so worried. I'm glad you're all right and sorry I was such a shit earlier." He stepped back, as if his own emotion embarrassed him. "Who was it?"

"Sam Dorset. I already talked to Chief Cole. He's useless. Look, get your scooter on the houseboat. We're outta here."

Wayra jumped down from the car and barked. Rocky's face lit up and he ran his hands over Wayra's head. "Wow, who're you?"

"He followed me from the hotel," Kate said. "I couldn't just leave him. So for now, he's ours."

"I hope he and Liberty get along."

The hawk hovered just above them, wings fluttering, then flew on be-tween houses. Wayra watched her until a strong scent distracted him, that of the man with whom Kate had had sex. Wayra understood this was the man's home and that Kate, her son, and the hawk lived out back, in the houseboat tethered to the dock.

Rocky pushed his scooter onto the houseboat, then started untying the houseboat from the dock. "Why're we moving from here? Rich didn't have anything to do with this, did he?"

"He told me not to make waves when I was about to call Chief Cole. He's . . . changed, Rocky. I can't explain it beyond that."

He gave her an odd look, skeptical, then said, "I'll move your car, Mom."

"Forget the car. And the cart. We'll come back for them tomorrow. I need you on the houseboat with me. Look, I know you think I'm paranoid and whatever, but we can't just stay here, okay?" She gestured toward the water, the fog. "That shit freaks me out. I'd like some human company as we navigate through it to the marina."

"Yeah, it freaks me out, too."

Minutes later, the boat began to move into the bayou. Wayra trotted out to the front deck and noticed the hawk perched at the edge of the open upper deck, watching him warily. *Are you the same hawk from the landfill?* He directed his question at the hawk, but she simply swiveled her head, looking away from him.

As the boat entered the thicker fog, which blanketed every small rise of land, he suddenly felt Charlie beside him, then saw him clearly, sitting near the railing, legs crossed. He puffed on his fat Cuban cigar. *The fog is filled with them, Wayra. If you could see what I do, you'd make them turn back.*

I don't have a say, Charlie. And unless you've got some specific alterna-tives, get lost.

Another man materialized next to Charlie, a short, squat man with Oriental eyes, a clean-shaven jaw, and a bald head. He wore a suit and tie and looked like a Wall Street guy. Then his attire shifted to jeans and a work shirt, like some down-home farmer dude from Kansas. He kept fine-tuning his clothing, the blue of the shirt deepening, his denim jeans shift-ing from dark blue to stonewashed to jeans with frayed hems. Victor, the chaser clotheshorse. Whenever he was uneasy, his clothes changed per-petually.

He was one of the thirteen on the chaser council, an ancient whose last physical life predated Wayra's birth by at least several centuries. *Wayra, good to see you again,* Victor said.

I'd like to be polite and return that greeting, Vic. But I know better.

You always were a cynic. Victor suddenly grew hair, as if he believed it might create a more congenial atmosphere between them.

I like you better as a bald guy, Wayra remarked.

Really? Why's that?

Buddha was bald. I have a fondness for Buddha.

Actually, Buddha wasn't bald, Wayra, but I'll leave you to your illusions. With that, Victor went immediately bald again and developed a protruding belly. *You should know, Wayra, that Dominica burned one of her own for saving his human host and annihilating two brujos. We recruited him, a surgeon in his most recent life. And Maddie was enormously courageous and helpful.*

So you've known all along that she was on Cedar Key? Wayra asked.

Not all along, no. But—

Wait a minute, Charlie burst out. *You two know each other?*

Oh, c'mon, Charlie, Wayra said. *I know at least six of the thirteen chasers on the council. I may know more than that and just don't realize they're on the council.*

But I bet you don't know that Victor was my mentor during the last few years of my life, Charlie said. *That he recruited me into the chasers.*

This bit of information astonished Wayra. He hadn't known anything about how Charlie had become a member of the chaser council. *Victor, I appreciate the update on Maddie, but unless you have some useful intel about how I can rescue her without Dominica bleeding her out, you can go away. I've known Dominica longer than any of you chasers. I understand the dynamics. I won't be dictated to by anyone who allowed this travesty to happen in the first place.*

Victor glared at him. The hawk abruptly swept down from her perch on the roof and dive-bombed the two chasers. Her shrieks brought Rocky to the front of the houseboat, but since he couldn't see the chasers, he didn't have any idea what was going on. He whistled loudly for the hawk and she glided down to his padded arm and clutched it, head moving right, left, her strange eyes impaling Wayra. Charlie and Victor faded away.

Wayra now felt certain she was the hawk he'd seen at the landfill, the hawk who had saved his ass. The fact that she just *happened* to live with

Kate and Rocky was exactly the kind of sign he'd hoped for, the synchronicity he so deeply needed.

Kate veered the houseboat close to the shoreline, where the fog thinned. The *brujos* within it watched them, pursued them, but the fog didn't move any closer to the houseboat until they rounded the eastern edge of the island. Then a pair of tendrils drifted over the side of the houseboat. One slithered toward Wayra, the other toward Rocky.

Wayra growled, bared his teeth, and leaped onto the ribbon of fog, breaking it into dozens of smaller bits. The pieces whipped back and forth, like the severed tail of a lizard, and finally dropped over the side of the houseboat. The hawk shrieked and dived at the long band of fog that threatened Rocky. The length of fog reared up, a pale cobra poised to strike, but the hawk tore through it, her beak ripping it apart.

What the hell sort of hawk was this?

Rocky ran inside, shouting at Kate to open the engine as wide as it would go. As the houseboat picked up speed, the hawk landed on the railing. Her shrieks echoed across the water, through the darkness, like a battle cry. Wayra dropped his head back and howled. The fog rapidly retreated.

Dominica stood in the back office, staring down at Sam Dorset, sprawled on the couch where Gogh's and Joe's hosts had put him. He snored loudly, his mouth partially open, his unshaven jaw giving him a raw, primitive look. Liam, who had been inside him, now hovered nearby, fretting like an old man.

I'm sorry, I didn't mean to do it, but I could smell sex on her, it excited me, I just couldn't help myself and—

"Shut up, Liam," Dominica demanded. "Just shut the hell up. Don't any of you get it?" She looked at Joe, Whit, Jill, Gogh. "You can't allow your hosts to drink alcohol or take drugs. Whenever a host takes any kind of mood-altering substance, *we* lose our way too easily. We need this hotel as our base. It's how we make money, how we fit into the community. Once the island is completely ours, we'll have to mingle with tourists. And what happened tonight and back in February just *cannot* be repeated. Ever. So as of right now, every *brujo* who has a host is responsible for that host's behavior. I've taught you how to control humans, how to manipulate them, how to isolate their essences, how to inflict pain on them when they misbehave. Use the tools I've given you."

"You're being kind of harsh, Nica," said Whit. "None of us is as ancient as you are, as proficient in the ways of the dead. We're learning."

"Yeah," Jill piped up.

"Liam nearly disrupted our entire operation," Dominica said. "So here's a new decree. From now on, if you can't control your host, then you don't deserve a host. It's as simple as that." The *brujo* net trembled and shuddered as her new decree was broadcast. "And my best advice to you in this regard is to limit what your host drinks. So Liam, get back into Sam and wipe his memory clean of what happened."

I already did that.

"You'd better be sure. You need to fiddle with his brain chemistry so his body absorbs the alcohol more quickly, and get him home. I don't want him here."

I don't know squat about brain chemistry. Before I died, I ran a convenience store.

"For Chrissake," she snapped, and backed up to a chair and sat down. Dominica plunged Maddie into a Snow White sleep so fast that her host never had a chance to fight it. Then she drifted out through Maddie's chest and spoke with Liam and the others mind to mind. *You're going into Sam with me, Liam, and I'm going to show you what to do. Then you're going to teach it to the others. That's your new assignment. Understood?*

Yeah, okay. I get it, you don't have to scream.

She had never had to explain such things to her tribe in Esperanza. Many of those *brujos* had been as old or nearly as old as she was and understood the human body. She initially learned about human physiology from a surgeon who had hosted her for a year. He never even knew he'd been seized; her purpose with him was simply to learn. Hadn't any of these ghosts been curious enough to explore the parameters of power in the world of the dead? Until she'd liberated them, hadn't they ever ventured somewhere other than their pathetic astral planes?

She drifted through the top of Sam's head and Liam followed her. Within minutes, she had shown him how to speed up the alcohol absorption in Sam's body and how to conduct a memory wipe correctly, focusing on the hippocampus and prefrontal cortex. Even though memory wasn't just confined to these two areas of the brain, this wipe would suffice for their purposes. It was possible that Sam might remember bits and pieces of the incident later, but in the long run it wouldn't matter. Every host they seized was damaged in some way, even Maddie. And the longer she hosted Dominica, the more damaged she would become.

The damage manifested in any number of ways. Sometimes hosts were so broken by *brujo* possession they went mad. Then the virtual metal room became their padded cell for the rest of their existences. Other times, hosts became psychic. Or psychotic. Or sociopathic. Some simply gave up, surrendering completely. Some were compliant and a few entered into a kind of symbiosis with their *brujos*. Those were the best kinds of hosts.

Maddie was not that kind of host.

At times, Dominica felt her hatred and revulsion of all things *brujo*, and on occasion Maddie dropped her guard and Dominica could dip into her memories. That had been more common in the early days of their relationship. Now, her guard seemed to be up most of the time. It was difficult for Dominica to read her at all.

Will you be able to teach these techniques to others, Liam?

Absolutely. It's easy. The—

Loud, insistent knocking at the door startled all of them. *Joe, see who it is and get rid of them.*

As he moved to the door, Dominica drifted out of Sam and slipped back into Maddie, waking her, animating her, and urged her to follow Joe. Since his host was the owner of the hotel, it was logical that he should deal with customer complaints, employee problems, anything related to the functioning of the business. Maddie was the front desk lady, the public relations person who always greeted customers with a quick, engaging smile, directed them to restaurants, rentals of kayaks, canoes, electric carts, and handed out maps, bottled water, and whatever else was requested. When necessary, as it was earlier tonight, she helped bartend and waitress.

Joe opened the door. "May I help you, sir?"

"Uh, yes. I'm the coordinator of the group that pulled in earlier today? From Georgia? Some of our passengers are quite concerned about what happened earlier. I'd like to speak to the management."

Dominica suddenly didn't trust Joe to handle this particular problem, so she swept past him, her hand extended. "Hi, I'm Maddie. I'd be glad to answer any questions you have." Dominica stepped outside with him, shutting the door behind her. She touched the man's arm, walking him over to the desk. "What's your concern, sir?"

His prissy mouth pursed, and he poked at his black frame glasses, pushing them farther up the bridge of his nose. "Well, we're a family group, as you know, and, quite frankly, some of the parents are concerned about the rape that occurred earlier."

"It wasn't a rape," Dominica said. "A customer had way too much to drink and walked into the women's restroom by mistake."

His eyes widened. "Ah, okay. That explains why the police didn't show up. I'll let the parents know. They were talking about checking into another hotel."

"Well, if they'd like to do so, we'd be glad to refund their money. And we do apologize for the worry that incident caused."

"Thanks very much."

He walked off toward the dining room and Dominica hurried back to the room where the others were. "Okay, let's get back to work, people. Whit, may I speak to you for a moment?"

When the others had left, she gestured toward Sam. "Someone should drive him home. Then I want Kate Davis found. Joe's host needs to apologize to her. He and Gogh frightened her."

"Why not just seize her? She's a goddamn pain in the ass. And it would be easier for her and Gogh to get along then."

"Find me the right ghost and we'll do it. A very strong-willed ghost. Like you."

"You're the only other *brujo* as strong-willed as I am, Nica."

He leaned toward her then, to kiss her, and suddenly Maddie seized enough control of her body to pull back, to jerk her arms upward. Dominica tightened her control on Maddie before she could shout out loud, but she screamed in her mind. *You let that fucker kiss me and I'll fight you so hard you'll be forced to bleed me out in front of a bunch of your kind.*

"Shut up," Dominica hissed, and was horrified when Maddie's body started twitching, jerking, her limbs moving in every direction, as though she were in the midst of an epileptic fit.

Alarmed, Whit moved toward her. "Nica, what is it?"

"She's . . . fighting me."

Dominica slammed her virtual fist into Maddie's pain centers, into a knot of nerves, and she fell to her knees, sobbing, body shuddering, foam filling the corners of her mouth, spilling down her chin. Her eyes rolled back in their sockets, and she went still. She had passed out. Dominica forced her into consciousness, made her sit up, and looked at Whit.

"It's over," she said quietly. "You and I can't do anything when I'm using her as a host. Find the right ghost for Kate. And one for her son." And for that strange hawk of theirs, she thought, but didn't say it. The hawk disturbed her and she didn't know why. "And let's step up the seizure program, Whit. Tomorrow, we seize the county coroner in Gainesville and get him out here to the island. And we seize a few state cops, the ones who drop by the bar when they're off duty. Let's up the ante. Ten to fifteen hosts seized daily."

Whit winked, aimed his index finger at her as though it were a gun. "I'm on it," he said, and strode quickly from the room.

Dominica sat there on the floor for a few moments, hating Wayra and all the others who had chased her from the mountains of Ecuador to this flat, strange spit of land on the Gulf of Mexico. But right now, she felt certain she was winning, and that was more important than her hatred, her need for revenge. It was all that mattered.

March 15-16

. . . .

Seven

Even at seven in the morning, the Island Marina offered zero privacy, Kate thought. It stood at the end of Dock Street, the tourist zone, and faced a tremendous parking lot that would fill steadily all day. On the far side of the lot were two more docks where surplus tourist boats were tied up. Across the street was a place that rented electric carts. And it was all exactly what she craved right now, the company of humanity in all of its myriad forms.

Her houseboat, *Someday,* was now docked in slip 13 and bobbed in the early morning swells. Powered by a single Mercruiser 228 horsepower engine, it was thirty-six feet long, with an inside cabin large enough for her and Rocky to live here comfortably. They had sectioned it off so they each had a small bedroom, enough space to give them some privacy. With the open upper deck, and the front and rear decks, they rarely got in each other's way.

At the moment, Kate sat on the back deck, sipping coffee, and tried to piece together everything that had happened yesterday. But whenever she thought about it, she was suddenly back in the restroom, fighting off Sam. Or she was facing Rich as he told her there was no need to call the cops, that she shouldn't make waves. She wasn't sure where to go from here, where to turn, what to do. The only thing she felt certain about was that she would not be returning to the hotel to bartend. It frightened her to even consider how she would make ends meet without her income and tips from the hotel.

She stared out across the water, mulling over her few options: draw money from Rocky's car fund, beg Annie for more hours at the café, or look for another part-time job. None of these options looked promising.

Kate watched the dozens of sailboats and fishing vessels dotting the expanse of water off to her right. A few noisy Jet Skis sped by, headed for the Old Fennimore Mill condos, a dozen three-story buildings smack on the salt marsh. Tourists, she thought. They were the only ones who used Jet Skis around here. Several colorful kayaks waited on the skinny, sunlit sand that was the public beach. The island playground was empty at this hour. Pretty soon, the guy who rented out the slips would show up for work, see the houseboat, and stop by to be paid, a week in advance. He would give her a discount because she discounted his drinks every time he came into the hotel bar. She wasn't worried about that. What worried her was everything else.

Suppose the slip guy was afflicted in the same way as Rich? Bean? Marion? Sam? The chief of police? Cedar Key was so small that it wouldn't take Rich too long to check the various marinas. What would she say to him if he appeared?

Kate rubbed her dry, aching eyes and wished she had gotten a good night's sleep. But by the time she'd finally crashed, Rocky had gone to bed, the dog was curled up in a ball on the back deck, the hawk had flown off somewhere, and she felt severed from her old life, adrift, directionless. She had gotten up at five to watch the sun rise and, by then, the hawk still hadn't returned, the dog was asleep in the kitchen, and Rocky slept on. Alone but not alone. It seemed to be the story of her life.

She walked out to the front deck and watched the trucks pulling into the marina parking lot, all of them hauling boats. Fishermen always got started early. A couple of the guys waved at her, locals she knew from the bar who hadn't been coming around much since the weirdness had started. Then a spiffy new black truck swung to a stop in front of her houseboat and Fritz Small, Zee's son, hopped out, a tall, lanky young man with tattooed arms. He looked like a redneck but had graduated with honors from Brown a couple of years ago. His wife, Diane, was with him. She was in graduate school in Gainesville.

Fritz waved and called out, "Morning, Kate."

"Hey, Fritz, Diane. What brings you guys into town so early?"

"The bass are running," Fritz said. "I, uh, just wanted to stop by and let you know that Dad will be dropping in to see you. He's completely lost his mind, so don't believe a word of what he says, Kate."

"Lost his mind? You mean, about this end-time stuff?"

Diane rolled her eyes and curled her long, dark hair around her hand, then flicked it over her shoulder. "This goes well beyond the end-time. He heard about what happened to you last night, with Sam Dorset, and he's going to tell you his crazy theories."

"Word sure gets around this island pretty fast," Kate remarked. "What's his theory?"

"It's total bullshit." Fritz tugged his baseball cap down lower over his forehead. "Just take it with a grain of salt." He leaned forward and patted her arm. "And take care, hear?"

And just like that, he and Diane hopped back into their truck and drove out of the lot. Kate stood there for a moment, frowning, sipping from her mug of coffee, then retreated to the back deck, not sure what to think. Less than half an hour later, she heard someone calling her name, got up again and moved to the side of the houseboat, where she could see the old man at the front. "Zee?"

"Who else would come calling with a bowl of hot grits and scrambled eggs, two forks, and a bottle of moonshine?" He patted the soft cooler slung over his shoulder, laughed, and came on board.

His stride seemed markedly slower than she remembered, his shoulders more hunched, his gray hair grayer, the pack on his back as prominent as a tumor. But he clutched the case that held his prized Stradivarius and the mirth in his rheumy blue eyes hadn't changed one iota. Kate hugged him hello, their mutual history a third presence that mitigated whatever differences they might have.

"Good to see you, Zee."

"You, too, hon."

As she stepped back from him, she felt certain that among all the people she knew on Cedar Key, Zee hadn't changed. The evil hadn't claimed him. How could it? It would have to find him first. He rarely ventured away from his wooded camp on the other side of the island.

Kate pulled another chair up to the table and Zee plopped his thin body into it. He set his containers on the table, placed the Stradivarius case carefully on the floor next to his chair. "Can I get you some coffee? Juice? Toast?" she asked.

"All of the above would be magnificent, thanks."

"Coffee black, straight up? Right?"

"You got it. And I'll add a splash of moonshine."

"And honey rather than jelly on the toast."

"Ah, Kate, you have your old man's memory."

Kate ducked inside the houseboat for plates, napkins, coffee, and popped a couple of slices of her homemade date bread into the toaster. When she rejoined Zee on the back deck, he had opened his containers of food and his moonshine, and stood near the railing, the gorgeous violin tucked under his chin, bow poised.

"Got yourself a favorite tune, hon?"

"Charlie Daniels. 'The Devil Went Down to Georgia.'"

"Perfect choice."

He got to his feet and began to play. The music exploded out across the water, into the early morning light, and transported her to a time when she and Jake had gone to a Charlie Daniels concert in Gainesville. Nearly half a million people had attended. But Zee's grasp of the music and his incomparable talent, combined with the perfect tone and pitch of the violin, far surpassed that of Charlie Daniels. Zee and the violin were one, their skins melted together, their souls joined, he knew all about the devil. And before he finished playing, the dog came out onto the deck, the hawk returned, and Rocky wandered out to see what was going on. Dozens of people gathered in the parking lot, along the other slips, and boaters drew in closer, everyone spellbound.

Years ago when Zee had played for Kate and her dad, Kate had held the violin and had seen the mark that designated it as a genuine Stradivarius: "*Antonius Stradivarius Cremonensis Faciebat Anno 1689.*" She had no idea where Zee had gotten it or the genuine bow or, for that matter, how he had paid for it. She'd always suspected that Zee was a multimillionaire, from a combination of luck and serendipity, but even those details ceased to matter as he played.

When he finished, applause erupted, horns blasted from the Jet Skis, and the sailboats and fishing vessels drew up to the houseboat, clamoring for Zee's autograph. He graciously accommodated all of them. When everyone had wandered away after Zee's fifteen minutes of fame, he leaned toward Kate and Rocky.

"Listen close now. That devil has traveled from Georgia to Cedar Key, and all them people who clapped and cheered know it just as well as me." As he spoke, he ran his hands lovingly over his violin, then returned it to its case, and attacked the food on his plate. In between noisy bites, he talked in a Southern drawl that was as much a part of him as his magnificent talent. "You need to get yourselves someplace isolated, where these fucks can't find you. I would like it if you and Rocky joined our community on the far side of the island, but I 'spect you won't do that, Kate. You're too much like your daddy that way. Your daddy and me were tight, but he hated my religious bullshit, his term, not mine."

"Slow down, Zee," she said. "Fill me in."

"There's no filling in, hon. That's my point. It's them against us." He pulled his pack off the chair, dug inside, brought out a semiautomatic weapon, and set it in the middle of the table. "Your daddy taught you how to shoot. Thirteen rounds in this sucker, with another twenty-six rounds in these two clips." He set the clips on the table. "Take it, Kate. I promised your daddy I'd look after you; this is the best I can do short of you and yours joining me and mine. The end-time is here this time." He dug into his pack again and brought out a small canvas bag. "There're a dozen grenades in here. Satan's legions are taking people on our island, using their bodies, and no one is safe."

Kate stared at the gun, at the bag that held the grenades, and wondered where he'd gotten them and if he'd been stockpiling weapons since Y2K. "Explain what you mean by taking bodies, Zee."

"I'm not sure how they do it, but I've seen it as it happens. Couple two, three weeks ago, I was standing in line at the Island Market. That fellow from the bank, Paul Crown, was in line in front of me, all spiffed up for work, you know? And suddenly he starts twitching all over, like he's got some nervous condition. I asked him if he was okay, and when he glanced back at me, his eyes changed. It was like watching ink being poured over his eyes."

Kate went utterly still inside. "But what *is* it?"

"Satan's legions, like I said."

"You mean, *demons*?" Rocky sounded incredulous.

"That's right, son."

Rocky shook his head. "I don't believe in demons."

"Spirits, then, evil ghosts. It doesn't matter what you call them. Sam Dorset and what he tried to do to you last night, Kate? Ain't Sam doing it. It's the thing inside of him. He got taken weeks ago. Bean over at the hotel? Same damn thing. At least half the hotel employees have been taken, the ones who are involved in the daily functioning of the place."

You're in danger, Maddie's note had said. *Speak to no one, not even me.* Did that mean Maddie had been taken?

I'm trying to protect you, Rich had said. *Please don't make waves.*

She knew Rich had been taken and if the same was true for Maddie, then why had both of them tried to warn her? Did that mean something of their humanity remained?

"Until now, you probably weren't on their list because you're just a part-timer." Zee leaned forward, his voice quiet and intense. "But after last night? You can be sure you've been targeted." His eyes went to Rocky. "And son, you haven't been taken because you're under the age of sixteen, least that's the way I'm figuring it. But even that may not hold right and true much longer."

"I don't believe in demons," Rocky said again. "And frankly, no disrespect intended, Mr. Small, but it sounds like science fiction to me."

"I tell you what, son. I wish it was science fiction. They took the major island players first—a banker, the mayor, the newspaper editor, hotel owner, police, some of the small business owners, the doc, the librarian. I've been piecing this together for weeks. I really got suspicious, though, when those two bodies were found under the pier and there was just a brief mention of it in the paper. Ask yourselves this: What happened to them bodies? Is anyone investigating?" He looked hard at Kate, then at Rocky. "No. They got rid of the bodies."

"How do you know that?" Rocky asked. "Did someone admit it?"

"Me and Frank Cole go back a ways. He's been chief of police on the island for—what? Damn near twenty years? Hell, I've helped him get elected a bunch of times. I ran into him one day and asked him flat-out about them bodies. You know what the asshole says to me? 'Ah, Zee, that's police business, don't worry yourself about it.' That's when I was pretty sure I was on the right track." Zee patted Rocky's arm. "Look, I'm not saying I got all the answers. But I've got some of the answers and now I'm giving them to you and your mom."

"Okay, so let's say you're right, Mr. Small. Then how come four of your people tried to run me off the road the other day? How do you know your own people haven't been taken?"

Kate heard the hostility in Rocky's voice, but was glad he'd asked the question.

"I know them four. They weren't part of our camp. But they'd been taken, all right, and they stole a cart from us. We got it back and sent them on their way."

"How?" Kate asked. "They could've taken you, right?"

"Only if they leaped out of the bodies they were using. But they weren't about to do that." He gave a small, wicked laugh. "We were carrying torches. They're scared shitless of fire. And we had AK-47s. A shot from one of them suckers is going to send you to the other world right quick. And the way I think it works for these demons is if the human host dies before the demon escapes, the demon is obliterated."

"But how can something that's already dead be annihilated, Zee?" she asked. "That doesn't make sense."

He looked suddenly and totally miserable. "I know. I sound like a fuckin' fruitcake. Fritz and Diane, they've just about had it with my theories. But everything I've told you is what I've learned, observed, pieced together."

"You're basically suggesting that we run out to an uninhabited island and hide," Kate said.

"Just to keep you safe from being taken until we've got our army together."

"Your *army*?" Rocky balked. "Why not report this to the feds? Or to the state police? Let them handle it."

"Because we don't know how widespread this invasion is, son. It's possible these ghosts have infiltrated the feds and the state police." He tapped the weapon, the bag of grenades. "Now put these someplace safe. If you need more weapons, come by the camp. My advice to you is to get your supplies and food as soon as the market opens. Make sure you buy extra gasoline and an extra tank of propane. Then you should hightail it out to Snake Key or Sea Horse Key. Both of them have plenty of mangroves and coves where you can drop anchor and not be seen." He pushed to his feet, shrugged on the backpack, carefully fixed the strap of the Stradivarius case over his shoulder. "Son, don't give your ma a lot of grief about this."

"Hey, I still have to go to school, to my job, to—"

"And I still have my job at Annie's Café," Kate said. "Just because we're moving doesn't mean life stops, Rocky."

"That's not what it sounds like."

"Reckon school is okay," Zee said. "Least for a while. As far as we can tell, no teachers have been taken yet. Don't know about the rescue center. Just keep a close watch, son."

"What the hell am I watching for, exactly?"

Zee brought his finger to the corner of his right eye. "The black eyes. That doesn't always happen, but when it does, it's incredibly strange. Then the twitching . . ." He twitched, a perfect imitation of how Rich had twitched last night. "And sometimes their mouths move out of synch with their words."

Rocky shrugged. He obviously thought Zee was as nutty as his mother. "Well, I gotta go shower. Nice seeing you, Mr. Small."

"You, too, Rocky."

Kate walked out to the front of the houseboat with Zee, the dog trotting along behind them. "He's going to give you trouble about this, Kate."

"I know."

"This evil, what's happening here, is hard to accept till you experience it yourself." He hugged her quickly. "You take care. Keep in touch. You got my cell number."

As Kate watched him cross the parking lot, she wondered who he had lost to this evil.

"Mom, you know this is total bullshit, right?" Rocky came up behind her, swung an arm around her shoulders. "I mean, Zee's been planning for Armageddon since Y2K. He's an incredible musician, but he may be crazy."

"We're moving, Rocky."

His arm slipped away from her, and his voice lost its softness. "I'm not moving anywhere. I'll stay with Amy. This is completely insane."

"Nope, you're not staying with Amy. I'll call her parents if you persist with this, Rocky. We'll stay out on Sea Horse. We've got a couple of Zodiac rafts and a skiff with electric motors, and we can keep the cart and the VW somewhere close to wherever we come to shore. I'll need to return to Rich's to get the car and the cart and would appreciate it if you would drive one of them. Then I'm going shopping for food and supplies. I'll meet you back here by noon."

"What the hell are we going to do out there all day? Forget it. I'm not going. I'll help you with the car and the cart, but I'm not going out there. Besides, I've got to work from noon to four."

"Then I'll meet you back here around then."

"You're not hearing me." He was practically shouting now. "I'm. Not. Going. Period."

Kate was now so livid that she fought to keep her voice quiet, even. "Yeah, you are. End of discussion."

She moved past him, certain that if she didn't get away from him quickly, she would say something she could never take back, that would damage their relationship irreparably. She hurried through the houseboat to pick up the weapons and grenades on the deck. She went into her bedroom, slammed the door, dropped everything on the bed. She sank to the edge of the mattress, hands gripping her thighs, forcing herself to take deep breaths, then exhaling slowly. Tears welled in her eyes, and she felt like throwing herself against the bed and sobbing. Yeah, like pulling a Scarlett O'Hara would solve anything.

Then she remembered something her father had said to her one afternoon years ago, when they'd gone fishing. *Trust what you feel even if you don't have facts to back it up, even if the people around you are saying you're crazy. It might just save your life.*

And just that fast, every doubt she'd entertained for the last six weeks disappeared.

Just outside of Gainesville, Sanchez pulled into Devil's Millhopper State Geological Park. He resented the stop; he simply wanted to get to Cedar Key and locate the redhead. He craved the opportunity to see her in person, to feast on the sight of her. That telepathic connection they'd shared, however brief, had ignited something between them. Sanchez had never experienced anything quite like it. It was as if they had stepped inside each other's skins, felt what the other felt in the most intimate, immediate way. Or, at any rate, that was how it had been for him.

Delaney had called him yesterday afternoon when he was on the road and told him to stay overnight somewhere and meet here at the park in the morning. He didn't want Sanchez to head into Cedar Key until they'd both met the FBI agent who had requested ISIS help. Irritating, but there was nothing he could do about it.

He and Jessie got out, he put his suitcase in the trunk, locked the car, and they headed for the half-mile trail where he was supposed to meet the two men. The park was actually a bowl-shaped sinkhole 120 feet deep that led to a miniature rain forest, a biological and ecological wonderland. No dusty paths here. A complex network of wooden boardwalks and stairs switched back and forth along the steep limestone slopes, past streams and lush vegetation. A sign announced that the half-mile nature trail where he was supposed to meet up with the two men only meandered along the top of the sinkhole. A second sign said that dogs on leashes were welcome.

Jessie had never been leashed. Sanchez didn't own a leash. "What the hell, girl. Just stay close, okay?"

She barked and immediately bounded ahead of him, racing along the boardwalk with her nose to the ground. So much for obedience. But in all fairness to her, she'd been in the car since they'd left Cocoa Beach more than two hours ago. They had stayed overnight with a former ISIS remote viewer who had left six months ago for a job with NASA. His friend's job with NASA was to remote-view Mars—for landing spots, sources of water, life-forms. *It beats looking for terrorists,* he'd remarked.

Unless they looked like Red, Sanchez thought. Except that Sanchez no longer believed she was a terrorist. He no longer believed they were dealing with a terrorist organization in the traditional sense of the word. He hadn't yet told Delaney about what had happened the night before last, when he was in his father's yard and Red had communicated with him. But he had given Delaney the location of this alleged terrorist cell and Delaney had sent him northward the next morning.

The one good thing about all this was that the events he'd seen through his sister had now changed. In that vision, Delaney had told Nicole he was flying to Cedar Key "tomorrow" and Sanchez was already there. In actuality, Delaney had flown his Cessna to the area first to meet with the agents investigating the bleed-outs and Sanchez hadn't gotten to Cedar Key yet. Free will prevailed always. What a viewer saw at any given moment was only the most probable version of events. And since the version he'd seen hadn't happened, perhaps the events that would prompt Nicole to demand answers from Delaney wouldn't happen, either.

His BlackBerry jingled as a text message came through. From Nicole.

Hermano, you said you'd stay in touch. What's going on? I haven't heard from you.

Typical, Sanchez thought, that she contacted him at the moment he was thinking about her. He quickly replied:

Sorry. Got caught up in stuff. Not on Cedar Key till later today. Promise to keep in touch.

You'd better. Don't want to punch Delaney. Luv u.

He trotted after Jessie, surprised that the trail around the sinkhole was crowded with runners, hikers with dogs, couples with dogs, families with kids. But it was Sunday, after all, the weather crisp, the sky crystalline, and Gainesville was a college town. No one called him on breaking the leash law or gave him dirty looks. Live and let live.

Near the end of the trail, he saw Delaney and another man leaning against the railing, peering down the chasm, talking earnestly. Delaney was hard to miss anywhere—a black man nearly seven feet tall. But next to him stood a short white guy with sandy blond hair graying at the temples. They looked like characters in a sitcom.

Jessie reached them first, nudged Delaney's leg with her snout, and he laughed and fussed over her. When Delaney introduced her to the fed and she raised her paw in greeting, the man didn't react. The guy either didn't like dogs or was humorless or both. It didn't bode well for this meeting. Sanchez suspected he would end up, once again, defending his ability. The bureau boys he'd dealt with in the past regarded remote viewing as fringe science, a joke, and a waste of taxpayers' money. But perhaps O'Donnell would be different because, as Delaney had said, he wanted results.

Sanchez walked over to them and the fed glanced from Jessie to Sanchez, gave a kind of gritted-teeth smile and stuck out his hand. "Tom O'Donnell. Bob's been extolling your abilities, Mr. Sanchez."

He didn't want to grasp O'Donnell's outstretched hand. But if he didn't, he would be perceived as an unfriendly SOB. So before he gripped the man's hand, he shut himself down psychically, the equivalent of hitting a circuit breaker. It hadn't always been that easy, but it worked. He didn't pick up squat. "My pleasure, Agent O'Donnell."

O'Donnell looked to be in his late forties. Although he was at least a foot shorter than Delaney, he appeared to be fit, a gym rat with muscles as hard as granite, a solid handshake, and piercing eye contact learned at Quantico. "So tell me about this terrorist cell, Mr. Sanchez."

They walked along the trail as Sanchez talked. He chose his words with great care, revealing enough so that O'Donnell didn't interrupt with questions or clarifications. But when Sanchez finished, O'Donnell zeroed in on the one detail that mattered personally to Sanchez.

"The redhead. Tell me more about her."

"There isn't any more to tell."

"But you think she's the head of this cell?"

"We're dealing with a nontraditional terrorist cell and she has been pulled into it inadvertently."

"What do you mean by that? What's a nontraditional terrorist cell?"

Prove yourself, Sanchez, he seemed to be saying. *Show me you know what the hell you're talking about.* Sanchez felt like a bug under a microscope and it pissed him off. "It means, Agent O'Donnell, that whatever profile you bureau boys have cooked up about terrorists is wrong in this instance."

"Really. And you say she was pulled in inadvertently? How can that be? All terrorists have the same choices the rest of us do."

"Terrorists are recruited for a variety of reasons—poverty, despair, hatred, cultural biases, religious beliefs. None of those things apply here. The redhead *didn't have a choice*. That's what the viewing revealed."

"I don't understand."

"In his first viewing, Tom," said Delaney, "he insisted this cell steals *bodies,* not identities. We aren't sure what that means."

Thanks to the contact with Red the other night, Sanchez now knew what it meant. But he wasn't about to enlighten either man yet. O'Donnell was silent for a few minutes, walking quickly, deliberately, like a man who knew that aerobic exercise might extend his life, but who resented every step, every deep lungful of air, every muscle that tightened. He followed Jessie down the boardwalk stairs, away from the sinkhole rim and into the sinkhole itself. Sanchez had the distinct impression that O'Donnell didn't even realize they were descending, that he was so wrapped up in his mental arguments that the downward spiral didn't register.

Halfway down O'Donnell seemed to emerge from his trance. "Here's the deal, Nick." He stopped, hands clutching the railing so hard that the tendons in the backs of his hands resembled the roots of small trees, pressing against the skin as though it were earth. "A couple of days ago, a dog uncovered a body in a landfill in Ocala. So we've got fourteen bodies now, all of them exhibiting the same virus. And this virus, see, is curious.

"It apparently mutates, but we don't know how. It's like nothing the CDC has ever seen before. They aren't sure how contagious it is, but are fairly certain it's spread through body fluids, like AIDS. They also think it may be what caused these massive bleed-outs. One theory they're looking at is that the virus is most dangerous when it mutates, and that's probably when the bleed-outs occur. Frankly, all these highly paid scientists and outside consultants are clueless. So the CDC intends to quarantine the area. HDS, FEMA, the bureau all concur. Initially, we were going to ask you to be embedded, but it's too dangerous. This virus is lethal and we don't know enough about it to advise you on how to protect yourself. So we'd like you to do whatever the hell it is you do in our headquarters just outside the quarantine area."

What the fuck. He didn't intend to be denied the opportunity to find Maddie. "Whatever I pick up outside the quarantine area won't be nearly as accurate as what I can pick up in the town, Agent O'Donnell."

O'Donnell looked irritated. "RV means *remote* viewing, right? I thought the whole point with RV is that you don't have to be on site, that you can do it anywhere."

"That's true." Delaney spoke up quickly. "But with some things, the closer to the target you are, the more accurate the information is."

That was bullshit, Sanchez knew, and read between the lines: Delaney wanted him to be on Cedar Key. "Especially with something like this. There're just too many variables that can get screwed up at any point along the line."

O'Donnell kicked at a stone on the boardwalk and shook his head. "I can't make the call on this one, guys. I have to ask my supervisor and he may have to go up the line to the CDC and DHS. In the meantime, you move into the headquarters and we'll set you up in a comfortable spot and you do your thing, Sanchez."

"Then you'll have to move me in, too," Delaney said. "I'm his monitor. That's how we work, like different halves of the same brain."

O'Donnell's phone rang, he glanced at the number. "Excuse me, I need to take this call."

He walked off and Delaney touched Sanchez's arm and tilted his head toward the stairs. "Let's talk." They moved quickly down another flight of stairs, Jessie leading the way farther down into the sinkhole. "I think we should head back to Homestead and do the RV from there. The idea of being stuck in some makeshift headquarters outside the quarantine zone with O'Donnell breathing down our necks doesn't appeal to me in the least."

That explained why Delaney had supported Sanchez. It didn't have anything to do with him thinking that Sanchez should head to Cedar Key. "I have to go to Cedar Key, Bob. The redhead contacted me the other night."

"What? *How?*"

"Psychically." He quickly told Delaney the rest of it, the truly weird stuff about Annie's Café and the hungry ghosts who were the real terrorists. "My sense is that the ghost in her is so ancient we don't have any context for understanding what's really happening on the island."

Delaney looked horrified. "Jesus, Sanchez. Are you sure that's what she said? Hungry fucking *ghosts*?"

"I heard her as clearly as I hear you right now."

"A terrorist cell of hungry ghosts. Holy shit. There's no precedent for this. Anywhere."

"Which is exactly why I'm going to Cedar Key."

"No way. Too dangerous. O'Donnell is right about that much."

Sanchez felt the rug being snatched out from under him. "I'm going, Bob, with or without your blessing."

"For fuck's sake, Sanchez, don't put me in this position."

"Hey, *I'm* the one going in, *I'll* be at risk, not you."

"You're going rogue, amigo."

"Tell O'Donnell I have to return to Gainesville to get our stuff. When will they impose the quarantine?"

"Tonight at the earliest, tomorrow morning at the latest."

"Good. Then I'll be on Cedar Key by the time the quarantine's in place. When I don't come back, you tell him I must've gone in on my own. That exonerates you."

"What's to prevent you from being taken by one of these mutants?"

"Nothing. I'm as vulnerable as anyone on the island. But she did say they're terrified of fire. Apparently they can be annihilated if the human host is killed and the ghost can't escape before the host dies."

Delaney rested his elbows against the boardwalk railing and stared off below, his expression inscrutable. "Christ, Sanchez. Be honest with yourself, okay? You want to go in because of this redhead."

"I want to understand what's going on."

"And the woman doesn't have anything to do with it," Delaney said and laughed. "Yeah, right."

She has everything to do with it. We connected, she and I. "If I'm there, I get answers more quickly."

"One condition. I'll give you a weapon and one of the cells that will be connected to the DHS communication system, and in return, you contact me immediately if she gets in touch with you again. And you keep me in the loop every step of the way."

"Sounds reasonable."

"And before we leave, see what you pick up on O'Donnell."

Sanchez made a face. "I was trying to avoid that, but okay. What'd you pick up from him?"

"See what you get, then I'll tell you."

Sanchez glanced back and saw O'Donnell trotting down the stairs toward them. "We need some time alone so I can get the weapon and cell," he said softly, and Delaney nodded.

"Sorry about that," O'Donnell said as he joined them. "It was my supervisor. Since I had him on the line, I ran your suggestion by him. He nixed it."

Sanchez shrugged. "That's fine. I've got to return to Gainesville to pick up my stuff and Delaney's. Where's the headquarters going to be?"

"Just north of the fourth bridge," O'Donnell said.

"I'll get back to your headquarters by late afternoon," Sanchez said. "How's that sound?"

O'Donnell offered his gritted-teeth grin and extended his hand. "Then we have a deal. Excellent."

Shit, here goes. Sanchez flipped on his psychic switch and his senses suddenly loomed like a gaping hole just begging to be filled with the detritus of someone else's psyche. When he grasped O'Donnell's hand, a rushing stream of images poured into him. Then the stream froze on a single image: O'Donnell, his face crayon red, demanding to know where the prisoner was and when Delaney had last visited her and had there been any word from that rogue Sanchez?

O'Donnell withdrew his hand, and the images dried up. "I suppose your dog will be joining us, Sanchez?"

"Always."

Once they were in the parking lot, they went to their respective vehicles and Sanchez and Delaney managed to get a few moments alone. Sanchez quickly related what he'd seen and Delaney's eyes widened. He blurted, "Okay, when I read him, I saw myself and O'Donnell interrogating a woman—I don't know about what—but she'd been brought into custody. And then I saw myself alone with this woman, a tall blonde, unusual face, and I was asking her about a note that a hawk had dropped at my feet. And then I helped her escape."

"Escape to where?"

"Beats the shit outta me."

"What'd the note say?"

"I don't know. I didn't see it. But we both picked up something that relates to a prisoner, and it's got to be the blonde."

And that meant it was more likely to happen, Sanchez thought. "You have that weapon and cell?"

"Yeah." Delaney opened his trunk, unzipped a small leather bag. "Keep in mind that four bridges connect Cedar Key to the mainland, all of them on State Road 24, the only way on or off the island. Bridge number four will be blocked and everything south of it will be quarantined. The Coast Guard will patrol the shorelines. A curfew will be in effect. It could get ugly, Sanchez."

"I'll be in touch regularly."

"Use your BlackBerry to videotape anything I should see. Send it to my personal e-mail address."

"You got it."

Delaney handed him the satchel. "Now get the hell outta here so O'Donnell won't see in which direction you're headed."

When Sanchez hit the road again, headed for the island and the mysterious redhead, his heart was on fire.

Eight

In the afternoon light, Cedar Key looked normal to Maddie—as normal, anyway, as anything could be to her these days. Long, narrow shadows crossed the road, the gulf waters reached outward toward the horizon, infinitely blue, as flat as a book cover. The temperature had climbed to a perfect 72 today, but the brisk wind blowing off the water promised a much cooler night. On her way across the bridge to Dock Street, she passed bikers, Rollerbladers, runners, lovers holding hands, people walking their dogs. Normal; it all looked so beautifully, wonderfully normal.

But it wasn't.

Dominica controlled her completely and the only reason she was on this bridge, on her way to buy coffee at the Island Café on Dock Street, was because Dominica was a caffeine addict and craved the stuff the way she did sex. Fortunately for Maddie, she loved the café's coffee, but couldn't let on. If Dominica knew that, Maddie would be denied even this simple pleasure. If she let on that Dock Street was her favorite block on the island, if Dominica realized that, she wouldn't allow Maddie anywhere near it. The point, always, was to tighten her grip over Maddie, to deprive her, increase her isolation, force her to remain subdued, compliant, and, ultimately, to break her. So she remained quiet and allowed herself to drink in the sights on Dock Street.

Lined by shops and restaurants, the entire street looked as if it had been constructed of old driftwood. Every building boasted a colorful, artistic sign rendered in lemon yellows, vivid reds, and luminous blues and violets. The places on the water sat on tall wooden pilings to help prevent flooding during inclement weather, their wide decks jutting out over the gulf.

Tourists strolled in and out of the shops and restaurants and dozens of stray cats snoozed in slices of warm light or played in the shadows beneath the buildings. When Maddie passed a group of them, they hissed at her and scampered away. Ever since Dominica had seized her, animals didn't just avoid her—they ran from her. And these cats sensed the ghosts within her and Mayor Peter Stanton, who walked with her, with Dominica.

He swung his long arms, his strides quick and confident. He wore jeans, a T-shirt, and a Cedar Key cap that shaded his eyes from the sun. Nothing about him revealed that his body was controlled by despicable Whit. He and Dominica chattered constantly, sometimes out loud, most of the time mind to mind. Maddie had been eavesdropping on their conversations, as she sometimes did, and had learned something new about Dominica: She didn't know how to swim and, as a result, was frightened of the ocean. Ironic, since she hoped to make an island a *brujo* enclave. It seemed inconceivable to Maddie that in the six centuries of Dominica's existence she had never learned to swim. Surely in all that time she had seized at least one host who had done so. Then again, maybe not. *Brujos* in general exhibited little curiosity.

Eavesdropping invariably left Maddie feeling soiled, defiled, and depressed at the hopelessness of her situation. It was best to just tune them out. After all, with Dominica so engaged in conversation with Whit, Maddie had a degree of freedom that enabled her to look at what *she* wanted to look at, to feel what *she* wanted to feel, to think her own thoughts separate from Dominica's overbearing influence. And after all these months of imprisonment within her own body, she'd become adept at hiding her thoughts and emotions.

As they passed the pier, the mayor spoiled Maddie's reverie by swinging his arm around her shoulders and speaking aloud to her. "Your hair looks gorgeous in this light, Maddie."

"You look like shit, Whit. You really should take better care of the mayor's body."

Oh, Maddie, that's not nice, Dominica chastised her and squeezed Maddie's vocal cords, tightening her control over her voice until she felt as if she were choking.

The mayor's arm slipped away from her shoulders. His hand trailed down her spine to her ass, cupping it, patting it, murmuring, "Nice, very nice. This is a valuable body, Nica. She could live well into her nineties."

Maddie struggled to break Dominica's hold on her, but the most she could do was wrench to the side, so Peter's hand fell away from her.

He threw his head back, laughing. "She really hates it when I touch her."

"She's a silly puritan," Dominica said.

Even after all these months, Maddie still wasn't accustomed to hearing her own voice when Dominica spoke. Wayra had once referred to it as the *brujo* schizophrenia, but to Maddie it seemed more like a multiple personality disorder.

"It's time she got over that, Nica." He took Maddie roughly by the arm, jerking her closer to his side, hooking his arm through hers so that his fingers could caress the curve of her breast without it being noticeable to anyone around them. "Beautiful," he murmured. "Young flesh is just so damn intoxicating."

"It feels wonderful," Dominica cooed.

Horror, disgust, and rage poured through Maddie, enabling her to briefly break Dominica's control over her. She snapped forward at the waist, fingertips brushing the tips of her shoes, then threw herself back and to the side, crashing into the mayor. Peter stumbled, his arms pinwheeled for balance, and he fell off the curb and sprawled gracelessly in the road.

With Dominica's attention focused solely on Peter, her control over Maddie loosened more than it had in months. Maddie lunged for the pier and dashed up the steps, startling fishermen, gulls and pelicans, a family with kids, barking dogs, and vaulted over the railing. Dominica fought to seize control of Maddie as she struck the water, but Maddie's emotional state was too wild, reckless, desperate, and it empowered her. And as her body started to sink, Dominica panicked and leaped out of her.

Maddie swam frantically, deeper and deeper. She tore off her jacket, her shoes, and everything sank down through the sunlit water. She moved fast toward the pier and the marina. In the pier's shadow, she wouldn't be visible to the people on land and would be able to surface for air. Thanks to her youth and the fact that she used to be a runner, her lung capacity was still fairly good. She didn't feel the urge to surface yet.

She swam east, her arms and legs propelling her forward. The salt water stung her open eyes. But she couldn't close them, she had to see where she was going, where the shadows were thickest. Sound traveled with astonishing clarity through the water—music from one of the restaurants on

Dock Street, the roar of a Jet Ski, the chug of a boat's engine. It meant she was nearing the marina and the pier.

As the pier's shadows closed over her, Maddie shot toward the surface, her head broke through, and she gulped at the air. It shocked her to realize her lungs breathed only for her, her heart beat only for her, her body belonged to her again. Her arms and legs, muscles and nerves, responded to her smallest desires. She had forgotten what it felt like. Sobs of joy welled up inside her.

Maddie treaded water for another minute or two, the chill rapidly eating into her. She estimated that she had to swim another hundred yards to reach the slips in the marina, but would have to swim much deeper because of the sunlight and the boats so that she wouldn't be visible or get hit.

She heard more shouting above her and when she glanced around, saw several kayaks and a couple of small boats combing the water around the pier, searching for her. She knuckled her burning eyes, sucked air deeply into her lungs again, and dived down.

Her plan was flimsy—find a boat onto which she could climb and hide. But how could she hide from Dominica? Other than her fear of oceans, fire, and Wayra, she was like the Catholic version of a god, anywhere and everywhere, ubiquitous, practically all-seeing, all-knowing.

As a ghost, Dominica could move through solid objects, could think herself anywhere in the universe. As one of the most ancient ghosts, a *bruja,* she could inflict excruciating pain on humans, kill them—or heal them. Maddie had known about these *brujo* abilities before she'd been seized, but in the past months, she'd learned the details intimately. In the Southwest somewhere, Maddie had cut her foot on a piece of glass, cut it so deeply that she could see bone. Within minutes, Dominica stopped the bleeding and the wound closed up and never got infected. Why couldn't the bitch turn that kind of ability toward what was good?

Many of Dominica's abilities had been learned throughout the centuries of her existence and Maddie doubted if her new tribe was capable of doing a fraction of what she could. Plunging a host into the deep sleep, performing a memory wipe, inflicting agony: She was still teaching this stuff to her new tribe. But the one thing even the new ghosts had mastered was the bleed-out. Maddie wasn't afraid to die; she already knew her soul would survive. But she didn't want to suffer as she died. Worse than any of this, though, was the prospect of being seized again, of being imprisoned within her own body.

Fueled by a mounting horror that her freedom was only temporary, Maddie swam hard and furiously, using up the air in her lungs more quickly. She became light-headed, her lungs ached and threatened to burst, the muscles in her arms and legs throbbed, her eyes burned more fiercely, her vision grew fuzzy. She kept swimming. When her peripheral vision went dark, she shot toward air and light and exploded through the water's surface.

She gasped and gulped, gasped and gulped again and again. Still treading water, she knuckled her burning eyes to clear her vision, but it didn't seem to help. Luminous orbs and wisps of what looked like discolored smoke drifted in the air around her. Only when the orbs and bits of smoke shot toward her did she realize they were *brujos* in their natural form. Shocked that she could see them, Maddie sucked air into her lungs and dived again, mentally screaming for help from Wayra, Sanchez, someone, anyone, who might be able to hear her and give her an edge.

One of the *brujos* pursued her into the water and glowed like a lantern. But it couldn't adjust to moving through water and quickly soared into the air again. Then a second and a third came after her. She was sure the *brujo* net shuddered and shook with the news that Dominica had lost control of her host, that her host, in fact, had escaped, and was up for grabs.

Being possessed by Dominica was awful, but at least Maddie was accustomed to her. Being possessed by a ghost like Whit would break her. She swam deeper, arms and legs moving wildly, her lungs already hurting, her eyes burning so badly from the salt water that she had to squeeze them shut. Something bumped into her on the right and she opened her eyes and saw huge shapes on either side of her. Dark shapes with fins. Sharks. Jesus God, they were sharks.

Maddie panicked. The sharks pressed up against her on either side, then suddenly lifted her until her head broke through the water, into sunlight and air. *Dolphins.* The rushing whoosh of air escaping from their blowholes nearly deafened her. Maddie grabbed onto the left dolphin's dorsal fin, sucked air deeply into her lungs, and hung on tightly as the dolphins went under again.

Kate felt as if she'd been abandoned. Rocky didn't answer his cell phone, the dog had taken off as soon as she'd returned to the houseboat with her food and supplies, and the hawk was, she hoped, with Rocky. She wanted to get out to Sea Horse Key before dark, so now she drove along Airport

Road in the cart, headed for the animal rescue center to fetch her son. Like he was still in grade school, she thought. If Amy was working, too, then Rocky was going to be embarrassed and super-pissed at her for picking him up. But until he turned eighteen, she was calling the shots.

The center occupied two acres of land along Goose Cove and cared mostly for injured aquatic birds. They also rescued doves, pigeons, turtles, iguanas, small mammals like squirrels, cats, a few dogs, even an occasional fox, and, of course, one hawk, Liberty.

Kate turned into the driveway and continued through the open gate to the main building. Rocky and Amy stood between his scooter and Amy's cart, embracing passionately. Kate drew up alongside them. "Hey, I hate to interrupt, but Rocky, we need to get moving."

He and Amy leaped apart, both of them looking guilty, and Kate wondered what else had been going on inside the building, on the grounds. "Hi, Kate," Amy said in her chirpy voice, tucking her long blond hair behind her ears. "We just finished closing up."

"Good to see you, Amy." That svelte teenage body, the tight jeans and top, the perfect skin, a cheerleader type, a diminutive beauty. "You two the only ones working on a Sunday?"

"Pretty much."

Amy's eyes flicked nervously toward Rocky, a clear indication that she understood what Kate was really asking—whether they'd had any supervision at all, whether they'd been screwing their brains out in the administration building. But Rocky, swept up in his anger toward Kate, didn't notice his girlfriend's angst.

"We're not done here, Mom."

"*You* are," Kate snapped. "Load your scooter in the backseat. I'd like to be out of the marina before dark."

"Why're you guys moving out to Sea Horse?" Amy strode over to the cart. "Nothing's out there."

Shit, Rocky, you weren't supposed to tell her or anyone else.

"Exactly." Rocky's anger turned his voice as brittle as dry twigs. He loaded his scooter into the cart's backseat. "But my mom believes that crazy asshole, Zee Small."

"So you really think we've been *invaded* by something?" Amy asked.

"I'm just taking precautions, Amy."

"Should I warn my parents?"

Rocky spoke before Kate could reply. "If you get freaked about something, you come stay with us." He gave Amy's hand a quick squeeze and got into the back of the cart with his scooter. "I'll call you later."

Amy blew Rocky a kiss, then swung into her own cart and followed them out of the center. The hawk swooped down over them and flew just above the cart. "You were supposed to keep that information to yourself, Rocky."

"She and I don't have secrets," he shot back. "And you don't have to come and pick me up like I'm eight years old."

"Then answer your damn phone."

"It's dead. I forgot to charge it last night. So let me get this straight. We're going to anchor off Sea Horse, then you're going to work?"

"Yes."

"And I'm supposed to stay out there on Sea Horse all by myself? How does that keep me safe?"

Good point. She obviously hadn't thought this out well enough. "You go to Amy's while I'm at work. We both go in on the skiff. But she has to pick you up and drop you off at the café."

"She will." He paused. "She thinks you're paranoid, Mom."

"I don't give a shit what she or anyone else thinks."

As they neared the marina, Kate saw a crowd gathered on the public beach, tourists and locals shouting and pointing at something in the distance. People snapped photos, took videos, but from the road she couldn't see what was going on. She turned into the marina, stopped in front of the houseboat. She and Rocky ran out onto the dock, where tethered pontoon boats bobbed in the water and throngs of gawkers watched a spectacle unfold about a hundred feet offshore.

A pair of dolphins carried a woman between them. She appeared to be gripping one dolphin's dorsal fin, while the other dolphin kept her feet elevated, so that it looked as if she skimmed the surface of the water. Kate couldn't see the woman's face, but even from here she could make out her curly copper hair trailing down her back, burning against her alabaster skin. Maddie. She looked like a mermaid, mythic, Neptunian, as if she had risen from ocean depths beyond human comprehension. Someone in a boat pursued her and the dolphins. Kate suddenly had an awful feeling about this.

"What happened?" she asked one of the old-timers standing next to her.

"That young woman supposedly leaped off the pier like she was hell-bent on killing herself. Way I heard it, she was with Mayor Stanton, and when he didn't see her come up for air, he and some others went out in kayaks looking for her. They were sure she'd drowned. But the dolphins saved her. Pretty amazing."

Mayor Pete Stanton. Zee had told her he'd been taken early on and Kate had no reason to believe otherwise. Had Maddie tried to force the evil out of herself by jumping into the gulf? But why would that work? Kate realized she just didn't have enough information to understand the nature of this evil, and until she did, she didn't want to be anywhere around here. She tapped Rocky's shoulder with the back of her hand. "Let's get outta here."

He emitted a shrill whistle, calling Liberty, and the hawk appeared just ahead.

When they reached the parking lot, Kate spotted Rich and Bean getting out of a cart, headed toward her. She pretended she hadn't seen them, and she and Rocky veered off toward the houseboat. Anxiety chewed through her. It horrified her that she was afraid of Bean, a man she'd known for thirty years, and of Rich, whom she had known since she was in kindergarten and who, for the last fourteen months, had shared her bed and her life in a way that no man had since she and Rocky's father had split. The faster she fled this island, the safer she and Rocky would be.

"Hey, Katie-bird, hold on." Rich's fingers closed around her arm. "You moved without saying squat to me."

Kate jerked her arm free and addressed her son before she even looked at Rich. "I'll be along in a few minutes, Rocky. Go ahead and get started."

He eyed Rich warily. "You sure, Mom?"

"Positive."

Rocky hesitated, then hastened on to the houseboat. Only then did Kate meet Rich's gaze. "Let me know how much I owe you for utilities and water. I can pay you next week."

He looked stunned. "That's *it*?"

The incredulity in his voice defied explanation. It was as if he had forgotten what had happened last night, what he'd said to her: *Don't make waves.* It reminded her of how Bean had acted that February night after his fuck fest in the bar. Selective amnesia. "Yes, that's it."

"But—"

Kate leaned toward him, sinking her finger into his muscular chest, and whispered, "I know what you are, Richie-bird."

She whipped around and ran toward the houseboat, ran through the crowd still fixated on the dolphin spectacle, ran even though she hadn't moved the cart to some location where she and Rocky could get to it. Rocky had started the engine and she jumped on board. She glanced back once, but Rich had vanished into the crowd.

The houseboat turned into the open water, headed into the dying sun.

Sanchez's motel stood at the end of First Street, an old rundown place that looked like it had been built in the fifties and hadn't been renovated in all the decades since. Business wasn't exactly booming—he and one other man were the only guests. But the motel allowed dogs and Jessie was sprawled comfortably on one of the beds. Sanchez stood in front of the wall map of Cedar Key, studying it.

The main island consisted of a grid of eight east/west streets, and seven streets, A through G, that ran north/south. From Fourth Street north, the Back Bayou cut into streets A through D. No matter where you were on the island, water was everywhere. He had no idea where he should begin looking for Maddie, and decided to walk around downtown first and see what, if anything, he picked up. Then he would head over to Annie's Café, where the hungry ghosts supposedly congregated every evening on the right side of the dining room.

Sanchez scooped up his room key and promised Jessie he would be back in a jiffy. She didn't even raise her head.

The moment he stepped outside, Maddie's silent scream for help tore through him, hammered against his temples. Sanchez spun around, trying to determine the direction. It seemed to be coming from the east. He raced up the street, past another rundown motel, past the entrance to Dock Street, into the marina parking lot. A large crowd had gathered near the water and even more people had spilled onto the beach, all of them watching something. In his head, he could still hear Maddie screaming, and was certain it came from out on the water, that she was what everyone watched.

He couldn't push his way through the crowd, so he ran along the outside of it, up a grassy slope to a condo complex and then down to a narrow, rocky spit of beach along the marsh. Even here, a dozen people stood around, gawking, pointing, shouting, taking photos and videos as though it were all part of a reality show.

Then he saw them, a pair of dolphins cutting in close to the marsh, with a woman clinging to the lead dolphin. *Red.* When the dolphins dived, she disappeared and he heard her silent scream again.

He snatched a paddle out of the sand and quickly pushed a yellow kayak out into the marsh. A thin black dog appeared out of nowhere and shot past him, splashed into the marsh, and started swimming. By the time Sanchez was calf deep in the water, the dog had disappeared into the tall reeds.

Sanchez climbed into the kayak and paddled furiously. The dolphins surfaced again and he caught sight of Maddie struggling to hold on, to breathe, her head whipping from one side to the other as though she were trying to determine where she was.

"Let go," he shouted. "It's shallow enough to let go!"

The dolphins made an abrupt turn and Red either couldn't hold on any longer or simply let go. She fell into the water. The dolphins swam off, arching in the dying light, diving, arching again, the whooshing noise from their blowholes echoing in the air, rhythmic, strange, mixing with a high, keening sound they made. Red didn't come up.

Frantic, Sanchez paddled the final twenty yards to where he'd last seen her. The kayak hit something—sand, a submerged island, rocks, a mound of shells, he couldn't tell what the hell it was. But it beached the kayak.

He scrambled out into water barely ankle deep and stood for a moment in the burning light of the setting sun, birds careening overhead, singing, cawing, crying out, squawking. He turned rapidly in place, eyes searching the water, the reeds, his head spinning, his senses out of whack.

He suddenly saw a dark-haired man splashing wildly through the shallows. Where had *he* come from? Sanchez then saw what the man apparently saw: Maddie floating facedown in the weeds, arms out on either side of her. She wasn't moving. Sanchez, closer to her than the man was, reached her first. He dropped to his knees in the shallow water, turned her over, lifted her head out of the water. Mesmerized by her beauty, by the dusting of ginger-colored freckles on her pale cheeks, by the perfect curve of her jaw, the seductiveness of her mouth, and all that luscious copper hair, seconds passed before he realized she wasn't breathing.

With her head and back resting against his knees, he pumped several times on her chest. *"Breathe, Red, breathe."* He opened her mouth, pressed his own against it and breathed into her, then pushed down on her chest. Breathe, press, breathe, press. Again. She finally bolted forward, coughing violently, her parrot-green eyes bulging in their sockets. She retched sea-water, coughed some more, sucked air in through her mouth. Sanchez helped her rock back on her heels, water lapped over her thighs.

"Red," he whispered.

"Sanchez?" She raised her bloodshot eyes to his.

He wrapped his arms around her, holding her close, tightly, aware of her breasts pressed against his chest, of the shape of her ribs, of the heat of her breath against the side of his neck, of her wet hair, strands of it curling against his arm. The dark-haired man reached them, flung his arms around them, and whispered urgently, "They're everywhere, amigo. Get out of here fast, run, run. I'll protect Maddie."

She clutched the sides of Sanchez's face, her eyes bored into his. "It's okay. Wayra's a friend. She . . . Dominica . . . leaped out of me. The real terrorists sit on the right side of Annie's Café. Remember that. Be there. Please," she whispered in a choked voice.

"I'll find you," he said hoarsely, and brought his mouth to hers, kissing her tenderly, swiftly.

The dark-haired man pushed him forward. "*Go.*"

Sanchez shoved the kayak off the sand, back into the water, leaped inside and paddled fast toward the closest stretch of shore. He stumbled up a boat ramp, glanced back once, but couldn't see Red or the man. He fell to his knees in a patch of grass, hands clutching his thighs, his wet clothes like excessive gravity that pinned him to the ground. *They're everywhere.* The ghosts? Was that what the man had been referring to?

He ripped off his shoes and wet socks and weaved his way up the street, anxious to get back to his motel room, where he could text Delaney. *And say what, Sanchez? You gave her mouth-to-mouth? You kissed her when the ghost named Dominica wasn't inside of her?* Even with what Delaney knew about what was happening here, that kind of information would land Sanchez in a padded room for sure.

His BlackBerry belted John Lennon's "Imagine," the tune he'd assigned to Nicole. He couldn't bring himself to talk to her, not yet, not this instant, and turned off his BlackBerry.

They surrounded him and Maddie, small, glowing orbs that dived at them like wasps. The orbs didn't touch them, but they probed, and Wayra kept moving back, back, his arms encircling Maddie, holding her tightly as he tried to get her out of the shallows, to shore, where they could run. The orbs sensed he was different, perhaps they even sensed, for the first time, that Maddie was different, that she was not just some random host their leader had seized.

"You don't want to be a part of this story." Wayra spoke quietly, his voice sharp. "It's far more ancient and powerful than you are. Dominica uses you by telling you exactly what you want to hear."

"No good, Wayra," Maddie whispered, tightening her arms around his waist. "The bitch is here. To your right."

Wayra saw her, a fat plume of discolored smoke zooming in on his right, just as Maddie had said. Before he could react, Dominica dived through Maddie's skull. He felt it the moment it happened, the instant Dominica seized control of her, and his arms dropped to his sides. He stepped back.

Dominica spoke with Maddie's mouth and vocal cords and used Maddie's hands, lifting them theatrically into the air. "Really, Wayra. I was, like, well, totally embarrassed you thought you could protect her just because your arms are around her. Since when was that one of our rules?"

"*Our* rules?" He laughed. "How you twist your memories, Nica. You and I never established any mutual rules or playing field. I don't collude with evil. What other lies have you told yourself about us? About you and me? How else have you edited your personal history?"

She winced; he knew his words struck her to the core. "We *brujos* can seize you here. You don't have any immunity on Cedar Key."

"Your tribe is new. They sense I'm totally alien to their experience. If they try to seize me, I'll show them just how alien I am and I don't think you want that, Nica. It would require you to explain too much. And I'm sure you still remember what it was like when I took your essence into myself in that greenhouse in Punta."

"You . . . you intended to obliterate me," she spat. "To crush me out of existence. You were so hateful."

"You're a plague."

"A plague," she repeated, and shook her head. "I'm a survivor. So what can you offer in return for Maddie, Wayra? What are you and your chaser buddies willing to trade?"

"You take the island, you give us Maddie in return."

She laughed hysterically, the last of the light setting Maddie's hair on fire. "Cedar Key isn't yours to give. It's already mine."

"Then do what you must, as will I." In a flash, he shifted and raced toward land.

Nine

Dominica watched the black Lab race through the marsh, a fleeting shadow in the starlight. A rushing tsunami of memories nearly crippled her. For a hundred and thirty-seven years, she and Wayra had loved each other, traveled together; they could have ruled an empire. How had it come to *this*, a standoff in a salt marsh?

"*You fool*," she shouted.

Her words drifted out over the marsh, filling the emptiness between them. Disgusted, Dominica forced Maddie's body to move forward. She slogged through the water, struggling not to think about the last time she had seen Wayra, outside a church in Punta, Ecuador, more than a year ago. He had tried to obliterate her by taking her essence into himself and shifting. She had saved herself by hurling out her most intimate memories of their centuries together and it was enough for him to hesitate.

In that instant of hesitation, she had fled. But she doubted if even her most intimate memories would prompt him to hesitate next time. After he had assaulted her in Punta, she had exacted her revenge by seizing Sara Wells, the woman he had loved then, and had killed her. He would never forgive her for that.

Her fear of the shifter remained, but as long as she occupied Maddie's body, he wouldn't dare attempt to annihilate her. He knew all too well how quickly and effortlessly she could bleed Maddie out. But Maddie's stunt deserved punishment. She had humiliated Dominica, who only last night had decreed that any *brujo* who couldn't control his host didn't deserve a host. She somehow had to turn this incident to her advantage.

She reached the rocky beach in front of the Old Fennimore Mill condos, grateful that the darkness hid her from the spectators on the balcony and along the beach who had witnessed Maddie's antics. *I should just bleed you out and be done with you, Maddie.*

Maddie didn't reply. Dominica sensed she was curled up in her virtual room, sobbing. *Save your tears. You'll have plenty to cry about when we get back to the house.*

Pain and more pain. Bring it on, bitch.

Such rage, Maddie. Here I thought you were weeping.

I wouldn't give you the satisfaction.

Dominica laughed, anticipating how she would make Maddie suffer, how she would break her. Yes, it might come to that. Breaking her spirit so completely that she would be the most compliant host Dominica had ever had.

Who was the handsome young man who gave you mouth-to-mouth, Maddie?

Silence.

Well, it doesn't matter. And I wouldn't get your hopes up about Wayra. Even the shifter can't fight a thousand brujos by himself.

Maddie had nothing to say about that. Just as well. Dominica didn't feel like talking to her, anyway. She climbed a shallow, grassy slope, hurried into the driveway in front of the house where she and Maddie had been living since their second week in town, and bounded up the creaky steps. She tore off her wet clothes and left them where they fell. She rushed into the bedroom for her spare cell phone and immediately called Whit.

"Nica?" He sounded anxious.

"I have her again, Whit."

"Password?"

"Pensacola."

She felt his relief.

"Excellent. The net is humming like crazy, though. Since you were unable to control your own host, many in the tribe are asking if last night's decree still stands."

She had expected this, but nonetheless felt angry and irritable that she now had to create some colorful fiction to explain what had happened. *You'll pay for this, Maddie.*

"What happened to me is precisely why it's vital that hosts are tightly controlled. I used myself as an example to illustrate the point. *I allowed her to escape.* There was never any doubt she would be seized again. The decree still stands. But additional training will be available for anyone who wants it." As soon as she spoke, the *brujo* net hummed and buzzed with the tribe's reaction.

You're such a goddamn liar, Dominica. You lost control of me because you weren't paying attention. And regardless of what you do to me, this body is still mine. If you do something that I find personally abhorrent, you won't be able to control me. Pervert asshole Whit copping a feel isn't going to happen again.

Dominica ignored her. "Whit, meet me at the house."

"Be there in a few minutes."

Dominica disconnected and stood there for a moment, staring out through the floor-to-ceiling windows that overlooked the gulf. The house sat on pilings fifteen feet above the water, and although it was small—just eight hundred square feet, most of it in one room—the view compensated for the lack of space. Stars popped out against the black skin of the sky, lights from downtown danced against the water, a slice of moon moved upward against the sky. It all looked lovely and oddly peaceful, but didn't lighten her mood.

She peeled off her damp panties and padded into the bathroom to shower. Within moments of stepping under the hot spray, of picking up a bar of organic soap, her irritation began to ebb. During the months she had used Maddie's body, she had developed a taste for *products*.

This century offered so many varieties of everything. The organic soap, scented with jasmine, soothed her. She loved the expensive organic shampoos that left her host's hair as soft as an infant's skin, and organic creams that kept her beautiful skin youthful. She even used a special foam product for shaving her legs and underarms, plucked her brows regularly, used a beet-red polish on her fingernails and toenails.

She tried to take good care of Maddie's body, but without making herself crazy. Maddie would argue that point, would say that *brujos* were unhygienic slobs who didn't bathe frequently enough, but Dominica felt it was a matter of perspective.

When Dominica had initially seized her, Maddie was a vegan. Within a few weeks, that diet proved too boring for Dominica and she gradually introduced fish, chicken, eggs, and dairy products into Maddie's diet. Maddie also had been a runner, her thighs and calves beautifully sculpted, hard as rock. Running didn't interest Dominica, so she compensated with daily bike rides, plenty of walking.

How different from her last physical life in the fifties, a kind of half life, forty years that she and her lover, Ben, had spent in the bodies of a husband and wife who were lawyers. In the fifties, exercise freaks and vegans were a rare breed. But because the ancient *brujos* were able to keep their human hosts at an optimum level of health, she and Ben didn't have to be runners and vegans.

Ben. She still missed him. Other than Wayra, he had been her lover the longest. Maddie's aunt Tess had annihilated him in Key Largo, in his host body, when Dominica and Ben had been pursuing Tess to kill her. She had seized Maddie, in part, to get even with her aunt.

Dominica took great care to keep her thoughts hidden from Maddie. She suspected the young woman was doing the same thing. In the early days of their relationship, memory bleeds were frequent and worked both ways. Now, it rarely happened. A part of Dominica missed those early days, when she and Maddie were just getting to know each other.

She scrubbed away the unpleasantness with Wayra, with Maddie's escape, all of it. When she was finished, she wrapped a thick, fluffy towel around her body, wrapped another around her hair, and stood in front of the closet, debating about what to wear. Something casual, perhaps with a shawl, since it was supposed to get considerably cooler tonight. She put on a khaki skirt, wrapped a black shawl around her shoulders, then folded the ends over her breasts and tied them in back. She brushed out her host's hair and blew it dry, eyeing herself in the mirror.

"You're really quite lovely, Maddie," she remarked.

Silence.

Footfalls echoed on the stairs outside and Whit strolled into the house without knocking. "Nica?"

"Back here," she called, and stepped into the bedroom doorway, one finger at her lips, her other hand lifting the skirt at one side, revealing Maddie's beautiful leg, thigh, making it clear she wasn't wearing panties.

His host's eyes went dark; Whit peered out of them completely now. He kicked off his shoes, tore off his sweater and shirt, and came toward her quickly, unzipping his jeans. "What're we doing?"

She untied the shawl so that it fell away from her host's shoulders and breasts. "We're going to break Maddie," she said, and dropped back onto the wonderfully soft bed, threw her arms out at her sides, and Whit ripped off the rest of his clothes and fell on her like the hungry beast he was.

Maddie didn't struggle. Her essence, her consciousness, vaulted from her body.

From the moment Dominica had called Whit and told him to meet her at the house, Maddie had suspected what her punishment would be. So when Whit had walked into the house, she was prepared. The moment they fell back onto the bed, she soared away.

Her consciousness moved upward into the early evening, looking for

Sanchez, Wayra. Without consciousness, her body would function at a physiological level, just as it did when people traveled out of body during sleep. But its animations, sensations, and emotions would originate in Dominica. Since Maddie refused to experience what amounted to rape, Dominica's ploy wouldn't break her. And she would be sure to block Dominica's memories of this encounter from her own awareness when she returned to her body.

She thought herself through town, focused on Sanchez, then Wayra, then Sanchez again, waiting for a telling tug. But the only tug she felt was north along State Road 24, the single road to or from the island. She seemed to be able to regulate her movement and altitude through her thoughts and desires. *Go here, turn there, lift up, drop lower.* She passed familiar landmarks—the Island Market, the Back Bayou, the first two bridges, then the third, and finally the fourth bridge. A cluster of bright lights beyond the fourth bridge drew her down. She hovered like a butterfly just above several large trucks and two dozen workmen who were erecting a barbed-wire fence across the bridge. Behind them was another crew putting up a concrete wall. A foot or two separated the two barriers. On either side of the bridge were two Coast Guard cutters.

It looked as if the area were being blocked off. But why?

Maddie thought herself west across the water to the Cedar Key cemetery, a place that everyone in Dominica's tribe avoided; cemeteries reminded them that they were dead. She drifted along the coast to the farthest reaches of the island, then south toward the island airport. She counted six more Coast Guard vessels, strategically placed around the four bits of land that comprised the island. She drifted over the airport, expecting to see choppers, planes, evidence of an invasion. But there were only three planes tied down, two single engines and one twin, and nothing on the runway. The airport didn't have a tower and the only planes that landed here after dark were those that belonged to the people who lived in the ritzy homes along the airstrip. They controlled the landing lights.

She picked up speed, returned to the fourth bridge, and thought herself to the other side of it. Access to the fishing pier was denied. Ditto with the boat launch. A handful of cars waited in front of a concrete wall while cops walked from vehicle to vehicle, talking with drivers, who handed over something, probably licenses and registrations. The first car made a U-turn and headed back toward Gainesville.

What the hell.

Maddie drifted in closer, hoping to hear what the cops were saying. At first, the voices sounded muffled, as though people were underwater. But the longer she hovered there, the clearer the voices became. The words they said differed somewhat each time, but amounted to the same message: *You'll have to turn back. This area is now under quarantine.*

Quarantine?

Her thoughts raced, and pieces of Dominica's immense and complex puzzle slammed together. Maddie guessed the bodies of people killed here in town had been discovered in the landfills. She suspected the autopsies had revealed an unknown virus or bacteria in every single victim. But it was actually a substance *brujos* created within their host bodies to facilitate their existence in the physical world. Her own body was filled with it. The mayor's body reeked of it. Bean, Rich, Sam, Marion, all of them had it. They were all contaminated with this *brujo* shit. She had no idea what the long-term effects might be. Dominica didn't seem to know, either. But if that was what the quarantine was about, then life on Cedar Key was about to take an abrupt ninety-degree turn into hell. Quarantine the place, isolate the people who hadn't been seized, drive them into hiding not only from the *brujos* but from the government as well. A quarantine would make it just that much easier for Dominica and her tribe to take over the island.

Alarmed and terrified, Maddie retreated—and snapped back into the bedroom. She stared down at her body and that of the mayor, grunting and humping each other like a couple of dogs. She felt strangely removed from her physical self, as though she were watching a movie, some clip of a porno film. She suspected the mayor's mind and soul had been broken some time ago. She hoped so, for his sake.

She thought herself away from the sordid scene and concentrated on Sanchez, on the way his mouth had tasted when he had kissed her, on what he'd said to her. *I'll find you.*

I'll find you first, she thought, and wheeled up through the roof of the house, out toward the moon, the stars, and then across town again. She found Sanchez leaving his motel room, an old motel that dated from the fifties. Most of the *brujos* ignored the place. It just wasn't the kind of motel where they would find hosts worth their time and effort. Even these young, reckless ghosts sought hosts who were young, fit, and sexually active. Tourists that fit that description didn't stay in this motel.

But idiosyncratic men with dogs did.

Sanchez and Jessie were walking toward a lime-green VW. Like before, the dog sensed her before Sanchez did. The retriever wagged her tail, barked, and tried to rub against Maddie. Sanchez whispered, "I feel her around, too. Red? You here or am I nuts?"

The island's being quarantined. That's going to make it easier for the brujos *to take over Cedar Key. Get out of here while you still can. Go by boat.*

"I'm not going anywhere until you're with me."

You don't even know me, Sanchez. You kissed some spaced-out chiquita who rode on dolphins. I'm a fucking mermaid, okay? Just leave. Now. Fast.

"For Chrissake, Maddie, don't tell him to leave."

Her grandfather, Charlie Livingston. Man in white. Man in white with cigar tucked behind his ear. Man in white who was no more substantial than she was. Man in white who was a member of the chasers and stood right next to her. Ghost, chaser, grandfather, whatever, his body looked solid. Did she even have the illusion of a body?

Maddie looked down at herself. Okay, this was good, she had a sort of body. Looked solid, felt solid; it would do.

"In this state, Maddie, you can look like Cinderella if you want to."

Cinderella? Was he serious? "Man in white who allowed this travesty to continue for months," she screamed, stabbing her hand at him. "Don't tell me what to say or not to say. You could've stopped this whole thing and didn't. And *Cinderella?* Christ, Charlie. At least choose a less offensive fairy tale."

Charlie drew back, eyes widening, obviously shocked by the vitriol in her voice. Maddie immediately wondered about the voice part of this equation. Technically, she was outside of her physical body but inside a body slapped together from her thoughts and beliefs or something. And she was in this situation because a ghost possessed her real body. In the event that she lived long enough to make sense of any of this, she seriously doubted she would ever tell it to anyone.

"You finished with your rant?" Charlie asked.

"My *rant*? Do you know what Dominica is doing with my body right now?"

"Your body is being used by the mayor of Cedar Key. But technically, it's not rape, he's, uh, having some problems. Besides, you aren't there. For that matter, neither is he. Now, are you going to hear me out or not?"

"Easy for you to say, Charlie. It's not your body that's being defiled."

"I don't have a body any more than you do right now."

"Whatever. Talk away. But the bottom line doesn't change. Whether I'm in my body or elsewhere is irrelevant. It's *my body*. And the bitch is using my body as a weapon against me. That's terrorism."

"Yes, it is. That's what they do, Maddie. It's how they've survived for centuries."

"'Survive.' That's a curious word, you know? In human terms, it implies breath, a heartbeat, warm skin. These fucks are *parasites,* Charlie."

"I can't argue with you. 'Parasitic terrorists' fits them perfectly." He paused and fiddled with his Zippo, flicking it open and shut. "What you did today was courageous."

"It was desperation, not courage."

"The fact that you were saved by a couple of dolphins has already added to your urban-legend status among the members of Dominica's tribe. Even though she's trying to spin this to make it look like it was intentional on her part, most of them know she lost control of you. No one—except Wayra—has ever duped Dominica in that way. You're her match. You've got to spin the narrative to *your* advantage."

"Great. Now I'm FOX News. The problem with my spinning anything is that she controls my vocal cords."

"Go back. Play on her fears. Be a Livingston. She won't survive it. Make her think she's winning, Maddie. That will make her reckless, careless."

"But she *is* winning. Once this quarantine is in place, Cedar Key becomes a *brujo* paradise."

"Or a *brujo* prison," Charlie said.

Another ghost came into view, an attractive woman with auburn-colored hair, soulful hazel eyes. She touched Sanchez's shoulder—and her hand went right through him. "Oh, I hate it when that happens," she said softly.

"The dog sees you, Jenean," said Charlie. "And Nick definitely felt it. Maddie, this is Jenean, Nick Sanchez's mother. She's helping us out with this *brujo* mess."

"You're a *chaser*?" Maddie exclaimed.

Jenean's quick, bright smile could light up the dark side of any planet. "No. I'm just helping out and trying to make amends to my son for everything I failed to do when I was alive."

"Can Sanchez see you?" Maddie asked.

"When I choose to make myself visible and when he's in the right frame of mind. At the moment, he's, uh, completely freaked out by what has been happening. He's quite taken with you."

"Why don't you stick with Nick, Jenean, and I'll get Maddie back to her body."

"Unless the mayor is finished with me," Maddie said, "I have zero desire to return to my body, Charlie."

Jenean looked sympathetic and patted Maddie's shoulder. "Just do what Charlie suggests."

It irritated Maddie that these two ghosts—her grandfather and Sanchez's mother—gave her advice about how to act, about the decisions she should make, about how she should feel. What the hell did they know about anything? Neither of them could feel what she did, could understand the horror of being imprisoned within your own body, of not being able to move your arms or legs in the way you wanted, of not being able to take a crap when you wanted, of not being able to do a damn thing unless Dominica allowed it.

"Please, no advice, okay?" Maddie said. "You two are more powerless than I am. At least I'm still alive." *Sort of.*

Charlie and Jenean exchanged a glance that suggested they were on the same page of . . . well, something. Charlie finally said, "The mayor's essence is withering up, dying. If he dies, Whit won't be able to use the body. He's having trouble performing sexually because of it. The only way *brujo* possession works is if the body is *shared* by the host's essence. Even if the host essence is broken, shriveled up in some virtual *brujo* cell, a *brujo* can use it as long as the essence is alive. When Esperanza was a nonphysical place, it was possible for a *brujo* to simply take over the body while the person's essence was gone. But once we brought Esperanza into the physical world, the rules changed."

"Suppose I stay out of my body indefinitely?" Maddie asked.

"Then eventually your body would die, Maddie. Even Dominica isn't powerful enough to animate a host body by herself."

"Does she know that?"

"She used to know. But until she seized you, it had been years since she occupied a body for any length of time and she may have selective amnesia about it. I think that's what tonight's punishment is really about. Her tribe is operating under the assumption that the bodies they seize are theirs to use however they want even if the host's essence dies."

"They're such *vile* beings," Jenean said, then wagged her fingers and followed Sanchez and the dog to his VW.

Charlie and Maddie moved across town to the house, drifted through the wall, and stood in the bedroom doorway. Maddie felt strange staring at her half-covered body, arms thrown over her head, her hair fanned out beneath her, the mayor lying beside her. In the moonlight that streamed through the windows, their bodies looked waxen.

"Jesus, I don't know what happened," Whit was saying.

"It's okay," Dominica told him. "Your host is in that age group, Whit. It's why so many of them take Viagra."

"Obviously, the next time we try this, I need a younger host." He sat up, swung his legs off the bed. "And you need to have someone other than Maddie."

"I know. It was a mistake."

"Let's get a bite to eat."

"I should get over to the hotel. Why don't you bring us takeout from Annie's Café?"

Charlie touched Maddie's arm—and she fought with herself about how it wasn't really a real arm, on a real body, even though it felt real—and tilted his head toward the bed. *You'll be okay now. I'm always nearby, Maddie. And remember what I told you. Play on her fears. Be a Livingston.*

Why should I do what you tell me to do? Why should I believe anything you say, Charlie? Aunt Tesso says you've been manipulating her since day one. She isn't here now, so you're manipulating me. Fuck that.

Then go ahead and stay out of your body, hon, and I'll be seeing you on my side of life right quick. Look, this is really complicated, okay? Chasers aren't gods and we're badly outnumbered.

Maddie hesitated. She didn't intend to die; she was just nineteen years old. She had stuff to do, places to see, she had dreams. Never mind that she couldn't think of a single goal except to free herself and see Sanchez again. Never mind that even if she liberated herself, she would be forever contaminated with this *brujo* shit coursing through her bloodstream. Never mind that she would be damaged. She refused to allow this bitch to steal her life any longer than she already had.

She slipped back into her body and apparently did it without Dominica being aware of it. She immediately erected a wall around her memories and her awareness. Even so, she felt Dominica's irritation that Whit's host had been unable to maintain an erection.

Maddie snickered, plopped back on her virtual couch, and covered her face with a pillow and laughed out loud.

Annie's Café stood in the crooked elbow of a salt marsh on State Road 24, a one-story place that looked as if it had been built of the same driftwood that Sanchez had seen everywhere else on Cedar Key. The tiny parking area was jammed with vehicles and he had to park the cart two blocks away, in a neighborhood of old Florida homes. He held on to Jessie's halter, making it clear that she shouldn't stray, and as they walked through the chilly air, he kept glancing around, hoping that Red would show up again. She didn't and neither did his mother, although he felt her around just as he had earlier out in front of the motel.

"Mom?" he whispered.

"Right here, Nick." She materialized for a moment at his side, then faded as a car turned toward them, headlights bright, glaring.

"You think the people in that car can see you?"

"You never know."

"So you're, like, what, my guardian angel now?"

The car passed and she came into view again. "I've been here over a year and have yet to meet anything with wings. Be careful in the café, Nick."

Like he needed his dead mother telling him that.

"I've got your back," she added, and faded again.

How could a ghost have his back?

Sanchez wondered about the dark-haired man who had told him to get out of the salt marsh. Wayra. He had Googled the name when he'd gotten back to the motel and discovered that in Quechua it meant "wind." The Quechua people predated the Incas and the language itself was still spoken in parts of Peru and Ecuador. He didn't know what, if anything, that meant in relation to what was happening.

His BlackBerry jingled, no song this time, just that obnoxious electric chord. Nicole's text message appeared:

ET, call home.

Hey, I'm here, he typed. *On Cedar Key. Am OK. How's dad doing? Did Carmen return?*

Yes to Carmen. Dad seems better. He won in dominoes today. Holler for whatever you need.

Interesting, he thought, that Nicole apparently had taken what he'd said seriously enough to keep texting and calling him.

Hugs, he typed, and signed off.

Sanchez, no longer gripping the dog's halter, entered the café through a screened porch that led to the wide outside balcony. It extended a hundred feet into the salt marsh, with tables on either side and another row straight down the middle. Every table was covered with a checkered plastic tablecloth, easy to clean, but ever so tacky. Burning torches, mounted on posts that extended upward from the railing, cast the area in a surreal light. Half a dozen customers had their dogs with them, and the dogs lay with paws draped over the edge of the balcony, watching fish jump, listening to the sounds of the marsh.

The hostess, a middle-aged woman in jeans and a sweater, showed Sanchez to a table along the railing, but close enough to the screened porch so that he could see the large group of customers on the right side. Red had referred to them as "the real terrorists." They looked like locals and tourists to him. Were the ghosts inside of them?

Assume nothing is what it appears to be, Delaney had texted him moments before Maddie had located him earlier today. *Stay with it. And send vid from the café.*

The group on the right was loud and boisterous and a couple of the men kept waving the waitresses over, shouting for more beer, more wine, more warm bread, more salads, more, more, more. They ate and drank like gluttons.

He surreptitiously snapped a couple of photos of the group, e-mailed them to Delaney, then to Nicole just for safekeeping. He brought one of them up, enlarged it. With the porch screen between him and the group, the photo lacked the detail he wanted. But the smaller torches inside the porch illuminated the area in a strange, pumpkin-colored light. Pale orbs floated in the air around the group. They looked like water droplets, but the lens on the BlackBerry was dry. Light leaks? Not likely. He glanced up, but didn't see anything in the air that resembled the orbs in the photo.

He pressed the video button, then stretched his arms above his head, a guy working the kinks out of his back, the BlackBerry cupped and hidden in his right hand. Ten seconds, fifteen, thirty. He lowered his arm, viewed the video. It had captured the balls of light, too. He e-mailed this to Delaney, with a note: *Any idea what these orbs are?*

Sanchez thought he might be able to get better photos if he went inside to use the restroom. Just as he was about to stand, an attractive blond waitress came over to take his order. Her nametag read KATE. "What can I get you to drink, sir?"

"A Corona. And I'll take the salmon Caesar salad."

"Great choice. I'll bring your dog a bowl of water and some treats, too."

"Thanks, I appreciate it. Excuse me, but I was wondering if you heard about the incident today with the woman rescued by the dolphins?"

She looked wary. "Uh, yeah. Who hasn't heard about it?"

"What happened exactly?"

"I'm not sure."

"Do you know who the woman was?"

"Why?"

"I'm a freelance journalist," he lied. "I'd love to interview her."

"Her name's Maddie Livingston. I used to work with her."

"Do you know how I can get in touch with her?"

"She works over at the Island Hotel, at the front desk." Then she scribbled something on her order pad, tore it off, and set it on the table. "Be back with your drink in a minute."

Sanchez picked up the slip of paper. *Island invaded by something that seizes human beings and seeks to live out their mortal lives. Evil ghosts. One of them is in Maddie. Everyone on the right side of the room is possessed by this evil. When the evil is fully in control of the human, blackness rolls across their eyes. Get out while you can.*

"What the fuck." He folded the slip of paper, slipped it down inside his wallet. He sat there a few minutes longer, arguing with himself. When to leave? Immediately? After he'd snapped a few more photos or taken more video from a better spot?

Photos and video first, he thought, and pushed to his feet.

Kate ducked into the kitchen and sent Rocky a text message. *Am telling Annie I'm sick, going home in 15 min. Ask Amy to drop u here.*

"Table four's order is ready," called the cook.

Table four, where twenty-seven of *them* watched her, their eyes shifting from blues and hazels and soft browns to obsidian black. She knew these faces—one of the local cops, a state trooper, two real estate brokers, a banker, Bean and his ex-wife, three artists who owned a co-op on Dock Street, the owner of a new restaurant on Second Street, a retired couple from upstate New York who lived out near the airport. For years, many of these people had moved in and out of her life as friends and lovers, bosses and customers. She knew their alcoholic preferences, food allergies, family dramas. And all of them were changed, possessed.

"Where's Annie?" Kate asked the cook as she picked up the tray.

"Went outside to take a call."

"Tell her this is my last delivery. I feel like shit, coming down with the flu or something, I'm going home."

"Home?" The cook's head snapped up. "You can't go home now, Kate. We've got more than fifty people out there and just you and Jen doing the tables."

"Give Annie the message."

Kate stepped out of the kitchen just as Peter Stanton, the mayor, lumbered into the dining room. He stood there a moment, his clothes as disheveled as his graying hair. At one time, he had been a handsome guy, trim and fit with a personality and smile that could charm any woman into bed. And there had been a lot of women, three wives, multiple affairs. He was a politician's politician, mayor of the island for nearly twenty years. But at the moment, he looked like a neglected backyard, his face gaunt, dark circles under his eyes, his jowls sagging. All the life had vanished from his eyes.

He saw her and hurried over. "I've got a takeout order, Kate."

"You'll have to wait a few minutes, Mayor Stanton. I've got meals to serve. We're busy tonight."

Kate moved past him, but he grabbed her shirt, jerking her back. She stumbled and the tray tipped and everything slipped off—plates, bowls, glasses, all of it shattering, salads, soups, pasta, ribs, pork chops, burgers, food splattering everywhere. Kate fell into Stanton, who toppled backward and crashed into a bussing cart. It slid across the room and crashed into *their* table and Stanton hollered, *"Seize them, seize all of them."*

Pandemonium erupted in the café. Customers at other tables leaped up, screaming, their bodies jerking and twitching as the evil seized them. Kate scrambled to her feet, grabbed one of the small, flickering torches and slammed it into Stanton's side as he lunged for her. The banker who held the mortgage on her houseboat hurled himself at her and she thrust the torch in his face, singeing his lashes and brows and beard, setting his hair on fire. He shrieked and slapped at his face and skull and the evil within flew out; she actually saw it, a pale, dancing orb of light. Kate drove the torch into it and it vanished.

The torch fizzled out and she grabbed another and set two tablecloths on fire. Zee had told her they feared fire, so she gave them fire—burning tablecloths, plants, food, clothing, napkins, paneling, chairs, tables, railings. Smoke rolled through the café in great, greasy clouds, flames leaping, dancing, hungry. Kate made a beeline toward the farthest edge of the porch, the goddamn zombies, demons, ghosts, horrors, whatever they were, dropping, burning, the air thick with orbs.

The second torch went out. She snatched a third out of its holder and clambered over the balcony railing, into the salt marsh. She set the tall reeds on fire and they burned fast, furiously, and emitted thick, dark smoke that provided her with a measure of cover. She hurled the torch away from her, back into the café, and raced over mounds of shells and soft sand, rocks and driftwood and gulf debris. She fled through marsh so thick that the tall reeds and grasses snapped back into her face and arms, their stalks covered with teeth like saws that sliced through her skin.

At some point in her panic, she realized she wasn't alone; the thin, black dog kept pace with her. Kate had no idea where he'd been or how he'd found her, but was grateful for his company. She made it to her wooden skiff, the dog jumped aboard, and she opened the outboard up wide and the skiff sped away from the café, the salt marsh, Cedar Key.

But Rocky was still back there, he hadn't answered her text. Her chest heaved with sobs, tears burned tracks down her cheeks. Where was her son? What the hell was happening to her life?

The fog began to rise. She had to focus, to concentrate. She knew the channels even at night. She'd been traveling them since she was old enough to stand up. She knew every island, every beach, every fishing spot. She knew where dolphins played, where manatees mated, where wood storks slept, where the water dropped off into impossible depths.

When she finally reached Sea Horse Key thirty minutes later, she brought the engine to an idle and made her way through channels where the water was deepest, behind mangroves so thick that the inner branches rarely saw the light of day. The skiff bumped up against the houseboat, anchored in a protective cove, beneath a braided dome of branches. She tied the rope to the ladder, then looked at the black Lab.

"I'll be back for you in a second, okay?"

The dog whined.

Shit, Kate thought, and scrambled up the ladder. On the balcony, she threw open the doors of the supply closet and brought out one of the wooden planks she and Rocky had used as a hurricane shutter for one storm or another. She wedged one end under the outer edge of the houseboat and let the other edge drop to the lip of the skiff. Then she called to the dog, snapped her fingers, clicked her tongue against her teeth. "C'mon, you can do it, you can do it, c'mon, dog."

The skinny black Lab raced up the plank and onto the houseboat deck. He followed her into the cabin, where she turned on an electric lantern.

She put out a bowl of water, emptied a can of tuna fish into another bowl. "No dog food, sorry." She picked up the lantern and stumbled into her bedroom, her fingers punching out Rocky's cell number. It rang and rang and rang until she reached voice mail. *It's Rocky. Leave a message.*

"It's me. Call. Immediately."

She turned the lantern down low, pulled off her shoes, and collapsed on the bed, the cell close to her head. She didn't even have the energy to cry. She yanked the quilt up over her body and shut her eyes. When she awakened hours later, she swept up her cell to see if Rocky had called. He hadn't. She groped through the dim light for a glass of water, found nothing, and had to get up. Kate picked up the lantern and made her way into the galley for a bottle of water. The fridge was propane fueled, so the water was cold.

As she turned with the bottle tipped to her mouth, everything within her went still and cold. On the floor of her living room, on the floor where she had last seen the dog, head against a couch pillow, lay a fully clothed man with long, dark hair. He slept on his side, hands sandwiched between his knees. She didn't have any idea who he was, had never seen him before. How had he found her? Where was the black Lab? *What the fuck's going on?*

Kate backed away from him, then ran into her bedroom and retrieved the gun Zee had given her, a Walther PPK, a weapon her dad had taught her to shoot. It was the only thing she and James Bond had in common, a semiautomatic. This would do, she thought, and slammed in the clip, crept back into the living room and lowered herself into the nearest chair, the gun aimed at the man's head.

She remained like that for more than an hour, the man motionless, Kate's eyes screaming to close. The hawk appeared, tapping at the balcony doors to be let in. Kate ignored her. *Go find my son,* she thought. *Find Rocky. Bring him home.* The hawk retreated.

The man finally rolled onto his back and his eyes opened. He stared at her, lifted up onto his elbows, and in a soft, hoarse voice said, "You've got it all wrong, Kate."

"Who are you? How the hell do you know my name? What did you do to the dog? Start talking or I'll blow your fucking head off."

Quarantine
March 17–20

. . . .

Memory is when an experience
continues to live within you,
haunting you,
like a hungry ghost.

—from *Yoga, Power, and Spirit:*
Patanjali the Shaman by Alberto Villoldo

Ten

Wayra didn't peg Kate as the type who made empty threats, so he started talking. "All right, where would you like me to start?"

"With your name. Start there. Then you can tell me where the dog is."

"Wayra. My name's Wayra. I—"

"What the hell kind of name is that?"

"It's Quechua."

"Quechua. Isn't that a language that was spoken before the Incas?"

"Yes. It's still spoken in parts of South America."

"Do you have a last name?"

"I haven't had one of those since 1162."

"Stop fucking with me, Wayra." She gestured with the gun. "Sit up, lock your hands on top of your head, and scoot over to the couch."

He moved slowly and carefully, doing exactly what she'd told him. "About the dog—"

"Shut up. I'm asking the questions." Kate backed up to the chair, then moved behind it. "How'd you find the houseboat? No one but Rocky and I know its location."

"I was in the skiff with you when you fled the café. I couldn't get out of it on my own, so you fixed a length of board between the houseboat and the edge of the skiff. You fed me a can of tuna fish and apologized that you didn't have dog food. Then you—"

"How . . . how can you possibly know any of that?"

"Isn't it obvious?"

"*Obvious?*" she practically shouted. "*Nothing* is obvious to me anymore. *Nothing* is what it appears to be. You must've been hiding on the boat somewhere and you . . . shit, you probably tossed the dog overboard."

The simplest explanation, Wayra thought, was often the most difficult to accept. "I *am* the dog, Kate."

"Yeah, and I am the walrus, thank you, John Lennon."

"If you would put your gun down, I'll show you."

She laughed, a quick, nervous sound. "Oh, this should be priceless. Show away, Wayra, but the gun's not going anywhere."

He hesitated, then shifted. When he looked at her again, she was backing away from him, her face the white of Wonder Bread, her entire body seized up with incredulity. Her weapon lay on the floor. "Oh my God . . ." The words spilled from her mouth in a hoarse, almost painful whisper. "I . . . I . . ."

Terrified that she might slip over the edge, sweep up the gun, and start firing, Wayra shifted again, quickly. His bones and muscles throbbed from two shifts within minutes of each other, but he was relieved that Kate was sitting in a chair now, gripping her knees, staring at him.

"Ho-holy shit," she stammered. "Are you . . . a . . . a werewolf?"

"No. A shapeshifter."

"Are . . . th-there more . . . of you?"

He shook his head. "I'm the last of my kind."

"I . . . wow . . ." She rubbed her hands over her face, pushed up from the chair, and walked around the cabin a couple of times, her breathing irregular. She finally paused in front of the fridge, reached inside, and returned with another bottle of water. She handed him one, sank into the chair, and ran her bottle over her face. Then she twisted off the cap, drank, and held the bottle tightly in her hands. In the glow of the electric lantern, she looked exhausted.

"My . . . worldview seems to be seriously flawed."

No more so than that of most humans, he thought, and tipped the bottle to his mouth, emptied it, and leaned back against the couch again, his legs stretched out in front of him. "How much do you know about what's happening on Cedar Key?"

"Enough to move my boat out here and hide. Enough to know the mayor and nearly every other power player on the island has been compromised by . . . well, Zee Small calls them 'Satan's minions.' I think of them as evil ghosts."

"Close."

"Which? The minions or the ghosts?"

"The ghosts."

As Wayra offered the condensed version of *brujo* history, Kate listened with rapt attention. She interrupted now and then with a question, but it was usually to clarify something he had said or to ask for more information. At one point, a tapping at the deck doors prompted Kate to get up and open them. A breeze blew through the houseboat, swollen with the smell of salt water and marsh, and a sparrow hawk glided through the doors, crying out, and circled the living room. It landed on the arm of the couch next to Wayra and stared at him. Recognition shuddered through him. "You're the hawk from the landfill."

The hawk fluttered upward and landed on Wayra's shoulder.

"Jesus," Kate breathed. "She's never done that with anyone except me and Rocky."

"She's your *pet*?" he exclaimed.

"Rocky rescued her last year, and after she was released from the center, she just ended up living on the porch. What do you mean she's the hawk from the landfill?"

"She was at a landfill in Ocala where I found the body of one of Dominica's victims. She went after a cop who was going to shoot at me."

"*Ocala?* That's, like, thirty-five miles from here." Anxiety tightened her mouth. "I thought she was with Rocky. Liberty is like his protector."

"I'm sure he's somewhere safe. Otherwise she wouldn't have left him."

As if in response, the hawk fluttered up from Wayra's shoulder, flew over to Kate, and settled on the back of her chair. "I can't look for him now, not in this fog," she said. "He knows not to come out in it."

"Dominica conjures the fog. It enables these ghosts to travel inside of it in their natural forms and makes it easier for them to seize the living."

The horror in her eyes was that of a woman who was just beginning to realize the true nature of her new reality. "In their *natural* forms? What does that even *mean*?"

"Their souls, spirits, essences, whatever you want to call it."

"The orbs," she said quietly. "At the café, I saw orbs. One of them . . . just vanished when I stuck my torch through it."

He nodded. "They call it annihilation, but you actually freed it to move on in the afterlife."

For a long time, she said nothing. She just stared at her hands, fingers threaded tightly together, her bottle of water pressed between her knees. When she finally spoke, her voice sounded small, uncertain.

"What else . . . do I need to know about these fuckers?" Her voice cracked, and she swallowed hard. "Zee Small said they can be obliterated if the host is killed and the *brujo* doesn't escape. He said they're afraid of fire. That certainly seemed to be the case tonight."

"It sounds like this Zee Small has figured things out on his own. That's impressive."

"At first, when he told me, I thought it was more of his religious bullshit. But yeah, he has figured out a lot of it."

"Anyone can be taken, Kate."

"Even you? A shifter?"

"*Brujos* have tried, but they find me distasteful. Dominica's little army here doesn't know what I am, so they've kept their distance."

"How can Rocky and I protect ourselves?"

"There's no magic here. Stay out of the fog, be sure you're armed, don't hesitate to use fire." He noticed how the hawk watched him, almost as if she were listening to his every word. Even though animals usually reacted to him in some way, he'd never experienced anything like this, especially with any kind of bird. "The bottom line is that they have a great advantage over the living. They can be anywhere, at any time. You won't find them in cemeteries and they stay away from hospitals. Dominica doesn't know how to swim, so it's unlikely that she would follow anyone into deep water. Her ghosts don't seem too fond of water, either, but it may be that it's simply easier for them to move through air. Once you're seized, they control you completely."

"Not in cemeteries," she repeated. "That's ironic. It's where everyone expects to find a ghost. If you're seized, is it possible to escape?"

"People have done it. But some are forever broken or profoundly changed. Others survive with their humanity intact. It all depends on what you are within yourself."

"Will Maddie survive?"

"I think so." But he hadn't been able to say that until this afternoon in the salt marsh, in those few moments before Dominica had seized her again. "But Maddie has been a prisoner within her own body for months. I'm not sure how much longer she'll be able to hold on to who she is. The—"

The hawk suddenly cried out and flew toward the French doors, circling, agitated, until Wayra opened the doors for her. She flew off into the darkness, silent now. It was then he heard what the hawk had heard. "Boats, headed this way," he hissed. "Turn off the lantern. Do you have another weapon?"

She turned off the lantern. "Just grenades. Christ, I can't see a damn thing. Lemme find a flashlight." Drawers opened and shut, then a narrow beam of light pricked the darkness. "I'll get a couple of them."

Kate hastened into the galley and Wayra slipped out onto the back deck. He heard at least half a dozen Coast Guard cutters out there and that meant there would be several people aboard each one, all of them armed. He crouched at the railing, watching, listening, smelling the air. His sense of smell wasn't as sharp in his human form, but even so, he caught the distinct scents of at least ten people on the two lead boats. The fog now crept into the mangroves, tongues of the stuff wrapping around some of the outer branches. *Brujo* fog? It seemed to be, but he sensed it lacked direction, that Dominica was so occupied with something else that the fog she'd conjured was on its own.

He heard the hawk just above him, on the roof or the upper deck, making a soft trilling sound. Her wings fluttered, and a feather drifted down onto the porch. Wayra picked it up, ran his fingers over it and marveled at the softness. He set it on the railing.

Kate dropped to her knees beside him and set a green camouflage bag on the deck between them. "Here," she whispered.

Wayra reached inside, his fingers trailing across the grenades. "How many?"

"Forty-two."

"Where'd you get them?"

"Same place I got the gun, from Zee Small."

The guy who figured things out before anyone else, Wayra thought. "Does he have more weapons?"

"Knowing Zee, he probably has an arsenal."

"Ultimately, we're going to need more than these grenades."

The boats out beyond the mangroves suddenly slowed down, barely idling. Through the mangrove branches, he could see their lights, reflected unnaturally in the thick fog, and estimated the vessels were less than a hundred yards away from the houseboat. He heard shouts, but couldn't distinguish the words.

"Let's go topside," Kate whispered. "We might have a better view."

Wayra plucked two grenades from the bag and followed Kate up the ladder to the left of the door. They emerged on the open upper deck, which nearly reached the tops of the mangroves. The hawk, perched on the back of a lounge chair, continued to trill and preen herself. She had alerted them to the approach of the boats, but didn't seem too concerned about them at the moment. Wayra took that as a positive sign.

He and Kate moved, hunkered over, to the railing. Except for explora-tory tendrils of fog near the island, most of the fog loomed like a wall about a hundred yards offshore, swaying, undulating, sentient. He heard the *brujo* litany: *Find the body, fuel the body, fill the body, be the body* ... At first, it sounded like the wind through trees. Then it sounded like finger-nails drawn over a chalkboard. And then it became the lascivious caress of callused palms over youthful skin, and the hawk suddenly lifted into the air, shrieking, and flew off toward the fog.

Wayra squeezed the bridge of his nose and tried to block out the litany. But he couldn't. He had known this sound since Dominica had joined the *brujos* centuries ago and learned to manipulate fog, conjure it, command it to act as a cover for her hostless followers.

"What *is* that sound?" Kate whispered.

"Her army. The ones who need hosts."

More shouting erupted from the boats, shots echoed, engines fired up, and above it all, the hawk's shrieks echoed across the water. Wayra stood in order to see what was going on. The wall of fog closed in around the two lead vessels and the hawk remained well above it, visible in the starlight, circling, shrieking, occasionally diving down toward it, then soaring up-ward again. It was as if the hawk understood what was going on.

The fog had thickened so much Wayra could no longer see even the shapes of the vessels inside it. But his imagination filled in the blanks. He knew what was happening, had seen it hundreds of times over the years. As the fog closed in around the vessels, the *brujos* within it were seizing hosts. He wasn't close enough to hurl a grenade, and if he grabbed Kate's weapon and starting firing, his shots would fall short and the fog and *bru-jos* would turn in their direction.

Wayra sank to the floor, hands pressed over his ears, and struggled to block out the wails of the people who were seized, their cries of shock and agony. Kate grabbed one of his shoulders. "Wayra, we need to help them, to—"

He took hold of her wrist, pulling her down to the deck. "They're being seized and we can't do anything. We're too far away to shoot or toss gre-nades, and if we expose ourselves, they'll turn this way."

"But—"

"If you're taken, your son will be unprotected. If I'm killed, Dominica wins and Maddie will be trapped for good."

In the ghastly glow of the lights in the fog, Kate's face looked ravaged with uncertainty, grief, rage. Her eyes filled with tears and she ran back to the ladder and vanished over the side. Wayra remained on the open deck a while longer, hoping he would be proven wrong, that the fog would roll in closer to Sea Horse Key and he would have an opportunity to hurl grenades and blast Dominica's minions into oblivion.

But it didn't happen. The wails and shrieks of the seized, the forsaken, the victimized, seemed to go on for a long time. How many? How many were being seized? A dozen? Two dozen? He tried to convince himself that Dominica wasn't winning, but he kept hearing what she'd said to him after she'd seized Maddie again in the salt marsh. *Cedar Key isn't yours to give. It's already mine.*

Sanchez and Jessie raced through a wooded area, sirens shredding the air around them. They came out on a dirt road that curved along the salt marsh. Starlight spilled across it, revealing a low fog that twisted through the reeds like some impossibly long, pale snake. On the other side of the road stood homes on concrete or wooden pilings, weekend places, rentals. All were dark, uninhabited, no cars in the driveways. He could still hear the sirens, and since the breeze had shifted direction, he smelled smoke from the burning café.

Sanchez loped toward one of the empty houses, ducked beneath it, and hid behind a Dumpster piled high with wood and other construction materials. Jessie dropped to the ground beside him. In spite of the chill in the air, she was panting hard. He drew his fingers through her fur, whispering to her, telling her what a good dog she was, running like that, never straying. "We're going to break in and find a place to sleep for the night."

She whined softly, but stayed close as he peeked around the Dumpster, checking out the rest of the road. It appeared to dead-end here, with one house on the cul-de-sac and another at two o'clock. No sign of lights or cars. He darted toward the stairs, Jessie close at his side.

The front door was locked, no surprise. Sanchez checked the obvious places for a spare key—behind a large ceramic pot, under the mat, on the upper edge of the door frame. Nothing. He shrugged off his jacket, wrapped it around his fist, and slammed it against one of the glass panes in the door. The glass tinkled as it struck the floor inside. He quickly knocked away the jagged shards, reached through the opening and turned the dead bolt. The door creaked as it swung open, and he and Jessie hurried inside.

Starlight streamed through the large windows, enough for him to see that the main part of the house was a single large room that held both the kitchen and the living room. He guessed there were bedrooms off to either side. Sanchez opened the fridge door and was relieved that the power was still on, that the fridge wasn't totally empty. Bottled water, ketchup, mayonnaise, mustard, butter, peanut butter, jelly. He grabbed two bottles of water, poured one into a bowl and set it on the floor for Jessie. As he guzzled from the other, he opened the freezer. Trays of ice, a loaf of frozen bread, two frozen pizzas. He hurried over to the pantry and found cans of tuna, fruit, vegetables, packages of ramen noodles and spaghetti, juices, more bottled water, bottled sauces, popcorn, even dog and cat food. Good, perfect, they wouldn't starve here.

He filled a bowl with dog food, made himself a peanut butter and jelly sandwich, gobbled it down as he went through the drawers. He found a flashlight, turned it on, aimed the beam at the floor, and moved restlessly around the house, checking the views.

From the master bedroom, he could see up to the curve in the dirt road. From the living room, he had a view of another section of the road, the salt marsh, the gradually rising fog, and the house at two o'clock. From the second bedroom, he gazed down into the cul-de-sac and at the house that occupied it. No lights on there, no car. It looked as if he were alone at this end of the road.

Sanchez opened the porch doors. The balcony was wide, long, and wrapped around most of the dome-shaped house. The smell of smoke was much stronger now, the squeal of sirens just as loud. The road remained empty of cars, people, even wildlife.

He shrugged off his pack, set it on the floor, and sank into one of the Adirondack chairs. He checked the cell phone Delaney had given him lifetimes ago in that parking lot at the state park. The damn thing didn't have a signal, but his BlackBerry did. Its signal was weak, but at least he had something. He texted Delaney: *Got out of café safely, am hidden in a neighborhood on the marsh. They're hungry ghosts, just like we talked about. Did u get the vid?* He pressed *send* and waited anxiously to see if the text went through. When it did, he kept staring at the BlackBerry, hoping for an immediate reply.

Minutes ticked by. Then Delaney replied: *Stay put. O'Donnell knows you went rogue. He thinks u tricked both of us. Quarantine now in place, just not formal yet. Got vid. More soon. D*

Sanchez started to answer him, but a text message from his sister popped up. *You okay?*

Google Maddie Livingston. Esperanza, brujos, Cedar Key. Quarantine about to be or already imposed.

A cart suddenly rounded the curve, four men inside. Terrified they might look up and see him and Jessie, Sanchez shoved his BlackBerry into a pocket, grabbed his pack from the floor. He and the dog slipped back inside the house.

Master bedroom. From here, he could watch them without being seen. The cart stopped in the middle of the road, and the four men got out. They passed around a bottle, appeared to be talking, but the sirens were still squealing and drowned out everything but an occasional laugh.

The driver gestured toward the left. Two men headed off in that direction, presumably to check the empty houses Sanchez had passed on his way in here. Then the driver and another man strode up the street toward the houses at this end. So who were they? Cops? They were wearing jeans and jackets. But even if they had been wearing uniforms, it didn't mean anything, not after what he'd seen at the café. He had to assume these four men were inhabited by the same evil that was inside those people at the café, inside Maddie.

He had a Glock 34 nine millimeter that Delaney had given him. During his training with ISIS, he had used this weapon most frequently. But his had been altered somewhat with a set of Dawson fiber-optic sights, with the rear sight adjusted for both windage and elevation. A stainless steel guide rod and heavier spring had been added, the trigger pull had been lightened, and some of the internal stock parts had been changed out with stainless steel to smooth up the action. An extended magazine release had been added, too.

The best news was that the Glock held eighteen rounds and he had three additional clips. In short, he had enough ammo to take out all four of these men. But Sanchez had never killed anyone before. Self-defense was one thing; picking them off from the balcony would be murder.

The front door was the only way out of the house. He slung his pack over his shoulder. "Let's move, Jess. Fast." She ran over to him, and as he opened the door, he caught hold of her collar with one hand. "Stay close," he whispered.

She whimpered in response and hugged his side. He wondered, not for the first time, whether she was a human soul trapped within a dog's body, voiceless.

They raced to the bottom of the stairs, then dashed right, around a fence that separated this property from an open field. Sanchez dropped into a crouch on the other side, his heart slamming against his ribs. His options hardly boded well for getting out of here. Low brush covered the flat, open field; nothing was tall or thick enough to provide a hiding place. The wooded area behind the house in the cul-de-sac seemed to be his best bet, but to get to it he would have to cross the road and would be exposed long enough to get shot.

Sanchez crawled to the edge of the fence, looked around it. One of the men trotted purposefully toward the only other house on this street, the place on the marsh. The other guy was stooped over, tying his shoe.

Do it now.

Sanchez dashed out into the road and Jessie tore toward the woods like a bat out of hell. She understood, she got it, thank God. Just when he thought he would make it, one of the men shouted, "Hey, you, stop where you are!"

Sanchez kept running, and the guy opened fire.

A bullet whistled past his head. Another bullet pinged against the road. Sanchez didn't wait for a third bullet. He opened fire, shooting blindly, and dived into the woods. He slammed against the ground so hard his breath rushed out of him. He lay there for a moment, stunned, then managed to roll onto his stomach.

Neither man was visible. Neither of them was shooting. Did that mean he'd hit one or both of them?

Sanchez raised his head slightly and a volley of gunshots exploded through the darkness. He scrambled back, unwilling to fire because it would expose his exact position. Then, suddenly, the other two men from the cart appeared, moving up the road, darting in and out of cover like commandos, boys playing Special Forces. Four of them, Christ. Four against one.

He leaped up and took off through the woods, just behind a line of trees that paralleled the road, and started firing, emptying his clip. He slammed in another and continued to fire. He moved so fast that by the time they shot back, he was gone. Then someone else started shooting, the gunshots markedly different—automatic rifle, assault rifle.

Sanchez couldn't tell if the shooter was targeting him or the men from the cart, so he hit the ground and rolled into the deeper shadows. Breathing hard, he rocked back on his heels, and was shocked to see that the fog from the marsh now rolled through the road. How had it risen so quickly?

Then the shooting stopped. He no longer heard the sirens. A tense, uneasy silence settled over the road, across the dark marsh. Sanchez felt that if he moved, if he breathed too loudly, the enemy would hear it and the final volley of gunfire would be it for him.

To his utter shock, one man came forward from the trees along the salt marsh. Sanchez couldn't see his face, but in the starlight his silhouette looked bamboo thin and he carried a rifle upright, tight against his chest, and had an identical rifle slung over his left shoulder.

"Guy with the dog, I know you're in these woods and can hear me," the man called. "These fucks are dead and so's the evil inside them." He stopped on the left side of the road and turned over one of the men. "This here boy used to work down at the local garage. Did some good detail work. Got taken back in late February." He moved on and rolled a body out from behind a piling. "This young lady worked as a secretary at the high school. She got taken late January, early February. Not sure why they bothered with either of these two, 'cept they needed someone to fix their cars and probably one of these sick fucks liked the young lady's body."

Sanchez crept out to the line of trees, glanced around quickly, warily, to make sure the man was alone. It seemed that he was. "Hey, mister," Sanchez called. "How do I know you're not one of them?"

"'Cause I just killed three of them and usually they don't kill their own kind, at least not like this. So here's the deal, boy. All this gunfire is sure to bring out more of them. A lot more. Between the fire and the gunshots and the government boats out there, you can bet your ass they'll be fanning out across the island, looking for those of us who haven't been taken. I've got a refuge, if you and your dog care to join us."

Jessie. He whistled for her and she barked and raced out of the dark and leaped up, tail whipping back and forth so fast he thought it might fall off. "Good girl, awesome. Stay close."

Sanchez and his dog left the safety of the trees and trotted out into the road. The old man who stood there with his two AK-47s reminded Sanchez of a crow, something about his stance, his arms pulled in like wings, the gauntness of his long face, a beaklike nose.

"Been watching you since you and your dog took off from the café. You saw what happened."

"The mayor went for a waitress named Kate and—"

"That girl has gone through some shit. Walk with me, huh? Name's Zee Small."

"Nick Sanchez."

They met in the middle of the road. Zee wore his long gray hair in a ponytail. His jeans looked like they hadn't been washed in about five years. No telling about his age—anywhere from early fifties to early seventies. The old man extended his bony hand and Sanchez shut down and grasped it. No images rushed into him, no psychic doors flew open. The only thing he picked up on the old guy was his fervently religious certainty about what was what on the island. It guided everything he did, every decision he made.

"Thank you for intervening," Sanchez said as they walked quickly, deeper into the woods.

Zee turned on a flashlight and kept it aimed at the ground. "We need the good guys, Nick. We're real short on them right now."

"How'd you know I wasn't one of them?"

"I was in the café, go there most nights. Food's good, gives me a chance to see these fuckers up close. When the mayor and Kate went at it, her with them torches, and you took off with this gorgeous dog of yours, I knew you were one of us."

"Because of the dog?"

"Partly that. These stewards of Satan's don't like dogs. Or cats. Or any other animal. But I also knew 'cause you weren't running from fire. You were running from *them*."

Just before the woods ended, they reached an old truck the color of soot and piled inside, Jessie perched between them on the front seat. The old man drove like a maniac on the dark roads, the two AK-47s resting next to him, upright against the seat.

"Where'd you get your weapons experience?" Sanchez asked.

"'Nam, lifetimes ago. Here's the weird thing, Nick. In a rice paddy out in the middle of who-knows-where in 1967 thereabouts, I met one of these

mutants. Yes, siree, this boy was one of ours and he was whacked. Kept trying to fuck all the women in this village, his eyes had gone dark eons ago.
The thing inside him was ancient, just like the thing inside that pretty redhead from the Island Hotel. Maddie. You met her?"

Sanchez didn't intend to tell the whole truth yet. "Yes."

"So what about you? Where'd you learn to shoot?"

"Quantico."

Zee slammed on the brakes. "You're a *fed*?"

"I work for the government, but that doesn't make me the kind of fed
you think I am."

"Yeah? What kinda fed does it make you, Nick?"

Here we go. Sanchez flicked his internal switch to the *on* position. "That
ring you're wearing. May I hold it?"

"What the fuck for?"

"You asked what kind of fed I am. I'm going to show you."

Zee hesitated, then worked the ring off his finger and dropped it into
Sanchez's palm. It was the easiest kind of reading for him, a gold ring that
held on to personal stories. Sanchez closed his fingers over it. No rush of
images, just a name, a single name lit up in neon. "Lydia." Her name unlocked the door to the rest of it. "She died a few years back, you went into
seclusion. I see you in the deep woods, distraught. She came to you in the
middle of the night, came right into your tent and lay down beside you
and you woke and . . . and—"

"Shittin' hell, son. I'll take that ring back."

Sanchez dropped it into Zee's open palm. The old man worked it back
onto his arthritic finger. "I read about you government seers on the Internet. Stargate."

The old man obviously wasn't the ignorant redneck Sanchez had assumed he was. "That was our former incarnation. We're now called ISIS."

"ISIS." Zee emitted a choked laugh. "Such fancy names. For me, Stargate was a TV show, a movie. Don't know about no ISIS. Lydia was my
wife. And yeah, she came to me in a tent about a month after she died while
waiting for a bone marrow transplant. After that, nothing for me was the
same. You see the dead, they lay beside you, they touch you and you feel
it . . . I gotta tell you, Nick, nothing in your life is the same again."

With that, he put the truck in gear and they drove on, without speaking, to the outer reaches of the island, and into another stretch of woods.

Eleven

In the predawn light, Dominica surveyed the smoking remains of Annie's Café. The entire building had collapsed. Charred bodies lay here and there, unrecognizable chunks of flesh and limbs. A tractor already moved through the area, scooping the debris into several dump trucks to be taken off the island. Two trucks had left already.

The tractor's bright lights exposed the utter ruin that despicable Kate Davis had caused. But the physical ruin concerned her less than the loss of eight members of her tribe, five who hadn't escaped their hosts when the roof caved in, and three who had been there to seize hosts and had been annihilated by the flames. For these deaths, Kate would pay dearly. Then there were four others who had been on another part of the island, searching empty homes, whose deaths by an unknown cause had resonated through the *brujo* web.

A cart pulled up alongside her and Whit got out. "Have they found her?" Dominica asked.

"Not yet. But she left the island yesterday afternoon, moved her houseboat elsewhere."

"There're dozens of islands out there where she could be, Whit."

"Right now, we've got a more pressing problem."

"What?"

"They're in the hotel courtyard, Nica, and need to speak to you."

"They?"

"New hosts of a peculiar kind."

She got into the cart with him and they headed for Second Street. She was grateful the fire hadn't leaped from block to block, consuming the entire island. With so many wooden buildings, it wouldn't have taken much. As it was, some of the firemen who were hosts to her kind had been so terrified of the flames they had fled the area. She, Whit, Joe, Gogh, Jill, even Liam had confronted their own fear of fire by taking over the job of the firemen, and had put out the flames. She didn't yet know how to deal with the cowards. She understood their fear; it was also her own. But she had confronted and conquered her fear. Why hadn't they?

When she and Whit walked through the gate of the courtyard, illuminated by the lights in the hotel windows, she was surprised to see a group of men and women in Coast Guard uniforms, sitting around two of the tables. Joe and Gogh were serving them food. All of them were hosts to *brujos.* New blood, she thought. The tribe had lost eight, gained ten. But where had these hosts come from?

"People, if you can listen up, please," said Whit. "All of you here know Dominica. She has some questions for you."

"I'd like to know how you came to seize these hosts," Dominica said.

The woman who stood hosted Luz, a *bruja* Dominica knew slightly. Her name meant "light." Dominica liked that. "A bunch of us were traveling in the fog between Cedar Key and some of the islands and saw Coast Guard cutters. Two of them were well ahead of the others so the fog enclosed them and we seized them."

"What are Coast Guard cutters doing in these waters, Luz?"

"According to our hosts, they're here as a result of a quarantine that was imposed overnight. They'll make sure that no one from the island escapes by water. Everything from the fourth bridge south is now blocked."

"A quarantine?" She looked over at Whit, her expert on all matters American. "Who has the authority to do that?"

"The Centers for Disease Control, FEMA, the Department of Homeland Security, the FBI, all of them, I guess."

"According to my host," said Luz, "DHS working in conjunction with the CDC. A substance was found in the bodies of some of the victims. An unidentified virus. They think it's due to a biological terrorist attack and until they know for sure how it's spread or how contagious it is, they've decided to sideline the island."

Dominica's first impulse was to attack these government boys en masse, seize all of them. But she realized that would make her look scared and weak. Besides, she could use this to her advantage. The locals wouldn't be able to leave. It would now be easier to control the town.

"Terrorists?" She laughed and kept on laughing, and pretty soon the other *brujos,* obviously surprised by her reaction, started laughing, too. "People, we're *terrorists.*" Dominica threw out her arms, welcoming the idea. "They've just conferred the deepest honor on our tribe. This country is so terrified of terrorists it forces its own people to go through machines at airports that render them naked. And when the passengers refuse, they're subjected to what amounts to sexual molestation. Terrorists are so feared that the military here invades other countries with impunity and pours trillions into their war machines while their own people are unemployed and hungry and losing their homes. Can you believe the favor they've done us? They have no idea what real terrorism is. We're going to teach them that."

"You're right," Whit breathed. "My God, you're absolutely right, Nica."

The *brujos* stole glances at each other, still confused. "But what will we do about food?" asked Luz. "Our hosts have to eat."

"We have plenty of food in the market for the time being. But we'll be sending groups of you out to raid the empty homes and bring back whatever food you find. The important thing is that with the island quarantined, those people who haven't yet been seized won't be able to leave. They're trapped. We're practically assured of victory now. A *brujo* enclave in the U.S. of A."

"I'll organize the food-hunting expedition," said Joe.

"What about the bitch who started the fire at Annie's?" asked another *brujo*. "Has she been caught?"

"Not yet," Whit said. "But we're going to double up on our search for her at first light."

"With our new additions, Whit, where do our numbers stand?" she asked.

He thought a moment. "Three hundred and nine."

"Let's see if we can push it to four hundred by nightfall." As soon as she said it, she felt the net trembling with excitement. Open season on humans. "But for now, the restrictions about children under the age of sixteen still stand. And no bleed-outs, please. We would have to put those bodies in freezers, and right now we need the freezers for food. Gogh, we're going to need specific groups to perform specific jobs other than food hunting and searching for Kate Davis. I'll give you a list of what needs to be done, and you work with Joe and Whit in picking out who does what. I'll need a couple of *brujos* without hosts to go out to the fourth bridge and see what's actually going on." She turned to Luz. "How many Coast Guard cutters are we talking about?"

"Probably between five and eight. It depends on how much area each boat is supposed to patrol."

"Any idea about what other kinds of reinforcements are being used?"

"My host only knows about the Coast Guard."

"Well, we'll find out. You can find accommodations for your hosts either here at the hotel or in one of the empty homes on the island. Once you've done that, report to either Gogh or Whit so we can assign you to one of the task groups. Any questions?"

Silence.

"Excellent." She gestured at Whit, Gogh, and Joe, and the four of them walked out of the courtyard. "Gentlemen, this is the best news yet. But we have to move quickly and efficiently." Never let it be said that her defeat in Esperanza had taught her nothing. "Our biggest challenge will be food and controlling the food and supplies we find in the empty homes and restaurants out on Dock Street. Everything should be brought to the Island Market and to the hotel. We may have to implement restrictions of some kind. Any members of the tribe whose hosts are fishermen should be put to work off the docks and beaches. Let's haul in as much fish as we can."

Whit said, "By the way, the two trucks that left already with a haul of debris have been turned back at the roadblock."

"Then we need to find another spot for the debris to be dumped."

"I know just the place," Whit said. "The airport runway. You and I can drive the trucks out there, Nica, and make sure these government types who are quarantining us can't land any planes."

"Brilliant. Let's get it done before the sun rises."

The task proved more arduous than she thought it would be. The runway was long and there was so much debris, some of it still smoking, that it took them half a dozen trips to cover most of it. A chopper might still be able to touch down, but only if the pilot was crazy.

Mixed in with the debris, of course, were body parts. Dominica thought they would attract vultures, rats, roaches, and other vile creatures, so she forced Maddie to walk into the debris to look for body parts and to deposit whatever she found in plastic bags. She resisted immediately, as soon as she plucked up the first bone, and fought hard to seize control of her body, struggled to scream, to hurl the bone. Whit stood there, laughing and shaking his head, enjoying the show. Dominica struck her nerve centers, causing Maddie such excruciating pain that her knees buckled and she rolled through the scorched wood and dust screaming.

Maddie scrambled onto her virtual couch, unable to resist or fight any longer, unable to hurl her consciousness outside of herself. Her body continued on without her participation, hands picking up body parts—a severed arm, a foot, a hand missing two fingers, a scorched leg bone—and dropping them into a green garbage bag.

The stench permeated her virtual world, the smell of death she had lived with all these months, the stink of Dominica. The *bruja* always had claimed that she couldn't possibly emit an odor, that she was just consciousness. But the reek of rotting eggs and decay was so pervasive that Maddie didn't think she would ever be rid of it. And it finally drove her out of her body, a screaming nothingness without mass or weight, invisible to the naked eye.

The rising sun punched a burning hole in the horizon. If she thought herself into that fiery orange hole, maybe she would emerge in some other universe where Dominica had never existed, where *brujos* were just the stuff of legends, fairy tales, the darker side of Disney. In that universe, she might be in vet school by now, following the path she had intended after her grandmother had moved her to Key Largo, after she had become a runner and a vegan and lost sixty pounds. But then, she never would have seen Esperanza, lived there, experienced the magic of knowing a shapeshifter, of living among people who, as Spock used to say, "lived long and prospered." She never would have understood the true nature of good and evil or of a reality with all its twists and strangeness.

Yeah, all of that was good. But in that other universe, she wouldn't be a prisoner in her own body, either, her sanity hanging by a thread so fragile that one more incident like this might break her.

Even now, as she soared through the gathering light, she considered not returning to her body, letting Dominica have it. Who cared? So what if she died? She wouldn't get stuck as Charlie and the chasers, Dominica and her ghosts, had. She would take up yoga in the afterlife, become a vegan again, find a mentor who would help her wade through all the mistakes she'd made in her short life, a mentor who would help her choose her next life, the right parents, the right circumstances that would enable her to achieve her spiritual and creative potential. Or something.

She felt a sharp, insistent tug at her left and followed it to a neglected building behind a barbed-wire fence. Several waterfront acres spread out around the building and as she drifted in for a closer look, she saw animals in cages, birds in a huge aviary. A zoo? Not on the island. This appeared to be the animal sanctuary she'd heard about—but had never seen before now. She dropped to the ground on virtual feet, in her virtual body, surprised that she didn't have to do anything to create this body, to maintain it. Was this how her grandfather Charlie did it? *Think yourself into being.*

Far above her, a bird cried out, and when she looked up, a sparrow hawk was spiraling toward her. It touched down on the roof of the building, staring at her as though it could really see her. Was that possible? Why not? She lived in a world of impossibilities.

Maddie stuck her nonexistent fingers in her nonexistent mouth and let out a shrill, sharp whistle. The hawk flew upward, circled her, then landed right at her feet. *It sees me, hears me.*

The bird keened and suddenly the door of the building slammed open and a tall, handsome kid barreled out. Rocky, Kate's son. And the hawk, of course, was Liberty. She had seen them several times at the hotel, and Dominica, she remembered, was afraid of the hawk for some reason. Rocky was obviously hiding out.

"Liberty," he whispered, and the bird flew over to him and landed on his outstretched arm. "I knew you'd come back. I knew it. I've . . . got a little food, sandwiches and stuff the employees left in the fridge, and bottled water. I started to . . . to leave last night, but heard all the sirens and shit and . . . and . . ." Then his face collapsed in on itself and his eyes filled up and he started to cry. The hawk keened and inched its way up his arm to his shoulder and then ran its beak gently through his hair, a caress.

It was a strange and heartbreaking sight. Maddie quickly lifted up, away from the kid and the hawk, and thought of Sanchez, Wayra, Sanchez, Wayra, either one, an ally, please. She ended up near one of the uninhabited islands off Cedar Key, and swirled down through the mangroves to a houseboat. Wayra was sitting on the back deck, a laptop balanced on his thighs, his bare feet pressed against the railing. An empty plate and a mug of coffee were on the table. He seemed very intent on what he was reading.

Maddie touched down next to him and shouted his name. He flinched, that was all. He didn't look around, didn't really hear her. He merely felt *something.* She stood in front of him and leaned into him, shouting his name again. This time he looked up, blinked his large, dark eyes. "Maddie?"

Yes, yes, right here, it's me.

But he couldn't see her, couldn't hear her. Not like Sanchez could. With Sanchez, it was like having a conversation. With Wayra, it was a game of charades.

"Wayra?"

Kate padded out onto the porch in jeans, a pullover sweater, and bare feet. She held a wrench in one hand, pliers in the other. "Can you give me a hand here? I'm trying to soup up the engine so we can get across the water fast as soon as it's dark."

"That won't be for another eleven or twelve hours, Kate."

She shrugged. "I know. I just feel the need to do *something* productive."

"Then let's fit a couple of those electric engines to canoes. You've got three of them in your storage area. No noise. Less cumbersome than moving the houseboat."

Her arms dropped to her sides. "Good idea. But I'd still like to ramp up the houseboat's engine. Be prepared for . . . well, whatever."

"Sure thing." Wayra pushed up from the chair. "We could try going over while it's still light out, working our way from island to island, but there would still be vast stretches of open gulf where we'd be exposed."

"I'm resigned to waiting until dark," Kate said.

Kate, can you hear me? Maddie stood between her and Wayra, frantically waving her nonexistent arms at Kate. *Hey, I'm here.*

Nothing. Not even a flinch. Maddie moved into the doorway, but Kate walked right through her.

As soon as Wayra went inside the houseboat, Maddie soared away, frightened now that even Sanchez wouldn't be able to hear her. She sought the luminous thread that had led her to him before, but something interfered with her ability to locate him, a low humming, a buzzing, that disoriented her. For a while, she drifted aimlessly, struggling to focus on his energy. She needed to connect with him, with someone who could hear her. She finally narrowed her search to a densely wooded area on the far side of the island.

In there, you're somewhere in there.

As Maddie descended through the trees, the buzzing noise ebbed. She slipped through branches, deeper into shadows, and landed as lightly as a leaf on the ground. She smelled smoke, then food, and wondered how she could smell anything at all. She followed the scents to a clearing deep in the woods. Tents and old rusted trailers encircled a campfire, barefoot kids and dogs ran around, several men and women cooked over large aluminum pots and pans, and two other adults were setting the food on a long table. Here and there in the trees, Maddie caught sight of heavily armed guards.

It looked like a gypsy encampment and she sensed that none of these people had been seized yet. She would have to shield this memory from

Dominica. With the quarantine in place, these people and any others who hadn't been seized would need to be extremely careful.

Sanchez, Sanchez, she thought, turning slowly, waiting for a tug in one direction or another. She finally felt it, coming from straight in front of her. She moved past the campfires, the long table set with platters of fish, grits, home fries, coffee. Two dogs barked at her, but neither of them followed her. She couldn't tell if they actually saw her or just sensed her. The hawk had definitely seen her. Why could the hawk see her but not the dogs? What about other animals?

She paused in front of one of the guards, a Rambo type with tattooed arms the size of tree trunks, and clapped her virtual hands inches from his face. No reaction. She noticed his weapon. She was no gun expert, but she'd watched enough movies to recognize the sucker as an AK-47. So despite the nomadic appearance of this camp, these people were apparently well-armed. She wondered how much they knew about *brujos*.

Maddie moved on, following the tug, and entered a thicker part of the woods. She found Sanchez fishing from a shallow bank with a skinny guy with a gray ponytail. Except for the AK-47 next to the old man, they looked like a couple of Huck Finns. Fortunately, they were fishing in an inlet and the trees shrouded them. She walked over and sat on the ground next to Sanchez. Jessie whined and Sanchez immediately glanced to his left, where she was sitting. *Red?*

Right next to you, Sanchez. A search is under way. Her minions are going house to house. You should probably tell these folks to put out the fires. Brujos have an excellent sense of smell.

"Hey, Zee," he said aloud. "Maybe the cooking should be done indoors from now on. Just in case these suckers have organized a search party."

"Sounds smart to me." He whipped out a cell phone, looked at it, snapped it shut. "No signal. Shit. You think the quarantine jammed the cell signals?"

"Probably."

Zee tapped his temple with the heel of his hand. "I'm getting sloppy in my old age, Nick. I shoulda thought of that cooking thing. I'll walk back and tell them to kill the fires."

"How fast can you move camp if you have to?"

The old man eyed Sanchez warily. "Why? You picking up something, son?"

Would he believe you if you told him I was sitting next to you? Maddie asked.

He might. He knows Dominica is inside your body.

She and pervert Whit are covering the runway with body parts and debris from the café. It's going to take them a while. The safest place for Zee's people is the cemetery. Brujos hate cemeteries.

"Just curious, Zee."

"Well, most of them trailers can be driven outta here like any vehicle. If we were in a hurry, we'd leave the ones on hitches behind."

"Is there another wooded area like this one?"

"There're several. But we've got an ELF field around this one that makes it tough for Satan's army to get in."

"An extremely low frequency field? What's generating it? Why does that work?"

"Don't have a clue why it works. But we've got high-voltage power lines around this woods, and that's what generates the field. Early on, one of the demons tried to get in and couldn't do it."

"You could see it?"

"Heard its wails of frustration and then its death wails. Watch my pole. I'll be right back."

Zee picked up his weapon and bolted to his feet with the spryness of a much younger man. *Is he right about the ELF field, Red?*

Yeah. No one else around here has figured it out, though. Dominica first encountered it in Otavalo. It's how she keeps a brujo captive who has broken one of her rules.

"How do you find me?"

I think of you and wait for a tug in a particular direction.

"Yesterday, with the guy named Wayra . . . what happened?"

She took me again. When it gets really bad, I leap out of my body. You're the only one who can hear me. Even Wayra can't seem to. He's on a houseboat with Kate, who worked at the hotel as a bartender. Her son is hiding out at this animal rescue center on Cedar Key. Shit, I'm babbling, you don't know them. How'd you end up here?

"Did Kate also work at Annie's Café?"

I think so.

"Then I met her last night." As he talked out loud, describing what had happened after he'd fled the fire at the café, the sound of his voice moved through her like cool water. It made her temporarily forget her actual circumstances and assuaged the agony Dominica had inflicted on her. Listening to him, she could almost believe there was some way out for her, a route to freedom she hadn't thought of.

Did you hear from Delaney after you texted him? she asked.

His head bobbed, just as it might do in a regular conversation. "Yeah. He said to stay put for now. At some point before I arrived on Cedar Key, some fed had come out here and installed a security video in the café. It transmitted images to a remote computer. That's what they're studying now."

What's there to study? It's obvious there was something wrong with the people on the right side of the café.

"I know. They've got the video I took, too. But trying to explain a concept like hungry ghosts to most of these guys is like trying to convince moon-walk doubters that we actually went to the moon. I doubt that Delaney is even trying to explain it that way."

She felt Dominica's attention shifting back to her, probing, searching for her. *Got to go, she's wondering what happened to me.*

"Wait. How can I come to you, Maddie?"

You can't as long as she's inside me. If she knows about you, she'll kill us both. She already grilled me about the guy who resuscitated me. She saw you kissing me.

"Jesus, Red. What can I do to help you?"

Right now, nothing. She touched his shoulder—and her hand moved right through him.

"I felt that," he said.

How about this? She moved in front of him, bent over, and touched her hands ever so lightly to the sides of his face so they didn't sink through him. Then she kissed him just as lightly. *Did you feel it?*

Smiling, Sanchez touched his fingers to his mouth and whispered, "I did. Like the soft threads of a spiderweb."

Then the old man loped back over, breaking the spellbound moment. "Got that taken care of. You looked like you were talking to yourself, Nick."

Maddie laughed and ran along the banks, her heart singing. She flapped her arms like the wings of a bird and thought, *Up, up, and away.*

She snapped back into her body so abruptly that it jerked forward and then back in the cart's seat, alerting Dominica that something unusual had just occurred. "What is it?" Whit asked.

Dominica rubbed the back of her neck. "It felt like whiplash."

"I'm only going ten miles an hour, Nica."

"I think Maddie has learned to travel out of body. Isn't that so, Maddie?"

Maddie scurried back into her virtual room with its small, pathetic virtual comforts, anxiety eating away at her. Could the bitch prevent her from traveling outside her body? From escaping in that way?

It was one thing to go along for months as a prisoner in her body, plotting and planning ways to reclaim her power and her freedom, never aware that she might have other options. But now that she'd learned to slip out of her body so easily and had found someone who could hear her, now that she wasn't so horribly alone, she knew that to be denied contact with Sanchez would kill her.

Twelve

Kate wore black—black jeans, black long-sleeved shirt, black windbreaker. She even tied a dark kerchief around her hair. Her weapon and an extra clip were in the pockets of her jacket. Wayra was at least six foot three, much too tall to wear Rocky's jeans, but she found a dark shirt and jacket that fit him, and with his black hair, she thought he wouldn't be visible out there on the water.

They climbed into the canoes, both equipped with electric motors that they couldn't use until they were out of the mangroves, in open water. Wayra led the way, paddling through the dense mangroves. Despite the chill in the air, insects hummed, mosquitoes dive-bombed them, and here and there fish splashed.

The news about the quarantine had hit the Web and, thanks to her wireless Internet card, her communications hadn't gone down. Official information was sketchy, but the parameters of the quarantine and the reason for it were spelled out. Wayra had explained that what the CDC believed was a virus was actually a substance that *brujos* prompted a host body to make so that physical life would be more comfortable for them. As if physical life, she thought, were a hostile environment like the moon or Mars. Maddie and all the others who had been seized would have the substance in their bodies for years, perhaps for their entire lives.

She now realized, of course, that Rich had already been seized the night they had sex and she wondered if she now had the substance within her own body. The CDC was theorizing that the virus was transmitted through bodily fluids. But if it wasn't really a virus, could it be transmitted through sex? The question disturbed her and begged for an answer.

They paused at the edge of the mangrove. No fog yet. And the moon wouldn't rise for another forty minutes. "I don't see any boat lights, do you?" she whispered.

"No."

"If we follow the current, we'll get there that much faster."

"You lead," he said.

"Hey, Wayra, you have any of those grenades? Just in case?"

"Four."

"About this substance that the ghosts cause their hosts to produce. If a *brujo* host has sex with someone who isn't a host, can this substance be transmitted that way?"

He didn't answer immediately and that worried her. "I honestly don't know, Kate. My inclination is to say no. But over the centuries, these ghosts have evolved in ways that have shocked me, the chasers, and anyone who knows anything about the ancient *brujos* of Esperanza. It was never an issue in Esperanza because no one was doing autopsies. When someone bled out, the rest of us knew what had caused it. It's entirely possible that Dominica has figured out how to make this substance transmissible that way. It might be why she has allowed this tribe to be so blatantly promiscuous. Maybe every *brujo* host who has sex with an uncompromised person is creating the inner conditions that facilitate that person's seizure. It could explain why her tribe has been able to seize so many with so little resistance."

"That's troubling."

"You're worried that you had sex with Rich when he was hosting a *brujo,* so you might have the substance in your body, too, right?"

"How . . . I didn't tell you about Rich."

"In my other form, my sense of smell is extraordinary. That night you fled the hotel, I started following you because I smelled that you had been with a man who hosted a *brujo.*"

"That's weirdly intrusive, Wayra."

There in the little cave of mangrove branches, in the thick, almost oppressive odor of salt water and swamp, he gave her arm a reassuring squeeze. "Look, we don't know anything for sure. Even if it's true, any *brujo* would find you utterly distasteful regardless of how conducive this substance made your body."

She actually managed a small, stifled laugh. "And why's that, Wayra?"

"*Brujos* like compliant hosts, people who tend to be passive, laid-back. It's why Cedar Key is perfect for her new tribe. But you and Maddie, in your hearts, are revolutionaries."

"Then why was Dominica able to take her?"

"Because she's the niece of one of the people who helped destroy Dominica's tribe in Esperanza. Vengeance is pivotal to her existence."

Kate didn't feel like any revolutionary. At the moment, she was just a distraught mother terrified for her son. "Let's go, Wayra." She pushed her paddle against a branch and the canoe whispered out of the mangrove, into the open water between Sea Horse Key and Cedar Key. She paused briefly to lower the motor into the water and turned it on.

The sky looked as if stars had been flung out against the blackness by some Olympian. The thin necklaces of clouds didn't do much to mitigate the light and she suddenly wished for black thunderheads and a horrendous downpour.

They aimed for the tip of the peninsula, where the runway was, and would travel along the eastern shore, through marsh and reeds, and come out behind Amy's house. It was the most logical place to begin their search. Rocky had supposedly been with her when Kate had gone to work at the café. If Rocky wasn't there, then they would continue into Goose Cove to the animal rescue center, the only other place he might be. Kate kept hoping that Liberty would show up and lead them to Rocky. But the hawk hadn't been back since she had flown off last night. She desperately needed to believe Liberty was with Rocky, protecting him.

As they neared the island, Kate was shocked to realize Dock Street was mostly dark. Always in the past when she had approached Cedar Key from this direction, at night, the glimmer of lights along Dock Street burned brightly, an invitation. Business and restaurant owners who hadn't been seized had probably gone into hiding and taken their food and supplies with them. Now they were hiding not only from *brujos,* but from the government as well.

By the time they reached the tip of the peninsula, the fog was thick, but low. It didn't seem to be coming in off the water, but clung to the land like a transparent layer of earth and rock. Even though it made her uneasy, she didn't feel it was an imminent threat. If anything, it provided a convenient cover for their canoes.

"Is it *brujo* fog?" she whispered.

"Yes." No hesitation from Wayra on that one. "But it's confused, disoriented, it doesn't seem to have any direction."

His canoe bumped into hers and he came alongside her, turned off his motor, tilted it back out of the water. Kate did the same. "You make it sound like it has a consciousness, Wayra."

"It usually does. But this fog is more like a self-organizing system that vaguely recalls being conjured. And right now, it's not threatening us. How far up the runway is Amy's house?"

Kate studied the shoreline. She had never approached the house by water, at night. She brought out her flashlight, turned it on, and shone it off to her left, locating the runway. It looked weird, misshapen, as if an earthquake had torn apart the asphalt, then someone had come along and tried to slap it back together again. "Wayra, something's wrong with the runway."

"Yeah, I see it. Let's stop here. I'm going to take a look. Take this." He passed her the small bag that held the four grenades, then his canoe pulled out ahead of hers, and bumped against the shore. He grabbed onto something, secured his canoe, stepped out. "Be back in a few."

With that, he dropped to his hands and knees and began to shift. It didn't freak her out like it had the first time she'd seen him do this. If anything, his transformation possessed a curious kind of beauty, each detail precise, perfect, sculpted from some arcane mathematical magic known only to nature.

His skin went first, black fur sprouting from the pores until it covered every part of him. Then his arms changed into a dog's legs, his hands became paws, his human legs shortened, his feet turned into paws. His bones cracked and popped and his spine seemed to rise and twist, as though it were actually some sort of serpent whipping from one side to the other. His nose, ears, and head went last, the bones moving, shortening, rearranging themselves so quickly that it looked as if his entire face were coming apart.

When the shift was completed, he moved along the runway, his slight body visible in the starlight, nose to the ground, to the upheavals in asphalt. Kate wished she could believe she had lost her mind. But her life had taken a sharp turn into the impossible that night back in February, when Bean and Marion had put on their spectacle in the bar, and now it was veering into such high strangeness she couldn't imagine where it might all be headed.

When Wayra returned minutes later, he was once again a man. "It's covered with the debris from Annie's Café." He climbed into his canoe and pushed quickly away from the shore. "It's a smart move on Dominica's part. Only a helicopter could land here now. Dominica made Maddie pick up body parts that were mixed in with the debris and Maddie fought her and lost."

"Lost how?" Kate paddled after him. "What do you mean?"

"Her consciousness left her body."

"She *died*?"

"No. She traveled out of body. It may be why she's been able to survive all these months."

When Wayra spoke about these kinds of things—out-of-body travel, shapeshifting, the history of Esperanza—Kate felt like Alice tumbling down the rabbit hole. Yet, she remembered that during the awful times at the end of her relationship with Rocky's father, she had taken up yoga and meditation, and one morning, she had found herself outside her own body, staring at herself as she meditated. She had sat down in front of her body and watched and listened and eventually couldn't stand the division anymore and had dived back into her flesh and bones. But the things Wayra spoke of went well beyond her brief out-of-body excursion.

As their canoes drifted along the shore again, moving toward Amy's home, Kate said, "Have you ever turned anyone else, Wayra?"

"Once. During the plague years. I came upon a heap of bodies waiting to be burned and saw two people in that heap who weren't dead. A mother and her son. I turned them both. It cured them of the plague and for ten years, maybe longer, the three of us made our way across Europe together. But the boy was never right in the head. He committed suicide, his mother blamed me and left. I never saw her again."

"How do you transform someone?"

"Do you always ask so many questions?"

Was he kidding? "Hey. I'm entitled. When we left Cedar Key yesterday, you were a skinny dog. Then I find a man on my living room floor and our hawk likes you. I really need some info here, Wayra." She knew she sounded nearly hysterical, that her voice had risen. But facts always helped her to accommodate what she didn't understand. "I need to know what the hell I've signed on to here."

"You haven't *signed on* to anything. You've just stumbled into a very old story, Kate."

They continued paddling parallel to the runway, speaking softly. "You didn't answer my question, Wayra, about how you transform someone."

"I don't know how. I haven't done it in centuries. I think it has to do with need, intent, and some profound instinct that I can't explain when I'm human, but which probably makes perfect sense to me when I'm not human."

"So are you dog or wolf?"

"Both. The man who transformed me was seventy-five percent wolf. What percentage does that make me? Does it matter?"

"You bet your ass it does. Are you, like, a werewolf? Is that it?"

"You already asked me that, Kate. Werewolves are rare. So are vampires. But shifters are the rarest."

"Where did the original shifter come from?"

"Shit, Kate, is this an interview?"

"I'm sorry. I'm just trying to understand everything."

"I've been led to believe that the first shifter was created in a lab in Lemuria."

"What's Lemuria?"

"A legendary continent like Atlantis that probably existed between 75,000 to 25,000 BC. It was located somewhere in the Pacific. Are we close to the house yet?"

"Just ahead. See those lights on that dock there? Her place is on the far side."

He moved out ahead of her, making it clear he didn't want to answer any more of her questions. She couldn't blame him. Kate paddled faster to keep up with him, her paddles splashing noisily. As she approached the property, she was struck by the size of the house, a sprawling place by any standard, the long, wide roof showered in starlight. Huge windows overlooked the water. No lights shone in the windows. But smoke spiraled out of the chimney, sweetening the air. She hoped Rocky and Amy were locked up inside with her parents, roasting hot dogs over the fire.

Please let it be true.

Their canoes bumped up against the empty dock. Kate tied hers to the ladder and climbed up, Wayra following closely behind her. They moved swiftly, angling through the dark shadows created by numerous trees along the side of the house—live oaks, pines, all of it thick enough to provide them with some cover. Then they approached the rear porch at an angle.

"Wayra," she whispered. "One more question. Have you loved anyone since you were turned?"

"What difference does it make?"

"It makes a difference to me."

"I've loved two women. Dominica, before she joined the *brujos,* and a professor at Berkeley, Sara Wells, whom I also knew in the life after I was transformed. But Dominica killed Sara during the battle for control of Esperanza."

He paused and glanced at her. In the dim starlight, his profile seemed majestic, and he looked as mythic as Maddie had when the dolphins had rescued her, not quite of this world.

"Anything else?" he asked.

"If we run into these *brujos,* how do we protect ourselves?"

"The same way you did at the café."

On the porch, Kate pressed her face to the glass in the French doors, but couldn't see anything. The door was unlocked, and the hinges squeaked as it swung open. She drew her weapon and she and Wayra entered together. The beam of his flashlight struck a tiled breakfast room, then the kitchen. The cocoon of silence felt tight, uncomfortable. The pantry door stood open, the packaged and canned goods in disarray, as if someone had gone through them rapidly, knocking stuff off the shelves.

The icemaker churned, puncturing the silence with staccato bursts like gunshots. They continued through an arched doorway to a family room, where heat from the fireplace kept the room snugly warm. Amy's naked parents lay in front of the couch, their bodies still intertwined. Both had bled out and their blood had pooled beneath them, turning the tile a tomato red. Kate's stomach turned inside out and she wrenched back, nearly gagging on the bile that surged into her throat.

"Rocky?" she shouted. "Rocky?"

She whirled around, clutching the gun, and moved quickly toward Amy's bedroom, terrified that she would find her son's dead body. Battery-operated night-lights along the hallway provided just enough illumination for her to see where she was going. The door to Amy's room was shut. Kate kicked it open, sighted down the gun, and stepped into the room. Empty, Christ, empty. Relief flooded through her, then horror. Had both Rocky and Amy been taken?

Kate checked the other bedrooms, but they all looked as if they hadn't been slept in for days. She opened the door to the garage, slapped the wall until she found a switch, flicked it. A dim light flared, revealing a Lexus and an electric cart. Kate went over to the cart—plugged in, the key in the ignition. It would get them to the animal rescue facility much faster than the canoes.

She hurried back into the family room, where Wayra was crouched next to the bodies. He had shut their eyes, covered them with a throw. "They've been dead a few hours."

"And the *brujos* who did this? Where are *they*?"

"Probably looking for new hosts. Let's get outta here, Kate. The moon is going to rise in a few minutes. It'll make us more visible out there in the marsh."

"There's a cart in the garage, charged up, with a key in the ignition. It'll be faster."

Wayra considered it, then shook his head. "We'd be too exposed. We don't know what sort of chaos is happening on the rest of the island. I think the canoes are actually safer."

Worried sick about Rocky, she yielded to Wayra's opinion, and they left the way they'd come in. Moments after they pushed off into the salt marsh, the moon crept up over the horizon, a bright yellow sliver, and she thought she saw Liberty circling through the light. But it couldn't be her. This bird didn't make a sound and didn't drop down to check them out, as Liberty usually did.

They paddled east, where the salt marsh was thickest, the reeds taller. Just as they neared it, lights suddenly impaled them, bright glaring lights that seared away every dark pocket of safety.

"*Halt right where you are.*" The man's voice boomed through a PA system, then engines roared to life.

Kate glanced back. An airboat bore down on them, its engine so loud she could feel the sound of it in her teeth. Coast Guard? Redneck? She paddled faster, harder, but was moving against the current now, an ant struggling through a pool of honey. Wayra, still ahead of her, slowed and glanced back. She gestured frantically with her paddle, *Go, go,* and his canoe vanished into the marsh.

She paddled wildly, but when she was within eight yards of the marsh, the airboat cut in front of her, its turn kicking up such turbulence that the canoe tipped, spilling her into the shallow water. Kate half swam, half stumbled, the bright light blinding her. She came up alongside her canoe, her weapon gone, her pack gone. Then the airboat swept in behind her and something sharp bit her between the shoulder blades. It stuck there, in her skin, her muscles, they'd shot her, my God, they'd shot her with a tranquilizer dart, as though she were some wild, intractable animal.

Kate reached back, trying to reach the dart, yank it out. Already, she could feel the effects of whatever was in it—time screeched into slow motion, her limbs felt weighted, as if filled with wet concrete, everything listed to the right, the left, and the world blurred. The airboat's engine went silent. The shouts from the men on board sounded drawn out, vowels and consonants rushing together. *Grrraaaaaaabbbbbbbbb heeeeeeerrrrrrr beeeeeeeffffffffooorrrreeee sshheee goooessss uuunnnddddeeerr.*

She pitched forward, the water closed over her head, and then there was nothing.

Wayra shifted as soon as he was out of the canoe and now raced through the marsh, tore across Airport Road, and plunged into a wooded area on Gulf Boulevard. He ran north, putting as much distance as quickly as possible between himself and the airboat. When he could no longer hear its shrieking engine, he slowed to a trot.

He worried about Kate, what had happened to her, but he couldn't go back there and risk being caught himself. Right now, his job was to find Rocky and Maddie. In a little while, he would double back toward the cove and check out the animal rescue center. If the kid wasn't there, he wasn't sure where he would look after that.

Wayra approached the edge of the woods to orient himself. Not a chance. None of the streetlights were on. He suspected it was Dominica's doing to keep people who hadn't been seized yet off balance. What else was she planning? Public beatings? Hangings? Executions? And how would she keep her new tribe in line?

He struggled not to despise her, but it was difficult to feel otherwise. She had killed people he loved, seized Maddie, and hurled his life into perpetual turmoil. For that, she deserved annihilation. Yet, even as he thought this, he knew that such emotions would continue to bind him to her energetically, just as he had been for centuries. He needed to gain a deeper understanding of why he had once loved her and why she had been such a fixture in his life for so many centuries after she had joined the *brujos*. And once he understood, he would have to forgive her. Only then would the tie between them be truly severed.

Wayra walked along the shoulder of the road, senses alert for the sound of cars, voices, the whisper of carts. But the road remained empty of any sign of humanity. Even though many of the dark homes he passed had cars parked out front, he guessed the residents were in hiding—in an attic, someone else's home, a condo—or they had fled weeks ago.

As he cut back into the woods, he suddenly heard a familiar keening and dropped his head back and howled. Moments later, the hawk fluttered down through the trees, landed on a low-lying branch, and dropped a large fish at Wayra's feet. It was wet, still alive, flopping around on the ground. Wayra bit off the head, killing it. Liberty flew down from the branch and landed on the ground. Wayra pushed the fish toward her with his nose and she pecked straight across the fish's midsection, creating what amounted to a dotted line, so that Wayra was able to tear it in half. He nudged the larger half toward her and they both got down to the business of eating.

In the centuries of his existence, particularly in the early years in Europe, he had shared food with other mammals, but never with a bird. It raised all kinds of questions about the hawk. Where had she come from before Rocky had rescued her last year? Why did she stick around the houseboat with him and Kate? Was she hosting a *brujo*? Was it all some clever ploy? But that seemed unlikely. Animals generally didn't provide the stimulation that *brujos* craved, and besides, he didn't sense any ghost inside of her.

When she finished her piece, she preened and made that same soft, trilling noise she'd made last night on the upper deck of the houseboat. Wayra licked his paws and cleaned himself, then stretched out against the cool ground, wondering how to communicate with her. She hopped over to him and touched her beak lightly against his nose, as if to say, *Hey, dude, listen up.* Then she took off, wings flapping, and flew low through the woods so that he could follow her.

When the woods ended, they crossed to another street, another block, and entered yet another thicket of trees, working their way back toward the airport. But on Airport Road, she turned east toward Goose Cove and the animal rescue place. As they turned into the loop around the cove, a pair of carts whispered by, their rear seats loaded with cardboard boxes that held food. He could smell it all, rice and beans, pasta and jars of sauces, even the frozen meats, chicken, turkey, fish, hamburgers, pork. They had potatoes, too, and fruits and vegetables that smelled like they were a bit too ripe.

He understood what Dominica was doing. She'd instructed her little army to raid every house on the island and take whatever food they could find. She knew that hungry hosts might endanger her plans and was preparing for a siege.

Even if Dominica had told her tribe to be on the lookout for a skinny black dog, they didn't pay any attention to him, and they never even saw the hawk.

As soon as the carts were out of sight, the hawk flew lower and touched down on the top of the facility's front gate, the only part of the fence where there was no barbed wire. Wayra considered shifting into his human form so that he could scale the gate. But he was exposed out here and no telling how many more *brujos* would be passing by with their carts loaded up with food and supplies.

He found a soft spot in the ground and started digging. The hawk keened a couple of times and flew off toward a cluster of buildings. The hole was finally deep enough for Wayra to wiggle under the fence and he raced toward the buildings. They formed an open square that faced dozens of cages with small animals inside and a tremendous aviary where birds now squawked and cried and shrieked at his intrusion. He was afraid their ruckus might attract attention from the *brujos,* so he quickly shifted back into his human form, threw open the aviary door, picked up one of the twenty-gallon containers of seed, and carried it inside. He hurled handfuls of seed into the aviary, then tipped the whole thing over and the birds converged, making an awful racket, but nothing as loud as it had been moments ago.

Wayra hurried out of the aviary and left the door open. He moved swiftly along the rows of cages, checking on the other animals. All of them appeared to be hungry—squirrels, opossums, several pathetically thin cats, three rabbits, guinea pigs, four iguanas, two dogs. All had been injured in some way and treated. But they had little or no water and obviously hadn't been fed in several days and were frantic to eat, to escape. Their respective foods were in containers outside the cages, so Wayra opened cans and jars and fed them all and left the doors to the cages open.

He found a hose at the side of the building, turned it on and filled a huge plastic tub in the middle of the courtyard. Once the animals had eaten, they began to venture from their cages in search of water.

Wayra found the hawk in front of a door that faced the cove, pecking furiously at the wood. He tried the handle; the door was locked. Wayra threw his body against it, but the damn thing didn't budge. He loped along the front of the building, paused briefly to pick up a large conch shell, and slammed it against the first window he reached. The glass shattered. The hawk flew through the opening, keening loudly, and Wayra scrambled in after her. She flew up a hallway and then through the door of an office at the very end.

Rocky, huddled in the back of a supply closet, smelled sick. Sweat poured down his pale face, he trembled and shook, his arms were clutched tightly against his body. Cluttering the floor around him were food wrappers, apple cores, orange seeds, part of a sandwich. An empty plastic bottle lay on its side, water puddled around it. The hawk cried out and Rocky's eyes opened slowly, dreamily.

"Lib?" His voice ground out of him, hoarse, gravelly. Then he saw Wayra and immediately snapped upright and scooted back farther into the closet. "Don't touch me, please don't fucking touch me, I won't say anything, I promise, just don't . . . don't go inside me again, you made me sick." He didn't scream. Wayra could tell he barely had the strength to speak, much less to scream. Tears coursed down his pale, hollow cheeks, his arms tightened against his body, his mouth puckered, trembled.

"Hey, it's okay." Wayra spoke softly and crouched in the doorway. "I'm here to help. My name's Wayra. Your mom sent me."

"Why . . . didn't she come herself?"

"It's too dangerous, Rocky." Wayra extended his hand. "Liberty and I will take you back to the houseboat."

"The . . . animals. The birds. I . . . I have to feed them . . . give them water."

"I already did. Grab my hand, I'll help you out of there." When the kid grasped Wayra's hand, an alarm shrieked inside him. Fever raged through him. "Did one of them seize you, Rocky?"

The kid collapsed against Wayra. He helped Rocky to a nearby chair, then hurried to a supply closet and found a blanket tucked on a corner shelf. He draped it around the boy's shoulders, but Rocky's body shuddered, his teeth chattered. Wayra jerked open desk drawers, cabinets, looking for aspirin, something to relieve the kid's fever. He located a bottle of Advil in one of the drawers, tapped two into his palm, and retrieved a bottle of water from the little fridge near the window.

"Swallow these. They'll bring down your fever."

The hawk fluttered and flew, keening and crying, and finally settled on the back of the kid's chair, and ran her beak through his hair, a caress that was gentle, loving. Rocky took the Advil.

"Were you seized?" Wayra asked again. "Is that what happened? Did one of these monstrosities take you?"

Rocky, still sobbing, covered his face with his hands and, for the longest time, didn't say anything. His shoulders finally stopped shaking, his sobs subsided. When he finally spoke, his voice was quiet, and his hands dropped to his thighs. "It . . . it came in the late afternoon. It was inside of Amy . . . and it . . . she . . . I didn't know it at first. She wanted to do it, to . . . to hook up . . . to . . . have sex . . . but she . . . then she started bleeding from everywhere, *everywhere,* from her eyes and ears, mouth and nose and skin . . . and . . . and it leaped into me, just *took* me. I . . . I don't know how long it was . . . was inside me. Hours, it felt like hours. It . . . sifted through my memories, I could . . . feel it doing that, stealing my memories.

"Then it . . . leaped out of me and I . . . not too long afterward, I started throwing up . . . I got hot . . . I . . . I . . . I wanted to fucking die. Amy was . . . there." He stabbed his finger at the corner of the room, where the floor was streaked with blood Wayra hadn't seen when he'd entered. "I . . . I dragged her body into the walk-in freezer." He stabbed his hand toward the metal door off to the right, knuckled his eyes, and in between sobs, stammered, "My mom . . . was right. Zee Small . . . he was right. It's . . . they . . . Satan's . . . demons . . ."

Shit. Advil wasn't going to do it. Rocky had had an allergic reaction to the substance that *brujos* created in their hosts. Wayra suspected it was a form of anaphylactic shock—and the *brujo* probably had found the environment too inhospitable and had decided Rocky wasn't a suitable host. So although the substance had saved him from being permanently taken, it might kill him.

"Okay, Rocky. I need you to focus. I need a boat, a kayak, something to get us to the houseboat. Does the center have any kayaks? Canoes?"

"A . . . canoe. With an electric motor." He drew the blanket more tightly around him and tried to keep his teeth from chattering. "We . . . use it to collect injured seabirds. I think . . . it's just outside the fence. On the beach."

"Okay. I'll be right back. Liberty will stay with you."

"No. I'm going with you. I . . . I don't want to stay here alone. Please . . . don't leave me, Wayra."

"Okay, I'm not leaving you, Rocky. Sit tight for a second." Wayra went over to the freezer, opened it. Amy was in there, all right, blood now frozen on her face, arms, and legs. He gently shut her eyes, turned her on her side, and stepped over her. Kate had told him that, according to Zee Small, the *brujos* hadn't been taking people under the age of sixteen. That had obviously changed. It alarmed him, but even more troubling was what Rocky had said about the *brujo* stealing his memories. That meant Dominica might already know where Kate's houseboat was hidden.

He quickly returned to the fridge and searched for any sort of human medication. Behind the food, he found three bottles of Augmentin, two Z-Packs, a bottle of erythromycin, and Benadryl pills. He wasn't sure if any of it would work, but took it all. He hurried, grabbed another bottle of water from the fridge, then twisted off the cap. He handed Rocky the water, a pill from the Z-Pack, and a Benadryl. "Take those, then we're leaving."

Rocky swallowed the pills, wiped his arm across his eyes. Wayra helped him to his feet. Somehow, they made it outside, where all the animals he'd released were now congregated around the huge plastic tub, sating their collective thirst. No squabbles, no fights. Wayra unlatched the gate to the beach, and helped Rocky out across the sand to the canoe. Once he was inside, he covered Rocky with the blanket, then pushed off from the beach. When he was knee-deep in water, he climbed inside and started the electric engine.

The engine was a bit more powerful than the ones he and Kate had used, but even so, he knew the trip would take at least an hour. "Hold on, kid," he murmured. Rocky stirred, but didn't speak.

The hawk flew just above them, their eyes and ears.

The fog had risen steadily in the ensuing hours and although it crept up close to the canoe, it didn't cover them. Wayra sensed Dominica's attention was still focused elsewhere, that she'd left the fog on its own, and it didn't know what to do when confronted with something as alien to its experience as Wayra.

The hawk steered them clear of an airboat, several cutters, and by the time they reached Sea Horse Key, Rocky's fever had spiked. Wayra got him onto the houseboat, to the living room couch, and covered him with blankets. He scribbled something on a sheet of paper and held it out to the hawk. "Find Kate. Get this to Kate. I know you understand me. I don't know how that's possible, but I know you do. Just get the damn thing to her. I'll take care of Rocky."

The hawk snatched the piece of paper out of Wayra's hand and flew out the open balcony doors. Minutes later, Rocky went into convulsions.

Wayra knew he would die without medical intervention, but there was no medical help out here and probably no one in this country who would know how to treat a *brujo* contagion. There was only his shifter blood, and he had just one choice.

He shifted into his other form, dropped his paws to the kid's chest, and instinct kicked in. He suddenly knew exactly what to do. He licked Rocky's face repeatedly, placed his right front paw on the boy's forehead, and light shot out of it. Then he sank his teeth into Rocky's neck until he drew blood.

Thirteen

Sanchez woke suddenly and bolted upright in his tent. Jessie stood at the opening, whining softly. He crawled out of his sleeping bag and moved over to her.

"Shhh," he whispered.

She moved along behind him as he unzipped the inner flap and peered out. Things looked normal, at least as normal as anything was here. No campfire, but dim, battery-operated lanterns hung from low branches here and there, providing just enough illumination for him to see that the picnic tables were empty, tents were zipped up for the night, trailers were sealed against the chill, the dark, the bogeymen.

He listened closely to the silence and realized what had awakened Jessie. The background hum of the power lines that he'd heard ever since he'd gotten here was conspicuously absent. Had the power on this part of the island gone down? Wasn't the ELF field from the concentration of power lines what kept the *brujos* out of here?

Sanchez made his way back to his sleeping bag and belongings. He put on his socks and shoes, shrugged on his jacket, slung the pack over his shoulder. He pocketed his BlackBerry and the useless cell Delaney had given him, picked up the Glock 34, slipped the extra clip in an inner pocket. He ducked outside the tent, Jessie right behind him.

At night, with just the sentries awake, the camp struck a stark contrast to what it was like during the day, when everyone bustled around, carrying out their specific tasks. The kids were schooled in one of the trailers, the men fished and killed wild game, and the women cooked and sewed and did the camp laundry in large tubs or in the washing machine in the camper where Zee, his son, and daughter-in-law lived. Their way of life seemed retro to Sanchez, the roles far too traditional for his taste. But it worked for Zee and his thirtysome followers, united for the end times.

Sanchez had sent Delaney a detailed e-mail about what he knew and suspected and had speculated about how the *brujos* might be defeated. Delaney hadn't responded. So before he had turned in several hours ago, Sanchez had e-mailed him again, demanding to know what, if anything, the government intended to do about defeating this strange enemy. This e-mail hadn't elicited a response, either.

Now he paused and texted Delaney. *Did u get my 2 e-mails?*

Almost immediately, a response came through.

O'Donnell is pissed u went rogue, filed a complaint with my boss. The CDC running this show. They believe the virus is a contagious, biological weapon. If u left now, u would b quarantined. Keep gathering info. They're talking about sending in hazmat unit. I'll give u ample warning. Use txt message. Safer.

Sanchez's fingers flew over the keypad. *Insanity 2 send hazmat. They'll b seized, bled out.*

He stood there a moment, staring at the BlackBerry, waiting for a response. Nothing came through. He quickly texted his sister: *Hiding out with a group that hasn't been seized. Am ok.*

Seized: She wouldn't have any idea what he was talking about. Sanchez navigated to Wikipedia and sent Nicole a link about *brujos,* djinn, and other legendary life-forms. Brujos *are hungry ghosts and they're all over CK. More soon. Luv u*

After a few minutes, Sanchez hurried on through the camp, anxiety eating away at him. Why hadn't Delaney replied? Was O'Donnell with him? Was that it? His sister would find the text message as soon as she woke up tomorrow morning.

He passed the now cold campfire, half-burned logs within a ring of stacked stones. It reminded him of the only time he, Nicole, and his parents had gone camping when he was a kid. It was somewhere in the Ocala National Forest, outside any of the designated camping areas. He and his old man had gathered stones like these, and his mother and Nicole had collected wood. The four of them had sat around the campfire that night roasting hot dogs and marshmallows, and it was one of the few times he could remember his parents laughing together. That night, he and Nicole had lain awake in their tent, whispering back and forth, excited at this unexpected turn in their parents' relationship. It hadn't lasted, but for those few glorious hours, he had learned the meaning of hope.

It was what he'd felt when he'd held Maddie out there in the salt marsh, and when she had been out of her body and had kissed him. Hope kept him here, not the agendas of the feds, of Delaney, of anyone or anything else. Just hope.

Beyond the circle of stones, he encountered the first of the sentries, a giant of a man with more tattoos than Sanchez had ever seen outside of fiction. He nodded at Sanchez. "Can't sleep?"

"Something woke me. When did the power go off?"

"About twenty minutes ago. Not to worry, brother. I alerted Zee and we've got additional security."

"So Zee is awake?"

"Man hardly ever sleeps." The guard gestured toward his camper, where a soft light was visible in one of the windows. "He's in there reading the Bible. Me, I'm not much of a reader, but I can tell you that I don't believe the meek will inherit the earth. The meek just get fucked over and here on Cedar Key they get taken by Satan's army."

"I agree. But if they get into the camp, what're you supposed to do?"

"Shoot to kill."

"Is that in the Bible?"

Tattoo Man grinned. "Don't know about the real Bible, brother. But it's in *my* Bible."

Sanchez moved past him and knocked at the door of Zee's camper. "Zee, it's Nick."

"Door's unlocked. C'mon in."

Sanchez opened the door and he and Jessie entered the camper. The dog went straight for the bowl of water and cat food set out for a cat or cats Sanchez had never seen. Zee was sitting at the kitchen table, not reading any Bible that Sanchez could see, but hunched over his MacBook, the only source of light in the camper. His thinning gray hair, loose from its pony-tail, stuck out wildly from every part of his head, as if he'd just crawled out of bed. A bottle of moonshine and a glass were in the middle of the table. "Power's out at this end of the island, Zee."

"Power's out all over the island. I'm on it. And before the sun rises, we're moving, Nick. I figure Satan's army cut the power 'cause they know it protects us. Just trying to figure out where it might be safest." Zee stabbed his thumb at Sanchez's pack. "You headed somewhere?"

"Yeah, out of here with everyone else. I think the cemetery is the place to go. These ghosts hate cemeteries."

Zee raised his eyes from his MacBook. "How do you know that?"

From Maddie. "I just do."

"Just like you knew about my wife." In the glow from the laptop, his face looked worn and leathery. The creases in his throat and forehead, at the corners of his eyes, seemed to be filled with this unnatural light. "You know God's speaking to you, right, son?"

"It doesn't matter who's speaking to me if the information is correct. I think we should move immediately. Are your son and daughter-in-law here?"

"Shit, no. They left this afternoon, told me I'm a fruitcake and they don't want nothing to do with me or the camp."

"I'm sorry, Zee."

He waved Sanchez's sympathy aside. "I told them their best bet is to get the hell off Cedar Key."

"Yeah? How?"

"Beats me. Coast Guard's got the island covered, road's blocked at the fourth bridge, no planes coming in or leaving."

"So what's your plan for defeating these mutants?"

Zee tapped the edge of his MacBook. "I've been mulling that over. I was going to run this past you when I was finished. Fire seems to be our best weapon against them. But if we have to burn the island to get rid of them, that's not winning."

"Suppose we got most of them in a particular area of town and then set just that area on fire?"

Zee splashed moonshine into his glass, sipped at it, sat back. "How would that work, exactly?"

Sanchez hadn't told him that he communicated with Maddie from time to time. "You know the redhead who works at the hotel? Maddie?"

"Sure. She's got one of Satan's stewards inside her."

"She's got the tribal leader inside her. From time to time, Maddie and I . . . communicate."

Zee frowned and sat forward, his dark, intense eyes fixed on Sanchez in a way that made him squirm inside. "Using this . . ."—he rolled his hand through the air—"seer ability you have?"

"Telepathy, mind to mind."

Zee's mouth twitched into a sly smile. "Can you and I talk that way? Sure would be easier, Nick."

"I doubt it. The evil within her seems to facilitate this communication in some way. I can hear her as clearly as I hear you now. The problem is that she doesn't have any control over this evil. Dominica, the evil inside of her, controls *her*. But we might be able to find a way around her."

The old man pushed the bottle of moonshine toward him and gestured toward the galley cabinet. "Grab a glass and sample some Zee Small moonshine, son. Loosen up this tongue of yours. Let's hear all about this telepathy shit."

As Sanchez pushed to his feet, gunfire exploded through the darkness, earsplitting staccato bursts that tore across the outside of the camper and shattered the window behind the table. Zee and Sanchez dived for the floor, then Sanchez rolled and crawled over to the window and positioned himself on one side of it. Zee snapped open a door under the galley sink, brought out what looked like a submachine gun, and stood on the other side of the shattered window. He slapped the lid of the MacBook, shutting it and killing their only source of light. Sanchez gripped the Glock so hard his fingers hurt, and dared to glance through the window.

Four pairs of blindingly bright headlights screamed, *We're here, bet you can't shoot us.*

"Let's show 'em what's what, Nicko," whispered Zee.

They opened fire simultaneously on the headlights.

The lights exploded, another window in the camper blew apart, and then Zee was on his cell, barking instructions to whoever was on the other end. "We're outta here, Nick," and he and Sanchez ran to the front of the camper, the dog at their heels.

Within seconds, the camper lurched forward like a dinosaur with indigestion. It belched and coughed and sputtered as it slammed over rocks, roots, low brush. It didn't move quickly enough. In the side mirror, Sanchez saw a truck closing in on them, its headlights gone, an inside light winking off and on like a firefly. He grabbed Zee's submachine gun and let it rip. The truck's windshield blew apart, the hood popped up, and the sucker veered out of control, tearing across the ground until it crashed into a tree.

"Good work!" Zee yelled.

A second truck raced forward, its passage covered by a constant barrage of bullets. One of the camper's rear tires blew—Sanchez felt it—and Zee struggled with the steering wheel to keep them moving. Sanchez leaped up and ran back through the camper to one of the shattered windows. For an instant, he had a clear view of the truck's driver, bent over the steering wheel, driving like a lunatic while his companion stood in the bed of the truck, firing over the roof. Sanchez took out the front and rear tires and riddled the side of the truck with so many holes it gave new meaning to the term "air-conditioning." One of his shots hit the gas tank and the truck exploded, chunks of flaming debris bursting out in every direction.

A heartbeat later, the camper swung out onto the road, rear end fishtailing, then tore into a curve, the flat tire probably shredding by now, and headed for Gulf Boulevard. Sanchez hung out the window for a better look. Trailers and vehicles from the camp popped out of the trees, one after another, like beings from some other dimension.

He pulled himself back inside, sank against the floor. His hands shook, an acrid stink clung to the air, and the wind whistled through the broken window. He pressed his fists against his eyes. *I just killed at least two men, maybe more. I'm no better than these* brujo *bastards.*

Jessie nudged him with her cold nose, whining softly, and Sanchez dropped one arm over her back and the other to his thigh. She sank to her belly, her head resting on Sanchez's knee. The weapon lay beside him in broken glass. "I think we're okay for now, girl." *Until the next attack, the next crisis.*

He squeezed his eyes shut, forcing himself to breathe slowly, deeply, until his hands stopped shaking and he felt calmer. When he opened his eyes again, his mother was sitting on the floor beside Jessie, her legs folded lotus style. The dog stared at her, but didn't make a sound. Jenean didn't look quite as solid as she had previously.

"You did what you had to do, Nick."

"I shouldn't have put myself in this situation to begin with."

"You'll be safe in the cemetery for a while. But Dominica is learning to overcome her fear of certain things, so that safety net may not last. You should have a backup plan."

"Like what? Just tell me how to get to Maddie without that ... that *thing* inside her killing her first."

His mother's ghost looked stricken and he had the sudden feeling that she knew only so much about these *brujos*. Her belief that she had to compensate for her lack of maternal support when she was alive had drawn her into a battle that wasn't hers. He reached for her hand, to give it a quick squeeze, but his own hand went through hers.

"Mom, you don't owe me anything. Really."

"Fire," she said. "That's how you have to fight them. Fire, like you and Zee talked about."

With that, she faded away and the camper stopped. "Nick," the old man hollered. "Get that cemetery gate open."

He told Jessie to stay, picked up the monster submachine gun, and opened the camper door. Fog twisted across the pavement, narrow bands of it that his movement quickly dispersed. But as he dashed to the gate, thicker ribbons of the stuff darted toward him like hungry snakes—from the right, the left. One piece wrapped around his ankle and a bitter cold penetrated his jeans, cut through his flesh, pierced his bones. Sanchez tore at it with his hands, then kicked the other piece away. He slammed the butt of the weapon against the rusted gate lock a couple of times until it popped loose. Sanchez pushed the gate open and motioned Zee and the others inside.

The fog didn't follow him through the gate. It remained just outside, smaller pieces merging to form longer, thicker tendrils. Low, thin veils of fog crept out of the trees on the far side of the road, swaying at first, then whipping across the pavement toward its counterparts. It was as if the separate pieces were controlled by the same brain, one piece calling to the other: *Join us, make us bigger and stronger, join us.* That was creepy enough. But then he heard what sounded like sand blown against trees, like fingernails drawn down a blackboard, and realized it was an insidious whispering: *Find the body, fuel the body, fill the body, be the body . . .*

And he suddenly knew it was these *brujos* in their natural form, trying to overcome their fear of the cemetery and seize him and everyone else in Zee's camp. It triggered an elemental terror in Sanchez. He aimed the monster weapon at the largest bank of fog and fired into it. The fog broke into a thousand pieces. Some pieces hastily retreated to the other side of the road, into the trees. Other pieces hesitated, coiling as if to strike. Sanchez fired into those and they burst apart like exploding stars.

The last vehicle in Zee's caravan sped into the cemetery and Sanchez quickly shut the gates and secured them with large rocks so they wouldn't swing open. A larger bank of fog now moved like a hula dancer just outside the cemetery. "You come anywhere near this cemetery again," he shouted, "and I'll unleash the artillery on you, and it'll be fire."

He backed away from the gate, spooked by how fast the fog swelled and thickened, and how loud the lascivious litany became. It scraped against his senses until he slapped his hands over his ears, then spun around and loped toward the circle of trailers and trucks.

It suddenly occurred to him that the cemetery might be a trap, the perfect prison for Zee and his followers until the *brujos* overcame their fear of this place.

Maddie's exhaustion clawed through her. Every time she didn't think she could lift another cardboard box out of a cart or the back of a truck and carry it inside the Island Market, Dominica tweaked her adrenal glands. Then for another ten or fifteen minutes, she zipped along, lifting, carrying, moving among the other hosts who entered and left the market.

The hosts were worse off than slaves, she thought. They were captives who no longer controlled their own bodies or actions, and some of them, she knew, were no longer around at all. She didn't sense the mayor's essence and suspected her grandfather was right, that the mayor was dying or had died at Annie's Café, and pretty soon the mayor's body wouldn't be able to sustain life. Whit would be forced to seize another host.

Of the core group of Dominica's *brujos*, Maddie felt she might be able to reach out to Richard, Kate's ex-boyfriend, and Bean, who owned the hotel. Both of them seemed to have held on to a fragment of their humanity. Their *brujos*—Gogh and Joe—didn't control them consistently. It was why Richard had been able to warn Kate *not to make waves,* and why Bean hadn't fired Kate in February, after his fuck fest in the hotel bar. She'd uncovered these two facts in Dominica's recent memories, and they defied what Dominica wanted Maddie and the other hosts to believe, that the *brujos* were like gods, all-knowing. The truth was that *brujos* could be duped, distracted, tricked, and a host's memories could be hidden from them. Maddie was proof of that.

The market hummed with activity. Dozens of hosts stocked shelves, dozens more outside unloaded food and supplies, and cars and trucks arrived every few minutes with food and supplies pillaged from homes. She decided to seize her chance.

Bean. Mind to mind.

Maddie carried her cardboard box into the third aisle, where canned goods were shelved, and crouched next to Bean, who was moving merchandise around so he could fit the contents of his box onto the shelves. While Dominica spoke aloud to Joe, the *brujo* within Bean, Maddie pushed her mind toward Bean's essence and brushed up against it like a gentle, cool breeze.

Bean, can you hear me? It's Maddie. Don't freak out, don't act surprised.

He didn't react at all. His hands kept moving and Joe kept using Bean's voice to converse with Dominica. Maddie tried again, pushing up against Bean's mind more forcefully. *Bean? You there?*

Holy shit, Maddie. I can hear you. Can they hear us?

Not while they're distracted with each other and everything that's going on. If any of us are going to live, we need to start fighting back.

Hey, I've seen what they do, these bleed-outs. No, thanks. And we both saw what they did to poor Von. Shit, they burned him alive.

He was already dead, Bean, and he didn't burn. He moved on in the afterlife. I saw him while you all were standing around the fire pit. He was with a guide. That's why you didn't hear him wailing. Dominica tried to make an example out of him, but it didn't work. He was a good man. There are forces at work here that are more powerful than she is.

Yeah? Where? All I see is death and destruction and chaos.

Fear is how they control us and fear is how Dominica controls them, so the first thing you have to do is stop being afraid.

You can't fight them. I've tried. Every time I fight this fucker, he inflicts so much pain on me I wish . . . I was dead.

One by one, we have to escape. The next time Joe puts you into a deep sleep, hold on to your anger and try to stay conscious so that when he leaves your body, you can bring yourself to full consciousness. Then run like hell and hide in one of the empty houses. Or race up State Road 24 and get out of the quarantine area if you can. Or better yet, start burning the town. That'll chase them out faster than anything.

Have you tried to contact anyone else?

I'm going to try Rich. Like you, he still holds on to some of his humanity.

If there's anything left of the man I know, he'll be on board. I think it would be more effective if we could all escape at the same time and burn these freaks out of here.

The only way to coordinate something like that is if we acted up simultaneously and forced them to put us into a deep sleep. But they each have separate places where they put us and I don't know if we can communicate like this when they aren't inside us. Let me work on it, Bean.

A commotion outside grabbed Dominica's attention and Maddie instantly pulled back from Bean, optimistic for the first time that there might be a way out for all of them. "Nica," shouted Liam, lumbering into the market, waving a camera. "There've been three more bleed-outs, two at a house over on the runway, and a body at that animal rescue place. But no one has come forward yet."

Liam, still hosted by Sam Dorset, the editor of the newspaper. Liam, who tried to force Sam to rape Kate the other night in the hotel restaurant. The revulsion Maddie felt for this *brujo* was up there with the revulsion she felt toward Whit.

"Who were the hosts?" Dominica asked when Liam reached her.

Other *brujos* gathered around to see the digital photos on the camera. "According to Sam, the ones in the runway house are the parents of a girl named Amy, Rocky Davis's girlfriend."

"Kate's son?" Dominica exclaimed.

"Yes."

"Excellent."

Liam clicked through the photos. In the first, the man and woman on the floor near a fireplace were covered with a quilt. Even so, it was obvious they had bled out; their bloody faces were fully visible. In the second, the quilt was gone, exposing their intertwined bodies, bloody and naked. The *brujos* murmured with excitement. They loved the carnage.

"Who covered them?" Dominica asked.

"Not me," Liam said. "I found them like that. I was checking the place for food and supplies."

"Was anyone else in the house? Human or *brujo*?"

"Nope."

"Let me see photos of the third body, of Amy."

"She was found in the freezer at the rescue facility."

He clicked to several photos of the girl. The *brujos* really enjoyed this one, crooning over the photo, oohing and aahing their approval. Amy lay on her side, which struck Maddie as oddly as her parents being covered by a quilt. Dominica seemed to find this strange as well, perhaps one of the few times she and Maddie had agreed on anything.

"These people weren't known hosts to anyone, were they, Whit?" Dominica asked.

He stepped forward clutching a sweating Coke bottle, his face so pale he looked as if he'd been locked inside a cellar for months. "I have no member of the tribe on record for these hosts. In all fairness, Nica, yesterday morning you instructed our members to raise the number of hosts to four hundred. I suspect that's why they were seized."

"I also said the rule still stands for not seizing anyone under the age of sixteen. So as of this moment, I'm asking anyone who knows about these blatant violations to come forward. The offenders will then be brought before the council."

Silence gripped the crowd. Liam pocketed the camera and suddenly leaned in toward Dominica and actually poked her in the chest; Maddie felt it, his fingernail pressing against her sternum. "*You* have misled this tribe, Dominica. You've been promising us a true ghost key, a place for our kind, but I don't think you can deliver. I think it's just all empty promises."

"I second that," shouted a woman on the other side of the market, someone Maddie didn't recognize. "Let's see a show of hands for everyone who thinks Dominica is misleading us."

Of the hundred or more people in the store, a definite majority of hands shot upward. *You're cooked, Dominica,* Maddie said and laughed.

Shut up, just shut the hell up.

You're cooked, Maddie shouted again and again. *Cooked, cooked, cooked.*

Dominica erected a barrier between them, so she couldn't hear Maddie's voice. It was exactly what she'd hoped the bitch would do. She immediately reached out to Kate's ex-boyfriend. *Rich, can you hear me? It's Maddie.*

He didn't seem to hear her. His *brujo*, Gogh, was too busy trying to calm the crowd. "Hey, hold on, people. Just hold on. Dominica has been honest with us from day one. From the beginning she told us this wouldn't be easy or simple, but that it was possible."

"That's bullshit," Liam shouted. "What she said was that if we followed her rules, she would show us how to use the power of the dead to control the living. From where I'm standing, people, it looks like the living are controlling the dead. The island has been *quarantined*. Did you see the pamphlets that were airdropped in town today?" He waved one. "Well, take a look. Everything south of fourth bridge is under a quarantine. The Coast Guard is patrolling the island so no one can escape. They think Cedar Key has been attacked by a biological weapon."

"Shut up, Liam," Dominica barked.

But Liam kept right on going, his voice progressively louder, uglier, stoking the frustration shared by many in Dominica's new tribe. "How the hell does a quarantine help us turn Cedar Key into a *brujo* paradise? Look at us, just look at us." He threw his arms out dramatically, a gesture that encompassed the madness in the market to shelve and store all the food and supplies that had been taken from homes all over the island. "Why're we doing this? Because Dominica told us to. What's the purpose? Dominica said it's to prevent our hosts from starving if the quarantine continues indefinitely. But what's next? Rationing of food and supplies? Is that the next step, Dominica? Rationing, with you or the council deciding who gets what?"

Keep shouting, Liam, Maddie thought, and suddenly, in spite of everything, she admired him, the only *brujo* to stand up to Dominica.

Whit strode into the middle of the crowd. As the island mayor, hosts knew him, recognized him; as Dominica's lover and her second in command, *brujos* knew him. But everyone, Maddie thought, also knew that Whit would need a new host soon. You could see it in his face, in the way he held himself, in his pallor. The *brujo* net trembled and shook with the realization that the essence of the mayor was gone, and that his body might not survive till dawn. He already looked like the walking dead.

"People, c'mon," Whit said in a soft, gravelly voice, patting the air with his thin, pale hands. "Give Dominica the benefit of the doubt here. Look what she has done for us this far. Until she arrived, we were a pathetic group of astrals, clinging to the physical plane because we didn't know shit from shinola. Now look at us, more than a thousand strong. Many of us are enjoying physical existence again through our hosts. We have purpose and direction. Dominica showed us how to do this. With a community as large as ours, there have to be rules, parameters."

"And that's why Von was obliterated? To enforce some goddamn rule that Dominica laid down?" Liam shouted.

"Von was annihilated because he saved his host and killed two of our own." Whit now shouted, too, but his voice sounded pathetically weak and Maddie knew the other *brujos* heard it, that weakness, that ebbing of his life force.

"Von was used as an example for the rest of us," Liam snapped, facing Whit, his host's face cherry red. "And how's she protecting *us*, Whit? We suffered several more annihilations tonight by that rogue group on the other side of the island. Have any of us heard her even mention *that*?"

More shouting erupted in the crowd. Insurrection in Dominica's tribe, Maddie thought, could only be a positive turn of events for her. But would it really come to that?

Whit raised his arms like an umpire calling for a time-out. "Pipe down." He sounded angry now. "Give her a chance to address this."

"I was about to mention it when you so rudely interrupted me, Liam," Dominica said.

"Then what about it?" demanded Jill. "How're we going to retaliate against Zee Small's group of Bible thumpers?"

"Right now, we've got them exactly where we want them," Dominica said. "They'll be easy to seize or herd in that cemetery. We need to get our supplies squared away first."

Liam turned to the crowd. "Is that good enough, people? Hell, no."

"Hell, no, hell, no," the crowd chanted.

"Chief Cole," Whit hollered, glancing around. "Take Liam into custody until he's cooled off."

Frank Cole, the police chief, marched forward, hoisting his cop belt like the self-important prick he was. Maddie couldn't remember the name of the *brujo* he hosted, but it didn't matter. Cole looked annoyed, angry, and clearly wasn't on Dominica's side. "I'm fed up with this whole stinking arrangement. For starters, someone outside the council needs to run the market, Dominica. I'll appoint two people to do it."

"You aren't the leader of this tribe." Dominica stabbed her finger at him. *"I am."*

"And you, Dominica, can be overthrown," Liam yelled.

Dominica's rage was so palpable that Maddie *tasted* it—an awful sourness along the surface of her tongue, a thickness in the back of her throat, a coating like plaque against the back of her teeth. Then her temples pulsed and ached, her nostrils flared, and Dominica leaped out of Maddie and into Sam, driving Liam out of his host and leaving Maddie stumbling around, floundering, her legs and arms like putty.

The last shred of civility in the crowd ruptured. Everyone shouted now and no one paid any attention to Maddie. She slipped down an aisle, her heart beating only for her again, her lungs breathing only for her. And with each beat, each breath of air, she reclaimed control of her limbs, her body.

She navigated her way through the crowd, up an aisle filled with bottled water, wine, beer, closer and closer to the door. She could smell the clean, chilly air from here. Beyond that door lay her freedom, Sanchez, Wayra, and a way back to Esperanza. Beyond that door lay her life, waiting for her.

As she approached the register, she forced herself not to move abruptly, erratically. She couldn't appear to be in a big fat hurry to escape this madness. She tucked her hair behind her ears and moved without looking around, moved through the chaos of *brujo* against *brujo*, through the screaming and shoving. Not much father. Three yards, she was just three yards from the door. Someone jostled her from the left, but she kept walking, eyes fixed on the floor.

Two yards.

The shouts and pandemonium reached a new level of madness.

Then she pushed open the front door and that first breath of freedom intoxicated her, left her almost giddy with glee. She flung herself across the street, faster and faster, arms tucked in tightly at her sides, legs eating up the pavement, her heart singing.

She charged up a shallow hill, certain she was going to make it, that she would find deep pockets of darkness where she could hide, that she would find Sanchez and Wayra, that they would defeat Dominica somehow. Winning was no longer the point. Maybe it never had been the point. After all, what did it mean to win against Dominica? Wouldn't there always be another Dominica somewhere to take her place? Another ancient *brujo,* another corrupt politician, another phony avatar who only enslaved the people? Wouldn't evil always be present, staking out its territory among the vulnerable and fearful?

Her only goal was to remain free, to survive. She ran faster, gulping at the air, drawing it deeply into lungs that breathed *only for her;* she must never forget how this felt. *Her* lungs, *her* heart, *her* organs, *her* body, *her* soul.

Just then, a truck barreled around a corner, four *brujos* inside, two holdout captives tied up in the back, a man and a woman who were gagged and blindfolded, dozens of luminous orbs floating in the air around them. The headlights exposed Maddie like a tumor on an X-ray.

The truck's brakes screeched, and Maddie dived to the right and struck the ground so hard that her breath rushed out of her. Stunned, she struggled to push up, but her arms felt weak, insubstantial. She tried to roll over, but her body wasn't listening. It was as if all the months of imprisonment within her own body had short-circuited her brain so that it no longer listened to *her,* to what *she* wanted. It was as if her brain waited for an order from Dominica.

Get up, run fast, flee . . .

Her body twitched and jerked, as though it couldn't understand her command. She raised her head, but it immediately plopped to the ground again. She started drooling, tears ran from her eyes, she tried to scream. Nothing worked. Maddie's fingers dug into the grass, down into the dirt, and she pushed upward with every bit of strength that remained in her body and managed to roll onto her back.

Her body shuddered and shook and she fell back against the ground, teeth chattering. Her arms jerked upward and wrapped around her body like wings. She suddenly went still, squeezed her eyes shut and thought, *Please. Listen to me. You're my brain, my body, my nervous system. I am now going to get up and run like hell. I'm in control of this body. Me, Maddie Livingston.*

Then even her mind went still. Something shifted inside her skull, muscles twitched, jerked, tightened. She sensed her nerves realigning themselves. And then, suddenly, she could move.

Fourteen

Insurrection looked to be imminent. Dominica stood there in Sam Dorset's body, Liam darting around her, raging, shrieking, a hundred or more *brujos* shouting at her, at each other, some of them already fighting. And for some reason, the words of Walt Whitman, which she'd read only today on her favorite blog, Gypsy Woman World, came to her: "Whatever satisfies the soul is truth." She knew her own truth. And it told her to stay with Sam a few moments longer, that he was her mouthpiece for information and news, the voice of journalism, and when he was host to someone other than Liam, he did this job well.

Whit hurried over to her, took her hand, Sam's hand, his host's face so pale that he looked as though he were already a ghost. "I'll take him, Nica," Whit whispered. "I can't survive much longer in the mayor's body. His essence is dead."

It wasn't supposed to be like this. In the old days, in the ancient days, a *brujo* could seize a host and keep that body even if its essence died. "Do it," she said. "Seize him and I'll chase down Maddie."

"You'll have to put the mayor's body on ice somewhere so we don't have another rotting corpse on our hands. In fact, we're going to have to bring in the dead and put all of them on ice."

"No problem. Just do it, Whit. Then control this crowd."

As Whit leaped out of the mayor's body and into Sam, the mayor's body simply crumpled to the floor. For moments, Sam's body accommodated both Dominica and Whit, and nothing worked right. His arms moved in different directions, and his legs refused to move at all. Then Dominica shot toward the ceiling of the market and out through the door, seeking Maddie, that little escapee bitch.

The first thing she saw was a truck idling at the bottom of the shallow hill in front of her, with a young couple tied up in the back of it, surrounded by hungry ghosts. The driver leaped out and ran toward a patch of grass where Maddie, dazed and confused, struggled to stand. Dominica dived into Maddie's skull with the ease of a scalpel through flesh.

"Shame, shame," Dominica cooed. "Honestly, Maddie. Give it up. You'll never escape."

Silence.

"Suit yourself."

Dominica quickly checked to make sure Maddie wasn't injured, then hauled her to her feet, slapped away the dust and bits of grass on her jeans, and turned to face the driver of the truck, Luz, still hosting one of the women from the Coast Guard. "What have we got here?" she asked.

"Are you all right, Dominica?" Luz asked anxiously.

"I'm fine, Luz. Two hostages? How magnificent. From where?"

"From Zee Small's camp."

Perfect. This fine young *bruja* had delivered Dominica from the rage within her tribe. She could use these hostages to prevent an insurrection. "Take them to the hotel. The tribe is going to vote on their fate."

"Fantastic," Luz gushed, obviously relieved that she hadn't injured Dominica's host and thrilled at the prospect that her hostages would bring her fifteen minutes of fame.

By then, Whit had led the crowd outside to see what was going on. "We have hostages," Dominica announced. "They're being taken to the hotel courtyard and everyone will vote on what we should do with them." Then, in a softer voice, she asked, "Where's Liam?"

"I don't know. I lost track of him in the chaos."

"If he's seen again, he's to be annihilated." She made sure these words were transmitted through the *brujo* net, and within moments, the net shuddered in response. "Liam has gone rogue."

"We have an opportunity here," Whit said, touching her arm. "Let's take advantage of it." With that, Whit, firmly ensconced in Sam Dorset's body, punched the air with his raised fist and screamed, *"Hang them!"*

"Hang them, hang them, hang them," the crowd chanted.

As the truck moved slowly forward, the crowd trotted along behind it, and their chant grew louder, more frenzied, rising and falling in the dark, chilly air. When the power within the collective madness of a crowd was harnessed, it could topple regimes, governments, countries. But the power within *this* crowd had surpassed her ability to harness or direct it. This power swept out through the darkness, a sentient, enraged being, an agent of profound change. It stoked passions too long buried, cut away at the oppressions and inhibitions her tribe had suffered when they were alive. Most importantly, these passions had turned away from *her* and focused on an enemy. The hostages. Whit's instincts were brilliant.

Whit drew up alongside her, his grin wild, exuberant. "I figured I'd give them something else to shout about."

"Good work. How is Sam's body?"

"Excellent. Liam didn't damage it. He actually took good care of it when he wasn't shitfaced. Excellent food, exercise, positive thoughts . . . Well, maybe not so many of those." He threw his head back and laughed, a full, exuberant sound that caused Dominica to smile. "Jesus, I love being physical in such a fine body."

He grasped her hand and their eyes locked. It thrilled her to see such desire in Whit's eyes, such blatant lust. "Soon," she whispered, and kissed the back of his hand.

He slung his arm around her waist, drew her to him, and they stopped there in the middle of the road, the chanting sweeping over them, past them, fueling their passion for each other. His hands slipped over her throat and breasts, her hips and ass, down her thighs. Dominica felt Maddie rising to fight her, gathering strength. Dominica tightened her control over Maddie, grasped the back of Whit's head and drew his mouth to hers. Warmth, the slippery dance of his tongue against hers, their hearts filled to bursting: She loved the one she was with.

Maddie didn't fight her. Dominica sensed the young woman was beginning to choose her battles carefully. And this one didn't seem to be worth the effort.

Whit broke the embrace first and he and Dominica skipped up the street together like little kids chasing fireflies. A pure moment, she thought. Now it would be deeply embedded in her memory—the slant of his head as he laughed, the pressure of his hand against hers, and the powerful chanting filling the very air she breathed. *Hang them, hang them;* a chant that had originated with Whit. She had chosen well.

They hurried to catch up to the edge of the crowd that pursued the truck.

He grasped her hand more firmly. "Do you think they'll vote to hang the hostages?"

"I hope so. But we'll see. We have to abide by their vote, Whit."

"I know. It'd be smart to keep them as backup hosts, Nica. But hangings will diffuse a potential insurrection."

Tonight she had learned how important it was for the tribe to feel they were part of a democracy, that they weren't existing under a dictatorship. But she also wondered to what degree her ghosts were influenced by the thoughts, needs, and emotions of their hosts. The locals on Cedar Key tended to be self-sufficient people, who knew nothing of *brujos;* the people of Esperanza had been cowed by years of *brujo* assaults and it had made them easier to seize, keep, maintain. Yet, the locals were also laid-back, live-and-let-live, lulled by the constancy of the gulf, by the size and isolation of the island, all of which made them easier to seize and hold on to. A contradiction.

Whit's shoulders twitched once as he adjusted his control over Sam, then he dropped her hand and moved out ahead of her, chanting with the crowd, his raised fist beating the air. Dominica felt proud that she loved the one she was with.

The truck pulled right through the open courtyard gate and more than a hundred of her tribe poured in behind it. A couple of hundred ghosts in their natural forms also drifted into the courtyard, the newer ghosts as luminous orbs, the older ghosts as bits of discolored smoke. These older ghosts were not the quality of the ancient ones in Esperanza, but they held promise, she thought.

The *brujo* net trembled with anticipation; her tribe wanted theater. Okay, she would give them theater. She forced Maddie through the crowd, to the porch of the old barracks where she felt at home, and climbed onto the railing. More hosts poured into the courtyard from the hotel's side door and just enough light spilled through the windows to create an eerie shadow quality to all who moved there.

Dominica held up her arms, silencing the crowd. "All right. Let's find out who these hostages are. Whit and Gogh, please remove their gags and blindfolds." It was likely that the men who hosted Whit and Gogh already knew who these hostages were; there weren't many people on the island whom their hosts *didn't* know. And if the hosts knew, then the *brujos* knew. But they played along for the sake of theater, drama, lights, action.

The two men climbed into the truck and tore away the gags and blind-folds from the hostages. The young man looked terrified, while tears rolled down the woman's cheeks. "What . . . what the hell is going on?" the man shouted. "All of you here know me. What're you doing?"

"What's your name?" Dominica demanded.

"Ask anyone here. They'll tell you who I am."

"He's Fritz Small, Zee's son," Joe said. "And the woman is Diane, his wife."

"Bean," sobbed Diane. "How can you be a part of this . . . this insane *mob*?"

"Bean's asleep," said Joe. "I'm in charge. Name's Joe. And Jill"—he pointed at Marion the librarian—"is my wife."

"*Was* your wife, till you knocked me off, you asshole." Jill exploded with laughter.

Fritz blubbered, "Jesus God. It's true, it's all true. My old man was right."

"What was that?" Dominica said, mocking him by holding her hand to her ear. "Your old man was right? About what, Fritz? *Us*? About what's happening on the island? So tell me, what kind of defense does your father have against us?"

The woman sobbed harder, tears coursed down her cheeks, snot ran from her nose. "We . . . haven't done anything to any of you. Please . . . let us go."

Dominica felt bad for the woman, for Diane. She looked nice enough. She could easily imagine the two of them having coffee down on Dock Street, gossiping as only women could about the island, the friends they had in common. Dominica couldn't recall the last time she'd had a close female friend. But the problem with most women was their fickleness, the way they twisted truth to fit some female goddess archetype that had nothing to do with the world she inhabited. Unlike Wayra, she didn't give a shit about Jung, synchronicity, archetypes, or the collective unconscious. Dominica was interested only in results.

"It's not up to me," Dominica replied. "We're putting it to a vote." She gazed out over her tribe. "How many would like to keep the hostages as backup hosts?"

Barely a third of the crowd raised their hands.

"A show of hands for all in favor of hanging," she shouted.

Hands shot up all over the courtyard and the chanting began again. *Hang them, hang them.* The chants of the crowd infused the air with a passion she hadn't seen since the final battle in Esperanza. Her new tribe demanded blood and blood they would get.

Dominica leaped down from the barracks railing and hurried over to Whit, Gogh, and Jill. "Jill, get us some rope from the supply room," she said quietly. "Whit and Gogh, bring the truck around under the lamppost. We'll hang them together."

Whit's eyes, as dark and slick as wet leaves, glinted with pleasure. "I think that big oak would do nicely, Nica."

The oak dominated the right side of the courtyard, its huge, graceful branches curving out into the center, leaves rustling in the chilly breeze. "Perfect." She turned and raised her arms, conjuring fog.

It crept in beneath the courtyard gate, rolled in over the fence, and wrapped around the trunk of the giant oak, eager, hungry. *Brujos* in their natural form immediately entered it, a fog as lovely as white silk, swaying with a kind of blissful anticipation.

Her creation.

Under *her* command.

As Whit brought the truck under the branches of the oak, the fog wrapped around its tires and began to rise toward the terrified couple. Diane wept noisily and kept trying to move closer to her husband. Fritz struggled valiantly to free his hands and feet, but only succeeded in losing his balance and toppled into his wife. They both fell to the floor of the truck.

The truck stopped and Whit and Gogh hopped out, climbed into the bed, and hauled the hostages to their feet. Just then, Jill barreled out of the side door of the hotel, waving two lengths of rope, and the crowd cheered and chanted again. The defiance Jill had displayed in the market was now gone, subsumed by the power of the collective. There was yet hope for Jill.

As Whit and Gogh held the two steady, Dominica fashioned a pair of nooses and leaped into the bed of the truck.

"You first," she said to Fritz, and fitted the noose around his neck as he screamed and squirmed and sobbed. She hoped that when he died, he went elsewhere. She didn't want him in her tribe. Over the centuries, she'd had too many screamers like him, complainers, ghosts who found fault with everything. When the rope was fastened securely around Fritz's neck, she ran her knuckles over Diane's soft cheek. "Such a pretty little thing."

The fog rolled closer, and the *brujo* litany whispered through the darkness. *Find the body, fuel the body . . .*

"Perhaps you both will join us when you pass," Dominica said. "It happens, you know. The transitional soul finds comfort in a tribe." She glanced at Fritz. "Although I have to say that I like Diane better than I like you, Fritz."

Diane's eyes bulged in their sockets, and Fritz screamed, *"Don't touch her; get your fucking hands off her!"*

"Now, now, Fritz, we *brujos* know how to share and that's something you'll learn if you choose to join us. The—"

Just then, Maddie's grandfather took shape beside Dominica. Charlie Livingston in his trademark white clothing, his Ben Franklin specs riding low on the bridge of his nose, a fat Cuban cigar tucked behind his ear. He looked as solid as every host in the courtyard, and although Dominica couldn't tell if the others could see him, Maddie did. She reacted immediately, fighting Dominica for control of her own body. But Dominica's control couldn't be broken, not right now, not with the collective madness of the tribe fueling her.

"This little charade has gone far enough, Dominica," Charlie announced.

"Get lost, Charlie. You don't have any control over physical life." Then she shouted, "Whit, start the truck and pull forward!"

"Hang them, hang them, hang them," the crowd shouted.

As the engine revved, another chaser appeared next to Charlie, a male Dominica had never seen before. Oriental eyes, bald as a turnip, wearing jeans, a pullover sweater, sneakers. The two of them sank through the hood of the truck, and the engine sputtered and died.

Whit kept turning the key, the starter whined and scraped, but the engine refused to turn over. Gogh leaped out of the truck and snapped open the hood. The chanting grew louder and louder, the fog thickened and swelled.

Fritz and Diane went mute with terror, the nooses around their necks already so tight that it wouldn't take much more pressure to strangle them.

Charlie materialized beside her again. "Release them, Dominica."

"You stupid asshole," Dominica spat, and turned to the fog. "Seize them! Bleed them out!"

The fog swept in, covering the truck, curling around the hostages' bodies, climbing into the branches. Shrieks of agony echoed across the courtyard and the *brujo* litany reached a crescendo, an orchestra of the damned. Then it was over.

The fog backed off so that all the others could see the hostages' bloody, lifeless bodies swinging from the nooses. The woman's neck slipped free and she dropped to the bed of the truck, into a pool of blood. "Whit, cut down Fritz. Then we'll need a couple of you to remove the bodies and wrap them in sheets. The back of the truck should be hosed out and the covered bodies placed back inside. We have a delivery to make."

Charlie looked livid and it made her smile. "We're winning, Charlie. Take that back to your chaser buddies in Esperanza."

"You've only won this round. The next round begins *now*." The air suddenly filled with cries and caws and the frenzied flapping of wings. A murder of crows descended on the courtyard, hundreds of them, maybe thousands, crows that were unnaturally large, mythic in size, their wingspans thirty, forty, fifty feet across, she couldn't tell for sure.

A tremendous white crow, twice the size of the others, swept in low over the courtyard. The flapping of its immense wings whipped up dust and dried leaves, creating dozens of miniature tornadoes that spun through the courtyard, tearing apart the potted plants, stripping branches bare, dispersing the fog. Now the other crows followed and the crowd scrambled for cover as the giant birds dived at them, cawing, snapping their dagger-sharp beaks.

Dominica jumped down from the truck, waving her arms to protect herself from being ripped apart, and shouted, "Get inside the hotel!"

Panicked, the crowd shoved through the side door, pushing at each other to get inside. As the crows dived at the stragglers, crying shrilly, *brujos* vacated their hosts and the liberated humans exploded through the courtyard gate, escaping into the streets of Cedar Key. Dominica realized the crows weren't hurting the living; it was just a ploy to scare the *brujos* from their hosts.

Dominica, already inside the hotel, threw open one of the windows and yelled, "*The crows won't hurt you! They're just trying to force you out of your hosts.*"

The white crow dived toward her and soared through the window, its impossibly long wings cutting right through the wooden frame and the walls as though both were made of water. Dominica lurched back, stumbled into the piano bench, and fell into the screaming crowd behind her. As the crowd scattered, Dominica slammed to the floor and the white crow aimed straight at her.

She scrambled back on her hands and knees, struggling to rise, but the crow kept diving at her, its flapping wings and dagger beak just inches from her body, eyes, hands. Other crows flew into the lobby, cawing, diving at the fleeing hosts until the terrified *brujos* vacated the bodies. Most of the liberated humans raced out the front door. A few, whose minds and spirits had broken irrevocably, stumbled around, alternately doubling over and moaning, then snapping upward and screeching.

The flock split in two and one part went after the luminous orbs and puffs of discolored smoke, the *brujos* in their natural forms. The giant birds slammed into them, snapped them into smaller pieces, clawed them to nothingness. Dominica heard their desperate, agonized wails as they were obliterated. But *brujos* couldn't be annihilated like this. It wasn't possible, it had never happened before. These crows were some chaser illusion, and illusions couldn't cause destruction.

Her feet found purchase and she vaulted upward just as the white crow swept toward her again. She flung out her arms. *"You're not real, you can't hurt me."* But the crow's beak grazed her right forearm, tearing open the skin, and Dominica dived behind the front desk to escape another attack.

All around her, those caws and cries echoed, and her *brujos* wailed as they were torn apart. Glass shattered, objects clanged and clattered and crashed, piano cords twanged. The birds were wrecking the lobby, dining room, bar, the kitchen. Then, between one breath and the next, a horrendous rushing sound sucked everything out of the air—oxygen, sound, even color, so that she saw the world only through her *bruja* eyes, black and white and shades of gray. Just as abruptly as it had started, it ended. Silence choked the air.

After a few minutes, Dominica grabbed onto the edge of the front desk and pulled herself upright. She glanced around slowly, taking in the unbelievable devastation. The lobby looked as if it had been turned upside down and shaken like a snow globe. Shards of glass and plates and bowls littered the surface of the front desk, the floor, the stairs. The piano bench lay on its side and had more holes in it than a sponge. The piano had collapsed, one of its thick legs sliced in two, and dozens of piano keys littered the floor. The wall mirror had shattered, the glass in the front door was gone, the screen flapped like a loose tongue.

Dominica moved unsteadily away from the front desk, barely aware that her arm was bleeding from where the white crow had grazed her. Shock kept shuddering through her, one wave after another. The door to the dining room had been torn off its hinges and the doorway was filled with debris—splintered chairs, more glass, silverware, pieces of dishes, lengths of torn tablecloths. Four of the broken humans, tourists, wandered around the lobby, shuffling through the broken glass, arms clutched to their chests. One of them, a woman, shuffled right out the side door and into the courtyard, and promptly fell to her knees, wailing inconsolably.

Brujos began to crawl from their hiding places, eyes wide with shock, faces pale. Whit ran through the front door and came straight over to her. "What the hell *were* those things?"

"Conjured by the chasers. Beyond that, I'm not sure." But she clearly understood their intent was to diminish the size of her tribe—either by infusing the *brujos* with such fear that it drove them from their hosts or by annihilating them, or both. "How many did we lose? Any idea?"

"I think between twenty-five and forty ghosts."

"And just that many hosts."

It could have been worse. The crows could have picked off her entire tribe. In fact, given another chance, they probably would do exactly that. She refused to give them another chance. "We're speeding up our schedule, Whit. In the next twenty-four to forty-eight hours, I want everyone in town seized, even people under the age of sixteen. Every member of our tribe should have a host. And no more hostages. From now on, every one of us with a host travels with a *brujo* in natural form so that when we encounter an uncompromised human, a *brujo* can seize that person. Now let's get a cleaning crew together and figure out what to do with the broken humans." She tilted her head toward the tourists wandering aimlessly around the lobby. "Then you and I have a delivery to make."

"I do think, Nica, that it might be time for you to bleed out Maddie and find a new host. We all saw that guy in white, the chaser, and his buddy. The net is humming with debate about whether your host has become a distinct liability."

"I'll make that call. If and when the time comes."

"But—"

"Look, Whit. I appreciate your feedback, your expertise, everything you do. But when it comes to my host, her fate resides with me and only me."

Fifteen

When Kate came to, she was on the cot against the wall, covered with a light blanket, a pillow under her head, her shoes side by side on the floor. She had no idea how long she had been in this room, on this cot, where it was, or how she'd gotten here. The last thing she remembered was being shot in the back with a tranquilizer dart by someone on the airboat. She knew that food had arrived twice, delivered by a man with a blurred face, and that she'd shoveled the food into her mouth and had fallen back against the cot again, unable to remain conscious.

But she was conscious now and slowly took stock of her surroundings. Small room, maybe twelve feet square. No windows. A nightstand bolted to the floor. It had a lamp on it, the light dim. An adjoining bath. She remembered stumbling into that bathroom at some point to relieve her bladder. She remembered a toothbrush, toothpaste, soap, a clean towel and washcloth, and remembered that she had showered. Beyond that, her memory yielded nothing at all about this place.

Kate sat up and swung her legs over the side of the cot. She noticed a table pushed up against the far wall, a chair at either end of it. On the table were a yellow legal pad and a pencil with a blunt tip. The walls were completely bare and the room lacked a radio, TV, magazines, books, everything that might anchor her in time. So she stood on legs that felt shaky and unstable and began to walk around the room.

When she walked like this, she entered into a kind of meditative state, and remembered that shortly after she had returned to Cedar Key, she had taken up meditation for the second time in her life. The course had been held at the library, taught by a bald man with beautiful eyes and a winning smile. One of the ways he had broken up the meditations was by walking through a garden outside the library, a sort of labyrinth of hedges and flowers.

Every week for eight weeks, it seemed she had walked farther and farther back into her own life, unraveling her relationship with Rocky's father, with her own parents, her childhood, her love for the island. Now she walked to unravel what had been happening on Cedar Key. As she unraveled that night in the hotel bar when Bean and Marion went at it, the door opened and two men walked in.

A short white man, a very tall black man. Shorty wore an FBI badge around his neck that identified him as Tom O'Donnell; the other guy wore a badge for ISIS, an organization Kate had never heard of, that identified him as Bob Delaney. They introduced themselves, O'Donnell pulled out a chair and gestured toward it. "Have a seat, Ms. Davis."

"I'm fine right where I am." She stood with her back to the wall. "Where the hell am I?"

"Outside of the quarantine area," O'Donnell said.

"Which tells me squat. Have I been charged with something?"

"We'd just like to ask you some questions."

"Hey, look, someone shot me with a tranquilizer dart. I deserve some answers before I answer any of your questions."

"The dart was unfortunate," O'Donnell said.

"*Unfortunate?*" Kate balked. "I could've drowned. It was a goddamn assault."

"You were in violation of the quarantine. They had their orders. And just so you know, we drew blood and you're free of the virus."

"You drew my *fucking blood*? What gives you the right to do *that*?"

"The quarantine," O'Donnell replied, and brought out an iPad, turned it on, set it in front of her. "We'd like to know about the incidents at Annie's Café, Ms. Davis."

Kate stared at a thirty-second video that covered everything from the moment Mayor Pete Stanton had grabbed the back of her shirt to when he had shouted, "Seize them, seize all of them" to when she'd held the second torch and begun setting everything on fire. The video wasn't the greatest; she guessed it had been taken with a cell. But it clearly showed her as the one who had started the fire. *Guilty as charged.*

"What would you like to know?" Kate asked.

"Why did you set fire to everything?"

"Didn't you hear what the mayor yelled? 'Seize them all.' What do you think he was referring to, Agent O'Donnell?"

"I honestly don't know. We were hoping you might enlighten us."

Shit. O'Donnell didn't strike her as the type who would believe anything she said. But she wasn't in the mood for lying. Kate walked over to the table and leaned in so close to O'Donnell she could smell the mint he sucked on. "Some people refer to them as demons. I don't believe in demons, so I think of them as evil ghosts. If you don't believe in demons or ghosts, then I suppose you can call them *bad fucking karma*, Agent O'Donnell. They crave all the sensory pleasures of physical life, so they seize the living for that purpose. That's what they've been doing on Cedar Key. One of them is in the mayor. In fact, all the people seated on the right side of the room in that video were hosts to these abominations. Fire annihilates them."

O'Donnell just stared at her, sucking harder on his mint. "Excuse me, but if ghosts are already dead, how can fire annihilate them? Where'd they come from? You'll have to be more specific, Ms. Davis."

More specific? Really? "Well, it's like this, Agent O'Donnell," and she started talking.

She went through the events in February, talked about the changes in Bean, Rich, others in town whom she had known for years. She didn't mention the shapeshifter, but told them about Zee Small's theories. And when she finished, O'Donnell pulled out the other chair and sank into it. Delaney remained standing, but the two of them exchanged a glance that probably didn't bode well for her immediate future.

"Look, I don't know how long you've kept me here, but my son disappeared the night of the fire at the café and I need to look for him. So please hurry up and decide whatever you need to decide." She looked over at Delaney. "You don't say anything. Why not?"

O'Donnell leaped in. "He's not here in any official—"

"Cut the crap, Tom." Delaney's response was quick, sharp. "She deserves an honest answer."

The man's eyes were the same rich, dark chocolate color of his skin. His intense gaze unnerved her. Kate felt as though he were strolling around inside of her, scrutinizing her soul, her psyche, the terrains of her heart. She looked down at the floor, away from him. "Honesty. Now there's an honorable place for the government to start." Then she raised her eyes and met Delaney's gaze. "So what's the *honest* answer?"

"You'll have a tough time convincing anyone in FEMA or Homeland Security or the CDC that *ghosts* are taking over the island. But at some level, many of them sense that an unknown virus has nothing to do with what's going on here. And that's why no one has gone into the quarantine area."

"Good thing. You'd be seized very quickly if you walked through downtown."

"We could call in ghostbusters." O'Donnell snickered at his own joke.

"Who took that video?" she asked. "How'd you get it? If there were security cameras inside Annie's—which I seriously doubt, it's just not that sophisticated a place—then they probably burned along with the building. That video looks like it came from a cell phone."

"It did," O'Donnell replied, and glanced at Delaney. "An agent went rogue and entered Cedar Key against orders. He was at Annie's the night it burned. But we also had another agent install security cameras at various spots on the island before the quarantine was imposed."

"So charge me or let me go, gentlemen. And if you're going to charge me, I'd like to call my attorney."

O'Donnell leaned forward, hands clasped against the tabletop. "You don't have an attorney, Ms. Davis. You can barely afford to pay your bills.

We know that your houseboat was moored behind Richard's place and then you moved it to the marina, and then you left Cedar Key. Why?"

Okay, this guy was beginning to piss her off. "I told you why. Rich changed. One of these evil ghosts claimed him. And one of them is in Sam Dorset, the editor of the paper, and that's the reason he tried to rape me. After it happened, Rich advised me not to call the police, 'not to make waves,' as he put it. And when I called the police chief—Frank Cole, another guy I've known practically my whole life—he told me he wouldn't arrest Sam until he'd slept off his drunk. Drunk or sober shouldn't make any difference. Frank was one of the first who got taken."

O'Donnell popped another mint in his mouth, pushed to his feet, and retrieved the iPad. "We appreciate your candor, Ms. Davis. We'll be back later with further questions."

Delaney, she noticed, wasn't as quick to get up. "Excuse me," she snapped. "Time is of the essence here. My son has been missing for . . . I don't know how many hours . . . and you're telling me you'll be *back later*? Do you have children, Agent O'Donnell?"

His blank look told her he didn't.

"What about you, Mr. Delaney? Do you have kids?"

"Yes. But I don't see what—"

"Put yourself in my shoes." She was nearly shouting now. "Your kid is missing in a quarantine zone, evil ghost shits have seized the locals—"

"And we saw those giant crows over the island," Delaney finished, his voice quiet, tense. He impaled O'Donnell with his eyes, just daring him to issue an order to shut up.

He didn't. O'Donnell looked like a man perched at the edge of an abyss, his eyes sort of wild as he sucked hard on his mint. "We don't know what those crows are about. We don't even know if they *were* crows. They were too big for crows. Enough about the crows, Bob."

Crows? Kate didn't know what he was talking about. It didn't matter. Delaney seemed to be in her court, but apparently couldn't say much with O'Donnell around. "I'd like to make the call to which I'm entitled. Immediately. Unless you charge me with something—or unless you plan to Baker-act me and send me to a padded cell—I have the right to an attorney."

"Cedar Key is under FEMA and CDC jurisdiction now," O'Donnell said. "Martial law. And that means that your civil rights are suspended."

With that, he headed for the door. Delaney held back, his eyes locked on hers, and reached into the pocket of his jacket. He withdrew something and pressed it into her hand. He seemed to hold her hand longer than necessary to pass her a slip of paper, his beautiful, dark fingers a shocking contrast to her pale skin. She slipped the piece of paper into the back pocket of her jeans and Delaney moved swiftly after O'Donnell without looking back.

When the heavy door shut again, the lock clicking into place, Kate ran over to it and hammered her fists against it, shrieking, "Hey, assholes, I'm entitled to an attorney . . ."

Her voice echoed. Useless, it was useless, she thought, and pressed her fists to her forehead, then began to walk again, faster, faster, her meditative state just beyond her or behind her, a shadow, out of reach. Didn't matter. She just needed to walk, to move, to find a spot in this little space where the video camera mounted inconspicuously in the corner couldn't see everything she did.

Could they hear her, too?

She assumed they could. She assumed they could peer through her clothes at her naked body, too. *TSA, hello. I am not your local terrorist. The terrorists have arrived and guess what? They look like us, they could be us when we're dead.*

Kate slid under the cot, lay there on her stomach, and dug out the slip of paper Delaney had passed her. She unfolded it, smoothed it out against the floor. "Rocky safe. Liberty will find you. Wayra"

She squeezed her eyes shut and held the note against her heart. "Rocky safe." But how had Delaney gotten this? Kate pressed her forehead against her hands, the note crumpled in her fist.

A long time later, a noise awakened her. It took her a moment to realize she was under the cot, hiding from the security camera, the piece of paper wadded up between her cheek and her hand. She quickly shoved it down inside her sock and turned her head, watching the feet of the man who entered her room. Large feet. His shoes, a pair of worn dock shoes, looked to be a size eleven or larger.

"Kate?"

"It's not a locked-room mystery, Delaney," she said. "There're only so many places in a room this size where I might be." She slid out from under the cot, brushed the dust bunnies from her jeans, sat back on the edge of the cot, and just glared at him.

"We can speak freely," he said softly.

"Yeah?" She gestured at the supposedly hidden video camera in a corner of the room. "Stupid is as stupid does."

He laughed. "It has a new loop."

"Why?"

He grabbed the back of one of the chairs and jerked it over closer to the cot. He flipped it around, sat down, rested his forearms along the back of it. "Because a hawk dropped that note at my feet."

Liberty.

"Help me understand what's going on, Kate."

"Excuse me, Agent Delaney. You're probably a really smart guy, but you wouldn't be able to grasp what I'm talking about, okay?"

"Really? Well, let's put that to the test. You and Richard, or Rich, as you've called him since grade school, became lovers when his marriage fell apart. He's basically a nice guy, but you aren't in love with him. He was company, the sex was good. When you were a kid, your mother worked at the hotel. Your old man was local color, an interesting guy whose passion was fishing. It wasn't catching the fish that mattered to him, but the ritual—alone in a boat, beneath a glorious sky, a Hemingway moment."

"Hemingway. Totally overrated. And how the hell do you know any of this?"

"It's my job."

"With this ISIS agency that I've never heard of?"

"Right." Delaney shrugged off his pack, set it between his feet, unzipped it, and brought out a pale blue and gray jumpsuit. "Put that on. And get this around your neck, where it's visible." He handed her a fed ID with a fake name on it. "We're outta here."

She cupped the ID in her hand, shocked to see her photo on it. "And how do I know this isn't a trap for me?"

"When I held your hand a bit too long? That's what I do. I read people that way. I get it, okay?"

"Get what, exactly? Spell it out, Delaney. Right now, I'm not even sure what *I* get and don't get."

He rubbed his hand over his face. "A redhead—Maddie—gave you something, a note, a warning. An old man came to your houseboat and warned you. He gave you weapons, too. That's when you moved your houseboat out of the marina to one of the other islands. You had so many warnings but you just kept going along with everyone else's agenda."

All true. She'd had ample warnings, and kept ignoring them, hoping they were wrong. "You're a *psychic* for the government?"

"A remote viewer."

"Isn't that a fancy name for a psychic?"

"Pretty much, although there're some subtle differences."

"And why're you helping me?"

"Because I believe you."

"How long have I been here?"

"Nearly twenty-four hours."

"Shit." *Rocky. What's happened to you, where are you, did Wayra find you?* She quickly slipped on the jumpsuit, flipped the hood over her head, fixed the ID badge so that it was visible. "What's this mean for you, Delaney? If you're caught?"

"I can kiss my life and career good-bye."

Kate followed him out of the room, into a dimly lit hallway. They were in a small concrete building with graffiti on the walls, a place she recognized that had once been used to store supplies for the fishing pier. She had played here as a kid, and somewhere on these walls, her ten-year-old self had scrawled her name.

They left through the back door, and in her first few moments outside, in a large parking lot, Kate filled her senses with the familiar smells of water, salt marsh, spring. A flock of silhouetted birds flew across the twilit sky. She didn't see a fence, soldiers, guards, nothing to indicate martial law. Just a single-wide trailer that stood to the west of the parking lot, which held two rows of electric carts and government vehicles. Delaney chose a cart with several boxes on the backseat, a broom and mop resting across them.

"I've got a canoe stashed in the salt marsh about a mile from here." His voice held a softness that seemed contradictory for a man of his height and size.

"Where're all the guards? FEMA? The CDC?"

"Set up right where the quarantine begins." He drove the cart out of the lot, onto State Road 24. "We're about a mile beyond that."

"O'Donnell didn't buy my story, did he?"

"O'Donnell understands that some very weird shit is going on, but evil ghosts are a stretch for him."

"But not for you."

"Frankly, I found it much stranger that a hawk delivered a note intended for you and knew to drop it in front of me."

"She's a smart hawk, for sure. But I agree with you. It's strange even for her."

"The hawk is your *pet*?"

"Not a pet, exactly. My son rescued her last year, and ever since she just hangs around the houseboat."

"Who's Wayra?"

A dog that followed me home and turned into a man. "He was helping me look for Rocky. We went into one of the houses on the runway, where Rocky's girlfriend lives, thinking he might be there with her. But we found a naked couple dead in front of the fireplace. They had bled out. Wayra knows a lot about these *brujos,* that's what he calls them. He's here because of Maddie. The ghost inside of her is one of the ancient *brujos* of Esperanza, Ecuador. She and Wayra are old adversaries."

"You realize how nuts that sounds?"

"Yes." And she hadn't even gotten to the part about a shapeshifter. She decided not to mention it. "It also happens to be true."

"But how do *you* know this guy?"

"I met him when he arrived in Cedar Key." Not a lie, exactly, but not the whole truth. "He helped me get out of the café the night of the fire. He apparently found Rocky."

Lights hit the cart's side mirrors. Delaney bit at his lower lip. "Shit. Another cart. Reach into the box right behind you, Kate, open the duffel bag, and grab one of the weapons and extra clips."

She twisted around, pushed the mop and the broom onto the road, opened the box. It held handguns, clips, handcuffs, handheld radios, a couple of cell phones. She plucked out a pair of nine millimeters, all the extra clips, passed Delaney the gun and half the clips.

"You know how to shoot that?" he asked.

"Probably better than you do. That colorful figure you mentioned—my dad?—knew as much about guns as he did about fish. Look, you don't have to put yourself at risk. Tell O'Donnell I took you hostage."

"He wouldn't believe it." Delaney turned abruptly into the trees on the right, killed the cart's headlights, and they both hopped out. He pulled a duffel bag from each of the boxes and they dashed through the trees, working their way farther north along the marsh, distancing themselves from the cart.

Their shoes sank into mud and muck, branches slapped her in the face, she heard fish jumping nearby. It was nearly dark now and she could barely make out the canoe. Fitted with an electric motor, it was tied to the branches of a scruffy bush, half hidden in the tall reeds along the water, the paddles on the floor. They dropped the duffels inside, she quickly got in, and Delaney pushed them off the beach and started the motor. It purred and quickly took them into the tallest reeds. Minutes later, a voice rang out. O'Donnell. "Delaney, don't be an idiot! The cutters are blocking your way outta here."

"Is that true?" Kate whispered.

"I don't know. But it doesn't matter. We have a way out. It took me most of the day to set this up."

O'Donnell kept shouting, his voice echoing through the darkness and across the water. An airboat came into view, the top of it about even with the top of the reeds. Once the tide came in, though, it would be visible. "That's where we're getting off."

"Hardly subtle."

"It'll do the trick."

They brought the canoe alongside the airboat, and Delaney killed the engine. He steadied it as she got out, passed her the duffels, then removed the electric engine and climbed aboard. He stashed the duffels and engine in a deep aluminum box anchored to the floor of the boat, dug out two pairs of goggles and two pairs of headsets. He passed her one of each. "Put those on."

She put on the goggles, slipped on the headset, they climbed into the tall seats, and moments later, the airboat exploded out of the marsh and into open water, engine roaring. The Zodiac tied behind their seats lifted into the wind like a sail, then throbbed like a giant heart against the floor of the airboat. A pair of Coast Guard cutters tore after them, but the airboat screamed onward, outpacing the cutters.

Bugs splattered against the windshield, smeared across her goggles. When they ripped through another marsh, Kate slapped her hand over her nose and mouth to keep the bugs and caterpillars out. "Where's your houseboat?" Delaney shouted over the racket.

"Sea Horse Key, directly west of Snake Key," she yelled back. "Go around the inside of Atsena, it's shorter, and may be too shallow for their boats."

The airboat swerved west, engine shrieking, a rising furl of water curving on Kate's side of the boat. She gripped the edges of her bench, terrified she might slide off into the water. As they shot away from Atsena Otie, she glanced back. In the light of the stars, she could see that one of the cutters was stuck, beached, and the other had slowed considerably. She couldn't hear their engines, not over the din the airboat made, but imagined they were straining.

"Keep going straight," she hollered. "The tide's low and there's a marsh coming up on your side where we can ditch the airboat and take the Zodiac."

He flashed a thumbs-up. Kate wished he could turn off the airboat's brilliant spotlight, but the risk of accident was too great if they couldn't see where the hell they were going. She kept shouting directions, turn here, turn there. When they reached the marsh, Delaney immediately turned off the engine, the lights. The darkness swallowed them, the airboat bobbed like a cork in the shallow waters, the night sounds closed around them.

Kate tore off her goggles, and she and Delaney stood at the same moment. Without uttering a word, they worked as if their brains were completely in synch. She retrieved the duffels, paddles, and engine, and he untied the Zodiac and dropped it alongside the airboat. He fitted the engine onto the back of it.

Just before Kate climbed down into the Zodiac with one of the duffels, she glimpsed a much smaller boat racing toward them. Delaney saw it, too. "Hurry, hurry," he whispered. "Get in." Then he drew a dark green tarp over the airboat, either end resting against the reeds.

It was too shallow here to use the engine, so they paddled fast, away from the airboat, and paused at the edge of the marsh, watching the smaller vessel. It had slowed and now moved south around Snake Key, probably checking out the mangroves in the cove. "I say we wait a few minutes," she said softly.

"Total agreement."

"You plan well, Delaney."

"I had plenty of help."

"From?"

"RV." He parted the reeds with his hand so that he had a better view of the boat. "I actually saw you the day I shook O'Donnell's hand outside of Gainesville, when Sanchez informed me he was going rogue. I saw myself interrogating you, then I was alone with you, asking about a note a hawk dropped at my feet. When I saw that hawk this morning, that's when I knew what was going to happen. Yesterday, after you were brought in, I made a point of touching O'Donnell and saw myself readying an airboat."

"Did you see how it turns out?"

"Uh, no. O'Donnell suspected I was reading him and moved away from me."

The boat rounded the tip of Snake Key and they lost sight of it. "Let's move to the other side of the marsh and head for Sea Horse," she suggested.

"We'll have to paddle until the water's a bit deeper and we're out of this shrubbery."

They paddled, but it wasn't easy. The shrubbery was thick, the leaves like saws. Some of the reeds had snapped in two and their pointed ends scraped and clawed against the sides of the Zodiac. Even though the boat was made of Hypalon, a durable plastic material, a puncture by one of these reeds would create a slow leak and they would probably sink before they got to Sea Horse. "You have any glue for this sucker, Delaney?"

"Nope. This part was a rush job. How far is it to Sea Horse?"

"From here, less than two miles. But it's all open water."

Kate heard something and at first thought it was another airboat. But Delaney touched her arm and pointed upward. A chopper swept in low across the gulf, its searchlights burning a path through the darkness, the *whoop* of its rotors growing increasingly louder. They pushed back into the marsh and Delaney slid lower in the boat. The Zodiac barely accommodated him when he sat up straight, but now his legs came along either side of her and his feet hung over the end. Kate leaned back against him, her head resting against his chest, his hands on her arms. He dropped his head back, and through the tips of the reeds, they watched the chopper make a wide circle around the marsh that hid them.

"Delaney, when you saw me in this vision or whatever it was, did that mean that what you saw would absolutely happen?"

"Never. In remote viewing, you only see what's most probable at the moment you see it."

He suddenly drew his fingers through her hair, a touch so gentle, so soft, that Kate felt it all the way to the tips of her toes.

"But I have to tell you," he went on, "that when I first saw you, I hoped like hell it would all come to pass." Then he leaned over her and touched his mouth to hers, a kiss so simple and yet so exquisite that she felt powerless to do anything except reach back and lock her hands behind his head, at the back of his thick, powerful neck. For long moments, it seemed that they breathed in perfect rhythm with each other, that their hearts beat as one.

Then the chopper moved in low over the marsh, sixty feet, fifty, forty, thirty, twenty, practically skimming the gulf, and gunfire tore through the reeds, chewed through the water. Kate instantly rolled to the right, onto her hands and knees, pulled the nine millimeter from her jacket pocket, rocked back onto her heels and shot blindly, without thought, into the sky, at the chopper. When she emptied the clip, she slammed in another. As the chopper circled in closer, she fired twice and the helicopter blew apart in midair.

The explosion reverberated across the water, through the marsh, a moving tide of violence. Pieces of flaming debris rained around them, igniting the tips of the reeds, which burned fast and hot. She just sat there, clutching the weapon, air bursting from her mouth in short, panicked staccato bursts.

"Delaney, we need to—"

He lay there bleeding, groaning, motionless, and she fell forward, her hands landing on either side of his head. "Delaney, Christ, what . . ." She lifted his head, begging him to speak to her, open his eyes, something, Christ, something. His eyes opened, but were glazed with pain.

"Side," he gasped, and passed out.

His shirt and jacket turned crimson. He was going to bleed to death here, in the Zodiac, where he had kissed her. A part of her actually believed she had caused this, that she was cursed, a purveyor and vehicle of bad luck. She loved Rocky and he had disappeared. She had loved Rich and he had become possessed by a *brujo*. This intriguing man had kissed her—and now might die. Kate started the engine and broke free of the marsh. Flaming debris rained down as she crossed the open water between the marsh and Sea Horse. She thought she heard a boat closing in on her and maneuvered the Zodiac erratically, a zigzag that hopefully would make her a more difficult target.

"Stay with me, Delaney, stay with me." She kept repeating these words, a mantra, a prayer.

Kate heard the hawk before she saw her, circling low, then flying in alongside her, keening loudly. When she plunged into the mangrove around Sea Horse, she cut the engine, tipped it out of the water, and paddled frantically. Liberty spiraled upward. Delaney hadn't moved. His blood covered her hands, saturated her clothes.

The instant Kate saw the houseboat, she shouted for Wayra, but he was already on the deck, probably alerted by the hawk, who keened nearby. "I can see you," he shouted, and shone a flashlight in her direction. "I heard the gunfire. Are you hurt?"

"Delaney is." Her fear for him choked off her words. She had some first-aid supplies on board, but was pretty sure that Delaney's condition went well beyond what first aid could do. "He . . . broke me out. Freed me from the feds."

The Zodiac bumped up against the side of the houseboat; she tossed the rope to Wayra, and he secured it to the ladder. She suddenly realized that getting Delaney out of the raft would be difficult. She estimated that he was six foot seven or eight, weighed well over two hundred and fifty pounds, and that she and Wayra might not be able to move him. Her hands, slick with his blood, kept slipping off him. He continued to bleed. She heard the wheeze of his breathing as she lifted his torso and Wayra grabbed his fore-arms and pulled.

They finally managed to get him onto the houseboat deck. Kate buck-led from relief, exhaustion, and sank to her hands and knees. Wayra dragged Delaney into the houseboat, leaving a trail of blood behind him. The ripe stink of Delaney's blood suffused her senses; she knew she would smell it for the rest of her life. Minutes ticked by before she could haul herself up. She stumbled through the open deck doors.

And what she saw paralyzed her—Rocky on the floor, his body caught between human and animal, like some scene from that movie *Altered States*. His limbs were human, his face was that of a dog or wolf, his eyes were wide open, lupine, a soft amber color, flickering here and there, roll-ing back in their sockets. And beside him was Delaney, Wayra hovering over him, one hand pressed to his forehead, the other welded to Delaney's chest, light shooting from his palms. He sank his teeth into Delaney's neck and Kate shrieked and lunged at him, and Wayra caught her and whis-pered, "Shit, Kate, I'm sorry," and slapped his hand against her forehead.

She swam into a dream. And in this dream, she was everywhere and nowhere. She wandered through memories that were not her own and ev-ery time she struggled to break free of whatever this was, she found herself at Rich's place, the last time they had made love, when the evil ghost had been inside of him.

And she knew that Wayra was changing her just as he had changed her son and was changing Delaney. With his mouth at her neck, she didn't have the strength or the will to fight him. She succumbed.

Sixteen

Wayra tasted his own urgency, a foul bitterness that coated his tongue, clogged his nostrils, threatened to choke him. He swept Kate's fallen weapon off the floor and pocketed it. He worked off her jacket, then lifted her and set her gently on the couch, on her back. He stared down at her, sickened by what he'd done.

He knew he'd bitten her for no other reason than to prevent her son from ever being alone, as Wayra himself had been for so many centuries. It violated every code he'd ever lived by and he deeply regretted it. His emotions had gotten in the way. But he couldn't undo it now and was grateful she would sleep through the transformation process. As the only uninjured and healthy one in this trio, her transformation would be complete in four to six hours.

He turned his attention to Delaney. Big man, nearly seven feet tall. Wayra guessed he weighed about two-seventy. That alone would lengthen the time of his transformation. But he was also badly injured. It meant his vastly improved immune system would slam into high gear to heal him first, just as Rocky's had. Then the transformation process would begin. No telling how long it would take. Rocky was twenty-four hours into the process. When Wayra had turned the mother and son who were infected with the plague, their transformation had taken two days. He hoped that wouldn't be the case for either Rocky or Delaney. He didn't think either of them had two days to spare. Wayra removed Delaney's jacket, tore open his bloody shirt. Christ, so much blood. It covered his right side like a second skin and made it impossible to tell the nature of the injury or how bad it was. He ran over to the galley sink, filled a pot with warm water, set it on the floor next to Delaney. He hurried into the bathroom and fetched clean towels and washcloths, Betadine and hydrogen peroxide.

He worked on the blood for long, tense minutes, wash and wipe, wash and wipe, until he could see the deep, gaping gash a bullet had torn across his rib cage. Wayra couldn't tell if the bullet had penetrated. If it had, then his body might expel it during his transformation or tissue would grow around it, encasing it forever. The bleeding had stopped. That meant the transformation had already begun. Wayra treated the wound with the peroxide and Betadine, then felt along Delaney's ribs to see if he could find any breaks. He didn't detect any. He hoped that if there were hairline fractures he couldn't feel, damage he couldn't see, the transformation would heal them.

Wayra found a shirt that was at least a size too small for Delaney, but it would have to do. It was important that his transformation, like Kate's and Rocky's, happened while he was clothed. That way, whenever he shifted in the future, he would always return to his human form wearing clothing, with his belongings zipped into pockets or whatever he carried. He didn't know why this was so, it just was.

He got up to check on Kate. Beneath her lids, Kate's eyes flickered back and forth, as if she were in REM sleep, dreaming. Good, this was as it should be. It meant she was accessing the vast collective pool of shifter history, the first step in a transformation unless the person was injured or sick. For Rocky and Delaney, the healing was first, then the history. Within this history lay the blueprint of transformation that their bodies would use, a blueprint now encoded in their DNA. The shape each of them ultimately took would be determined by the nature of their individual consciousness.

Even though it had been centuries since Wayra had turned anyone, the information about the process surfaced with shocking clarity and speed. He suspected it was that shifter blueprint at work.

Wayra didn't have any idea how Delaney would fit into this picture. Maybe he wouldn't. If he survived, he might choose to turn a woman and form his own pack. Or perhaps he, Kate, and Rocky would form a pack. That part of it was out of his control.

As he drew a cover over Kate and then turned to Rocky, he noticed the hawk. She watched him warily from the back of a kitchen chair, those bright amber eyes so sentient and aware that he felt if he reached out to her in his other form, they would connect in some way. When he crouched beside the boy, the hawk fluttered to the floor beside him and drew her beak across the side of his thigh.

Wayra reached out and stroked her head with his fingers. She made that soft, trilling sound he'd heard several times now, the equivalent of a cat's purr, then flew back to her perch on the chair. Wayra's gaze lingered on her for a moment, puzzling over her, then he turned his attention on the boy.

The infection that had sent Rocky into convulsions was gone now, but his transformation was hideous to watch. It was as if he were caught in some terrible evolutionary loop—his feet and hands in the midst of conversion, fingers and toes disappearing into the knobs of his fists and ankles to create what would eventually become his paws. His head was no longer human, and at this point it was difficult to determine what kind of dog—or wolf—he might become.

He figured Rocky would emerge first, then Kate, then Delaney. They would possess the rudimentaries of what they could do as shapeshifters, but he would have to teach them the nuances. As their creator, he was obligated to do so. But he sure as hell couldn't teach them what they needed to know while they were on the houseboat. They had to be outside, on land, in a wooded area or some comparable spot so that their initial sensory perceptions were of the wild.

Wayra walked out onto the porch, the hawk following him, and listened to the darkness. Night sounds, that was it. Yet he had heard gunfire, boats, and the explosion of the chopper. Surely that would prompt another chopper to be sent out, more boats, a rescue mission, something. He climbed the ladder to the upper deck, the hawk flying on ahead of him, and peered out over the tops of the mangroves. Fog stretched across the gulf, five feet high and still climbing, so much fog he couldn't even see water in any direction. That explained why there was no rescue mission.

But would the young *brujos* who traveled in this fog seize hybrid humans? Unknown. He hoped they would avoid his trio just as they had avoided him. Regardless, he had to risk moving them to land or his shifters might end up like that boy he'd turned hundreds of years ago, never right in the head, eventually committing suicide.

The mangrove where the boat was anchored never gave way to solid land. So he would have to move along the shoreline, which meant his shifters would be more exposed to the fog, to the south side of the island where there was a lighthouse, a beach, and thickets of trees and brush. Or he could head for the old cemetery on Atsena Otie Key. But that would mean three or four miles of open water, a less appealing choice.

Wayra whistled for the hawk and the two returned to the cabin. Not much had changed with his three charges. He made sure they were as comfortable as possible, then went over to the tiny pantry and brought out the torches he'd made earlier in the day. He had wrapped rags around a couple of broomsticks and a mop stick and now he saturated the rags in gasoline. He slipped several packs of matches in his jacket pocket, left a box of kitchen matches on the counter, and helped himself to one of the torches. Just in case. He turned down the battery-operated lantern, picked up another and carried it into the pilothouse with him. The hawk stayed with Rocky, Kate, and Delaney. He was certain she would warn him if there was any significant change.

He set the lantern on one of the benches, stood the unlit torch in the corner, reeled in the anchor. He started the engine, kept it just above idle, and didn't turn on any outside lights. Instead, he shone a flashlight through the window, orienting himself as he navigated to the edge of the mangrove. At this level, the fog was the same thickness and color as clam chowder. It pressed up against the front of the boat, drifted across the pilot-house window. He didn't hear the *brujo* litany, didn't sense anything inside it. Was it just ordinary fog? That seemed unlikely. He brought the power up and the houseboat chugged out into the fog, away from the safety of the mangroves.

Wayra headed along the eastern shoreline of Sea Horse and the fog quickly swallowed the houseboat. He felt like Jonah in the belly of the whale, the beat of the boat's engine the throb of the creature's heart. *Chug-chug, chug-chug*, a monotonous rhythm. He turned off the lantern, the flashlight, and noticed there was enough illumination within the fog—light from the stars or the moon—for him to see. But there was nothing to see, just the pale soup of the fog.

He navigated using the compass, the depth finder, the GPS. On the GPS screen, the houseboat pulsed a bright red and moved along the dark shadow that was Sea Horse. Two miles into the journey, something in the fog changed. He sensed it, an anger, a malevolence. And then he heard the litany: *Find the body, fuel the body . . .*

The hawk suddenly shrieked and Wayra slammed the engine into high gear. The houseboat sped ahead, but it didn't move quickly enough to out-run the fog. The stuff drifted through the wood, the glass, seeped through any minuscule crack or hole it could find. Tongues of it wrapped around his ankles and the cold bit through his skin, muscles, into his bones. Wayra lit the torch and touched it to the long rope of fog that ran from the wall to his leg. It broke apart, and the separate pieces swiftly retreated. Wayra brought the engine to idle and rushed into the cabin.

The hawk flew around wildly, shrieking, her wings flapping hard as she dived toward the windows, where fog pressed up against the glass, then drew back, afraid of her. Wayra raced over to the windows on the right, thrusting the burning, smoking torch at the glass. The fog retreated as though it didn't perceive the glass, then dived toward it again, intent on gaining entry.

Suddenly, Charlie Livingston and Victor materialized in the middle of the room. Charlie looked the same, the guy in white, Mr. Clorox. But Victor was so agitated his clothes went from Grecian tunic to jeans to a Wall Street three-piece suit to shorts and a T-shirt. His eyes changed shape and color, and Wayra knew none of this boded well for him.

"Vic, Charlie, good to see you both. I hope you're here to help."

"We're going to cover you all the way to Goose Cove," Charlie said. "This fog is filled with some older ghosts that are hungry enough to sample the four of you. Dominica sent out a call and an appalling number of these bastards answered."

"Just do it," Wayra said, and thrust his torch at the window again.

Charlie and Victor raised their arms at the same time and evaporated. A moment later, the world erupted with caws and cries, squawks and a high-pitched keening. Birds. Hundreds of them. Wayra couldn't see them until the fog rolled away from the houseboat with astonishing swiftness and then shock tore through him. Thousands—not hundreds, but thousands—of gigantic birds spread out against the starlit sky, and spiraled steadily downward toward the houseboat until they created a black veil that hid it from view. The hawk flew wildly around the room, then followed Wayra into the pilothouse and pecked at the side window until he opened it. She flew out and joined the birds.

Crows.

On the GPS, the blinking red light that had been the houseboat was replaced by a dark, undulating mass. Now and then, a bank of fog approached the dark mass, but the crows immediately attacked it and the fog either dispersed or fled. He imagined that the *brujo* net hummed like crazy right now, alerting Dominica to the presence of the tremendous crows.

Black crows and a single white crow.

Anxiety gnawed at him. Would it work? If not, then his trio would be more vulnerable than they would have been if he'd stayed where he was. It terrified him to think that in his eagerness to do the right thing for the people he had transformed he might have made a choice that could kill them.

For the second time tonight, Sanchez and everyone else in the camp heard the crows and scrambled onto the top of their trailers and trucks, heads thrown back, faces turned toward the sky. But this time, the birds weren't over Cedar Key. They swept in a massive wave across the starlit sky and looked to be headed somewhere out into the gulf. Zee swore they were headed south to Sea Horse, but Sanchez didn't know the area well enough to agree or disagree.

At one point, he and Jessie wandered away from the crowd and walked down to the finger of land that jutted into the water. Cemetery Point. Fog blanketed everything beyond it, and even from where he stood, he could hear the lascivious voices—*find the body, fuel the body . . .* He slipped his BlackBerry from his jacket pocket, turned it on, and found three text messages from his sister.

WTF?

Call me!

I called Delaney's boss, he put me in touch with some fed named O'Donnell, nasty SOB who refused to answer my questions. I'm contacting a reporter at the Miami Herald *and telling him there's a story for him on CK. Let the* Herald *blow this one wide open,* hermano.

"Shit," Sanchez murmured, and quickly punched out Nicole's number. To his relief, the call went through and she answered on the first ring.

"Jesus, Nick. I thought you might be dead."

"The cell signal is erratic. Put your reporter friend on alert, but he shouldn't come anywhere near here. I'll send you videos when I can." Then he gave her a thirty-second summary of what was going on.

"Giant *crows,* hungry ghosts, possession? You realize how insane this sounds, Nick?"

"Yeah. And every word of it is true. I'll be in touch, Nicole."

"Nick, wait. Dad was asking about you. What should I tell him?"

"The truth, just as I told it to you."

As soon as he disconnected, he tried Delaney's number for the umpteenth time. It rang and rang until he reached voice mail. At the tone, he left a message. "Where the hell are you, Bob? We're pretty much trapped in the cemetery, surrounded by this fog shit. Call. Text me. Something. Either phone, both are on."

Sanchez tried O'Donnell next, using the fed cell phone. To his utter shock, the call went through and O'Donnell answered on the second ring, his voice angry. "Nick? If Bob Delaney is there with you, I'd appreciate it if you put him on."

"He's not with me. I've been trying to get in touch with him. I could use some help here, Tom. The—"

"*Help?* You fucking went rogue on us, Sanchez, and I intend to get your ass fired."

If he had been threatened like this two weeks ago, he would have panicked. Now it barely made an impression.

O'Donnell rushed on. "And Delaney's job is on the line, too, and we're going to file criminal charges against him. You know what that SOB did? He busted out that waitress who started the fire at the café."

Kate, the blonde. Sanchez suddenly felt certain she was the woman Delaney had told him about when they'd last seen each other at the park, the day he'd gone rogue.

"Kate Davis violated the quarantine and we brought her in. Thanks to that video you sent from the café and our security video, she couldn't deny she'd set the fire. So she gave us some cockamamie story about evil ghosts possessing people on Cedar Key and how they're terrified of fire and—"

"The story's true, O'Donnell."

O'Donnell exploded with laughter. "For Chrissake, you sound just as nuts as she did."

"Old saying, Tom. You hear the same bullshit, wacko story from at least two sources, then maybe it's not bullshit or wacko. If you don't wrap your head around *that* truth very soon, you're going to be fucked along with the rest of us."

"Whatever weird kinda shit is going down on that island is about to stop, Sanchez."

"You can't stop them, Tom."

His guffaw this time sounded close to hysteria. "Just watch us."

With that, he disconnected. Sanchez stood there, replaying the conversation in his head, hoping it didn't mean what he thought it did: an attack by air, hazmat units sent in, calling in the National Guard, the military, no telling how over the top O'Donnell might go.

"Nick?" Zee came up behind him. "You look thoughtful, son."

"We're the proverbial sitting ducks here, Zee. The cemetery is a haven for us right now, but it's also a trap. The fog's got us boxed in all the way around. We need to create some chaos to distract that shit, then see if some of us can get out by water and make it into town. The Island Hotel is their headquarters. If we burn that sucker to the ground, it would be a good start."

"We've probably got more artillery than some third-world countries. We're now nearly forty strong. If we're smart, we can do this even though they number in the hundreds."

"It might be a slaughter, Zee."

"Might be. Unless we take out the redhead. If we do that, the entire tribe goes down. The tribe gloms around her."

All the sound suddenly drained from Sanchez's head. *Take out the leader. Take out Maddie.* He realized Zee wasn't just tossing out ideas. He had thought about this, discussed it with people in his group, believed it was possible. Sanchez pushed to his feet. "No. That's not an option. Not for me."

"Now just a goddamn minute, boy." Zee stood, one hand gripping the strap of his AK-47, the fingers of his other hand sliding through his thinning hair. "You don't go giving me orders. The—"

"I'm not *giving you* orders, Zee. I'm telling you what *I won't do.*"

"Sweet Jesus," Zee breathed. "You're in love with this woman. You . . ." His free hand moved randomly through the air, as if seeking a phrase or concept to which he could anchor himself. "You've connected with this woman through your telepathic stuff and fallen for a *fucking illusion.*"

Sanchez grabbed Zee by the arms and immediately wished that he hadn't. *Stuff* poured into him, the detritus of Zee's family drama with his son and daughter-in-law, his anxiety about his group of misfits, about the end-time, about his beloved island being invaded and possessed by the dead. And then he saw Zee's endgame, a bullet slamming into Maddie's forehead, right smack between her eyes, a shot that blew out the back of her head and instantly annihilated Dominica, who wouldn't be able to escape Maddie's body before she died.

"You miserable old fuck," Sanchez hissed, and gripped his arms more tightly. "No one's killing her—not you, not these goddamn mutant ghosts."

Zee jerked his arms free and shoved Sanchez away from him. Jessie, who had never even growled or barked at anyone, abruptly snarled and leaped at the old man, struck him in the chest, and Zee lurched back, tripped over something, and crashed to the ground, the retriever's paws still glued to his chest.

He struggled to push her off, but couldn't. "Get your dog off me, Nick, or I'll shoot her head off."

Sanchez grabbed hold of Jessie's collar, pulled her off Zee. "It's okay," he said softly. "I'm okay, back off, Jess, back off."

He dropped to his knees beside her and wrapped one arm around her neck and trailed the fingers of his other hand through her still-raised fur. She finally relaxed enough to whimper and lick his face. She backed away from the old man and sat against Sanchez's legs.

"I saved your goddamn life, son," Zee spat as he pushed to his feet.

"And I'm grateful. But if you threaten my dog again, Zee, I'll wring your scrawny neck. And if you even entertain the idea of shooting Maddie, I'll shoot you first. I'll deal with the Maddie situation on my own."

Zee flung his arm out toward the fog, the water. "Yeah, go right ahead. And we'll find your sorry ass bled out on a road or in a boat somewhere."

Sanchez whistled for his dog, and they moved quickly away from Zee, from the camp, out to the very tip of Cemetery Point. He stood there, staring at nothing, the cold water lapping at the toes of his shoes. The old man's words echoed in his skull. *You're in love with this woman.* Was he? But how? They had enjoyed a single kiss in a salt marsh. They had—

You followed her here.

Yes, he had. And he'd gone rogue to do it.

Either the old man is right or he isn't. Which is it?

Sanchez rubbed his hands over his face, then his arms dropped to his sides and he just stood there, feeling miserable and alone as the fog offshore swayed and swelled and laughed at him.

Seventeen

Shortly after the gigantic crows had appeared—then disappeared—Dominica urged Maddie up Second Street, toward the hotel. Whit, still in Sam Dorset's body, was with her, holding her hand. Maddie knew what the bitch had in mind. The attic. She and Whit intended to put Maddie and Sam in the deep sleep so they could tend to *brujo* business. Only horror awaited her in that attic—ten to twelve hours or more in a comatose state, her bladder filling, her body becoming dehydrated, her essence suspended in some dreamless place without light or color.

"She's resisting," Dominica was saying to Whit.

"So is Sam."

"Should we provide them with an impetus to move more quickly?"

"That sounds like fun," Whit said.

Dominica began to bring on the pain, doing so with such dark glee that Maddie refused to stumble, to scream, to fall. Then Joe and Jill raced across the street toward them, Joe shouting and waving his arms. "Nica, Whit, the feds have entered the quarantine area."

The pain abruptly stopped and Maddie went still inside. She immediately felt the *brujo* net tremble and shake with the news.

"Where are they?" Dominica snapped.

"Headed in on 24," Jill replied, her eyes shiny and bright with excitement. "A pair of Hummers."

"How many inside?" Whit asked.

"Eight, maybe ten," Joe replied. "Hard to tell. The windows are darkly tinted."

"Very nice." Dominica's voice—Maddie's own—sounded silken, seductive. Then she raised her arms, conjuring the fog, and sent out a call to all *brujos* without hosts. *We now get even for the way the hangings were disrupted.*

The fog rolled in swiftly and filled rapidly with the voices of the dead. *Find the body, fuel the body . . .*

Dread poured through Maddie—and Dominica felt it and laughed. "Oh, Maddie, Maddie," she cooed. "Now you'll see what fun we hungry ghosts have. Let's move off to the side and let the tribe go wild."

The four of them stepped back into the shadows, beneath the awning of a consignment shop. The fog swelled and thickened until it filled the entire road. It swirled up over the curb and climbed their legs, spiraling like vines. Its cold dampness seeped through Maddie's skin, into her ankles, shins, knees, and encircled her waist and breasts like the arms of a lover. She instantly recoiled and struggled not to fight it, not to resist, to just let it be. *Know your enemy.*

A strange silence gripped the air. Then the growl of engines punctured it and, moments later, the Hummers' headlights illuminated the fog, so that the stuff looked as if it were lit from within. Joe snickered and rubbed his hands together, Jill giggled nervously, Whit slung his arm around Dominica's shoulders. Maddie hated the weight of his arm, the way his fingers trailed through her hair, but she didn't fight it, didn't move.

The Hummers moved up the street like lethargic monsters. In the backwash of the headlights, she could see four or five silhouettes inside the lead vehicle. *Don't come any closer,* she thought. *Turn around, flee.* But the Hummers kept coming, the litany of the hungry ghosts a chorus the people inside the vehicles probably couldn't hear.

Then the lead Hummer stopped and the second Hummer pulled alongside it. The fog swayed and billowed with anticipation, waiting for the word from Dominica that the *brujos* within could attack, seize, do whatever they wanted. The driver and passenger doors opened on both Hummers and men in hazmat suits emerged, armed to the hilt with assault rifles—and flamethrowers.

Most of the *brujos* within the fog understood what flamethrowers were and the fog now retreated slightly, the net humming with their collective alarm. *They don't understand what the fog is,* Dominica told them. *Seize them.*

But the fog retreated even farther, pulling away from the vehicles, the armed men. Maddie sensed Dominica's anger and confusion that the *brujos* weren't doing what she commanded them to do. Her arms flew up, a dramatic flourish, and she shouted through the *brujo* net, *Seize them now.*

Dominica was so focused on communicating with her tribe that her control over Maddie loosened and Maddie lurched forward, waving her arms, and screamed, "Get out of here now, fast, they're going to seize you, bleed you out, go, go . . ."

Two of the men in hazmat suits dived back into the Hummer closest to her. The others just stood there staring at her, a wild woman racing into the street, shrieking. One of the Hummers lurched forward and a man's voice boomed over the PA, *"Get the fuck inside, this is a suicide mission."*

Three men spun around and ran toward the Hummers, their gaits awkward because of their suits, but the rest of them advanced through the street, toward her, their flamethrowers and weapons trained on her. She felt as if she had stumbled onto a sci-fi movie set, where the guys in the suits breathed like Darth Vader, great labored breaths amplified in some way by her terror.

Then someone struck her from behind—Whit, it was Whit, she could smell his sweat, the odor of his excitement—and she pitched forward and struck the ground. Dominica seized control of her again and leaped up and she and Whit raced for the alley. A moment later, gunfire chattered across the road where Maddie had been sprawled, the cloth awnings over two shops burst into flame, and Dominica shouted, *"Take them, take all of them, show them our power."*

Those words, *show them our power*, were exactly what the *brujos* needed to hear. The fog rolled over the men, swallowing them completely, and in the glow of the headlights Maddie saw them stumbling around, tearing at their suits, ripping off their helmets. They howled with agony and fell to the road, twitching, jerking, bleeding out. Maddie's horror escalated, but Dominica controlled her so completely that when Dominica moved her forward, she couldn't stop it, her legs obeyed.

She stopped by one of the fallen men, swept his weapon off the ground and aimed it at him as he writhed on the ground. *Shoot him,* Dominica commanded. But Maddie's finger refused to pull back on the trigger. It seemed to be the only part of her body *she controlled.*

"*Shoot him,*" Dominica screamed out loud.

Maddie's finger twitched, but didn't pull back.

Whit grabbed the gun out of her hands and shot the man repeatedly, then marched up through the road, firing at the men on the ground, riddling their bodies with bullets. Maddie just stood there, tears coursing down her cheeks, tears that belonged to *her*, tears that spilled even when Dominica yelled, "Whit, the Hummer!"

He spun and fired repeatedly at the Hummer that shot toward him. Bullets pinged and ricocheted off the grill, the windshield, but the monster kept racing toward him, and Maddie thought, *Yes, yes, hit him, hit the fucker, please,* and immediately felt guilty because it meant the Hummer would hit Sam Dorset, poor Sam, as trapped in his body as she was in hers.

Whit leaped out of the way and the Hummer sped past him. He fired again and one of its tires blew and the vehicle swerved erratically across the road, back and forth, back and forth, then spun around the corner, onto State Road 24, the fog pursuing it.

The second Hummer, with just one man inside, sped away. Maddie's knees buckled—buckled in spite of Dominica's control, buckled from exhaustion, despair, ruin. Dominica triggered Maddie's pain centers, kept trying to jerk her to her feet, pull her up, get her moving. But nothing worked. Her body simply shut down.

She was barely conscious when Whit and Joe lifted her up, supporting her on either side, and headed toward the hotel. And the deep sleep. Dominica continued to use her vocal cords, her mouth, barking instructions about moving the bodies to the hotel's kitchen freezer, where the mayor and a few others still lay in icy repose.

Then Maddie blacked out.

*   *   *

Wayra made it to a spit of beach near Goose Cove. Behind the sand loomed a thicket of pines, barely visible in the darkness, but he could smell them. No fog, the crows had gone silent—or left. He turned off the engine, pressed the button that lifted it from the water, and allowed the tide to move the boat forward until it struck the sand. It would be light soon. He wanted to get Rocky, Kate, and Delaney into the trees before the sun came up.

It suddenly occurred to him that moving Delaney was going to be a major problem. How had that fact escaped him? Pulling Delaney into the houseboat from the deck was one thing. But to move him from the houseboat to the trees would require picking him up, and Wayra knew he couldn't lift the man by himself. Would it be enough to just move him to the back deck? He would be surrounded by the wilderness of the island, the nearby trees, and his senses would be sharp enough to detect whatever wild scents he needed to become fully integrated into his new form. It might work. He decided to move all three to the deck. Then the first three shifters in nearly a thousand years would awaken together.

Wayra anchored and returned to the main cabin and picked up Rocky. His transformation was nearly complete. Some of his fur was starting to appear, a shiny blond and black mixture that swirled into a distinct pattern, like soft ice cream in a cone. His ears were coming in, his snout was almost fully formed. Wayra carried him to the deck and set him down. The hawk flew down to the railing and landed close to Rocky.

He sensed she'd returned because the crows had left.

He went back inside to get Kate. Some of her fur was visible now, too, black marble striated with various shades of brown. It was still too early to tell what her form would be, but at least she and Rocky would awaken together. As he slid his hands beneath her, she made a strange, gurgling noise in her throat, her eyes flew open, and promptly rolled back in their sockets until only the whites showed. She passed out again. Was it pain or just part of the process?

The only thing he remembered of his own transformation was that the initial agony had plunged him into a comatose state. When he'd come out of it, he was alone, terrified. He had wandered for days, struggling to understand new sensations, thoughts, and memories that rushed through him. His shifters wouldn't have to endure such a thing. They would have each other and he wouldn't abandon them as his creator had done.

He returned to the cabin for Delaney, took hold of his forearms, dragged him out onto the deck, and left him alongside Kate. He stared at them, this new generation of shifters, and felt a strange kind of pride. By the time their transformation was complete, they would know most of what he knew—about the history of Esperanza, shifters, chasers, *brujos*. They would know that the first shifter back at the edge of time had been a mutant, the product of genetic experimentations on the continent of Lemuria, the equivalent of the biblical Adam whose Eve had been normal, ordinary. They would understand that the longevity of their race enabled them to move back and forth in time, but it would take training to teach them how to master that kind of travel.

He felt like a proud father. Except for Kate. It disturbed him to look at her, to think of what he'd done. He crouched beside her and brushed strands of her blond hair away from her changing forehead. "Forgive me," he whispered.

She stirred, as if she'd heard him, but didn't wake up.

Wayra went back inside the cabin to get the other two torches. He planned to secure them at either end of the deck and to replenish his spent torch and place it at the front of the deck. He hoped that just the threat of fire would keep these hungry ghosts at a distance so that he could grab a few hours of sleep.

In the kitchen, he replenished his spent torch with dish towels and Delaney's bloody shirt. He doused all three torches with fresh gasoline, so that just the flame of a match would ignite them and create a formidable weapon against any *brujo*, of any age. He opened the fridge, looking for bottled water that his trio would need as soon as they awakened.

The hawk started screaming.

He dropped everything he held and raced out onto the deck. Liberty flew frantically from one end of the porch to the other, diving at small fog clusters on either side of the deck, trying to drive them back. But the fog moved persistently toward the hybrid humans, *his new shifters*.

Unarmed, Wayra moved toward the cluster of fog on the right and took it into himself, sucked it right into his mouth, down his throat, into his lungs. It was like inhaling a personal history, except that it burned and then became an agonizing pulse in the center of his chest. He pounded his chest with his fist, struggling to drive the pain back. He moved quickly to the other side of the deck and sucked in this fog, too, down into his cells and blood, down into the very marrow of his bones, and began to shift.

Within the fog he swallowed, some of the *brujos* fled. Others were too stupid, young, or naïve to flee—and they were obliterated, crushed by Wayra's transformation from human to other. But suddenly he couldn't breathe. Something monstrously huge and hard, like chunks of stone, blocked his air passages. He started choking, the world tilted to the right, the left, his peripheral vision went dark. He stumbled forward, fists pounding his chest, trying to dislodge whatever it was. Blackness swam across his vision, his knees gave way. He was unconscious before he hit the deck.

Maddie came to in the attic.

A dim light was on and it didn't illuminate the dust, the grime on the tiny rectangular window, the scuff marks on the filthy wooden floor, the ceiling and walls with their peeling paint. She had spent untold hours in here, restrained on the cot, where the air stank of endings, terror, urine, despair. In here, her life was truly on hold, her consciousness imprisoned. But now there were two other cots in the attic, bolted to the floor as hers was, as though hosts were psychotics who had to be strapped in and shut up.

Whit, in Sam's body, was in here, too. Dominica had convinced herself that she loved Whit as she once had loved Wayra, a mythic love that transcended life and death, time and space. Never mind that it was total bullshit, that Dominica's feelings toward Wayra had been precipitated by the ways in which he was different from her, as though he were a kind of trophy.

Look at me, look at this shapeshifter who loves me, it means I'm special, has a shifter ever loved you? Her feelings for Whit were merely convenience. He was here, available, and he was nuts about her. Whit, who was now touching Maddie's body, whispering sweet nothings to Dominica, who fell for it.

If Dominica won, Maddie shuddered to think how things might evolve. At the nightmare end of the spectrum, hosts might eventually unionize, demand rights, sit at the bargaining table with *brujo* reps. They might hammer out agreements on how long a *brujo* could occupy a host, the health benefits for a host, the parameters of what a *brujo* could force a human to do. Aside from the obvious problems with this horror, *brujos* lied. They lied for all the same reasons that the living lied—to save their own asses, to make themselves look better, to escape punishment. Forget unions and compromise. Once you compromised with a *brujo,* you pretty much sold your soul.

"It'll be light soon," Whit said. "Our calling card should be delivered shortly."

"Good. We'll follow them, make sure they do it correctly."

When Whit wrapped his arms around Dominica, Maddie didn't resist, didn't shriek, didn't try to seize control of her body. She simply didn't have the energy. Even if she'd been able to fight, it wasn't worth it, not when she was this close to being put into a deep sleep from which she might escape. If anything, Sam Dorset's fondling and kisses and Dominica's soft moans of pleasure only fueled Maddie's rage. Then Dominica uttered words she'd stolen from Gypsy Woman's blog and Maddie felt like vomiting. "All that's within my heart, I say to you each time I look into your eyes."

With that, Whit fell onto her, and they groped at each other's clothes and bodies and Maddie's rage collapsed into terror as she realized that what she'd thought would be a few fondles and kisses was about to become full-blown sex. She *reached* for Sanchez, reached and reached, but nothing happened. She tried to vault out of her body, but couldn't do it. Panicked, she struggled to recall how she'd fled her body before, how her consciousness had broken free of her physical self and soared. *Up and out, up and out, up and out, c'mon, please . . .*

She couldn't do it. But she suddenly felt Sam's essence, his consciousness, fighting Whit. Maddie reached out to him. *Sam, it's Maddie. Don't fight him. Cling to your rage when he starts putting you into the deep sleep. It'll keep you conscious. Maybe we have a shot at escaping.*

Maddie? Christ, I can hear you, I . . . I'm so sorry, I . . . knew what he hoped to do and I . . . I just don't have the strength to fight him, he inflicts too much pain . . .

Just endure it. They're going to plunge us into the deep sleep, Sam, and if you can cling to your awareness, we can get out of here.

I'll try. I'm so sorry this is happening to you, I'm so incredibly sorry for what I . . . tried to do to Kate and now . . . now to you, but it's not me, Maddie, it's not me . . .

I know, Sam. I know. I've lived with this abomination inside me for months.

They can't hear us, can they?

Not right this second. But as soon as they're done with us, they'll be more aware. Just do what I'm telling you, Sam. Anger, rage, your passionate desire to be free . . . it'll trigger chemical reactions in your brain that will help you remain conscious. Just pretend that you're sleeping.

I—

He stopped abruptly and in the ensuing silence, Maddie felt everything she didn't want to feel—Sam pumping away inside her, Whit using Sam's voice to groan like a pig, her own voice crying out. She desperately wanted to tear apart the pleasure Dominica enjoyed with *her* body. But her exhaustion drove her, instead, into her virtual cave.

She put on a Led Zeppelin album and cranked the volume up as high as it would go. The music pounded and throbbed against the walls of her consciousness and Dominica bolted away from Sam and slapped her hands over her ears.

"Jesus, she's playing Led Zeppelin so loud I can feel it in my teeth."

"Ignore her," Whit said, reaching for her again, nuzzling her neck.

"It's impossible to ignore her. We should get moving, Whit."

"I know. It's just nice being with you like this, Nica. And neither of our hosts resisted too much until now. Maybe they're adapting to the rules."

"They might as well. It'll make life easier for all of us."

"Listen, once we've got the entire island and all those assholes in the government, let's move in together."

Oh, sure, by all means, Maddie thought. *Move in together, kill each other.*

One final embrace, then they got up, dressed, and Whit went over to one of the cots and stretched out. Dominica stretched out on the cot again. "See you soon, Whit. Be sure to put Sam in very deep. It may be hours before we return."

Dominica began to fiddle with Maddie's brain and blood chemistry and she steeled herself against it, conjuring every terrible thing the bitch had done to her all these months—sex without her consent, unbearable pain, the horror of being a prisoner within her body, the endless hours strapped to this miserable cot, so deep within the Snow White sleep that she didn't even dream. And that was just for starters.

As Dominica flooded her body with endorphins, raised her sugar levels, slowed her heartbeat, Maddie's fury escalated into a murderous wrath that she held tightly within. Even so, she could feel her body shutting down, surrendering, losing the battle.

She grasped onto those moments in the salt marsh when Sanchez had held her, kissed her, when her lungs had breathed only for herself, when her heart had beat only for herself. She clung to those moments outside the Island Market, when she had been free. She took those sensations and emotions with her as she fell into the abyss of darkness.

The Final Days
March 21–22

· · · · · · ·

It turns out that an eerie type of chaos can lurk just behind a façade of order—and yet, deep inside the chaos lurks an even eerier type of order.

—Douglas Hofstadter

Eighteen

The sun peeked up over the horizon and showered the bank of fog in a reddish light that made it look as if it were bleeding. The sight unsettled Sanchez. Even worse, though, was how the first light allowed him to grasp just how huge the fog was. It seemed to stretch at least half a mile on either side of the cemetery. Although it still hadn't entered the cemetery, Sanchez felt it was just a matter of time and was likely to happen sooner rather than later.

In just the last few hours, the fog had grown bolder and now covered Cemetery Point. Technically, the point wasn't part of the actual graveyard, where the headstones and mausoleums were, and so far, the fog hadn't ventured into that area. Zee had ordered everyone to move themselves and their vehicles into the graveyard and had set up a fully armed perimeter security. They hid in trucks, in trees, on top of the trailers, and crouched behind the outermost gravestones. Zee's private army. Even Sanchez had been drafted.

He and Jessie huddled in a cart not far from the gate, the AK-47 between them, a carton of grenades on the floor in front of the passenger seat. Zee still had it in his head that his army could defend their territory—the cemetery—against these *brujos*. He had lost sight of the fact—or perhaps never recognized it as strongly as Sanchez—that they were prisoners here. The *brujos* had them right where they wanted them, where they could seize them in one fell swoop.

Even when Sanchez tried to interpret these events as he might a dream, he reached the same conclusion: Armageddon was just around the bend. It wasn't the end-time Zee and his group foresaw, but could very well be their personal end-time.

Sanchez suddenly heard multiple vehicles racing up Gulf Boulevard. Holdouts? Probably not. The fog was so pervasive you couldn't outrun it.

He started the cart and moved closer to the gate. A vehicle appeared in the fog, a dark shape, maybe a truck or jeep, moving fast.

As it approached the gate, he saw it was a large dump truck. No one opened fire on it. Their orders were to shoot only if threatened—in other words, if a vehicle barreled through the cemetery fence or gate or the fog crossed into the graveyard. The dump truck didn't slow, didn't stop, just kept on going, but something was rolled out the back of it. The fog instantly covered whatever it was, as if the *brujos* within had to sniff or taste or claim it. Then the fog rolled swiftly away from it, retreating all the way across the street, into the trees on the other side.

"What the hell." Sanchez leaped out with his weapon and ran over to the gate.

In the middle of the road lay two bodies, their legs tangled in the sheets. A man and a woman. She was sprawled on her stomach, the man lay on his back. Blood saturated their clothes, clumped like the dregs of sleep in the corners of the man's eyes and dried under his nose, on his lips, beneath his ears. They had both bled out. Despite the blood, Sanchez recognized Fritz, Zee's son, and knew the woman was Fritz's wife, Diane.

He told Jessie to stay, whistled shrilly to warn the others, and unlatched the gate. Sanchez walked quickly out into the road, his heart drumming, his hands frozen on the assault rifle. Forget interpreting any of this as a dream; the whole thing had collapsed into nightmare country.

He trained his weapon on the fog on the other side of the road, some of it visible through the trees. He couldn't hear the *brujo* litany, but sensed the ghosts within the fog chattering among themselves. They didn't number in the hundreds. Dozens, perhaps, but not hundreds. A positive sign, he thought, unless this group was just a scouting party. He felt these ghosts were at the lower end of the hierarchy in the *brujo* army, the ones who were still confused by the fact that they were dead but conscious. Some of them had seized locals early on, locals who had known Fritz, fished with him, gone boating with him, done business with him over the years. And the memories of those hosts remained vivid in their collective consciousness. They understood that Fritz's death meant Zee and his little army would attack and perhaps they weren't too keen on fighting this battle.

Sanchez stopped beside the bodies. He didn't want to touch them but couldn't stand the sight of their open eyes. He knelt and shut Diane's eyes first and immediately saw how she and Fritz had died, cannibalized by *brujos* within a fog, bled from the inside out. He also saw the larger picture, the cheering audience, Dominica's tribe in their host bodies and in their natural forms, the despicable mutant ghosts.

He couldn't bring himself to touch Fritz's eyes. He didn't want any more details of their deaths. But the highways of blood that crisscrossed his eyeballs compelled him to close Fritz's eyes, and as he did so, he saw that Dominica had intended to hang the two, but that something had interfered. So she had instructed the fog to attack. The images Sanchez saw of the attack were so hideous and brutal that they continued even when he was no longer touching Fritz, as though they were permanently etched into his brain cells, his DNA. He felt what Fritz had felt in his final moments, the agonizing explosion of capillaries, veins, arteries, organs, a body turned against itself, an immune system that hadn't just failed, but had collapsed completely.

He suddenly heard, *There's something older than the chasers and ultimately it will save you.*

The images dried up and by then Sanchez was doubled over gasping for breath. His mother materialized beside him and gripped the back of his neck tightly; he could feel the pressure, the warmth of her hand, just like the hand of a living person. Her breath brushed his cheek and he caught the fragrance of her skin, her hair, all of it intensely *real, there, present.* Had she spoken to him about something older than the chasers? Or was it something he'd picked up from Fritz?

"Get up, Nick," his mother whispered. "Fast. Don't let them think you're weak."

His head ached and throbbed, his vision blurred, he felt like he might puke, he didn't want to move. But he didn't intend to get seized, so he stumbled to his feet, swept up his weapon, aimed it at the fog. A cart filled with men from Zee's camp drew alongside him, and the driver hissed, "Get the bodies loaded fast."

As half a dozen men hopped out of the cart, Sanchez moved in front of it, aware that his mother remained nearby but was no longer visible. He eyed the fog on the other side of the road. "Stay the fuck back." He spoke sharply but quietly. "We don't intend you harm. We only want to bury our dead."

The chatter got louder, pulsing and thumping against his temples. The fog crept out from the shadows of the trees, eddying, swaying, but didn't move any closer to him, the cart, or the bodies. Jessie howled and raced back and forth along the inside of the fence. Sanchez kept his weapon trained on the center of the fog until the cart whispered toward the cemetery, the bodies of Zee's son and daughter-in-law on board. Then he backed away, slowly, his stomach knotted, his trigger finger aching.

Just before he reached the gate, the fog sprang across the road like some wild, hungry beast, moving so swiftly that thick, long tongues of the stuff wrapped around his knees. An arctic cold bit through his jeans and pierced skin, muscles, bone. His knee joints felt as if they were ripped apart and tossed into a shredder. His legs collapsed beneath him. He slammed against the dirt road, lost his grip on the rifle, and it clattered just out of his reach.

Sanchez rolled, struggled to vault to his feet, to run, but the fog formed a cold cocoon around his chest, thighs, and ankles that prevented him from getting up. His mother shouted, her voice needle sharp. But even as she shouted and he struggled to hear her exact words and to break the hold of the fog, something entered his body through his skull. He felt the *invasion,* the *violation,* the utter and complete *desecration* of his mind, body, soul. His mother's voice faded away.

He didn't know how long this hungry ghost was inside of him; it felt like lifetimes. He realized this was Dominica, the *bruja* who had held Maddie captive for so many months, and she tasted him, read him, sipped from his being as though he were a cup of hot, milky chocolate. His RV experience, his ability to read whatever touched him, leaped to his defense. He tasted *her,* read *her,* plundered, and plunged into her deepest memories. But he swam through madness. Most of her memories weren't linear, weren't connected to anything else. They existed as isolated islands of pleasure or despair, of hope or hopelessness, sweeping contrasts. He gleaned what he could and fled the weight and confusion and lunacy of her memories.

As she tried to accommodate herself to his body, it triggered something in his immune system that made it easier for her to adjust to physical life. *The virus.* This was the virus that O'Donnell and the CDC and FEMA and all the other government agencies believed was a biological weapon.

Sanchez started laughing. He couldn't help it. The real terrorists weren't amorphous enemies in the Mideast, they were the dead, the ancient dead, like this *bruja* whose existence dated back so many centuries he couldn't count them all. The harder he laughed, the more difficult it was for her to seize control of his brain, his organs, and especially his lungs and heart.

Breathe for me, she whispered, her voice strangely seductive. *Let your heart beat for me.*

Keep laughing, Nick, his mother shouted at him. *Keep laughing.*

Who's this bitch? Dominica demanded. *Your mother? Your alcoholic mother is giving you advice?*

Even though his body was paralyzed, he continued to laugh, tears coursing down his cheeks, and Dominica's soft, slippery voice moved around inside him. *So you're the man Maddie thinks she loves, Sanchez? What a worthless piece of shit you are, you and your empty life, your alcoholic mother, your temperamental father, your sister with all her intellectual pretensions. But you would make a great host for Whit, so we haven't seen the last of each other, you and I.*

Zee's people opened fire on the fog then and Dominica leaped out of him, the fog withdrew, his mother was gone, and the rising sun burned against his back. He pushed up from the dirt and lurched back through the cemetery gate, his monstrous thirst like that of someone who had wandered through a desert for days, sucking at every oasis the mind fabricated. When the gate clattered shut behind him, he collapsed against the ground, his dog whining and dancing around him, licking his face, leaping at him.

Someone clasped his hands and started pulling him across the ground. Sanchez's eyes popped open. Zee Small stood over him, tears of grief for his dead son and daughter-in-law brimming in his rheumy eyes. He picked up Sanchez, carried him to a cart, set him gently in the back. "You are one weird fucker, son. But we protect our own and I'm mighty relieved we don't have to bury you, too."

Sanchez desperately needed to speak, to tell Zee what had happened, what he'd experienced, to tell him he knew what could conquer these ghosts, that it might be as simple as laughter. But a strange inertia claimed him. His last thought before he drifted away was, *Shit, that mutant was inside me.*

Dominica reluctantly withdrew with the fog, then she and Whit drifted free of it and moved upward, over the cemetery. They coasted just above the treetops, where they could see the pandemonium below them—men and women shouting and running around, people carrying the bodies of the dead into the largest trailer, two men carrying an unconscious Sanchez into another trailer, the guards mobilizing around the cemetery. They scurried like ants whose nest had been penetrated.

She wanted Sanchez, wanted him as a host for Whit. How perfect would that be? The two of them in the fine bodies of Sanchez and Maddie.

They're terrified of us, Whit. Let's drift down and terrorize them some more.

No, thanks. I don't do cemeteries.

C'mon, Whit. Don't tell me you're like all the others in the tribe. What's there to be afraid of?

I'm not afraid, okay? I just don't like cemeteries.

Bullshit. You're afraid! But why? You're dead. Nothing can hurt you.

I'm NOT dead. I'm conscious, I can think and plan, I have desires, I laugh, I feel.

She had heard this argument countless times throughout her existence and it still amazed her that any ghost could actually believe it. *I have news for you, Whit. Only the dead need hosts. Without a host, none of the physical pleasures are available to you. You can't touch or be touched. You can't taste food or smell or see and your hearing is truncated. Consciousness uses your memories to fill in the gaps, that's all this is. And sooner or later, if we're going to round up the people in this camp, we're going to have to go into that cemetery and attack them.*

If you're so goddamn brave, let's see you go down there, Nica.

With pleasure.

She immediately regretted her bravado. But now that she'd made such a big deal out of this, she couldn't back out. She'd hoped that Whit would descend with her, that they could give each other strength and perhaps overcome their mutual aversion to cemeteries. She should have sweet-talked him, approached it more gently, cajoled him. But the nuances of relationships had always escaped her.

Dominica disengaged from the *brujo* net and slowly drifted down through one of the trees, through branches and leaves. Waves of revulsion swept through her. During her last physical lifetime in Spain, she had been buried after her death, and her consciousness had awakened inside the coffin as dirt was being tossed onto it. She hadn't understood what had happened, thought she'd been buried alive, and had screamed and screamed. She had even dived back into her lifeless body and struggled to animate it. When that hadn't worked, she had tried to shoot through the coffin's lid, but couldn't. So she had drifted inside that tight, black space, alternately screaming and sobbing and listening to the *thump thump thump* of dirt hitting the lid.

When her horror and panic had grown too great for her to sustain her awareness, she had passed out. A long time later, her consciousness had become aware again and she understood that her body had died but her consciousness lived on. With that understanding, she was able to leave the coffin. She had shot out through the lid, up through the ton of dirt, and into the world again. Wayra had been waiting for her.

For centuries, she'd believed her aversion to cemeteries was unique to her. But once she had commanded her tribe in Esperanza, she understood that every ghost held this loathing for cemeteries. It was simply a part of what ghosts were. She had conquered her fear of fire long enough to help extinguish the blaze at Annie's Café, so she could conquer this loathing, too.

Determined, she drifted about halfway down the trunk of the tree and then just couldn't go any farther. It was as if she had descended miles beneath the ocean floor and the pressure felt as if she might implode. She shot upward again, back through the branches, the leaves, and hoped that Whit hadn't been able to see her, that he would believe she'd made it to the ground.

He was waiting for her, and she felt his awe and astonishment. *Nica. You did it. Was it . . . awful?*

Worse than you can imagine. That much, at least, wasn't a lie.

I . . . I just don't think I can do it.

We can both do it without any problem if we're in our host bodies.

What about the others who don't have hosts? Will they be able to travel within that fog and enter here?

I think so. There's strength in numbers.

If you're strong, the tribe will be, too.

After you were put to death, Whit, what happened to your body? Was it buried or cremated?

Jesus, what kind of question is that?

I'm just curious. I was buried and became conscious in the coffin. She told him the rest of it, except for the part about Wayra. *That's where my loathing for these places started.*

Silence, then: *I was burned. I . . . saw it happening, saw my body inside the crematorium. I thought I was still alive. I mean, I could think and feel . . . I—* His voice broke off.

Then you have nothing to fear here. Will you try it with me, Whit?

He hesitated. *If our essences are merged and if we're away from the graves and mausoleums, then I can at least try it, Nica.*

She moved her essence toward his and they merged. The intimacy lacked that of physical lovemaking, but was the closest thing a *brujo* in its natural form could experience to intimacy, comfort, and communion. She immediately felt his anxiety and knew he felt hers as well. But she hid the truth about what had happened when she'd tried it alone. She, after all, was the leader of this tribe and was expected to accomplish and achieve things the others could not, acts of heroism to which they might aspire. If he realized she was as cowardly as they were, she would lose the tribe.

They drifted together toward Cemetery Point, where the land jutted out into the water, the salt marsh. Tendrils of fog eddied and swayed across the rocks. She braced herself for that terrible internal pressure; he nearly separated from her and shot for the sky. But he didn't. And the internal pressure didn't materialize. As they touched down, they drifted apart and hovered uneasily just above the rocks, separate beings fighting their separate demons.

Dominica knew this water was a brilliant blue, but her perceptions registered only shades of gray. She knew the air smelled of salt and earth, but she smelled nothing at all. The living could stand on these very rocks, open their mouths, and taste the salt in the air. Although she could hear the cries of the gulls and the shouts from the cemetery, these sounds lacked the rich texture of what the living could hear. In her natural *bruja* form, her perceptions, like her relationships, lacked nuance.

It's not so bad, is it, Whit?

Not right here, on the rocks, where I can see the water and the sky. But if we were over there, where the graves are, and that was all I could see, I don't know if I could do this.

Even if you're smack in the middle of the cemetery, you can always see something else. Trees. Flowers. Grass. Sky. Let's try it.

Whit drifted away from her. *Not right now. I've had enough, Nica. I'm ready to be physical again.*

Do you think you'll have any problem coming in here in your host body? I can do that.

He sounded certain of this. But the proof would be in actually doing it. If Whit was to rule the *brujo* enclave with her, he couldn't be a coward. Well, that wasn't quite right. She was a coward, but could hide the fact. He would have to do that or confront his fears. Either way, he couldn't be seen as compromised, fearful, uncertain of his next step, his next decision. The tribe trusted Whit's host, Sam Dorset, as they once had trusted the mayor. But Whit himself would have to earn their respect and coming into this cemetery would be the first step.

Let's go reclaim our hosts, Whit.

Nineteen

Maddie swam toward consciousness like a salmon struggling upstream. She knew if she didn't reach the surface, everything would be lost, Dominica would win, and she would be trapped forever.

She latched on to her rage and it lifted her.

She grappled for memories of love and surfaced into a subtle awareness that she was in the attic, on a cot, breaking free of the deep sleep.

She remembered the kiss in the salt marsh, Sanchez in all his trusting glory, and snapped forward, gasping for breath. She struggled through the mush in her brain, heard her limbs popping and cracking. But her lungs now breathed only for her, her heart beat only for her. She was free, *free.* Maddie swung her legs over the side of the cot.

For moments, she just sat there, gripping the sides of the cot, her mind assaulted by images of the men in hazmat suits, bleeding out in the middle of downtown, of Sam Dorset controlled by Whit up here in the attic, of— A steel door slammed shut in her head. She couldn't allow the horrors to keep her paralyzed. She curled and uncurled her toes, flexed her fingers and wrists, lifted her arms, moved her legs, sucked air into her lungs. She listened to the deep, steady beat of her heart and nearly wept with joy that her body functioned only for herself.

I'm free free free and so outta here.

Her running shoes stood side by side on the floor, and Maddie quickly put them on. When she stood, her knees felt as if they were filled with water, couldn't sustain her weight, and buckled. She struck the floor and stifled a sob of frustration. *Get up fast, you need to get out of here.* Maddie gripped the edge of the cot, pulled herself to her feet, and weaved over to the other cot where Sam lay in the deep sleep.

"Wake up, Sam, c'mon," she whispered, shaking him by the shoulders.

He muttered and groaned and turned slowly onto his side, as though his mind and body were mired in honey. Maddie forced him to turn onto his back and slapped him across the face. He pushed up onto his elbows, shaking his head like a dog with fleas. His eyes squinted open, his murmurs melted together. Maddie helped him sit up all the way, moved his legs until they hung over the edge of the cot.

"Sam," she whispered urgently. "We're *free*, okay? They're gone and you need to get up and walk so we can get the hell outta here. Do you understand what I'm saying?"

"Y-yes. But—"

"No buts. C'mon, here're your shoes." She slipped on his left loafer, his right. "I'll help you stand. It's not far to the door. It's light outside now, so we're going to have to sneak out through the kitchen and into the alley. And then into some other alley and get as far away from the hotel as possible."

"If they . . . find us . . ."

"They won't find us if you move your goddamn legs. Put your arm around my waist. Okay, good. Left foot, right, you're doing fine, not much farther to the door. We're going to take the back stairs to the kitchen, then go out that rear door that opens to the alley. You with me, Sam?"

"I'm moving, I'm okay, I'm so . . . sorry for what happened, Maddie, for what I did to—"

"It wasn't you, Sam. Forget it. Focus, just focus."

"I feel like shit, I need to take a piss . . ."

"Keep moving." They reached the door. "Just stand right here for a second. I want to check that old bureau. Maybe we stuffed our packs in there before they put us under. Shit, I can't remember." She remembered removing her shoes, keeping her jacket on, but couldn't recall what had happened to her pack. Had Dominica performed a quick memory wipe before she'd plunged Maddie into the deep sleep?

Maddie jerked open the drawers and rifled through old place mats, old clothes, old linens, old dusty *stuff*. No packs, nothing useful, of course not. Dominica had been thorough. She hurried back to Sam, cracked open the door, and they started down the old, sloping stairs.

They reached the second-story landing, but when they heard voices nearby, just up the hall, they ducked into a storage room. Pitch-black. But she'd been in here often enough while working at the hotel to know her way around. Stacked on the shelves were linens, towels, pillows, bedspreads, blankets, and quilts. Two large bins on wheels overflowed with dirty bedding and towels that had been sitting here for weeks.

Maddie patted her way across the wall until she located the handle for the oversized door to the laundry chute. She pulled it open and a thin watery light appeared at the very end of it, in the hotel cellar. Not a cellar, exactly, not like those in Esperanza, more like a postscript. It was below the kitchen, on the ground floor. Maddie knew there was an exit from there into the alley. The chute dropped about twenty-five feet, and the bin beneath it was empty.

She scooped dirty sheets and towels out of the overflowing bins and shoved them down the chute, creating a nest in the bin for her and Sam to land in. But would it be enough to prevent a hard landing that might snap a foot or leg? *Add more, play it safe.*

"Sam, give me a hand here. We're going down the chute but we need more stuff to land on."

He didn't reply.

Maddie glanced around. Just enough light trickled through the chute door and into the storage room for her to see Sam slumped against the wall, hands pressed to the sides of his head, as if he were holding it in place. He gave no indication that he'd heard her. Maddie went over to him, gripped his arms. "Sam. Pay attention. We're going down the chute. From there, we can get out of the hotel and—"

"And to where, Maddie? Don't you fucking *get* it? There's no place to hide from them, no place where we're safe, no—"

"Fine. Then stay here, where they're sure to find you. I'm outta here."

She quickly scooped more laundry from the bin, dropped it down the chute. When the bin below looked satisfyingly full, Maddie swung one leg over the edge, then the other. "Sam?"

"They'll find us," he said.

"They'll find *you,* for sure."

She pushed off and dropped with shocking speed from darkness into a dim light. She landed feet first in a mountain of laundry, sank to her knees, looked around uneasily, making sure she was alone. The light came from a bare bulb hanging from the ceiling on the other side of the room, and between it and her stood three more overflowing bins of laundry. One of them sat beneath the chute from the kitchen like a giant open mouth waiting for leftover food. It held dozens of tablecloths and napkins. Stacked next to a laundry sink on the other side of the room were plates encrusted with old food, stained glasses, used silverware. Some *brujo* either disliked kitchen detail and had decided to get even with his boss or had suffered memory loss about where the kitchen actually was. Regardless, the neglect didn't surprise her.

The sheets on which that Disney World group had slept hadn't been changed since they had departed. These bins had probably been filled since January, Maddie thought. The kitchen upstairs was so filthy a health inspector would puke. But that was the *brujo* way, a disregard for basic cleanliness and hygiene.

As Maddie stood, Sam landed beside her in the nest of sheets and towels.

"You're right." His voice vibrated with tension, fear. "Staying here is certain death."

"They may find us anyway, but at least we'll know we tried."

They scrambled out of the bin and crossed the room to the alley door. Maddie unlocked it, and they peeked out. Brilliant sunlight sliced into her eyes, the chilly air nibbled at her skin. A scrawny cat darted through the light and shadows and vanished behind a garbage can spilling over with bulging bags of trash. The alley in both directions was as empty as her hope had been for months.

She and Sam slipped out into the March morning and ran like the refugees they were. They stopped when the alley emptied into State Road 24, and huddled back against the wall, arms clutched to their chests for warmth. Just up the road lay Island Market, definitely under *brujo* control. The tribe also controlled the small museum, gas stations, bed-and-breakfast places, and motels along this road. It didn't mean *brujos* guarded these locations right now, but she scratched them off her list of possible hiding places.

"Now what?" she whispered. "It's your island, Sam."

He looked cold and scared. "On the next block, that half-finished church. They're terrified of churches."

Brujos feared cemeteries and fire, and Dominica didn't like oceans because she didn't know how to swim. But to her knowledge, they weren't afraid of churches, crucifixes, or garlic. These ghosts weren't like vampires. Maddie didn't argue with Sam, though. Maybe he knew something she didn't. Maybe, through Whit, Sam had access to information that she simply couldn't reach in Dominica. The dead shared among themselves in ways the living did not. The *brujo* net was evidence of that, a telepathic connection that guaranteed company and compassion for any ghost, anywhere, once they tapped into it. The living also had this same sort of net, but they were so divided in their religious and cultural beliefs that they rarely tapped into it. Most of the living didn't even know it existed.

They dashed up the road, then across it, and ducked into the church. No roof, just two incomplete walls. The bright sunlight spilled across the unfinished altar, the sawdust-covered floor. Construction on the church had stopped back in January, in the early days of the *brujo* incursions, when the carpenters had been seized by young, naïve ghosts who just couldn't wait to try out the newfound powers that Dominica, queen of the *brujos*, had described to them. The carpenters, of course, had short-circuited almost instantly, three of them bleeding out, the rest still wandering around in the tribe, their minds and spirits broken.

She felt the church was the wrong place to hide. "Sam, we need to keep moving."

"Whit won't come in here. Some preacher tried to convert him before they electrocuted him, and as he died, he vowed he would never set foot inside a church ever again. He brought that into death with him. He brought that fear with him when he died."

Undoubtedly true. Dominica had issues like that, too, but she had died so long ago she could barely recall them. Whit had been dead for just six months, so the stuff he had brought into death with him was fresher, raw. Still, Maddie didn't want to stay here. "Let's head into those trees." She pointed west, where there was no wall, just tremendous oaks and pines and homes barely visible through the branches. "It's an older neighborhood. We can hide in one of those houses."

Sam backed into an unfinished confessional. "I'm staying right here." His face came undone, and he began to cry. "I . . . I need to confess, to . . ."

Great, Sam Dorset, ex-Catholic. Maddie hurried over to him. "Sam, listen to me. You're not responsible for what Whit made you do, okay? *You* weren't doing those things. Whit was. You have nothing to *confess*."

He covered his face with his hands, his body shaking with silent sobs. "I'm . . . staying here."

"Fuck that." She grabbed his hand and yanked him to his feet so fast that he stumbled in confusion. "You're leaving with me."

"*We can't go out there.*" He screamed the words, wrenched his arm free. He backed toward the confessional with short, uncertain steps and kept his fisted hands out in front of him, as if he intended to punch her if she moved toward him. "They'll find us, track us down, bleed us out." His expression was that of a man so traumatized by *brujo* possession that rational thought had deserted him.

"Jesus, Sam," she whispered. "Okay. Okay. Take care of yourself."

Maddie turned and trotted west across the church, toward those towering oaks that beckoned, toward that older neighborhood in which she might hide until she could figure out what to do. In her grandmother's old neighborhood in Key Largo, the trees had been palms, Norwegian pines, gumbo-limbos with their thick trunks, their reddish bark. She felt a pang of nostalgia for that place, for the life she'd had before her aunt Tesso had come out of her coma, before she'd known anything about hungry ghosts.

She dodged blocks of concrete, stacks of bricks, piles of wood. She lingered briefly at the edge of the trees, hoping Sam would change his mind and join her, and glanced back. He was still sitting in the unfinished confessional, head in his hands.

"Sam," she called. "I wish you'd reconsider."

He raised his head, gazed at her for a moment, then suddenly shot to his feet, hands flying to his throat, and shrieked, *"Run, Maddie, they found me, run, run for all of us."* He started to choke, she could hear it, his desperate, dying gasps for breath.

She tore away from him, from the church, and plunged into the trees, stumbling, terrified she would be next.

Her head ached from hunger, her stomach growled constantly, her bladder was filled to bursting. But she didn't dare stop. She raced across two yards, ripped through an empty house, clambered over a rusted fence, and dropped into another thicket.

She doubled over, gasping for breath. *Move, just move, anywhere, fast.* But move where?

When she reached out to Sanchez, to her grandfather, to Sanchez's mother, she couldn't find any of them. Maddie suspected that Dominica had provided the connection, that she was the switchboard, the engine that made telepathic contact possible. *You're on your own.* Nothing new there.

She ran through the woods, arms tucked in at her sides, ran because she didn't know what else to do. When she finally slowed to catch her breath, she found herself on a twisting dirt road along the salt marsh.

Homes with metal roofs rose on wood or concrete pilings on either side of her, all of them apparently deserted. No cars, no people, no dogs, not even a stray cat.

Maddie ducked under one of the houses on the marsh side of the road, relieved her aching bladder near some bushes, then crept up the stairs to the front door.

Locked. *Shit.* She removed the screen of the closest window and kicked the glass. Fissures spread through it, tributaries to nowhere. She kicked it again, the glass shattered, and she crawled inside.

Maddie hurried to the sink, spun the faucet, and drank straight from it, sating her terrible thirst. She threw open the pantry door, looking for anything edible the *brujos* might have missed. Packets of trail mix, a can of tuna, a few bottles of water, that was it. She popped open the tuna and scooped it out with her fingers, shoving it into her mouth as she stood there in the middle of the kitchen, looking around.

Stuff lay everywhere—clothing, broken dishes and cups, paintings and photos that had been torn off the walls. The couch and its cushions looked as if a madman had gone after them with a butcher knife. The rocking chair's legs had been chopped off and tossed in the fireplace. This was what *brujos* on a rampage did when they pillaged for food and supplies, senseless destruction that made them feel like gods. Her eyes fixed on the sliding glass doors on the other side of the living room and the wide porch beyond it that offered a stunning view of the marsh.

No boats out there. Maddie crossed the room, opened the porch doors, stepped out and walked right to the end of it, where she had a view of the road. Empty, empty, empty. Violent shudders tore through her, and the empty can of tuna clattered to the floor. She sank into the nearest chair, gripped her knees, the armrests, her knees again. A sob escaped her and she pressed the back of her hand against her mouth to silence it.

No self-pity allowed. If Dominica found her this time, if she seized her again, she would kill her. *Kill* her. *Bleed her out.* Maddie thought of what the fog had done to Fritz Small and his wife, how it had covered them, consumed them. She thought of poor Sam in the confessional. *Run, Maddie, run for all of us.* Dominica ruled through fear. Maddie knew if she succumbed to fear now, then she deserved to be seized again.

She moved swiftly to the other end of the porch, where she had a different view of the road, then went inside the house again, desperate for a plan, a strategy, something. She made her way to the master bedroom, picked up the phone. Dead. A computer monitor rested on the desk, but she didn't see any computer, keyboard, or mouse. Maybe the owners of this place had fled early on and taken the computer with them.

Maddie jerked open the closet door and rifled through the clothes, looking for something that might fit her. She found a shirt, jeans, a heavy jacket, good hiking shoes that probably would fit her. In the bureau, she helped herself to clean underwear, a pair of socks. Shower. Her body screamed for a shower to get rid of Whit's stink, Dominica's stink, the stink of her imprisonment for all these months.

She didn't find any towels on the racks in the bathroom and the linen closet was bare. She returned to the bedroom to look in the closet again. She found towels on an upper shelf, helped herself to one, and several washcloths fluttered to the floor. When she stooped over to pick them up, she saw boxes from the Apple store pushed back against the wall, partially covered by slacks and jeans and a bathrobe that hung on hangers. Maddie quickly pulled the boxes out, and there, on top of one of them, with a big red ribbon pressed to the top, was a MacBook.

Someone's present. Excited, she brought it out and carried it over to the desk. *Please work, please let there be wireless.* Lid open, power on, laptop booting . . . The computer had been set up already for whoever was supposed to get it, a time-saver for her. She clicked on the icon for the AirPort in the upper corner—but not a single wireless network was indicated. So much for that great idea, she thought, and decided to shower first and then move the laptop to various parts of the house in the hopes of picking up a network from one of the other houses in the neighborhood.

In the bathroom, she set the clean clothes on the back of the toilet, turned on the shower, spun the faucet to maximum hot, stripped off her soiled clothes. For a long time, she just stood under the hot spray, the needles drilling into her skull, her skin, and refused to think too far into the future or too far into the past. She placed a time limit on the future and the past: sixty seconds. She could handle a minute on either side of the present.

Dirt and grime swirled down the drain and she told herself it represented her defilement, the horror of her imprisonment, spinning down the drain, *away.* She needed symbols now, something mythic and powerful to snap her fully back into herself.

She felt marginally better when her clean bare feet pressed against the fluffy bath mat, when she pulled on her clean clothes and socks and slipped her feet into shoes that held no memory of Dominica. Maddie ran a brush through her hair, marveling at how silken it felt, how the strands squeaked between her fingers. It felt magnificent to be clean again.

She scooped up her old clothes from the floor, picked up the laptop, and went into the kitchen. Here, she dumped her soiled clothes in the trash, set the laptop on the counter, tore open a packet of trail mix and munched on it as she clicked on the wireless icon again. Not a damn thing in range. As she picked up the laptop to move it, she felt a protrusion in the side—a spot for an Internet card. So where the hell was the card?

Excited again, Maddie returned to the bedroom closet and checked inside each of the Apple boxes. At the bottom of the second box was a small container with the Internet card inside. Maddie tore it open and raced back into the kitchen. She inserted the card in the slot, clicked the icon, and just that fast, she was online.

She quickly navigated to Gypsy woman's blog, the spot where Dominica usually began and ended her day. Gypsy's poetry about forbidden love, lust, and passion spoke to that part of Dominica that craved someone to love and loved the one she was with. She even commented on the blog as Nica.

Maddie studied Gypsy's photograph, a stunning woman in her early sixties with wide, dark eyes, her hair a wild mass of curls, rings adorning her fingers, bracelets climbing her arms. She looked like a gypsy. A risk, she thought, but what the hell. *Undermine Dominica from several fronts.* She clicked on the e-mail link and wrote:

My name is Maddie Livingston. Please read this—http://en.wikipedia .org/wiki/esperanza—so you'll understand what I'm about to tell you.

On your sitemeter, you'll find an IP that appears several times a day. Location: Cedar Key, an island on Florida's gulf coast now under quarantine. The woman from that IP comments as Nica.

If you read the Wiki article link, then you know a battle was fought against *brujos* last summer. My aunt Tess, tessl@gmail.com, was instrumental in that battle, which now continues on Cedar Key. The leader of the *brujos*—Nica—has formed a new tribe and they have seized nearly everyone on the island. I know how nuts this sounds. E-mail Tess for verification. She's an ex-FBI agent.

Could you please post this poem I've attached? It might stop this bitch in her tracks.

The poem was simple and awkward; a poet she was not. But Dominica would get the message. Maddie signed it, *Wayra*.

Then she sat there, thinking. Dominica knew her various e-mail addresses, her Twitter and Facebook passwords, her contacts. But as far as Maddie knew, Dominica had never rifled around too deeply in her computer knowledge. So unless she'd learned to hack into computers while Maddie slept, she probably didn't know the hotmail addresses for Tesso and Wayra. But she might be able to bring up that information, so Maddie created a new Gmail address and wrote both of them through those accounts. She figured Tesso would get the message first. She checked her e-mail whenever something popped up in her in-box. Wayra rarely checked his. But just in case he was ahead of the curve, she thought, he would know the score. She instructed both of them not to reply.

She deleted her current Twitter and Facebook accounts, then created new ones and sent a duplicate of her Gmail message to Tess's and Wayra's Facebook pages, then shorter messages to them both through Twitter. She powered down the laptop and slipped it inside the pack to take with her.

Once again, she moved restlessly around the house, checking that the doors—front and balcony—were locked, but that was stupid, of course, since the window was shattered and locked doors and sealed windows never kept out a *brujo*. She needed a weapon—fire would be best, preferably a flamethrower, but a gun would do nicely, too.

She checked under the kitchen sink for lighter fluid, matches, old rags, and found all three. Now, a broomstick. In the kitchen pantry, she helped herself to something better than a *wooden* broomstick—a metal mop stick longer than any broom equivalent. She quickly wrapped rags around it and set her new weapon near the door to take with her when she left.

A careful search of the rooms uncovered nothing useful. In the hallway, though, she discovered a padlocked door—a storage area, a closet, a place where the owner undoubtedly stashed all valuable belongings that renters might steal.

She needed a hammer.

In the kitchen, Maddie rifled through every drawer and cabinet until she found a toolbox that held a large, heavy hammer. This would do. It took three hard blows to the padlock before the sucker popped open. She scoured the boxes, the cardboard containers, the neatly arranged suitcases of stuff. She found a small cardboard box that held a few canned goods and packages of ramen noodles. She set that aside, then unzipped one of the suitcases and tore through the contents. She removed a sweater that looked like it would fit her, stuffed it into an empty backpack. Maddie unzipped yet another suitcase, flipped open the top.

"Bingo," she whispered.

All sorts of hunting and fishing knives were arranged neatly inside. From a side pocket, she withdrew an X26 Taser and charger that led her to believe the owner of the house was or had been in law enforcement. She selected a knife with a serrated edge, plugged the Taser into the wall, and set her backpack on the kitchen counter.

She moved out onto the balcony again. Road still empty. The two closest houses, both across the street from her, were definitely deserted. No vehicles were parked in front of either of them. She didn't recall seeing a car or cart parked under this house, either, but had noticed a storage shed that might hold a bike. Even a bike would be preferable to leaving here on foot. She didn't have any idea where she would go yet, but the dense woods to the north of the house looked promising. The trick was to keep moving, to make herself less accessible to Dominica, to find holdouts. The last she knew, Sanchez was with Zee Small's group, but where? And was he still with them? Or had all of them been seized?

If they had all been seized, then . . .

No, don't go there, don't think it, don't drop it into possible scenarios.

Maddie added a bottle of water to her pack, shrugged it on, then unplugged the Taser from the wall. She zipped the charger into an inner compartment and slipped the Taser into a pocket of a jacket she'd taken from the closet. She checked the road again, gazed out over the salt marsh, looking for boats. Nothing.

On her way out the door, she swept the hammer off the counter, doused her torch with lighter fluid, and flew down the front steps, into the light, the songs of birds, the emptiness of this tiny neighborhood.

She ducked under the house, where the storage shed was. No padlock on this door. But the shed was rusted and old, and when she slammed the hammer's prongs into the metal around the lock, she tore a hole in it. She struck it again with the prongs, pulled. The lock mechanism popped out, and the door swung open. The shed held a lawn mower, gardening tools, two dusty baseball caps, several lamps, a trunk, two bikes with flat tires, and a tire pump. She gathered her hair up, pulled on one of the dusty caps. Hiding her hair might buy her a few more moments.

Then she pushed the bike out, set it against one of the pilings and proceeded to pump up the tires.

As she inflated the last tire, the birds suddenly went silent and Maddie glanced around uneasily, looking for the reason. There, coming up the road toward her: a cart with two men inside. She didn't recognize them, but why should she? Since Dominica had plunged Maddie into the deep sleep yesterday the tribe probably had seized another fifty or a hundred hosts.

Had they seen her? If so, it wasn't as if she could pretend to act like Dominica. *Brujos* always knew when a human hosted one of their own. She might escape them on the bike. But if they were accompanied by a *brujo* in its natural form, she wouldn't get far. Even if the men were alone, her location would be broadcast through the *brujo* net as soon as they saw her and Dominica would seize her again.

She grabbed her torch, darted to the far side of the shed, her back to a hedge, her stomach twisted with fear. Their laughter rang out as they neared the house and she suddenly wished she had stayed inside or tried to escape them on the bike.

Coward, whispered that soft, inner voice.

She dug the Taser from her jacket pocket, lit her torch, leaped onto the bike, and pedaled wildly toward them, shouting, "Hey, *brujo* fuckers!"

The two men seemed startled to see her, a madwoman racing out from under a house, waving a flaming mop stick. They were either stupid or arrogant or both and simply stopped their cart and leaped out and one of them yelled, "Dominica wants you back, bitch."

They apparently believed their presence and shouts would reduce her to a blubbering state in which they could easily capture her and drag her back to Dominica, to the hotel. She kept barreling toward them, one man a middle-aged Humpty Dumpty, the other string-bean thin, around her age. They kept hollering and waving their arms and moving toward her.

As she neared them, she swung her flaming mop stick and whacked Humpty so hard across his bulging belly that the stick, the *metal* stick, bent like a straw. Another whack and it snapped altogether. The flaming part of it flew off, arced through the air, and landed in the road. Humpty gasped and stumbled back, arms clutched against himself. The younger, thinner man lunged for her, and she slammed into him with the bike.

The impact destroyed the bike's front wheel, Maddie catapulted over the handlebars, String Bean fell back into Humpty, and both of them crashed to the ground. Maddie landed on her side, and pain flared in her arm. She ignored it, vaulted to her feet, and hurled herself at String Bean. She Tasered him in the crotch and he shrieked and shuddered against the ground, as if in the throes of a seizure, then passed out.

Humpty scooted back across the dirt and the gravel, his feet struggling for purchase, and even as she moved toward him, she could see the ensuing struggle between him and the *brujo* inside him. She didn't have any idea what a Taser might do to a *brujo*, but there wasn't time to think about it. Humpty screamed, "You're gonna die, bitch, you're gonna die, the whole tribe's looking for you."

He got up clumsily, his feet jerking this way and that, as though his host were starting to fight back, and kicked out with his right leg. His boot grazed her hip and she stumbled. Crimson poured across her vision and she threw herself at him and Tasered him in the neck. He didn't even shriek. His eyes rolled back, his bladder let loose, he crumpled to the ground.

Adrenaline pumped through her, the inside of her mouth turned bone dry. Maddie scooped up her broken mop stick, raced to the electric cart, and took off into the woods. She glanced back twice to see if they were chasing her, but neither guy had gotten up yet. She didn't have any idea what had happened to the *brujos* within those men, but if they'd vacated the hosts, then she had to assume they were pursuing her and that one of them could seize her at any moment.

The cart moved faster than she could run, but it couldn't outrun a determined *brujo*. She set the broken mop stick upright against the edge of the passenger seat and, driving with her knee, wrapped some of her spare rags around the stick, soaked them in lighter fluid, and lit it. The torch burned brightly. She lifted it in her left hand, waving it in the air around her just in case *brujos* were after her. A lunatic with a torch. Was this how she was doomed to live from now on? Would she be looking perpetually over her shoulder, arming herself with primitive torches or flamethrowers, Tasers or guns? The only way she would ever be rid of Dominica was to annihilate her.

But how?

Burn the town. Start with the hotel.

The idea of returning to the tribe's headquarters filled her with dread.

Besides, burning the town would only cause the *brujos* to leap from their hosts or bleed them out and take off.

And she wouldn't be able to do it alone.

But whatever she did would have to be done alone. For all she knew, holdouts like Zee Small's group might have been hauled in while she was in the deep sleep and she might be the only uncompromised person left on Cedar Key. Her life now reminded her of *I Am Legend,* and she was the only human left on an earth populated by vampires.

Will Smith she was not.

Vampires these ghosts were not.

Like vampires, though, they were vulnerable, not the gods she once thought they were. And Dominica, because she had existed for so long, was vulnerable in ways that younger ghosts were not. Her vulnerabilities were emotional: She was vengeful, hungry for power, and always loved the one she was with. She feared Wayra because he could destroy her by either disappearing her back in time or taking her into himself and shifting, and she probably feared him even more now that Maddie had escaped. Dominica truly desired a *brujo* bastion. Maddie might be able to manipulate her emotions in one or two of those areas, but so what? It wouldn't destroy her.

Think, think. She knew the answer to this, Dominica had lived inside her for months, they had shared psyches, histories, emotions, thoughts, ideas, even sex. Maddie knew her better than anyone, even better than Wayra. She could seize humans, take over and heal their bodies, inflict excruciating agony, plunge her hosts into the deep sleep, kill them. But she was no longer human, didn't fully understand twenty-first-century America, and hey, she couldn't multitask.

In Esperanza, she had given an order to her tribe and her minions—most of them very old ghosts and some of them ancient ghosts—carried it out. Here, she didn't have nearly as many minions and among them were only a few—Whit, Joe, Jill, and Gogh—whom Dominica trusted and who had any inkling of what was actually going on. Liam used to be the fifth of her trusted *brujos,* but he had fallen permanently out of favor.

And just like that, Maddie had it. If there was too much going on at once, Dominica could delegate only so many duties, responsibilities, and crisis management to these four ghosts. At some point, she would have to do everything herself and wouldn't be able to because she *couldn't multitask.*

Maddie started to laugh. She laughed until the trees blurred, and then she slammed on the brake and leaned over the side of the cart and puked. The contents of her stomach covered the ground. She pushed pine needles over the mess with her foot, lifted her head, wiped her hand across her mouth, dug out a bottle of water and drank deeply, washing the taste of puke from her mouth, sating her thirst.

Can't multitask. That's it. Create chaotic eruptions all over Cedar Key.

She started the cart and drove fast through the trees. When she reached the edge of the thicket, she looked out, hoping to see a street sign. There. "Bay Street, Bay Street," she murmured. "Where the hell is Bay Street?"

Memory coughed it up. She was just below the third bridge, off State Road 24. The homes located on the small roads on either side of the main highway belonged to locals. Artists, fishermen, shop owners, restaurant workers, retirees. Most of them had fled early on, been seized, or perhaps joined Zee's group.

Maddie stopped the cart in front of the first house she saw, broke inside, and spent fifteen minutes pillaging the place. As she was about to leave, she realized her right arm ached terribly, and when she removed her jacket, she saw that her shirt sleeve was sliced open just above the elbow and soaked with blood. She rolled up her sleeve, and blood dripped down the inside of her arm. She tore off her shirt and stared at her wound, a three-inch horizontal gash. When she lifted the flap of skin she nearly passed out. Bone, she thought she could see bone.

When did this happen?

Maybe when she'd been thrown off the bike.

She weaved down a hallway in her bra and jeans, her jacket and bloody shirt draped over her shoulder, her pack clutched in her left hand, her good hand. In the bathroom medicine cabinet, she found gauze, Betadine, Band-Aids, hydrogen peroxide, alcohol, Neosporin, a bag of cotton balls. In a cabinet drawer, she uncovered a sewing kit with needles, thread, a thimble, safety pins.

Clean and close. She selected the thickest thread, coarse and midnight black, and threaded the sharpest needle. She knew the needle was wrong, that she needed what her grandmother had used to stitch Maddie's foot when she'd sliced it open on jagged glass during a barefoot run on the beach. But she would make do with what she had.

She opened the bottle of alcohol and dropped the needle into it, careful to keep the thread draped over the lip so it didn't slip away from her. She didn't have the time to find and thread another needle. Already, her hands shook, her vision blurred. Maddie sat on the floor, her back against the wall, and went to work on her injury in earnest now—cleaning it, letting it bleed, sopping up the blood, cleaning it some more, alternately squirting it with Betadine, hydrogen peroxide, and Betadine again.

Even if she managed to stitch it shut, she worried about infection and whether the cause of the injury was rusted. Her procedure was hardly hygienic and she couldn't recall when she'd had her last tetanus shot. What a dark irony it would be to survive *brujo* possession only to die of lockjaw.

The instant the needle pierced the skin at the top end of the slash, she choked back a cry. When she tried to stick the needle in even farther, so that she could stitch from deep under the slice, her vision swam into blackness, and she nearly passed out from the pain. Frustrated, disgusted with herself, she pressed the needle in deeper, deeper.

I'm gonna puke. She forced herself to pull the needle through, as though her flesh were a piece of fabric. Up, across, in, one stitch, two, three. She paused at some point to sip water, to dab Betadine on her stitch job. Then she resumed her stitching until she had thirteen tiny, neat stitches. Her hands shook so terribly that it took her a while to tie off the thread.

Already, the skin around the slash looked angry, puffy, bright red. More Betadine, a dab of antibiotic salve. Then she bandaged the injury with gauze, and rifled through the cabinet for antibiotics that might fight the infection. She found a container of Augmentin that had expired two years ago, eight pills inside, and popped one. At 500 milligrams apiece, she would take another this evening. Or two more.

If she lived that long.

She rested afterward, sitting against the wall with her eyes shut, her arm throbbing, and after a while, she forced herself to stand, to find a clean shirt. She shoved her bloody shirt into the trash, put on her jacket, and moved out into the rest of the house to take inventory.

Dominica's tribe had taken most of the food and beverages, but not the rags, the containers of kerosene and lighter fluid, the brooms and mops. She loaded everything into the back of the cart and moved on to the next house, the next, and the next. She didn't take just rags. She took glass bottles, towels, linens, feather pillows, aluminum foil, Saran Wrap, matches, anything that might give her an edge.

At the end of nearby Pine Street, she found a two-story house with a one-car garage that backed up to the water. On the first and second floors, large windows overlooked the bayou, so she would be able to see fog if it formed and boats if they approached. The second floor boasted front and back balconies, and when she sat on the floor in the middle of the master bedroom, she had an unimpeded view of the bayou on one side and of the street on the other. If anyone or anything came near the house, she would know. If *brujos* arrived in their natural form, she probably would sense them and she would fight them with fire.

That was her plan, at any rate. The big question was whether she could survive long enough to implement her plan.

As she unpacked her pillaged supplies and carried them up to the master bedroom, her arm continued to ache and throb, but the bleeding seemed to have stopped. Maddie took it as a sign that her luck would hold. But signs, she thought, were the last refuge of desperate people.

She went back downstairs and drove the cart into the trees behind the house. On her way upstairs again, she detoured into the garage and discovered a few more useful items, including an F-150 Ford truck with huge tires and a mean-looking grille across the front. No key in the ignition, of course not. Too damn easy. She checked the usual spots where people hid keys—the visor, the inside of the fenders, beneath the steering wheel. Nothing.

But on her way back upstairs, she found the car keys hanging from a decorative hook in the hallway. Maddie grabbed the keys and raced up the stairs to the master bedroom. She spread everything out on the floor and quickly went to work. She intended to create so many weapons and booby traps that Dominica would need tens of thousands of ghosts to handle the chaos.

Never again would Dominica or any other hungry ghost use her, defile her, subjugate her, demean her, or keep her imprisoned within her own body.

Twenty

Wayra came to in his human form, in a bed of dead leaves and pine needles, covered by a light blanket, his head resting in the lap of the loveliest woman he'd ever seen. Long hair, the color of cinnamon, framed her exquisite face, light brushed her high cheekbones, an astonishing feather tattoo ran the length of her neck on the left side. Her tawny eyes seemed familiar to him, but he knew he'd never seen her before.

His first thought was that he had died, Dominica had won, and this woman was something he'd conjured in the afterlife.

Then she ran her long, cool fingers across his forehead, brushing his hair back. The touch felt real, but he wasn't sure that *she* was real until he drew his fingers through her hair, thick and luxurious and as soft as an infant's skin. His thumb traced the curve of her chin, the arch of her brows, the bow of her mouth. He even touched the magnificent tattoo and could almost feel the feather pulsing and throbbing with life.

Wayra looked into her eyes again and suddenly understood. She had the eyes of the hawk. "It's not possible," he breathed.

"You were never the last of your kind, Wayra."

She slipped under the blanket with him, fitted her body against his and, for long moments, simply held him. He could feel the beat of her heart, the warmth of her skin, the soft whisperings in her mind as she reached out to him, one shifter to another. Slowly, hesitantly, his arms wrapped around her, and for the first time ever, Wayra embraced one of his own kind, ending centuries of loneliness.

A breeze skipped through the trees, rustling the branches, rearranging sunlight and shadows, and a strange peace suffused Wayra. It was as if all these centuries of his existence had culminated in this single discovery, that he was not the last of his kind, that somewhere along the nonlinear progression of his existence, he had accepted a lie as truth.

"But how can you exist?" He whispered the words, afraid that if he spoke too loudly, this fragile reality would shatter and she would disappear. "No chaser has ever spoken of you."

"There's a great deal the chasers don't know or understand." She kissed him and the intimate contact enabled their minds to instantly open to each other.

He learned that her name was Illary, Quechua for "rainbow," and that she was aeons older than he was. When she was changed at the age of sixteen, she was a close friend of Mary Magdalene and one of Christ's disciples, part of a group of noblewomen who supported Christ financially as he traveled through Galilee and Judea. He saw her early years as a human disciple of Christ, then as a hawk that was never far from Christ or Mary Magdalene. After the Crucifixion, Illary and her creator, the man who had turned her, had left the Holy Land and gone in search of others of their kind.

During their journey to Esperanza seven hundred years later, Illary's creator had been killed by a hunter's arrow. She had finished that journey alone and had arrived in Esperanza shortly after the city was brought into the physical world five hundred years ago. In all the centuries of her existence, she had turned only one person, a man whom she had loved as Wayra had once loved Dominica. He, too, was killed by a hunter's arrow and had joined the *brujos,* just as Dominica had done. But her lover, unlike Dominica, had left Esperanza willingly and now ruled the largest tribe of *brujos* in Europe and Asia. Illary had not seen him for more than a thousand years.

Her loneliness throughout all these centuries had so far surpassed his own that he didn't understand how she had managed to remain whole, sane. She heard his unspoken question and another chapter of her life opened to him—centuries spent in Europe in her human form, when she had nearly forgotten her shifter history and rationality was her refuge. He saw that she had been married and widowed dozens of times and none of her partners had ever known the truth about what she was.

Their clothes slipped away, her naked body covered his, and Wayra felt as if he'd fallen into a dream from which he never wanted to awaken. She drove out the bitter taste of the *brujos* he had taken into himself. In their lovemaking, each delicate taste and sensation enabled them to travel more deeply into each other's respective histories, down through decades, centuries, millennia, until they reached the collective memories of their race. Images swirled through them, around them, some of them so strange and alien that Wayra had no context for them: red rivers, a sky with twin suns, glacial peaks, oceans of unimagined depths, a continent of bold, pulsating blues at the edge of time.

A magnificent bird with a seventy-foot wingspan flew between the twin suns. On a vast savannah beneath those suns loped a gigantic African bush elephant. In a rushing scarlet-colored mountain river, a monstrous-sized wolf hunted for fish. On a sunlit leaf as big as a full-grown man, a Goliath beetle soaked up the day's warmth. Just above it, a tremendous butterfly suckled from the center of a gigantic orchid, its luminous red and blue wings opening and closing with elegant grace. At the edge of a vast ocean, a huge saltwater crocodile lay in the shoals, water lapping at its sides. In the depth of that ocean, a whale-shark moved with a stealthy silence, and alongside it swam a Chinese giant salamander and a colossal squid, its tentacles ten miles long.

Mammals, amphibians, insects, reptiles, invertebrates, fish, birds, all excessive in size: Were these the original shifters? The prototypes? Where was the place with the twin suns?

Still locked together, they rolled through the fallen leaves and pine needles, their bodies now slick with sweat. His fingers tangled in her hair, his mouth moved against her neck and breasts, his tongue inscribed secret codes against her skin. When her body arched against his and she cried out, her voice rose into the murmur of the breeze, the whispering of the leaves. Wayra drove on to his own completion and all the exhilarating and alien images instantly evaporated.

A long time later, they lay side by side, fingers intertwined. "So tell me how it can be that you exist," he said.

Illary rose up slightly, one hand supporting her head, the other hand resting lightly against his chest. Her dark hair cascaded over one shoulder. Wayra drank in her beauty; she intoxicated him. "Shifters predate humanity on the planet, Wayra, and everything you think you know about your genesis is wrong and you've been lied to—by your creator, by the chasers."

Wayra wished he could feel anger about this, but in truth, it didn't surprise him. She explained that in the beginning, there were seven tribes of shifters, the ones he'd seen. But by the time of Lemuria, science was intervening and some of the shifters' kind became genetic experiments, created in laboratories. But the dog/wolf shifters were not created in any lab; they were among the original seven tribes.

She talked for a while about the ancestral memories of shifters, how those memories stretched back to the dawn of time before humanity, before chasers, *brujos*. "And ultimately, those memories, the knowledge we carry, makes us more powerful than chasers."

He threaded his fingers through hers and held their hands up to the light. Her hand was lovely, the fingers perfectly formed, her skin a pale brown, café au lait. "But if the chasers are the ones who rewrote our history, can we trust them?"

"*You* tell *me*. You've worked with them, I never have. It's why I didn't reveal myself when they were around."

It took Wayra a while to answer his own question. "Over the centuries, I've met six of the thirteen who sit on the chaser council. Charlie and Victor are the only two I trust but that trust isn't constant. I've known Victor since shortly before the decision was made to bring Esperanza into the physical world. He voted against it, as I would have if I were a chaser. He was overruled. So yes, I trust him in that sense."

"And Charlie?" she asked.

"I met him in the year or two before he made his transition. The chaser council had been observing him for a long time, studying the connections in his life. They knew there was a possibility that his daughter, Tess, would be critically wounded in her work and felt she would be an excellent candidate to be the first transitional soul in five hundred years to enter Esperanza, thus breaking the *brujo* stranglehold over the city. So the chasers recruited Charlie before he died and my job was to guide him during his meditations and dreams. Once he made his transition and joined the council, I came to know him well. Of all the chasers on the council, at least from what I know of them, he's closest to human life and obviously still has family here in the physical. He means well, I trust him to do the right thing, but he can be manipulative. He hasn't been a chaser long enough to have anything to do with burying our true history. I doubt if he even knows about it. During my travels here, he's been helpful."

"And both of them were responsible for those huge fabulous crows."

"I've never seen them do anything like that before. I suspect they violated chaser rules by meddling like that, but it's long past the time to violate the chasers' unfathomable code."

"They may be helpful to us. But for now, it's best to keep my existence a secret from them."

"These other shifters. Do you have any idea where they may be?"

"None. But until the day I saw you at that landfill, I didn't know you existed, either, Wayra. My sense is that a confluence of events and circumstances will eventually make them known to us."

Maybe, he thought. But maybe not. Maybe there would be no confluence in their lifetimes. It exhausted him to try to follow the timelines, the connections, the magnitude of what he had just learned. He changed the subject. "How did you end up on Cedar Key? With Rocky and Kate?"

She stretched out against the leaves again, one arm tucked under her head. "I left Europe after the Second World War broke out and returned to Esperanza. I spent weeks at a time in a place called the stone forest, searching for direction, guidance. One night in a cave, I had a vision of a place on the water. A fishing village. I felt it was an island to the north, in the U.S. In the distance, across an expanse of water, I could see twin stacks that emitted smoke. These structures were huge; I had no idea what they were. Or where they were. But I knew that in this place, I would uncover more about shifter history, that it was part of my destiny. So I stayed in the cave until I had another vision, of a long finger of land surrounded on three sides by water. I later realized it was Florida."

"How did you narrow it down to Cedar Key?"

"Patience and time. I had nothing but time. In the late seventies, I ended up in Gainesville. In graduate school. One weekend, in 1978, I came to Cedar Key. From the fishing pier, I saw the twin stacks that had been in my vision. It was—"

"The Crystal River nuclear plant," Wayra finished. "It's visible from the pier."

"Yes. It became operational in March 1977. It took me more than twenty years, Wayra, but I found the place in my vision. Cedar Key pretty much became my hawk home from then on. When I went back to the stone forest five years ago, I had another vision, of a young woman and her son. Kate and Rocky. The first time I saw Kate, I recognized her—but not him, he was too young. In my vision, he was older, as he is now. I studied them, watched him grow and mature. I was desperately lonely and considered living with them as a hawk, just for the companionship. I also knew they were connected somehow to my destiny.

"Last year I was out on one of the smaller islands, feasting on crabs. A group of drunken fishermen saw me and thought it would be fun to snare a hawk. The hook went through my wing. I managed to bite through the line, but the hook was deeply embedded in my wing. I could barely fly. I somehow made it back to Cedar Key, to the beach in front of the animal rescue center where Rocky worked. That's where he found me."

Wayra stroked the underside of her wrist, his heart aching for her.

"You realize that he and Kate and Delaney are the new generation of shifters, Wayra."

"If nothing goes wrong." He explained what had happened when he had turned the mother and her son during the plague years. "I couldn't bear for that to happen this time, Illary."

"That was long ago." Her fingernails traveled lightly down the side of his face. "Everything has changed since then. I don't know Delaney, so I can't speak for how his transformation may evolve, but I don't think Kate and Rocky will be a problem."

"Except that the only reason I turned her was so that Rocky wouldn't be alone."

"It was the right thing to do."

"She may not agree."

"You don't understand the depth of her love for her son. Trust me, you did the right thing."

He hoped she was right, but it wasn't as if he could change anything at this point.

Leaves fluttered down through the air and caught in Illary's hair. He wanted to know everything about her, every piece of her long history, every emotion, every twist and turn in her journey. "Europe. Tell me about Europe in the twenties and thirties."

"Exciting. But strange. For a time, when I was married to a man in Zurich and barely remembered my own history as a shifter, I went through therapy with Carl Jung. I told him my dream about the scarabs. Do you know that dream, Wayra?"

Wayra had read everything Jung had written. He owned a copy of Jung's *Red Book,* which wouldn't be sold until next year. He had read the eloquent calligraphy in German. The dream to which Illary referred had triggered the basis of Jung's theory of synchronicity. And it had come from a woman whose insistence on logic and rationality had become so rigid and dominant in her life that it choked off her cure. He couldn't imagine Illary as that woman and said as much.

She laughed and turned her head, bits of grass and leaves and pine needles stuck to her hair. "Wayra, by that time I had been alive for a thousand years. I had lost count of how many times I'd been widowed. I can't have children. Rationality was my sanctuary. Yes, I was that woman. And when the beetle appeared at the window, I suddenly understood what I am. All my dim shifter memories burst forth with vivid brightness and rushed back. I've never allowed myself to forget any of it again. It's why I've spent more time as a hawk than as a woman." She paused. "Should we check on the new shifters?"

Wayra pulled her closer to him. "They'll be fine for a while longer. I want to know more and it's easier when we do this mind to mind." He kissed her once more and lost himself again.

Kate knew something was happening to her mind, body, and soul. But she couldn't stop it, couldn't mitigate it. It felt like a force of nature, something so powerful and transformative that she could only be swept along, swept up, and had no choice but to endure the excruciating pain.

The pain was sometimes specific—her hands and feet, for instance, felt as though they were burning. Her head pulsed and throbbed, the migraine to end all migraines. Her nose ached, her skin felt as if it had been set on fire, her tongue and teeth felt as though they had been cut out, extracted, and replaced with something else.

The air she tasted and smelled was filled with history. She could sense a fox pissing on a pile of pine needles in a forest, but had no idea where the fox or the forest were in space or time. She sensed a house built on this same patch of pine needles, could envision the people who had lived and loved inside this house, but didn't have any idea where in time or space the vision occurred. And so it went for what felt like hours, days, months.

Gradually, the pain subsided and her senses continued to expand. She became the honeybee flitting from flower to flower, taking away not only some delectable nectar, but the entire history of the flower, its petals and leaves, its stalk, even the history of the soil in which it grew. She became the caterpillar and the butterfly, the eggs and the birds, the humans and their children. Her senses now told her everything she needed to know about her environment, but almost nothing about what was happening *to her*.

Behind all the immediate sensations flowed information that inundated her, forced her to realize her reality had changed dramatically and irrevocably, but she had no idea what that meant in practical, daily terms. When she struggled through the labyrinth of her own memories in an attempt to piece together a coherent picture, a narrative that made sense, she couldn't do it. Her memory of what had come before this moment of pain, this instant of sensory overload, this breath of life and beauty, was just a blank, a darkness that stretched even beyond Google's infinity.

Google. What the hell is Google?

Something huge.

Kate latched on to that, the idea of a google, of something bigger than the sum of its parts, a holographic universe in which each part might not only reveal the scope of the larger picture, but contain it as well. She could see its structure—the Indra's net that mystics talked about—but she had no way of expressing this unity.

She finally opened her dry, aching eyes.

She was sprawled on her back in a densely wooded area, the shadows of the trees greater than the sunlight that spilled through the leaves. The sight captivated her, the way the encroaching light penetrated these deep shadows, changing the mood and texture of the woods itself. The leaves turned from dark green to a soft, celery green. She could see the life force pulsating in the leaves, the branches, the very bark. Insects flitted around through light and shadow and she could see their pulsating life force as well.

Kate turned onto her side and stared in horror at her long legs and paws covered with short, soft gray fur flecked with rich brown. *Shit fuck what's happened to me?* She began to shake uncontrollably and squeezed her eyes shut, certain she was locked in some terrible nightmare. Shudders swept up one side of her body and down the other. Her teeth chattered, her nose ran, she struggled to wrap her arms around herself, but couldn't seem to do it. When she opened her eyes, her long legs and paws twitched and jerked, her muscles screamed for real movement, she thought she might vomit.

Kate leaped up and tore toward the marsh, her powerful legs covering the distance in seconds flat. At the edge of the water, odors inundated her, the smells of various life forms that lived in the marsh—tiny fish swimming through the sunlight, dragonflies flitting from stalk to stalk, crabs scampering to and from the shore, and, much deeper out, manta rays, dolphins, sharks. Then there were the scents of the wading birds and the noise of their cries and chatter, blue herons and wood storks, egrets and gulls and pelicans. Their voices gave way to a celestial music, a celebration of life. The sensory feast briefly paralyzed her.

She looked—and there was her reflection, a beautiful, sleek greyhound with human eyes. She touched her paw to the reflection and the ripples broke it up.

Holy shit, it's real, I'm changed, I'm a shifter like Wayra, he pressed his hand to my forehead and light came out of it and then he sank his teeth into my neck and I've gone around the bend, I'm in meltdown, I'm—

Rocky, where was Rocky?

The last thing she remembered was seeing her son on the floor of the houseboat, his limbs human, his face that of a dog or a wolf. *Jesus God.*

Kate raced back into the wooded area where she'd come to, but didn't see anything in the shadows. She sniffed at the air, drawing the smells deeply into her lungs. A sensory tsunami crashed over her, and for long, terrible moments, she felt as if her brain were short-circuiting. Then, gradually, she realized she could separate the smells of nature—water, grass, trees—from those of animals. It took her a moment to determine the distance and direction of several powerful animal scents, then she ran toward them, darting over fallen branches and protruding roots, into an area of the woods where the pines grew so tightly together it was as if they were joined at the hips, a family of multiple Siamese twins.

She spotted a large dog with thick fur the color of sand striated with black, and when she silently screamed her son's name, the dog's head snapped around. His ears popped upright, straight as little church steeples, and his lips furled back, exposing his ivory-white fangs. Kate stopped. *Rocky, it's me.*

Mom. He howled as he tore toward her, and there in the shadows they danced around, sniffing and licking at each other. When he spoke, his words came to her in rapidly moving images, a movie of the mind. He had been hiding in the animal rescue facility when Amy, hosting a *brujo,* had appeared. The *brujo* had bled her out in front of Rocky, then seized him, infecting him. By the time Wayra had found him, he was dying and the shifter had changed him to save his life. Kate started to ask how the change had saved his life; she was a bit short on details. But the knowledge abruptly flowed into her awareness: the shifter immune system. It was why Wayra had lived so long.

But why had Wayra changed *her*? She hadn't been injured. She had freaked out at the sight of her son caught in some fucked-up biological nightmare, yes, definitely. She vaguely recalled screaming and rushing toward Rocky. But she hadn't threatened Wayra. She hadn't presented a threat to anyone. *So, why?*

Her question, once again, brought an answer. Wayra didn't want Rocky to ever be the last of his kind, to suffer the excruciating loneliness that he had. She appreciated that Wayra had saved Rocky's life, but shouldn't he have *asked* her before changing her?

Well, yeah. But when would he have done that, exactly? When she had dropped from exhaustion at moving Delaney onto the houseboat or when she rushed toward Rocky, screaming like a banshee?

She understood Wayra's whats and whys. And honestly, did she really mind being something other than a bartender? Did she really mind that one of her options in life was being able to run forty-five or fifty miles an hour, discern the ancient history of the soil on which she walked, and that she had access to knowledge that seemed to date back to the beginning of time? Did any of that really bother her?

No. She wished she could say otherwise, wished she could be enraged that such a thing had been thrust on her. But the bottom line—and right now everything for her was a bottom line—was that, except for giving birth to Rocky, her transformation was the most magnificent thing that had ever happened to her.

What had happened to Delaney? He had been badly injured when she and Wayra had gotten him onto the houseboat. Had Wayra changed him, too?

She had a bad feeling about it. Rocky picked up on her alarm, and they loped back through the woods, headed for the houseboat. *What's your first memory of all this, Rocky?*

Coming to in the woods and being assaulted by the odors. I went to look for you, Mom, but got distracted by a scent that consumed me.

Before the marsh came into sight, the odor of the air changed dramatically. She smelled terror, hostility, rage. And then she saw the rising fog, a long, thick bank of it forming a kind of barricade between her and Rocky and the marsh, where the houseboat was.

She felt Rocky's uncertainty. *Can it seize us?* he asked.

I don't know. But if we're moving like the wind, it's probably less likely. How fast can you run, Rocky?

Let's find out.

With that, he raced ahead of her and Kate dashed after him, rapidly closing the gap between them, then pulled out ahead of him and plunged into the fog first. The bone-piercing cold shocked her. A litany of voices thundered in her skull: *Find the body, fuel the body . . .* She felt the *brujos* within the fog trying to invade her, seize her, but they apparently found her distasteful and strange and broke away from her. Just the same, the fog rolled after her, pursuing her, the voices of the dead rising and falling in a maddening staccato rhythm. The fog brushed up against her tail, tasting but not trying to seize her. Then she reached the other side of it, and a moment later, Rocky burst from it like a bullet.

Fifty yards later, just short of a small clearing, they stopped. It took her a moment to process what she was seeing—a tremendous jet-black Great Dane backed up to a tree, an electric cart blocking him on either side, four men in each cart, and two large, armed men standing in front of him.

"Shoot the thing," one man in a cart shouted. "It's probably got rabies or some shit like that."

Kate didn't recognize the man who hollered, but she recognized both of the armed men when they glanced around—a state deputy who drank vodka straight up whenever he dropped by the island bar, and his college-age son. No question that they had been seized and that the Great Dane was Delaney. She could smell him as clearly as she could smell the *brujos* within the deputy and his son—and inside the other men. Delaney was about to spring and she knew the two men would shoot him. She doubted if even a shifter's immune system could save Delaney from shots fired at point-blank range.

She raced, howling, along the left side of the clearing and heard Rocky's echoing howls on the other side. And, more distantly, she heard a third howl. *Wayra*. Only one of the men in the carts was armed and he shouted, "Coyotes," and raised his rifle.

"There's no coyotes on Cedar Key," the deputy said, laughing. "That's dogs. Maybe this guy's buddies." He thrust the end of his rifle toward Delaney, who snapped at the rifle and swiped at it with his massive paw.

Kate didn't hear the rest. She wasn't even sure if he uttered anything more. The wind roared in her ears, she exploded out of the trees and leaped. By the time the deputy and his son saw her, it was too late. She struck the son so hard he fell into his father and lost his grip on his rifle. The deputy's rifle went off, the explosion echoed through the trees, and the shot flew wild. Delaney seized his opportunity and jumped at the two men, knocking them both to the ground, pinning the deputy beneath his massive paws and trapping the son under his father's body. As Rocky went after the armed man in the cart, Kate landed on the other side of the clearing.

Shouts rang out, one of the carts started to move away from the clearing, and Liberty suddenly swept down over the vehicle, shrieking, wings flapping madly, her dagger-sharp beak and claws ripping chunks of hair and skin from the men's heads and arms. All four men jumped out and took off into the woods, the hawk and Rocky pursuing them. Wayra came barreling out of the trees in his human form, waving torches and shrieking like someone possessed. He hurled one torch at the fleeing men and another at the remaining cart; the torch landed in the lap of the armed driver. The young man scrambled out, slapping at his clothes, and the *brujo* within him fled; Kate could see it, a puff of discolored smoke.

Around them, beyond them, the dry pine needles and leaves on the ground caught fire. Kate knew it wouldn't be long before the trees caught, before the entire woods was burning. Delaney apparently sensed this, too, and leaped off the deputy and his son. They were no longer armed and the *brujos* within them, terrified by the proximity of the flames, forced their hosts to their feet, and ran. The screaming man with the scorched pants stood there clutching his head, eyes wide with shock, shrieking, *"It's gone, it's gone, dear God, it's gone."* His face crumpled like cellophane and he fell, sobbing, to his knees, arms covering his head.

Kate trotted over to him and licked his face until his sobs subsided and he turned his head, struggling to catch his breath, to speak. "I . . . didn't . . . do anything . . . I . . . what . . . kinda dog . . . You . . . knew I . . . had one of them inside me. You . . ."

"You're safe now," Wayra said when he reached them. "What's your name?"

The man rocked back onto his heels, his eyes bright red, and looked from Wayra to Kate and back to Wayra again. "Friends . . . call me Ebo. I'm . . . a tourist . . . I . . ." He pressed his fists into his eyes and tried not to cry. "Got seized . . . three days ago . . ."

"The thing that seized you is gone," Wayra said gently. "They're all gone. But they're going to alert Dominica and the others about where you are, where we are. We need to get moving."

He looked desperate. "And go *where*? These bastards are everywhere, there's no escaping them, no—"

Wayra crouched in front of him. "Listen to me, Ebo. I'm deeply sorry for what has happened to you. You've stumbled into a very old story. But I assure you there *is* a way to escape them. You can travel with us, or you can get off the island on your own. My advice to you is to flee while you can, head toward the fourth bridge, where the quarantine blockade begins."

"I . . . I can make it on my own. The tribe is . . . targeting . . . groups. That's how these mutants found the dogs. They . . . got a tip about the hawk. Dominica hates that hawk, she knows it belongs to that woman who has the houseboat, and she sent us . . . to check things out. We saw . . . the houseboat . . . then that huge dog . . . She . . . Dominica . . . told us to shoot all dogs, especially any black Labs."

In other words, Kate thought, Dominica had ordered her tribe to shoot Wayra on sight.

Ebo waved his hand toward Kate. "I . . . don't understand . . . The greyhound, the Great Dane . . . that other dog that jumped on me . . . are they yours?"

"Not mine, no," Wayra said. "But I'm responsible for them right now."

A cart came toward them, Delaney and Rocky now in their human forms with Delaney driving, the hawk perched on the back of the rear seat. Kate stared at them, mystified that they'd been able to shift. How did they know what to do?

"Get in," Delaney hollered. "The fire's catching fast."

"What happened to the dogs?" Ebo asked as they piled into the backseat.

"They'll catch up to us later," Wayra said. "Is the redhead still in charge of these mutants?"

"I haven't seen her since last night. I think she . . . she was put into the deep sleep. That's what they do when they . . . well, you know."

Wayra nodded.

The cart whispered forward, not exactly moving at the speed of light, not even moving as fast as she could run. Kate thought of her life as a bartender, as Rocky's mother, Richard's lover, her parents' daughter. None of it made sense anymore. And yet all of it, in some odd way she would never be able to explain, made perfect sense. She was still Kate Davis, but now she was more than that woman, more than all of those roles she had lived. Kate Davis, she thought, had become more than the sum of her parts. She was like that holographic universe she had seen during her transformation.

When they reached the edge of the wooded area, Delaney pulled up just short of the road and they all got out. The road was empty of cars, sounds, empty of humanity. She felt deeply uneasy; the smoke was too close, thick, pervasive. But her real unease stemmed from her desperate craving for her human body, her human senses, her human bones and skin and identity. Suppose she could never change back?

You'll figure it out, Kate.

Delaney, inside her head. It was one thing to communicate like this with her son, quite another to communicate like this with the man who had kissed her in the Zodiac raft lifetimes ago, making her feel things she hadn't felt in years, kissing her right before he nearly had bled to death in her arms. She wanted to resist it, just on principle. But what was the point? At the moment, she was a greyhound who could run like the wind, whose sense of smell enabled her to travel into unimagined worlds, a shifter with DNA that seemed to perform like some intricate circuit board, connecting her to others of her kind. Why resist the experience?

How'd you figure it out, Delaney?

It's not so different from RV.

C'mon, your body changed. Your DNA changed. You became a dog.

I became a shifter. I think it's the physical manifestation of the work I've been doing for more than twenty years. It's the next step.

What happens now?

His response wasn't immediate. He stood next to her on the side of the empty road, and let his hand drop to her back. He scratched behind her doggie ears and drew his fingers lightly down her spine. Strange, pleasant sensations coursed through her.

I think Wayra has to give us some guidelines on shifter life, Kate.

Wayra told Ebo how to get to the fourth bridge, Delaney tossed him the key to the cart, and Wayra pressed it into Ebo's hand. "Go, while you still can," Wayra said.

"But . . . what about the three of you? How're you going to get out?"

"Don't worry about us."

Ebo threw his arms around Wayra, thanking him repeatedly, then jumped into the cart with the terrified eagerness of a traumatized puppy. He pulled away from them without a single backward glance. Kate and the others remained where they were, the hawk fluttering above them, until the cart was out of sight. Then both Delaney and Rocky dropped to their hands and knees and began to shift, the most grotesque and beautiful thing Kate had ever seen.

Their hands and feet, arms and legs, went first, bones cracking and popping and rearranging themselves. Their thumbs, then their fingers, retracted into their hands and their hands became paws with claws. Even as fur sped across their paws and up their legs, their spines cracked and popped, their necks thickened and shortened, their heads started to change. It looked agonizing, but neither of them emitted a sound.

In about ninety seconds, their transformations were complete. Rocky howled, and Delaney trotted over to Kate; he was now a magnificent Great Dane, obsidian black except for two perfectly white paws, left front, rear right. He nuzzled her side with his head. *We have to look at this as an adventure or we'll plunge into madness.*

Rocky added, *Madness? Are you kidding? This is awesome.*

"We should find a safe place where we won't be disturbed for a few hours," Wayra said, and then he shifted, too, his transformation occurring between one heartbeat and the next.

The hawk cried out and flew above them, circling, soaring. They followed her, a pack of very strange dogs loping west across Cedar Key.

Twenty-one

Dominica and Whit thought their way back to the hotel and up toward the attic. Dominica knew she'd left Maddie way too long in the deep sleep. But the excursion in the fog, to the cemetery, had delighted her. Seizing Sanchez, plugging into his memories however briefly, had been an unexpected bonus. Even her and Whit's experiment in bravery, entering the cemetery, had been illuminating. But they should have returned to the hotel attic sooner. She fully expected to find Maddie and Sam in bad shape. Dehydration, soiled clothes, mental confusion. What she did *not* expect was what they found—empty cots. Her shock incapacitated her, then collapsed into fury.

Without Maddie, she had no weapon against Wayra, the chasers, no means to wreak havoc on the lives of the people who had annihilated nearly everyone in her tribe in Esperanza. No way to get even. She didn't understand how Maddie had escaped. Dominica was sure she'd put her into a sleep deep enough to last ten or twelve hours. And yet, maybe not. Maybe, in the aftermath of her and Whit's lovemaking up here, she'd gotten careless, too cocky, too certain of victory.

What the fuck, Whit said. *I put him way under.*

We can find them, Whit. Just focus on Sam's essence.

Tense, unpleasant moments passed. *I don't sense him, but I feel the escape route he took.*

Dominica focused on Maddie. Due to the young woman's agitation at the time, her high-strung emotions, she was able to track Maddie's movement to a storage room, down a laundry chute, and out a side door. She and Whit thought themselves along the escape route, then crossed State Road 24 to the unfinished church. Here, the psychic residue of Maddie's path was exceptionally strong. She'd been scared, relieved, starved, thirsty, desperate. Her emotional and physical needs had driven her out of the church, leaving stubborn Sam behind in . . .

Here, Nica, here he is.

Sam was slumped in the nearest confessional, his head thrown back like that of a man in the throes of an epiphany. But the only epiphany he'd experienced was a bleed-out. Someone in her tribe had found him and finished him off. Never mind that bleeding out a host was illegal. The laws she'd laid down were rescinded immediately and good riddance to Sam Dorset, who had been nearly as problematic as Maddie.

Maddie ran west, Dominica said. *She saw the bleed-out happen.*

We can find her.

How ironic that he echoed her exact words about finding Sam. *I'll seize her and you seize that delectable Sanchez and I guarantee you neither of them will ever object to our having sex.*

Whit's essence rubbed up against hers, a sorry excuse for an embrace, but the best that *brujos* in their natural forms could achieve. *I like that idea, Nica. It may be the best idea you've had in the last twenty-four hours. With the right hosts, we can just leave if things get too crazy on the island.*

Leave? She had no intention of leaving. Except for the details—holdouts, the mounting garbage, zero infrastructure, dwindling food and supplies, and the fact that she lacked a host—Cedar Key was hers. She wasn't quite sure yet how she would get rid of the CDC, the FBI, the Coast Guard, and all the other feds outside the quarantine zone. But she had faith that she would figure it out. It disturbed her that Whit even mentioned leaving.

I'm not leaving here, Whit. This is the brujo *enclave.*

Not right now, it isn't.

But it will be.

He didn't respond for a few moments. *Do you have any idea what Liam is doing, Nica?*

Liam? Who cared about him? He was without a host. He was an outcast, a pariah. *Liam can't hurt us, Whit.*

Not yet. But when he's passionate about something, he can be convincing. And he has convinced an impressive number of brujos *that you're not up to the task of leading us. It all started in the market. His followers grow hourly.*

How many followers?

I don't have exact numbers yet, but at least a hundred. And they aren't interested in having hosts, at least not here.

Dominica filed the information away, and her mind clicked into gear. *Forget Liam. Right now, the bottom line is that you and I need hosts. We have several dozen backups in the hotel courtyard. Let's choose and get moving with our plan.*

What plan?

The plan that somehow ended with Cedar Key as a *brujo* bastion, the plan that would happen with or without Whit, even though he was the one she loved right now. *I'm not ready to discuss it yet. Let's go select our new hosts.*

As they thought themselves back to the Island Hotel, she felt Whit's moodiness, his sullenness, his withdrawal from her, the walls he erected. He was pissed that she hadn't confided in him about her plan. She hated the distance between them. She longed to merge her essence with his, and prompt him to forget his questions and concerns. She had no intention of seizing any feds, of battling them, unless they entered the town again and then they would be bled out, just like the men in the hazmat suits. Her only goal was to secure the town, to make sure that every last *brujo* in the quarantine area had a host. Once that had happened, she would summon others of her kind again, put out a call to them, and invite them to seize the feds. She refused to sacrifice a single member of her new tribe to any fed.

That had been one of her mistakes in Esperanza. Back then, she hadn't known that she could summon other ghosts. Her tribe had been so large that she never had the need for reinforcements. She felt certain that once she secured Cedar Key, everything else would fall into place. But she couldn't explain this to someone like Whit who, when he was alive, was victimized by American authority—cops, attorneys, feds, the legal and prison systems.

They drifted into the hotel courtyard, where several dozen men, women, and children were being held as backup hosts. In the light of day, the selection looked pathetic—the elderly whose terror had reduced them to blithering heaps, several young children who fussed and cried for their mommies, and a handful of potential hosts in their late twenties to late forties who looked fit and were in various stages of denial, defiance, grief. This was the group among which she and Whit drifted.

The children were guarded but not restrained as the adults were. Some adults, the screamers, were gagged. So far, one man had attempted to escape and he was now locked in an upstairs room, gagged and tied to a bed.

Choose, Nica, whispered Whit.

Maybe you should return to the cemetery and seize Sanchez while I seize one of these young women.

Uh-uh, not just yet. I'll return with a host, thanks. Once we've got hosts, then we can herd Zee's group out of the cemetery and I'll seize Sanchez.

Then how about if I choose a host for you among these possibilities and you choose one for me?

Whit's essence rubbed up against hers again. *Perfect.*

One moment he was sullen, the next moment he was loving.

They moved from host to host, scrutinizing the backups. It was like a display case in a bakery, where you examined all the delectable choices, the sweet scents driving you nearly half mad with indecision. *I'll take that one and that one and this one, too.* She finally settled on two possibilities.

One young man, a tourist, looked like a gym rat, a much younger Bruce Springsteen with killer biceps and soulful eyes. He was maybe thirty. He had beautiful hands that spoke of sensuality and strength. The second possibility was a man going gray in the temples, his body lean and mean, that of a runner, she guessed. He looked like an Olympian god, a bold, square chin, eyes a Windex blue, a seductive mouth that, at the moment, held a grim defiance rather than fear or surrender. He looked like a CEO, a commercial airline pilot, a Wall Street banker, a physician. In short, he looked like a leader.

Him. Take him, Whit. Our tribe will listen to him.

Whit studied the man, then drifted in to taste him. The man felt it and tried to wrench away, but his hands were cuffed to the arm of one of the heavy iron decorative benches and his feet were lashed together with rope. *A small dot-com CEO who made millions when the company was sold to Google. Name's Kevin. He's here looking for property. And a woman.*

He's come to the right place.

He's mine.

It delighted her that Whit approved of her choice. Maybe he understood her better than Ben or Wayra had.

What about a host for me, Whit?

Over here.

They drifted across the courtyard to a large oak that dominated the area. Of the four women tied to the trunk of the tree, he chose the one whose body appealed to Dominica, a looker in her late twenties. Short, black hair tucked behind her ears. Dark, angry eyes. She wore hiking shorts and shoes, and a shirt with a low scoop neck that promised a glimpse of her ample breasts. Not a skinny thing, not overweight, but pleasingly tall, perhaps five foot ten. She had a ring in her right eyebrow, wore an armband of metal bracelets that reached halfway up her right arm. She looked, Dominica thought, like some Amazonian warrior. She tasted the woman, something that had been strictly forbidden in Esperanza.

The taste was enough to extract a minimum of information. Lynn from Key West. Thirty-six and single. Ex-prison librarian, ex-teacher, ex-social worker, ex-Macy's clerk, ex-bartender, and not necessarily in that order. The point was that she rarely finished anything she started and might be easily enlisted to the *brujo* cause.

Well? Whit asked.

I'll take her, and Dominica ordered both Lynn and Kevin to be released. Then Dominica slipped into the woman on her left side, seizing her so swiftly and expertly she didn't have a chance to react, to fight. It took Dominica a few minutes to adjust her essence to the woman's body, to seize control of her lungs and heart. But once those lungs breathed for her and that heart beat for her, she located Whit on the other side of the courtyard, adjusting his essence to that of his host. Dominica was so attracted to the host she had chosen for him that she hurried over and took his hand.

Lynn and Kevin. Kevin and Lynn. "We chose well, Whit."

"Oh, but is he ever pissed, Nica."

"He'll get over it. He likes the way my host looks."

"He does. He really does." His eyes traveled the length of her body, head to toe and back again. Then he grinned. "Just the promise of something with your host makes him compliant." He slung an arm around her waist and pulled her against him, whispering, "Nica, assure me that you have a plan, that's all I'm asking."

She realized this was Whit's way of making up to her, of apologizing for his sullenness. "I do," she said. "I have a plan."

He nibbled at her ear, igniting such desire in the body of her new host that she felt like making love to him here, right now, in the courtyard. But Gogh interrupted them, the expression on his host's face tense, tight. He still occupied Richard, Kate's ex-boyfriend, the bartender at the Island Hotel. "We've got some problems."

"Lighten up, Gogh." Dominica spoke dismissively. "It's never as bad as it looks."

"Yeah," Gogh said. "It's worse. Along Gulf Boulevard, the woods are burning."

"Get the fire department—"

"*There is no fire department,* Dominica. There's no garbage pickup, no police, no city government at all, okay? Anything goes here. If that fire is going to get put out, *we* have to do it. If the garbage is going to be picked up, if food and supplies are going to be delivered to stores, if anything is going to be imported or exported, *it's up to us to do it.*"

His face turned beet red, he was nearly shouting, and she suddenly understood that she had overlooked the obvious. In order for Cedar Key to be a *brujo* bastion, it had to be a tourist bastion as well, with a booming economy. Who would want to visit a place where the garbage wasn't picked up, the fire department didn't work, and the police department was dysfunctional? All the chinks she had identified in the abstract a while ago now became quite personal, immediate, urgent.

"Fix it," she snapped. "You and Whit fix it now."

Whit linked his host's arm through Gogh's and they sauntered off like a couple of Wall Street shysters to discuss nuances, ramifications, details. Dominica went inside the hotel, delighting in her new host's body, in its quiet compliance. Lynn from Key West had an excellent body, young and fit, and might prove to be an excellent host.

Dominica headed for the lobby computer. She went online, to gypsy woman's blog. The latest entry inspired her. It showed a bare-breasted woman dancing, a flowing scarf entwined in her arms, and Dominica could almost feel the sensual touch of that scarf against the woman's skin. And the simple words struck to the core of Dominica's heart: *In dreams I taste you still.*

Even though she no longer slept or dreamed, it was how she'd felt about Wayra for centuries after he'd left her. These days, not so much. During those moments in the salt marsh, Dominica had understood the depth of his hatred for her and of his commitment to rescuing Maddie and defeating her and her new tribe. His heart was just as vengeful as hers, she thought. He intended to get even with her for killing Sara Wells, the woman he'd supposedly loved longer and more profoundly than he'd ever loved her.

Apparently she had been deluding herself for centuries by thinking that the best relationship of her existence had been with Wayra. It was her oldest relationship, but the one with Ben had been the best, the most stable, the most normal. They had even enjoyed a full married life in the fifties, both of them as attorneys. He had understood her. He had never sought to change her, as Wayra had. And Maddie's aunt Tess had annihilated him in a hotel in Key Largo.

That deserved retribution, bleeding out Maddie, an act of retribution for Ben.

She started to type a comment, but a new post suddenly popped up at the top of the page, an image of Dalí's melting clock, a place where time no longer counted, then the words:

Nica,

> Once upon a time,
> When you were mine,
> Love was a lie,
> Our phony tie.
> Now your lust
> Is a tragic bust
> And we are just
> Dust to dust.

Yours always,
Wayra

Dominica read the entry twice, certain he had written it. That tongue-in-cheek closing—"yours always"—was the same one she had used in letters she'd written to him over the centuries. Had he posted it by hacking into Gypsy's blog? Of course he had. She couldn't imagine him contacting a stranger and *asking* her to post it on her blog. He would never willingly draw an outsider into this battle.

Then it hit her. Wayra hadn't posted this. He hadn't even written it. Maddie had. She knew which of Dominica's buttons to push, knew how to phrase things, to make Dominica doubt the validity of her own perceptions, knew how to rip open her heart—and she knew how to hack. In her life before Dominica had seized her, Maddie used to write software and freelanced as a hacker specialist—someone who went after hackers.

Dominica hit the comment button and typed: *Maddie, Maddie, you are so fucked.*

Then rage overtook her. She shot to her feet, lifted the lightweight monitor and hurled it. The monitor shattered against the far wall in a satisfying display of glass and plastic, a forensic treasure trove of rage. She jerked open the door to a storage unit, grabbed a baseball bat that someone in this hotel once used with his or her son in Little League games, and went after the remains. She slammed the bat against the monitor again and again, reducing it to smithereens. Then she went after the computer itself and felt the first blow all the way to her toes.

"Nica?"

She paused, glanced at Whit. She realized her host was sweating, breathing hard, her heart hammering. "What is it?" she asked crossly.

His gaze flitted across the bits of plastic and metal that littered the desk, the floor. "What're you doing?"

"Getting even."

He didn't ask what she meant. He knew better. "A fire truck and one of the police cruisers are on their way to the fire in the woods."

"We still have cops?"

"We do now. Hosts who think they're cops, who're armed. We've got eight dump trucks, enough to crash through that cemetery gate and take those holdouts. If you conjure fog during the attack, it will help lessen the collective fear of the cemetery."

She dropped the bat. "And we have plenty of weapons? Real weapons?"

"We, uh, do, yes."

She heard the hesitation in his voice. "What else?"

"A small group had a confrontation with some dogs—and a hawk."

She disliked what this bit of information told her. Dog and hawk implied that Wayra had found support with Kate and Rocky. Had Maddie found *them*? Did it matter? What were these pathetic few against her larger tribe?

"We herd Zee's people, we don't bleed them out," she said. "They're to be brought to the hotel courtyard and kept here as backup hosts."

"Those were my exact instructions." Whit took her hand and brought it to his damp, cool mouth. His eyes, shining with a kind of primal wildness that excited her, locked on hers. He pressed her back against the edge of the lobby desk, his hands on her breasts, her buttocks, his mouth teasing hers. She felt such an intense and abrupt desire for him that when he unzipped her host's shorts, she didn't resist, didn't push him away, didn't admonish him about sex in such a public place. What the hell did she care about a public place? She craved Whit's touch and his passion for her only ignited her passion for him.

"Not so fast," she whispered.

But it was as if he hadn't heard her. He took her with several hard thrusts, grunting, shuddering, and she was left high and dry, her disappointment so acute she felt like screaming. Afterward, Whit clung to her like fire, his breath hot against her neck, his mouth burning against her skin.

Beyond them were other hosts, scurrying around, everyone with a job, a task, an *assignment*. No one looked at them, no one noticed her shorts pooled around her ankles. No one cared. *It doesn't matter*. Dominica recognized a kind of beauty in that blindness, that indifference to her and Whit's particular yearnings, and felt she had entered Gypsy's world of unbridled lust.

But Gypsy reminded her of the poem from Wayra that he hadn't written—but might have—and she pushed Whit away and jerked up her shorts, zipped them. Then she sank her index finger into his chest. "Next time, it's a bed, and *you* satisfy *me* first."

Whit looked mortified. "You weren't satisfied?"

"No," she snapped, and moved away from him, through the lobby to the waiting vehicles outside.

The soil, loose and dry, made it quick and easy to dig graves for Fritz and his wife. But for Sanchez, the preparation of the bodies for burial seemed to take forever. They had to be cleaned up, the blood washed away, their clothes changed, rituals observed. Sanchez finally wandered away from the group, into the trees, and sat on the cold, hard ground. He crossed his legs lotus style, shut his eyes, and struggled to contact Fritz's spirit or that of his wife, but failed to connect with anything at all. He tried to contact Maddie, his mother, Charlie, but every avenue was blocked to him.

He finally opened his eyes and looked slowly around the camp. Trucks and trailers and cars encircled the cemetery like wagons in a caravan. Open pit fires kept pots of food and coffee warm, women carried laundry hampers in between trailers, hung clothes out to dry on a makeshift clothesline, or hurried with their partners or spouses into and out of the trailers where the bodies were being prepared for burial. Then there were the guards, dozens of them positioned at various points outside the camp, vigilant, ready.

But not ready enough. He understood that Zee planned to attack the *brujo* stronghold after dark, when he felt they would have the advantage. But Sanchez couldn't squelch his rising anxiety that they needed to get out of the cemetery long before then. When Dominica had seized him and he had read as much of her as he could stand—he had caught snippets of her intention to raid Zee's camp. But it seemed she had to overcome her fear of cemeteries to do so. And it wasn't just *her* fear; this fear apparently was endemic to all of these hungry ghost mutants.

Sanchez felt guilty for suggesting this place to begin with, but at the time, Maddie had told him that *brujos* feared cemeteries and it had seemed like their safest bet. That element had obviously changed. One of the things he'd learned when Dominica had seized him was that she—and perhaps some of the other ghosts as well—could conquer her fears and aversions. It was the equivalent of a living person breaking a habit like smoking—not easy, but not out of her reach, either. She'd conquered her fear of fire long enough to help extinguish the blaze at Annie's Café, and it wouldn't surprise him if she conquered her aversion to cemeteries long enough to enter and attack the camp.

Sanchez got up, whistled for Jessie, and they loped back to their tent. He shoved his clothes and belongings into his pack, checked the clip in his Glock; it was full, eighteen rounds. He slipped it into his jacket pocket and put three additional clips into his pack that had come from Zee's munitions supply. More than seventy rounds, enough to make a difference, he thought, and felt disgusted it had come down to this, weapons and ammo. He suddenly longed for the RV room in Homestead, for the relative simplicity of his life then, a life that he knew might be forever lost to him now.

He slung the pack over his shoulder and made his way across the camp to Zee's trailer. Just as he started up the steps to the front door, it slammed open and one of the women swept past Sanchez with clothes draped over her arm. Zee stuck his head outside, his face cherry red with anger. "Her clothes have to be beautiful, you hear?" he yelled. "No jeans, no T-shirt, something feminine and soft!" Then he blinked and looked at Sanchez. "You off to somewhere, son?"

"You have a few minutes, Zee? We need to talk."

"Not a good time, Nick. We're trying to get the bodies prepared for burial."

In a soft, urgent voice, Sanchez said, "You need to bury the bodies fast so we can get the hell outta here. I have a bad feeling about staying here."

Zee rubbed his unshaven jaw and stared at Sanchez for a moment longer, his rheumy eyes so unspeakably sad that Sanchez had to look away. Then he shut the door and came down the steps to where Sanchez stood. "Is it God talking through you, son?"

"I never said God spoke through me, Zee. I just feel we need to leave immediately. Bury your son and daughter-in-law now, tell your people to get ready to move out, into town, and to be fully armed. We'll burn the town and take them down."

"That's our plan, but for after dark when we'll have the advantage of—"

"That goddamn fog was already aggressive this morning. They're just regrouping, Zee. Give me some of your men and we'll move out now, giving you time to bury Fritz and—"

Gunfire cut the rest of his sentence short, a continuous, explosive chatter from the AK-47s the guards carried. Zee's head snapped up, the Bluetooth connected to his ear burst with chatter that even Sanchez could hear, and he raced into the middle of the camp, waving his skinny arms. *"We're under attack, get to your posts."*

But for long, terrible moments, no one in Sanchez's field of vision moved. People glanced around in confused terror, as if none of them knew where their posts were supposed to be. Sanchez dived for the ground and rolled under one of the trailers, his dog following him. They scrambled along on their bellies until they were behind one of the massive tires. Jessie trembled with fear and Sanchez flung one arm over her back, murmuring, "Good girl, stay close." Then he peeked out from behind the tire.

Eight dump trucks had crashed through the cemetery gate, flattened part of the fence, and now tore into the cemetery, spreading out like a cancer. Fog thickened and rose on either side of them, then in front of them, creating a shield of white soup that obscured their precise location. But before the vehicles disappeared, Sanchez saw enough to know that Zee's people were seriously outnumbered. The trucks all had rear beds that held eight, ten, maybe as many as a dozen people. And within the fog, he could hear dozens more *brujos,* their litany so horrifying and alien that fear paralyzed him. Run or stay? Cower or fight and hope for the best?

No-brainer. He now knew what it was like to have one of these things inside his body. He didn't intend to ever have a repeat experience.

Sanchez rolled out from behind the tire again. He could make out vague outlines within the fog, dark, rapidly moving shadows, and he targeted the closest one, and opened fire, emptying his clip. The vehicle suddenly veered off to the right, the fog parting like some biblical sea, and flipped over. Two men in the truck's bed were hurled out, struck the ground, and didn't move. Sanchez rolled back behind the tire, tore off his pack, dug inside for the additional clips. He slammed one into the Glock, rolled again, and fired at whatever he saw, one side to another. When he emptied the clip, he loaded again, took hold of his dog's collar and moved toward the far end of the trailer.

Jessie got the idea and nipped at his hand, making it clear he didn't have to restrain her; she knew the drill, she would follow him. They crawled quickly over dirt and grass, chaos bursting around them: blaring horns, shrieks, shouts, gunshots, explosions, total pandemonium. At the far end of the trailer, Sanchez spotted one of the dozen mausoleums in the grave-yard and knew he could make it. "Okay, Jess, you have to stick close."

She whimpered, drew her tongue over the back of his hand. When he crawled out from under the trailer and leaped up, so did she. They raced through a thin fog, through the stink of smoke. He heard several of the vehicles closing in on him, and dived behind the mausoleum. Jessie landed beside him and Sanchez leaped up, the massive marble structure shielding his body, and shot blindly. A heartbeat later, a truck careened past the mausoleum and crashed into a small, wooden structure, tore a hole in the side of it, and slammed into the mechanism that powered the cemetery sprinkling system.

Suddenly, sprinkler heads all across the cemetery popped up out of the ground like living things and whipped into action, shooting great, power-ful gushers of water in every direction. The hosts who were nearest to the gushers were knocked off their feet, others were driven back, some ran for cover. The stupid *brujo* fog didn't seem to know what to make of these gushers, so it—or Dominica—used the moisture to create more fog, thicker fog, fog that both blinded and shielded him and Jessie.

They dashed through the fog to Cemetery Point. Jessie leaped into one of the canoes and Sanchez frantically pushed it off the beach and into the water and jumped in. He switched on the electric motor, but nothing hap-pened. "Shit, shit," he muttered, and checked the battery connection. He hit the switch again and again, then the engine hummed to life.

He opened the engine up wide, but the boat was just a simple canoe with a puny electric outboard—soundless, but puny—suitable for fishing on a calm day, not for escaping the madness in the cemetery. Long ropes of fog pursued them, whipping away from the land and across the surface of the bayou like water serpents. One strand lifted up out of the water, dropped into the boat next to Sanchez's feet, and quickly wrapped around his ankles. He tore the shit away with one hand and with the other he fired the Glock into that part of the strand that still trailed in the water.

The fog there didn't just break apart—it *fell* apart, as if he'd struck its brain. The boat whispered on through the salt marsh, sometimes hidden, sometimes exposed. Sanchez brought out his BlackBerry and activated his GPS so he could see exactly where he was in relation to land. Not only did the service work, but it was like looking at a map during an RV session in which he was supposed to pinpoint a target. He suddenly believed that Maddie was somewhere below the third bridge, and that she'd broken free of Dominica.

But as soon as he felt this certainty, he doubted it. His ability was capricious enough to surrender to desire, to create images and scenarios that would never manifest themselves because they had no basis in reality. Just the same, he continued toward the general area below the third bridge. When he neared the salt marsh with the tall reeds and lush growth that would hide him, he cut the power. The bayou quickly went shallow, forcing him to tip the engine out of the water. Since he didn't have paddles as backup, he drifted with the current.

Thirty yards from shore, he ran into a sand dune. It was low tide. He swung his legs over the side of the boat and sank to his thighs in muck. He pulled one leg out, stepped forward, sank again. Jessie barked and paced the length of the rocking boat, eyeing the water warily. "C'mon, girl," he coaxed her. "A short swim and then a short run. You can do it."

But in the end, she sat back, whining and pawing at the side of the boat and Sanchez had to lift her out and set her in the water. Then she raced for shore, splashing through water and muck. They plowed through the last few yards together and collapsed on a tiny dune of low brush and crushed shells. Sanchez felt so spent, so totally exhausted, that he shut his eyes. When he opened them again, the sun was much lower against the horizon, his stomach cramped with hunger, his mouth felt like a fire pit, dry and sooty.

He rocked back onto his heels and saw a dune buggy tearing toward them, toward him and Jessie. He flung his arms around her and they scooted down behind the dune, below the level of the brush and reeds. Jessie didn't move, didn't whimper. The dune buggy flew past them, the echoing laughter of the people inside a seductive call: *Join us, laugh with us, physical life is fun.* Seductive, he thought, unless you'd been seized and knew the truth. Possession by one of the *brujos* made death look inviting.

He didn't know how many minutes passed before he finally got to his feet. He felt washed out, like some old codger coming off last night's drunk. His thinking had gone fuzzy, his head and eyes ached, he craved sleep. He and Jessie trudged up the dunes. They weren't high dunes, but felt like Everest. His calves hurt, his feet hurt, he was a goddamn mess. He needed water, food, a respite. He tried not to think about the chaos and carnage he had fled. But suddenly, it was all he could think about. Visions exploded in his skull—real or imagined, the effect on him was the same, a crippling guilt that he had not stayed behind to fight, to defend the camp, to help the man who had saved his ass.

He crawled the last thirty feet to a wooden porch, up three steps, to the sliding glass doors. And there, he collapsed, he just couldn't move another inch. Jessie whined and pawed at him, licked his face and neck, insisting that he crawl another few feet to the doors. Sanchez reared up on his knees, pressed his palms against the glass and pushed left.

The door rattled open and he and Jessie made it inside the quiet house. He slid the door shut, eyed the comfortable-looking couch on the far side of the living room. It listed, the room blurred, and he knew he wouldn't make it. He crumpled to the cool tile floor, the side of his face resting against his hands, and shut his eyes. His dog stretched out alongside him, a warm, familiar shape against his side.

He dreamed in great, sweeping mythic themes, everything excessive, large, boldly colored. But when he woke, he recalled only the myth and the grandness, no specifics. He was thirsty enough to lick his own sweat, and weaved toward the kitchen.

Faucet on, he guzzled, then jerked open the door of the freezer and grabbed a handful of ice. The chill shocked him when he rubbed the cubes over his face and neck, and down his arms. Then it felt good and he popped a piece of ice in his mouth and sucked on it. He filled a bowl with water and set it on the floor for Jessie. She lapped it up.

Sanchez shrugged off his pack, dug out his map of Cedar Key and smoothed it out against the floor. *Where is Maddie?* He ran his hand slowly over the map, trusting that his body would show him her precise location, something more than *below the third bridge*. If his talent failed him, maybe Charlie or his mother would help out. But nothing happened. No tingling, no warmth in his hand, and his mother and Charlie were apparently out to lunch.

He tried again. And again. But he was so attached to the outcome, he picked up nothing at all. He didn't give up. He knew he could do this. He had done it before. But first, the zone. He had to sink into his zone, find the place of *no space no time*. But distracted by noises, hunger, thirst, and his own angst, his consciousness just couldn't seem to sink deeply enough. He kept thinking of his original impression, that she was below the third bridge. Then even that faded from his mind.

When he finally reached his zone, he moved his fingertips over the map without looking at it, and felt the warmth. Strong. Immediate.

His eyes popped open and he stared at the map.

Pine Street neighborhood.

Nothing on Cedar Key was very far from anything else, not as the crow flew. He estimated the Pine Street neighborhood was within a mile or two of his location. But getting there without running into any more roving bands of *brujos* would be a challenge. Sanchez shoved the map in his jacket pocket, stood on legs that felt like they were made of Silly Putty, and opened the sliding glass doors.

A slight breeze kicked in off the water, the smell of it familiar to him now. Fish, seaweed, sand, a faint residue of heat from earlier in the day. Go find her, he thought, and stepped outside, his dog right behind him.

Twenty-two

Maddie worked feverishly until her stomach growled, her bladder ached, until her eyes felt like they'd been stung with dust. She knuckled them and raised her head.

Long, narrow shadows, like elongated cartoon figures, fell into the room. All sorts of strange weapons surrounded her, most of them crude, built from half-remembered stuff from the Internet aeons ago, before she ever knew *brujos* existed, back in Key Largo when algorithms had spoken to her the way words spoke to writers or images and color spoke to artists.

She had torches, crude firebombs, odd-looking firecrackers that would create distractions. None of it would defeat Dominica's tribe, but she might be able to create such chaos that they would be driven away, off the island, into the fed zone outside the quarantine. She placed the first load of weapons in a cardboard box and carried it downstairs to put into the truck.

In the kitchen, she paused and rifled through the pantry and fridge, searching for something to eat. Dominica's people had taken just about everything that was edible, but had left behind a half-full jar of peanut butter, a few slices of bread, some frozen goods. She found a piece of bread that hadn't gone moldy, slapped some peanut butter on it, squirted honey across it, and gobbled it down as she hurried into the garage.

The truck was a monster. It boasted a large, open console below the dashboard and another one between the two front seats. There was also plenty of room in the passenger seat and on the floor in front of it for her backup weapons. The torches would lean against the passenger seat, within easy reach. And just in case she needed it, she dropped a bottle of lighter fluid into one of the cup holders with a box of kitchen matches and several lighters.

When she'd emptied the box, she set it on the hood to take back inside with her for the next load, and walked around the huge truck, checking the tires. The huge tires raised the vehicle four or five feet off the ground. Lights and gun mounts graced the roof, the sun roof slid open at the touch of a button. The truck was obviously used for hunting, probably in the Everglades, by some redneck weekend warrior.

She hurried back inside the house to put the rest of the weapons into her box. The light was fading fast from the bayou. It wouldn't be long before the fog rose. And tonight, she thought, the fog would be brutal, thick, ugly, hostile, aggressive, intent on blood. Fear flooded the back of her throat, that awful taste of bitterness and bile, and it all suddenly felt impossible, weighted, onerous.

No matter how she struggled to spin things in her own head, she was about to take on a tribe of vicious, hungry mutants, most of them so clueless that they simply carried out Dominica's orders and never questioned anything. Except in the Island Market that night. *Which night? Was that last night?* She didn't know. Linear time hadn't existed for her since Dominica had seized her. But she remembered the events, how Liam had confronted Dominica, how he had *dissented.*

Where was Liam now?

Didn't matter. She couldn't hang her hopes on some rebellious ghost, especially some young ghost like Liam who really didn't understand what had happened to him, where he was, who or what Dominica was. And she couldn't hope that Wayra or Sanchez would find her, that she would be rescued like some princess in a tower. That just wasn't going to happen. No guy in any universe she knew of ever thought a woman would rescue *him,* so where had this idea come from that a woman would be rescued by a man?

By the time she finished loading the truck, the sun nearly touched the horizon. She dreaded dusk. She would have to raise the garage door so she could drive the truck out of here. Just the thought of it brought back the taste of all the crippling fear that had kept her captive in her own body for so many months. What a weak little shit she was, allowing Dominica to use her body as she had because she was so terrified that if she fought the bitch, she would bleed out, she would die.

So what if she died? Death was nothing. You weren't obliterated, weren't reduced to dust. Her months with Dominica had taught her that. Energy couldn't be destroyed. And in death, you learned that mythic battles were being fought on levels that might or might not have anything to do with you.

It didn't matter if you grasped what these battles were really about. If you got sucked in, as she had, you had to deal with the situation as it was, not as you wished it existed. If she opened the garage door and found Dominica's newest host staring her down, so what? What did it change or not change? Nothing, absolutely nothing. She would still be herself, Maddie Livingston, willing to fight to the death to maintain her freedom.

Bring it on, bitch.

Just the same, she couldn't overcome her need to check the driveway and the road for cars, people, *interlopers*. Since the garage lacked windows, she grabbed one of her torches, put a lighter in her jacket pocket, and slipped through the door that opened into the fenced side yard. Her arm ached intermittently, as if to remind her of the possible risk. She dug another pill out of her jacket pocket, swallowed it with a gulp of water from a bottle.

She moved past a withered garden, tomatoes rotting on vines, dead clusters of cauliflower, and unlatched the wooden gate. She crept up the walkway, sticking close to the hedge. The sun had sunk so close to the horizon that its dying rays nearly blinded her. She raised her hands to shield her eyes and walked out to the end of the empty driveway. Dark pools of shadows spread out beneath the large trees on either side of the road. Nothing moved out there. Even the air stood still. It unnerved her.

Maddie listened closely to the cries of birds seeking a roost for the night and periodically heard what sounded like gunfire. All day, she'd heard sporadic gunfire, but she still couldn't tell its direction. It might be a good sign, might be a pocket of holdouts who understood that Dominica couldn't multitask. It might also mean the bitch was winning. It reminded her that although she had a lot of firepower, she didn't have a single gun or flamethrower.

A screech of tires startled her and when she glanced around for the source of the noise, a pickup careened around the corner, aimed straight toward her, two men in the back of it. Maddie fumbled for the lighter in her pocket, lit the torch and ran for the side yard. But the truck moved so much faster than she did that it pulled even with her before she reached the gate. She hurled the torch at the truck, it flew wide, and the two men leaped out and tackled her.

The three of them slammed against the ground and the two *brujo* hosts tore at her clothes, laughed, rolled her this way and that as though she were some cute toy found at the doggie park. Her horror triggered the release of adrenaline that flooded through her muscles, her blood, her very being, and enabled her to vault upward, breaking their hold on her.

Maddie kicked one man in the groin and he stumbled, clutching himself, and crashed into the trunk of a nearby tree. The second man grabbed her jacket, jerking her back. Maddie wrenched free, spun, and punched him in the face. The blow split open her knuckles, but she felt the satisfying snap of his nose. Blood gushed from his nostrils and he lurched back, stunned, hands flying to his bloody nose. The third man, the driver, launched himself at her from the side, struck her hard, and they both hit the ground.

Panic exploded inside her, she couldn't move, her attacker's body trapped her against the ground. She couldn't reach the Taser in her pocket, but her arms swung free and she beat her fists against his skull, yanked at his hair, clawed at his face and eyes and throat. He just laughed and sank his knuckles into her ribs and seized the sides of her face with such force that her head was immobilized.

"Dominica wants you back." The words spilled from his mouth in a cloud of spittle and fetid breath. His eyes had gone dark, the way a host's eyes always did when a *brujo* was fully in control. "And I'm taking you back to her and we'll hang you in the courtyard with the holdouts from that cemetery camp and how sweet it will be." Then he pressed his mouth to hers and dug his thumbs into her cheeks, forcing her to open her mouth. When he thrust his tongue inside, Maddie chomped down hard.

His blood poured into her mouth, hot, sticky, a squalid taste, and he shot to his feet, shrieking unintelligibly. Maddie flipped onto her stomach and spat out blood and a large chunk of his tongue. She struggled to rise, to lift up on her elbows, but her right side, where he had punched her, screamed with pain. Her arm now bled, the stitches had torn or just weren't holding. *Shit, get up, fast, into the garage . . .* But the first man, the guy with the injured balls, now came at her, his homicidal *brujo* eyes stuck to her like Velcro.

She knew how this would unfold. He would reach her before she got up. He would beat her, assault her, the *brujo* within him would seize her.

No way.

Maddie pushed up and rose unsteadily to her feet. Pain shot through her side, blood rolled down her arm. In the last of the dying light, she swayed like a frail branch, but when the man hurled himself at her, she dived for the torch, swept it up, grateful that it continued to burn, bright, savagely hot.

The next thing she knew, the two zombies moved toward her from either side. Physical exhaustion nearly crippled her, but emotional horror galvanized her. She swung her torch at the first man and struck him across the upper arm, setting his sleeve on fire. On the backward swing, she hit his companion in the throat and the *brujo* inside of him fled—and propelled itself toward her.

Maddie thrust the torch through the puff of discolored smoke, impaling it, and it suddenly was no more. Just like that, without so much as a whimper, the *brujo* was gone, extinguished, liberated, like Von. The host lay writhing on the ground, hands grappling at his injured throat, then his body convulsed and he went still.

I killed him, I killed this poor fool, my God, what am I?

No, the *brujo* had bled out the host before she vaporized it.

She heard noises behind her and whirled around and faced the driver. A bib of blood covered his mouth and chin; he had torn off his burning shirt and snorted like a bull.

"*C'mon, fuckstick,*" she screamed.

He charged her. Maddie swung the torch, but he was ready for it. He caught the metal stick with his right hand and yanked it away from her with the ease of a parent snatching a box of matches from a two-year-old. He hurled it over his shoulder and the torch landed on the dry hedge and instantly ignited it. He was oblivious to it.

Maddie tore away from him, toward the truck, blood now streaming down her arm, her side throbbing with pain, and prayed the key was in the ignition, where Dominica insisted that all keys for *brujo* vehicles must remain. She jumped inside—and there it was, the key, exactly where it was supposed to be. Now she had a chance. She started the truck, slammed the gear into drive, didn't flinch or hesitate. She aimed, the truck did the rest.

When the truck hit the man, she felt a sickening crunch, as if the impact snapped him in two. Hurled back, in the slow-motion weirdness of her perceptions, he looked like a snow bunny without the snow, arms thrown out at his sides, his expression seized up with astonishment and shock. He hit the ground and didn't move. She didn't see any discolored smoke or mist drift out of him and knew the *brujo* within him had died as well.

Horror and panic overwhelmed her simultaneously and Maddie slammed on the brakes. *Tick, tick,* whispered the engine. *Let me move.* Maddie slumped over the steering wheel, sobbing like a mental patient. She was no longer sure whether she had killed the men—or whether they had been killed by the *brujos* that inhabited them.

The stink of smoke roused her and she raised her head from the steering wheel. Embers from the burning hedge had set the dry grass on fire. It sped across the ground like a luminous serpent, igniting whatever it touched. Maddie scrambled out of the truck and ran over to the weapons the men had dropped. One was a handgun, the other a rifle with a scope. She slung the rifle over her shoulder, pocketed the handgun. She forced herself to check the dead men's pockets for additional clips, didn't find anything. She returned to the truck and searched it for additional ammunition. She found a small leather duffel with two extra clips for the handgun and one clip for the rifle.

My luck is turning.

Maddie tore into the side yard, through the garage, and up the stairs for her pack and whatever else she could grab. On her way back down the stairs, she lit one of the other torches. When she reached the ground floor, she set fire to a couch, then the chairs, throw rugs, anything that would burn hot and fast. In the kitchen, she paused long enough to turn on the gas burners, the gas oven. Terrified the entire house would explode before she got out, she raced into the garage, tossed everything into the truck, raised the door, and backed out into a darkness lit only by fire.

The house blew apart before she reached the end of the road. Flaming chunks hurtled skyward like special effects in a movie and landed in neighboring yards long abandoned. More dry vegetation burst into flame.

She watched part of it in the rearview mirror, then turned around to see it head-on.

Your world, Nica. Burning like Armageddon.

Even as she thought this, guilt besieged her for killing two men whose only crime was being in the wrong place at the wrong time, through no fault of their own, and for destroying other people's property. Even if she hadn't killed them directly, her presence had led to their demise; she was at fault.

As for the property, she didn't have any idea how else to create the kind of chaos that would shove Dominica over the edge. She watched as low-hanging branches caught fire. Pretty soon, old porches would go up like tinder. Windows would implode, roofs would collapse. She didn't hang around to witness the total devastation of the Pine Street neighborhood.

She turned onto the next street, Magnolia. Deserted neighborhood, everyone had either fled or died. She stopped long enough to light one of the rags shoved down deeply into a glass bottle filled with kerosene, and hurled it out the window. It landed in a withered flower bed, burst apart, and last summer's beauty became tomorrow's nightmare.

"I'm sorry," she whispered to the people who had once lived there, to the lives that had unfolded here.

Her truck moved on down Magnolia, a lone machine of destruction. She lit and tossed, lit and tossed, apologizing each time to the people whose homes she destroyed, to the trees and plants and grass that burned. *Create chaos, create chaos.* It was the only plan she had.

When she finished with Magnolia, when everything on the street was aflame, she moved on to Cedar Street. *Light and toss. Again. Again.* And she kept apologizing and now she cried, too, cried for the months and the dignity Dominica had stolen from her, cried for her own losses and for the destruction she caused.

Everything around her now burned. Smoke rolled across the road, trees and houses crackled and hissed as they went up in flames. Maddie sped toward State Road 24, swung left, tires screeching against the asphalt. The headlights impaled a cart with a man and a dog in the front seat. A dark-haired man with a golden retriever.

Sanchez and his dog? Would the dog stick with him if he was hosting a *brujo*?

Maddie braked, grabbed the handgun, flicked off the safety, threw open the door and stepped out. She didn't move away from the protection of the open door as she targeted Sanchez. The cart had stopped and Sanchez was out, moving toward her, his weapon trained on her. He didn't speak, his stride never faltered, his gaze remained fixed on her, steady.

When he finally spoke, his voice was quiet but firm. "You look like Red. But if Dominica's inside you, then I'm going to put a bullet through your goddamn forehead."

"You look like Sanchez. But you may be a host. We could just end up shooting each other."

Sanchez stopped three yards from her. "You're bleeding pretty bad. But even *brujo* hosts bleed, right?"

Before she could reply, the retriever trotted toward her and stopped at her side, barking, tail whipping back and forth. Maddie glanced at the dog, at Sanchez, at the dog again, and released her left hand from her weapon and ran her fingers through Jessie's fur. Emotion nearly choked her. For the first time in months, a dog allowed her to pet it. Jessie knew Dominica was not inside her and apparently her judgment was good enough for Sanchez.

"Got room for two more, Red?"

Overwhelmed, Maddie could barely manage a whisper. "Sanchez."

He came over to her, drew his fingers through her hair, wiped dirt and soot from her cheeks. He covered her face and nose and mouth with small, light kisses, like the brush of a butterfly's wings. The parts of her that had grown hard and knotted during the months of her imprisonment now melted away.

"When I smelled the smoke, I followed it," he said. "I knew I'd find you in the midst of it."

"I . . . killed two men, hosts . . . I . . . They ambushed me outside this house . . . I . . ." To her utter horror, she started sobbing. She pressed her fists against her eyes and suddenly saw herself as Sanchez probably did, a crybaby. "Shit, I—"

"I'd hug you, Red, but you're bleeding pretty bad."

Then he kissed her deeply, a kiss so sublime she gave herself over to it completely. Only the moment existed, the sensation of his mouth, the feel of his body against hers. Maddie hugged him tightly with her good arm, hoping this instant never ended, that she wasn't actually still imprisoned within her body, dreaming these moments so vividly that they seemed real.

He broke the embrace first with a sharp inhalation. He looked badly shaken. "You did what you had to do to stay alive, Red."

"Did I?"

"Yes."

The certainty in his voice caused her to realize that when he'd kissed her, he'd seen something in his mind's eye. It explained why he'd seemed so shaken. "You viewed me," she said.

"It happens unless . . . I shut down. I wasn't shut down."

"What else did you see, Sanchez?"

He touched her injured arm and turned it over so the blood running down the inside was visible. He worked her jacket off, unwound the gauze. "Who stitched this?"

"You see any helpers here, Sanchez? I stitched it."

"I'm no doc, but I've got some EMT experience and your stitches look like the work of a pro. But they weren't tight enough." He pulled a blue and white kerchief from his back pocket and wrapped it tightly around her forearm. "This should help until we can stitch it up again. You have antibiotics?"

"Yeah, outdated by about two years."

His eyes met hers, held hers, locked onto hers as though he were drowning and frantically searching for a safe harbor. "Maddie, Maddie," he whispered, and drew her gently into his arms, but without touching her injury.

She suddenly didn't care if she ever breathed or moved again. Her hands moved over his neck, through his hair, down his spine. She didn't give a shit if they stood here all night and into tomorrow. Then he spoke again, his voice soft, certain, strong and strange.

"I saw the horror of what you've lived since she seized you. I don't know how you stayed sane. She . . . took me briefly, Red." He stood back from her. "Outside the cemetery, when they dumped off the bodies of Fritz and Diana. While she struggled to make my lungs breathe for her and my heart beat for her, I read her, just like I read you now. But with her, it was . . . deeper, horrifying. I saw what happened to you in the attic, saw—"

She touched her fingers to his mouth, silencing him. "Good came out of it. It gave me the strength I needed to escape."

He grasped her hand firmly. "The fire's moving fast. Let's get elsewhere."

"The only way to defeat her is to create so much chaos that she's overwhelmed."

Sanchez stared at the stash of weapons inside the truck. "Where'd you get all this?"

"I made most of it."

"Jesus, Maddie. And the rifle?" He picked it up.

"I got it and the handgun from the . . . the two men I may have killed." She pointed at the duffel bag on the passenger seat. "In there is additional ammo for the gun and the rifle. I don't even know what kinds of weapons these are."

"The rifle is a semiautomatic, an AR-15. The handgun is a nine millimeter. Where the hell did Dominica's people get weapons?"

"Once they seized the chief of police and the cops, it was easy. How much ammo do you have?"

"Not enough. Just a single clip left, eighteen rounds. But with what you've got here, we've got a chance."

They rearranged the weapons so the passenger seat was clear and there was room in the back for Jessie. Sanchez started the truck, drove over to the cart and retrieved his backpack. He handed it to Maddie, who dropped it in the back with the dog, then they continued south on State Road 24.

"They took hostages from Zee's camp," Maddie told him. "They're in the hotel courtyard. They're probably being held as backup hosts."

"How . . . do you know that?"

Maddie explained what had happened when she was ambushed back at the house. "This *brujo* talked about how sweet it would be to hang me along with the hostages from the cemetery camp. His exact words. But the last time Dominica intended to hang someone—Fritz and his wife—the chasers showed up and prevented it. Then the giant crows came. I don't think Dominica will try hanging again. If we can create enough chaos on the island and then downtown, these *brujos* may be so freaked out by fire that we'll be able to get into the courtyard and free the hostages."

"Those crows were too immense to be normal crows, Maddie. What the hell were they?"

"Supernatural birds. That's the only explanation I have. The chasers can do stuff, but they don't do it often enough to suit me." It suddenly occurred to her that he might not know about the chasers or what Wayra actually was, what Esperanza was, might not know much about any of it, and she didn't know where to begin explaining. "You know about the chasers?"

He nodded. "I know enough—that hungry ghosts and chasers have been locked in battle for thousands of years, that Esperanza is unusual in a lot of ways, but I'm lacking on specifics. Ever since I first viewed you, I've been able to see and talk to my mother's ghost and she's supposedly friends with your grandfather, Charlie, who's one of the chasers." He spoke quickly, as though he couldn't get it out fast enough. "The first night I saw my mom's ghost, I was playing an Esperanza Spalding CD . . ."

"A synchronicity," she said, snapping her fingers.

He looked shocked. But she couldn't tell if it was because she had recognized the synchro or that she knew about synchronicity. "Yeah, exactly." Something new entered his expression, a kind of awe. "I once felt like the lone weirdo in the universe, Red. Now I don't." He flashed a quick smile. "No offense. I've got a shitload of questions, beginning with what's more ancient than the chasers?"

"Maybe the shifters."

"The shifters," he repeated. "Like werewolves? Vampires?"

"Similar, but different. Wayra is a shifter, a dog/wolf hybrid who is also human. But he's the last of his kind, born at the tail end of the twelfth century. I used to think the chasers are older than that, but I'm not sure now. The shifters may be older. They may be the ancient ones, the true repositories of knowledge. Shit, I don't know, Sanchez. I'm kinda fucked up from all these months with Dominica."

"The guy in the salt marsh?" he exclaimed. "Wayra? He's a shifter?"

"Yes."

"Christ Almighty. I . . . saw this thin black dog dart into the marsh and then there was Wayra and I never saw the dog again. What else should I know, Red?"

"I wish I could give you the *Reader's Digest* version, but even that would take days."

"It's a date, then. Agreed?"

For the first time in months, Maddie laughed. "Agreed."

Sirens peeled away the silence—fire trucks, closing in. Sanchez turned off the headlights, swerved abruptly right, across the empty road, and raced into the trees. Blackness swallowed them. The truck pounded through low brush, slammed over protruding roots, and when they were in the heart of the blackness, hidden from view by anyone on the road, Sanchez stopped.

"The fire threatened them enough to send out the fire trucks," he whispered. "And maybe the cops."

"There're only two fire trucks on the island. The last I knew, the firemen and cops were all dead or compromised. We have to assume they're all *brujos* with guns."

"Whatever. We want them out here, not in town."

Through the trees, Maddie could see the red lights of the fire trucks and, right behind them, the spinning blue lights of a pair of cop cars. "They've gotten it together enough to investigate."

"As soon as they're out of sight, let's create some more chaos for them."

The vehicles sped past them, sirens at full tilt, and Maddie pressed her hands over her ears to block out the relentless shrieks. When the lights vanished, she whispered, "Let's go."

Sanchez started the truck and tore back out onto the road. Just short of the second bridge, he turned right into a small neighborhood that backed up to the bay. Deserted houses, not a light anywhere, no sign of humanity. Just like the other neighborhoods, Maddie thought, and hoped whoever had lived in these homes had escaped.

He stopped parallel to a vacant lot on the water, where a FOR SALE sign leaned to the left. Across the street from it stood an abandoned SUV, an Explorer. "I've got the car, Sanchez."

"I'll take the field." He turned slightly in the seat, talking to the dog. "Jessie, you stay. Guard the truck."

"You talk to her like she understands you," Maddie said.

"She's smart," he said.

"Maybe she's a shifter."

Sanchez looked at Maddie with an expression that didn't bode well for a future for this relationship. "She's a dog, Red. A retriever. The species exists to please their humans."

"That's such bullshit. No species exists just to please someone or something else. That's how the *brujos* think, okay? That's their MO. And if you buy into that crap, then we're fucked, Sanchez. All of us."

His legs were already outside the truck, but his body remained behind the steering wheel, his head turned toward her, his expression tight, inscrutable. She knew that if he didn't grasp this basic truth, then she would get out of the truck and proceed on her own, toward whatever the future held.

"I don't know why I said that. I don't even believe it. Jessie does what she does because it pleases her, it makes her happy. She's the most joyful creature I've ever known."

Was he just saying that to placate her? He read her expression and shook his head. "No, I'm not, Maddie. I don't live that way."

She leaned toward him and cupped his face in her hands. "What a refreshing change you are, Sanchez."

"Ditto," he said, then kissed her, and she wrapped her arms around him, her desire for him deep and pervasive. But her terror overpowered everything else. She scooted back and they sprang out opposite doors.

Maddie loped across the street to the Explorer. During the battle for Esperanza last summer, an Ecuadoran guy who had lost both parents to *brujos* had shown her a few pyrotechnic tricks. She never thought she'd have to use any of them again, but was grateful those memories hadn't been destroyed by Dominica.

The SUV was unlocked. Maddie popped the lock on the gas cap, hurried to the rear, spun the cap. She pulled rags from her jacket pocket and soaked them with lighter fluid, then shoved them down inside the gas tank. She brought out her lighter, glanced back. Sanchez had set the field on fire and now loped toward the truck. She waited until she heard the engine turn over, then flicked her Bic and held the flame to the rags. It caught—and she raced back to the truck and threw herself inside.

"Fast!" she hissed.

The truck went from zero to sixty in seconds flat, the V-8 engine roaring.

The Explorer blew.

Wayra's alarm escalated by the second. Great plumes of smoke rolled across Cedar Key, ash blanketed the air, the shriek of sirens was almost constant now. He still had to find Maddie and the hawk hadn't returned yet. She had flown off half an hour ago to gather information about the fires and the situation downtown and now he feared that something had happened to her.

He and his pack moved warily through a deserted neighborhood at the far end of Cedar Key. He didn't sense any specific threat, yet the very air he breathed reeked of everything Dominica stood for, chaos, destruction, death.

Kate loped alongside him, her long, sleek greyhound body rippling with tension. *She's winning, isn't she, Wayra?*

I don't know.

It smells like she is.

"Yeah, it does," Delaney said out loud, and Wayra stopped and glanced back.

Delaney and Rocky had shifted into their human forms, so Wayra and Kate did, too. They all stopped beneath the drooping branches of an old cedar tree. "This isn't our battle, Wayra," Delaney said. "My job is to find

Sanchez and get the fuck outta here. Forget the mutant queen of these *bru-jos*. Let her have the goddamn island. My plane's at the airport."

"You're right. It's *not* your battle. Take Kate and Rocky and fly back to Homestead. You'll be safe there for a while. I'll find Sanchez and Maddie and get them out of here."

"Just hold on a minute," Kate said. "I'm not leaving Cedar Key. This is my *home*. I intend to fight these *brujo* bastards till they're gone."

"Yeah?" Delaney shot back. "And how're you going to do that, exactly, Kate? And even if we win this battle, then what? You're a shifter now. That changes everything. Tell her about it, Wayra. Tell her about how it changes everything you do and think and feel. You taught us the basics today, but you failed to address the emotional and spiritual changes this triggers." His eyes slipped back to Kate. "You think you can go back to bartending at the Island Hotel?" He laughed, a quick, nervous sound. "Or that Rocky can finish high school here?"

"What about you?" Kate said. "You can't go back to remote viewing and your life in Homestead. What the hell are *you* going to do?"

He looked suddenly miserable. "I . . . I don't know."

Rocky, blowing into his hands to warm them, suddenly spoke up. "Wayra saved my life. I owe him. He also saved your life, Delaney."

"Shit," Delaney muttered, running his hands over his face.

Wayra realized that what Delaney had said was true. He had taught his shifters the basics, but had avoided all the intricate, complex issues of living as a shifter. "None of you owe me anything. You're now more than what you were. Bob and Rocky, I changed you both because it was the only way to keep you alive. Kate, I changed you so that Rocky would never be alone, but that sentiment was due to my own experience, and for that I owe you my deepest apology. Each of you has to do what your heart dictates."

Just then, the hawk swept down through the smoky darkness and landed on the road. Relief coursed through Wayra, but before he could say anything, before he could express what he felt, the hawk unfurled her wings and instantly transformed, a process so singularly beautiful that Wayra couldn't take his eyes off her. Until this moment, the other three shifters hadn't known the truth about the hawk and they just stood there, staring, mute with shock.

Rocky broke the silence. "I knew it. I knew you were special." And he threw his arms around Illary, and she hugged him tightly, then slipped an arm around Kate and drew her into the embrace.

"Thank you both for everything you have done for me."

Delaney glanced at Wayra, brows lifting as if to say, *Thanks, dude. You kept this from us, too.* "If this is a group hug, then Wayra and I should be included," Delaney finally said.

For long, weird moments, the five of them stood there on the deserted road, on this burning island, hugging each other—and solidifying the bonds that united them. Illary was the first to break the circle.

"Fires are burning all over the island. About two dozen of Zee Small's group are being held in the island courtyard. We might be able to free them if we can create enough distractions."

"If we free them, we need to get them the hell out," Delaney said. "We'll have to get them to the airport."

"The runway is blocked with debris," Kate said. "You'll have to clear enough of it to take off."

"And there are so many *brujos* between the hotel and the airport that they would be easily seized," Illary said. "Can you bring the plane closer to the hotel?"

"Maybe to the marina," Delaney replied. "I can land short if I'm flying low. But the plane can only carry six people with baggage safely."

"We just have packs," Rocky said. "If the seats are removed and your tank isn't full, how many can you safely take?"

Delaney thought about it. "Maybe ten. Big maybe."

"A flight to Gainesville won't take more than twenty minutes," Wayra said. "You can make two trips if you have to."

"We could meet you at the corner of Fourth Street and A, which becomes Dock Street," Kate said. "That would give you a longer area for take-off and the street is wide enough to accommodate the plane's wings."

"All right," Delaney said. "I'll give it a shot."

"And after Gainesville?" Wayra asked.

"Homestead," Delaney said.

"We need a way to stay in touch," Wayra said. "Does everyone have a cell?"

"Rocky and I lost ours," Kate said.

"I've got mine." Delaney slipped his cell from the pocket of his jeans and looked at it. "Weak signal."

Wayra brought out his cell. "My signal's weak, too. But weak is better than no signal."

"I need a first mate." Delaney glanced at Kate and Rocky. "A navigator."

"Me," Rocky said.

Wayra noticed Delaney's immediate and well-disguised reaction. He had hoped Kate might volunteer. But to his credit, he didn't let on. "Then let's get on it, kid."

Kate looked distressed about Rocky joining Delaney, but didn't say anything. She hugged her son. "Be careful, Rocky."

"Not to worry, Mom." He stepped back. "Love you."

Delaney and Rocky shifted and loped off through the trees, headed toward the southwest part of the island where the airport was. Kate stared after them until they disappeared from view, then turned her attention to Wayra and Illary. "So tell me, my shifter friends, how are we going to free two dozen hostages guarded by *brujos* and how're we going to find Maddie and Sanchez?"

"Not in our human forms," Wayra replied, and shifted.

A moment later, Kate and Illary shifted, too. The hawk lifted into the air, flying low above the road, and Kate and Wayra followed her.

Twenty-three

Sanchez drove the truck like a lunatic, careening around corners, racing through deserted intersections. When the sirens closed in on them, he plunged into a wooded area, killed the headlights, and he and Maddie slid down low in their seats.

"*Brujos* are driving those vehicles," she whispered. "The firemen and cops were seized weeks ago."

Sanchez reached for her hand, brought it to his mouth, and kissed the back of it. "We'll use the guns only if we or others are threatened, agreed?"

"Absolutely. Where to next?"

"The airport. If Delaney is still alive, that's where he'll be. His plane is tied down there."

"If he's been seized or is dead, can you fly the plane out?"

Delaney had given him half a dozen lessons, so he could probably take off and land, but anything beyond that was out of the question. He said as much.

"The runway is covered with debris from the café. We wouldn't be able to take off."

"We'll move the debris."

She tightened her grip on his hand as flashing red-and-blue lights strobed through the trees. "*Brujos* are scared shitless of fire. They won't muster the courage to tackle the flames."

Sanchez released her hand and peeked over the top of the seat. "They're gone. Let's get moving."

"Airport?"

"Right. Unless you have another plan?"

She ran the back of her hand across her mouth. "Not at the moment."

Sanchez leaned toward her, kissed her again, and for a short while, they melted against each other, their hearts seeming to beat as one. He pulled back first. "When we escape this place, we'll find a bed with fluffy pillows . . ."

"And a thick comforter . . ."

". . . and a hot shower . . ."

". . . and privacy . . ."

He gave her hand a quick squeeze and started the engine, turned on the brights, and sped out of the trees.

For seconds, no more than that, his entire body sang. He not only had found Red, she was every bit as magnificent as he had hoped. Then headlights exploded in the rearview mirror, the side mirror, nearly blinding him, and Maddie shouted, "*Cop car, brujo cops.*"

The cruiser slammed into their rear fender, the impact threw them both forward, Jessie howled, and Sanchez nearly lost control of the truck. He spun the wheel, the truck zigzagged into a one-eighty, and he floored the accelerator. As they shot toward the cruiser, Maddie yelled, "Get alongside him, Sanchez, *I can shoot out the tires.*"

Sanchez turned, heard the truck's fender clatter to the road, and Maddie opened fire. Her second shot took out one of the cruiser's front tires and the driver skidded across the road, brakes shrieking, and crashed into the closest trees. The horn blared, and in his head, he could see the driver slumped forward, injured or dead.

Maddie pulled her head back inside the truck, slammed another clip into her weapon, then turned around, peering out the back window. "No lights, Sanchez. But if the *brujos* survived, they'll be coming after us."

"Shit, are there any more torches?"

"No. Go left, take this left, fast. Then a right, another left, it'll throw them off."

The tires shrieked into a turn, into a deserted neighborhood the fires hadn't reached yet. He took the first right, another left, moving just as Maddie had suggested. By the time he found his way out onto State Road 24 again, they were less than a mile from the airport.

Kate and Wayra loped across the sandbars beneath the first bridge, making their way toward the back bayou. Illary flew just above them, their scout, their eyes.

With the tide low, mounds of sand were visible, stepping stones through the salt flats. Some of the mounds held reeds and brush that hid her and Wayra, some held only crushed shells and tiny crabs that scampered around, looking for food, or burrowed into the wetness. The crisp air alternated between an uneasy silence, the piercing squeal of sirens, and erratic explosions, which seemed to be coming from behind them.

Once they reached the back bayou, they ran along a vast stretch of sand where the tide had receded completely, then turned to the dry land behind buildings that had stood here for most of Kate's life. Cafés, restaurants, art stores, an old motel, a fish market, colorful wood and concrete structures that served as memory landmarks for her. Even the Island Market, which she could see now, held childhood memories of her Sunday walks with her father, when they headed over to the market to buy bait for a day of fishing. Darkness swam in the market's windows.

They jumped onto an old dock shrouded in brush. A couple of small fishing boats were tied up, wire mesh cages for lobster and crabs stacked at one end. The entire area was deserted. They trotted up the pier to the road, Fourth Street, and stopped. The north side of the hotel property was one block over, a straight shot from where they were. Illary circled above them, vigilant, and spoke to them shifter to shifter.

I'm going to check out those explosions. From here, it looks like it's safest to dig your way under the hotel fence, and go in through the barracks. I'll meet you in the hotel courtyard.

Stay in touch, Wayra thought at her.

Always, mi amor.

Wayra didn't sound just smitten, Kate thought. He sounded like a man who had found the other piece of his soul. *What does Illary mean, Wayra?*

"Rainbow," in Quechua.

What's my shifter name?

I don't know yet. That's for another day. Maybe you'll still be Kate. In five hundred years, that name will sound as odd as Illary does to you now.

Five hundred years. That would be 2509. Right. She couldn't wrap anything around that. As Kate, Homo sapien, she had figured she would be lucky to hit retirement and Medicare. She couldn't fathom five hundred years in the future. At the moment, her goal was to stay alive long enough to chase these mutants out of Cedar Key.

As they dashed across the road, the explosions now sounded much closer. Kate felt the constant wail of sirens in her bones, her teeth. The smoke drifted toward this end of the island, and within it she smelled the panic of small wildlife, rodents, and insects struggling to flee the area. She could even smell the alarm of creatures in the marsh as they moved farther out into the bayou and then into the gulf.

Her eyesight astonished her. Even with this thick blackness, she could see everything clearly. She had heard that greyhounds had the best eyesight of any breed, that they were actually called sight hounds because sight was how they hunted. But this was like having bionic vision, and she suspected it was due to the shifter part of her, not to the greyhound part of her.

When they reached the other side of the road, they moved through a backyard littered with junk—a broken-down yellow school bus without wheels, a small rusted trailer, stacks of tires and wire mesh cages, two carts with flat tires, and heaps of trash—some of it in bags, most of it just loose. They kept to the deeper shadows, Wayra's black coat camouflaging him much better than her fur camouflaged her. And perhaps that was what the *brujos* saw first, a flash of pale gray where there should be only blackness, movement where there should be only stillness.

The first gunshot passed inches above her head and struck the school bus. The second shot kicked up dirt and pebbles just behind her. Kate dived under the small trailer and an instant later, Wayra joined her.

Two of them in a cart, Kate. We can easily outrun them. Head for the trees at the side of that condo. We don't want them to see us digging under the hotel fence.

I'm ready.

Kate burst from under the trailer and tore toward the trees Wayra had indicated. Even though the *brujos* fired repeatedly, she was moving too swiftly. Thanks to the absence of light all over the island, they probably couldn't even see Wayra.

She and Wayra reached the trees just moments apart, but this small thicket of widely spaced pines wasn't sufficient to hide them for long. They ran to the back of the building, past more overflowing garbage cans and Dumpsters that brimmed with trash, and emerged on the far side, near an alley.

That alley eventually leads into one behind the hotel barracks, Wayra. Let's go.

They made it into the alley, and when she looked back, there was no sign of the men in the cart. These particular *brujos* apparently lacked the ability to plan or strategize. Instead of trying to anticipate what she and Wayra might do, they simply continued on the same trajectory.

Kate led the way through one alley after another until they reached the wooden fence behind the barracks. They dug fast, dirt flying out behind them, the hole growing wider and deeper until it could accommodate them. Kate wiggled under first and emerged close to the barracks kitchen; lifetimes ago, she had found candles and wax on the kitchen table and, in the trash, that first piece of paper: "Yes, annihilation by fire." And then the other slips of paper. She now knew it was related to *brujos,* that fire could annihilate them, and suspected that Dominica and several other members of her tribe had voted on annihilating one of their own by fire.

They slipped inside the dark kitchen, went over to a small, dirty window, and peered out into the courtyard. The hotel had gone dark, and the only source of light came from a few stars the clouds had missed and from a fire pit in the center of the courtyard. A dozen or more *brujo* hosts sat around it, laughing and swigging from bottles of booze and beer, music blasting from a CD player on a table, a heavy-metal piece cranked up so high it made her eardrums ache. Party time, celebration. These *brujos* acted like the battle had been won already.

The hostages were tied to trees and tables in three different parts of the courtyard—four men in the center, four women near the fence, and four more men on the far side of the courtyard, close to the hotel, and another dozen scattered throughout the courtyard. Kate spotted Zee immediately, tied to the oak in the center, his head lolling toward his chest. He looked injured.

As Wayra turned away from the window, he shifted into his human form and Kate did the same. The process, only the fourth time she'd done it, was still painful and took considerably longer than Wayra's transformation. And now, as before, it took her several moments to adjust to the loss of sensory richness available to her in her canine form.

"The only way we can free those people is to create a major distraction that scatters the hosts," he said. "Just like Illary said."

"Fire."

"Right." He threw his arms out at his sides. "We set the barracks on fire."

"Jesus, Wayra. Before we're done here, this entire island will be burned to the ground."

"You have a better idea?"

"No."

They moved quickly through the old kitchen, gathering up anything and everything that was flammable. A can of lighter fluid, a container of Drano, a few rags, old dish towels, newspapers. Wayra jerked open a drawer in the counter and brought out four kitchen knives. The blades were dull, but they would have to do. They each pocketed two of them. Then Wayra picked up the container of Drano and started squirting it around the room.

Kate created a trail of lighter fluid that led to a nest of rags soaked in the stuff. She created another trail that led to the wooden chairs and table, where she placed pieces of rolled-up newspaper that she also saturated in lighter fluid. Before they were finished, they had crisscrossed the kitchen with enough flammable material to take down the entire barracks and the hotel next to it. She worried that they would be too close to the building when it went up, that flaming debris might be hurled into the courtyard and injure or kill the hostages. But it was too late for a plan B.

"Okay, get outta here, Kate. I'm turning on the stove burners and lighting a match. Stay close to the fence. As soon as the *brujos* panic, head for the women closest to the fence."

"I'll take the men in the middle of the courtyard, where Zee is. He knows me. Whoever finishes first should get to the group tied up closest to the hotel. We should try to get out the front gate."

As she turned to leave, Wayra said, "Illary was right about you and Rocky. She said neither of you would have a problem with being turned."

"A *problem*? Regardless of how this ends up, Wayra, I want you to know you've given me the greatest gift of my entire life."

He looked surprised, then grinned and shooed her out of the kitchen.

Kate backed toward the door. "Be careful."

"*Siempre.*"

Her Spanish was a bit rusty, but she was pretty sure that word meant "always."

She hurried out onto the rickety side porch, the knife now clutched in her hand. The music pounded the air with relentless fury, drowning out every other sound. Kate pressed through the hedge that grew along the fence, hunkered over, and moved quickly forward, heart drumming hard, beads of sweat rolling down the sides of her face despite the chill. When she was just beyond the fire pit and the drunken *brujos,* she glanced back and saw the flames licking at the windows of the barracks kitchen and Wayra hurrying along behind her.

One of the men at the fire pit suddenly shouted, "*Fire! Fire in the barracks!*"

"*Get the hose!*" yelled someone else.

They scrambled in various directions, looking for the hose, then the windows burst, and a gigantic fireball slammed through the roof like an exploding sun, clouds of black, greasy smoke trailing behind it. Flaming debris was flung a hundred feet or more into the night sky. The sides of the building ruptured with such ferocity that chunks of stone and flaming wood sped like deadly missiles in every direction.

Pandemonium erupted in the courtyard. The *brujos* scrambled for safety and stumbled around drunkenly, knocking over chairs and empty bottles, shouting simultaneously. Someone tripped over the fire pit and it toppled, spilling burning logs and scorching hot embers that quickly set weeds and dry leaves on fire.

The hostages who were still conscious screamed for help and struggled to free themselves. Kate dashed out into the middle of the courtyard, arms covering her head to protect herself from raining debris, and dropped to her knees in front of Zee. He looked bad, one eye swollen shut, bruises on his face and neck, his lower lip swollen, dried blood under his nose and in the corners of his mouth. She sensed he and the others were locked in various stages of terror, physical injury, emotional trauma, psychic and psychological chaos.

"Kate? What the hell." His words slurred. "Hope I'm not dreaming."

"You're not." She started cutting at the ropes that bound his hands to the tree. "How many of them are in the hotel?"

"Dunno. But they're in the hundreds now. The bitch in charge, not sure where she is. But unless we get off the island, we're all fucked, Kate. They killed Fritz ... and Diana and ... and when they raided the cemetery, they ... burned my violin."

The Stradivarius. "I'm so sorry, Zee. For everything." The knife wasn't sharp enough, so she bore down harder, moved the blade faster, and the ropes began to fray. "As soon as you're free, help the others. I've got an extra knife you can use. Then get out through the gate. A plane is going to fly us out."

"A government plane?"

"It's a private plane. Cessna. Look for it in the marina parking lot."

The rope came apart. She quickly handed him the extra knife and started to work on the ropes around his ankles. "Help the ones closest to the hotel, Kate. I can do this."

"Tell the others about the plane, Zee."

The top of the oak had caught fire, the leaves burning fast and furiously, branches snapping, falling. She kicked branches away and moved to the far group of hostages. She freed one, moved to the next, and was suddenly yanked back as though she weighed no more than a mosquito, and hurled to the ground. Her knife flew from her hand, she landed hard on her ass, and Rich stood over her, jaw clenched in a grin. In the firelight, he looked hideous, his features seized up with tension, the tendons in his neck like tight cords. "Katie-bird, I knew I'd see you again."

"*Fight it, Rich,*" she screamed, scooting back, feet scrambling for purchase. "*Fight it!*"

His body jerked as he sought to regain control of his own body. One arm and leg moved toward her, the other arm and leg moved in the opposite direction so that he resembled a grotesque marionette. Even his expression reflected his terrible struggle—one eye rolling around in its socket like a loose marble, the other fixed on her with a terrifying intensity.

"*Fight it,*" she shouted again, and leaped to her feet and swept a burning branch off the ground and thrust it at him.

He laughed, an awful choking sound, and grabbed it away from her with his bare hands, apparently oblivious to the fire against his skin, to the destruction around him, and hurled it behind him. "Fire doesn't scare me, Katie-bird, and frankly, I think I'd prefer you as a host."

Just as Kate leaped back from him, the hawk swooped down, her piercing call echoing through the burning courtyard, and attacked him with her beak and claws. He screamed, his arms flew up to protect his face, and he tripped over a body behind him and went down. For a moment, Rich just sat there, stunned, and then he began to bleed from the ears and eyes and mouth as the *brujo* inside him fled.

Kate's horror enveloped her. She rushed forward to catch him, hold him, to stem the bleeding. But a powerful instinct demanded that she drop to her hands and knees and shift. It wasn't an instinct she could resist or ignore. It was as overpowering as thirst, hunger, self-preservation. She dropped to the ground, began to shift, and the *brujo* that had been inside Rich slammed into her before the transformation was complete.

All external sounds and sensations rushed out of her. But she *felt* this *brujo*, *heard* him, *tasted* him, *smelled* him, and his history was as open to her as hers was to him. Gogh, this was a ghost named Gogh, a young, naïve ghost that had taken Rich back in early February; she actually saw it in Gogh's memory. She also saw him in the barracks kitchen with other ghosts, voting yes or no about the annihilation of a *brujo* that had saved his host and caused the deaths of two members of the tribe. She saw the annihilation ceremony on one of the nearby deserted islands and how one of the hosts refused to be involved and had left.

Then all traces of Gogh vanished—no taste, smell, voice, presence, nothing at all. She realized his essence had been freed to move on into the afterlife.

A breath later, her change was complete and she felt shaky, disoriented, strange. She remembered what she had seen in the collective shifter memory during her transformation, how Wayra once had taken Dominica into himself and it had nearly killed him. And he had told her about taking a *brujo* into himself in the same way on the houseboat and how he'd passed out. So why had she been able to do it without suffering as he had? Was Gogh still inside of her and merely hiding?

She didn't know and there wasn't any time to think about it. Sounds and sights and sensations abruptly rushed back into her world. The hotel now blazed, flames raged through the lobby, and the intense heat blew out the glass in the upper-story windows, then the windows in the lobby that still had glass. Bright orange tongues of fire leaped out the shattered windows and curled up the sides of the hotel, reaching for the roof, the sky. Flames danced along the fence to her left and raced along the top of it toward the gate where the liberated hostages were crowded, ramming their bodies against it to escape the pyre the courtyard had become. The gate, eight feet tall and topped with a heavy wood lattice, didn't budge.

Kate looked around frantically for Wayra or the hawk, but didn't see either of them. *Shit, we're trapped.*

"Scale the gate," Zee shouted.

Kate shifted into her human form, her change much faster now, with just brief discomfort. The smoke was so thick it burned her eyes, and around her, people were coughing, shouting, moving one of the tables and some of the heavy iron chairs over to the gate. The chairs were set on top of the table and two men climbed on top of them and beat at the wood lattice with their fists until it splintered and cracked and finally gave way. Up and over, up and over.

We're going to get out of here.

Dominica, Whit, and two dozen of her most loyal followers watched the chaos on Second Street from the roof of the library. She was still using the body of Lynn from Key West, Whit continued to use the body of Kevin, the ex-CEO, and her followers were fortunate enough to have their original hosts.

Three buildings over, another group waited on the roof of the police station, a third group occupied the roof of the Cedar Key Museum, and other, smaller groups were positioned in the marina, on Dock Street, on the roofs of condos. And when the hostages began climbing over the gate and the burning fence, Dominica's group opened fire.

Zee's people fell like birds, tumbling into the road where they lay twitching, dying. Others limped off into the darkness and would be picked off by other members of her tribe or taken by *brujos* in need of hosts.

Beyond this area, out past the fourth bridge, some of the lower astrals she had summoned earlier now seized the feds, feasting on them, living through them, enjoying the immense pleasures of physical existence. Her reinforcements, her backup, her plan B. Except not that many ghosts had answered her call, maybe a few dozen in all. Why so few?

"Fog," Whit hollered. "We need fog, Nica."

She raised her arms, calling to the fog, but nothing happened. She tried again. And again. And then, within the *brujo* web, she heard laughter, Liam's laughter. *You no longer command the fog, Dominica. It obeys the one with the greatest number of followers and right now that's me. Right now, my ghosts are taking those you have shot and we're healing them, as you taught us. And then we're releasing them, whole and able to take up arms against you and your brutes. And those other ghosts you summoned from the lower astrals? Most of them joined me. You have twenty-five of them, that's it. And they'll desert you as soon as they learn how incompetent you are. And I now conjure fog in which the living can hide from you. Watch, Dominica, as the fog rises at the end of Second Street to provide them with cover. Watch and weep.*

Stunned, Dominica leaned slightly over the edge of the roof and saw the fog rising at the end of the street. Impossible. She had commanded fog for all the centuries of her existence. No such rule existed about fog obeying the one who commanded more *brujos*. That was a lie, a chaser lie, and Liam had fallen for it. Even so, how was he doing this? Through the chasers? Were they facilitating this?

The chasers are using you, Liam. Her words were broadcast throughout the *brujo* net, just as his were in his attempt to undermine her, overthrow her.

Chasers? Liam laughed again. *There's no such thing. Or if there is, I've never met one.*

Those giant crows, Liam. They were conjured by chasers. She heard a background chatter, that of other *brujos* considering this new information. She rushed on. *You're a young, naïve ghost who couldn't find your way out of a grocery store, much less lead a tribe.*

Young and naïve is preferable to ancient and bitter. You've lost whatever vision you once had, Dominica. You're vengeful, cruel, a petty tyrant. All who follow me dealt with so many petty tyrants in their lives that they want no more of it. We're going to fix what you ruined here. It's time for you to leave.

Get lost, you stupid shit. You may command the fog for the moment, Liam, but without me, there's no brujo *net. I created it and I can destroy it. I now order all who follow me to disconnect from the net.*

Whit and the others with her on the library roof immediately disconnected from the net. She felt it, their energy blinking out like stars. Then, up and down the street, as others disconnected, she felt the turmoil in Liam's group, heard their protests, their questions, their doubts. *What's she doing? How can she do this? You told us you were the leader, that you could defeat her. How will we talk among ourselves? How will we communicate?*

Yes, indeed. Like any ghost that lacked a central switchboard, she thought, Liam's ghosts would have to learn how to communicate one on one, not the easiest thing to do when you had been dependent on the *brujo* net.

Good riddance, Liam, she whispered, then proceeded to destroy the *brujo* net in the same way she had created it centuries ago. She summoned her most powerful intentions and hurled them into the greater forces available to the dead in the hereafter. She clapped her hands twice, sharply, and the *brujo* net went dark.

Whit and the others on the roof all stared at her, aghast, awed. "My God, you actually did it," Whit breathed.

"Now what?" Jill asked. "How're we supposed to talk to each other when we don't have hosts?"

"Reach out, be firm in your intentions, believe it can happen, and it will. One of our rights in the afterlife is to be able to draw on its inherent power. You don't need the net to do that. It takes practice, that's all." And infinite patience, she thought, but didn't say it.

"What will happen to Liam and his group now that they can't communicate with each other?" Joe asked.

"The group will be thrown into total chaos. Now let's go claim our island. Jill, you and Joe bring the vehicles around."

"And do what?" Joe asked.

Wasn't it obvious? Had he—had all of them—lost the capacity for independent thought? "Gather up the dead and the dying and dump them at the edge of the quarantine area. We still have a small number of *brujos* who need hosts and I'm sure there are some among the freed hostages who are healthy enough to be seized. After all, where can they possibly go? If they try to drive off the island, they'll be seized by visiting *brujos* or arrested or shot by the feds. If they try to escape by boat, they'll be caught by *brujos* or the Coast Guard. So let's tie up our loose ends and then start cleaning up our enclave."

As the others headed downstairs, Whit took her hand and pulled her against him. Her host, Lynn, didn't resist. She actually seemed to be attracted to Whit's host, Kevin. "I love you, Nica," he whispered, his mouth warm against her ear, her cheek. Then he kissed her and she melted against him and allowed herself a few moments to love the one she was with.

Wayra raced after Illary, who flew low enough for him to follow her, but high enough to locate Sanchez or Maddie or both of them. He knew that Maddie had liberated herself from Dominica; he'd discovered that fact in the courtyard, from one of the female hostages he had freed. The only reason she would be out here near the animal rescue center and the airport would be to hide or to find some way off the island.

After freeing the hostages, he and the hawk escaped the courtyard. Now they were closing in on the animal rescue center.

A cart's headed toward you, Wayra, three brujos *inside. They're agitated about what's happening downtown.*

He veered into a front yard, paused behind a tree, and flattened out against the ground, watching the *brujo* cart as it approached. What Illary referred to as "agitation" smelled deeper than that. It stank of that peculiar fear that only a *brujo* could feel when its existence was threatened. Their combined odors told him nothing about the source of their fear, but he felt certain it wasn't just about the fire.

When the cart whispered past him, he leaped up, keeping pace with the hawk as she turned north and then west along Airport Road. As he rounded the curve in the road, now close to the house where he and Kate had discovered the bodies of Amy's parents, a familiar stench hit him. *Brujo* fear. *Tell me what you see, Illary.*

A cart and an airplane with people outside it. I'm going in for a closer look.

But what she didn't see and Wayra did because he was on the ground, was the rear end of a truck protruding from a mangrove. He ran over to it, sniffing at the tires, the branches and water around it, and caught a dog's scent and that of Maddie and Sanchez. The two of them together, here? How?

He pursued their scents down the beach and saw them, flattened out in the shallows behind a mound of reeds, the dog next to Sanchez, he and Maddie, her hair covered with a baseball cap, watching eight *brujos* taunting Rocky and a tall black man. He suspected other *brujos* in their natural forms hovered nearby. All that stood between his shifters and the *brujos* was equipment they had removed from the plane and several heaps of debris that had been cleared from the runway. Wayra didn't know if Maddie and Sanchez were armed, but even if they were, they were badly outnumbered.

As Wayra approached, Maddie turned her head—and saw him. She shot to her feet and raced toward him, her arms thrown open. Even though she didn't make a sound, her body was fully visible to the *brujos,* that young woman whose long and perilous journey with Dominica they knew nothing about. All they knew was that she had hosted Dominica.

Wayra leaped at her, hoping to knock her to the sand, but one of the *brujos* opened fire and the bullet with Maddie's name on it slammed into

Wayra's right side, punctured his right lung, and exited his other side, a clean sweep that nonetheless rendered him irrelevant. He collapsed, his breath an excruciatingly painful wheeze, and felt blood filling the cavity of his chest.

Fuck.

Twenty-four

For Maddie, everything seemed to happen in a grotesque slow motion, each interminable moment vivid and horrifying. As Wayra's paws struck her in the chest, knocking her to the sand, a single shot rang out, echoing up and down the beach, and Wayra's airborne canine body twisted and fell to the ground.

Now she scrambled toward him on her hands and knees, gunfire exploding around her, the same words spilling from her mouth again and again. *"Please don't be dead please don't be dead . . ."*

When she reached him, she saw the agony in his open eyes, the blood seeping through his clothes. Then his body went berserk, fluctuating wildly between animal and human, fur one moment, skin the next; legs and paws, then a human foot, a human hand; a human ear, an animal snout. His shifter immune system had kicked into gear and she knew that if anything could save him, it would. She leaned over him, struggling not to sob as she whispered, "Stay with us, Wayra. Stay with us."

As Maddie tore off her jacket to slip it under Wayra's head, a hawk—keening shrilly—suddenly landed on the sand next to Wayra. Rocky's hawk, Liberty. Her wings fluttered frantically and her plaintive cries tore into Maddie's heart and soul. This was the cry of a mother who had lost a child, a lover who had lost a partner. And then the hawk transformed into a tall, lovely woman whose eyes brimmed with tears. "Please. Don't touch him right now." She sank to the sand and lifted Wayra's rapidly changing head gently onto her lap. "His body needs a chance to stabilize."

"My God," Maddie breathed. "You're a *shifter*?"

Only then did she realize the gunfire had stopped. She glanced around and saw Sanchez, Delaney, and Rocky running toward them, with Jessie dashing along in front of them. The retriever reached them first and immediately went over to Wayra and licked his face and Illary's hands, then stretched out alongside him in the sand. Sanchez dropped to the ground next to Maddie and slipped an arm around her shoulders. "I thought . . ."

Maddie squeezed his hand. "Wayra took the bullet."

"His body," Sanchez said, staring at Wayra. "What's happening to him?"

Illary kept moving her hands gently over Wayra's face. "He's struggling for his life."

"Who're *you*?" Sanchez asked.

"She's a shifter, like Wayra," Rocky said, and crouched beside Illary, his eyes fixed on Wayra. "What can we do, Illary?"

Huh? How do they know each other? Maddie started to ask, but Illary spoke first.

"His temperature is dropping. Can you get something to cover him, Rocky?"

"You bet. There's a sleeping bag in the plane." He loped off toward the plane and returned moments later with a lightweight sleeping bag that he drew gently over Wayra's body.

"Shouldn't we get him to a hospital?" Delaney asked.

"Humans can't fix this," Illary replied. "His immune system is the best physician. He needs time before we can move him to the plane. Is enough of the runway cleared so you can take off, Bob?"

"You all know each other?" Maddie exclaimed.

"Uh, yeah," Delaney said.

He didn't elaborate and Illary continued as if Maddie hadn't asked the question. "Downtown is on fire. Dominica had some of Zee Small's people tied up in the courtyard. Wayra, Kate, and I freed them. I don't know how many actually escaped, but they need to be rescued. Kate is back there with them."

"We're not going anywhere without you two," Delaney said.

"Absolutely," Maddie agreed. "We'll wait until we can move Wayra into the plane."

"My mom and Zee can take care of themselves a while longer," Rocky said.

"Sanchez, Rocky, can you guys give me a hand?" Delaney asked. "We need to move those bodies and the rest of the equipment off the runway."

The men left and Maddie and Jessie stayed by Wayra. "Will he live?" Maddie asked.

Illary looked down at Wayra, her hands now sweeping through the air just inches from his head, his body. A pale light emanated from them, so they seemed to glow like moons. She shook her head as though her entire existence hinged on the answer to that question. "I don't know."

"Will that light heal him?"

"It might help. You should know, Maddie, that Kate, Rocky, and Delaney have all been changed."

"Changed? What do you mean?"

"They're shifters."

She might as well have said they were all aliens from Pluto. Stunned, Maddie just sat there listening as Illary continued to speak in that same quiet voice, explaining what had happened.

"No wonder Dominica never seized either Kate or Rocky," Maddie said finally. "She always seemed afraid of you, so she must have sensed something."

"If Wayra dies, Dominica will learn the true meaning of terror," Illary whispered. "I promise you that."

As soon as Kate, Zee, and the others in his group climbed over the courtyard gate, a torrent of gunfire mowed down half of them. Men and women pitched forward. "Keep running," Zee shouted. "Head toward the Old Fennimore Mill!"

The fire still hadn't reached the Fennimore, a condo development of a dozen buildings on the marsh. None among them had a weapon, so the most they could do was flee the immediate area as quickly as possible and remain hidden until Delaney and Rocky landed in the marina parking lot. From any of the upper condos on the south side of the marsh, they would be able to see the plane as it approached.

But before they even entered the Fennimore property, fog rolled in off the marsh and rose up quickly around them, boxing them in so they couldn't see more than a few inches in front of them. Kate stopped in the midst of it, her body tense, and listened for the lascivious litany of the ghosts within. She didn't hear or sense anything. It seemed to be just ordinary fog, yet she felt sure it was sentient, aware. But if it wasn't a *brujo* fog, then what the hell was it?

"We should get inside one of them condos," Zee whispered, pausing beside her. "We know what this fog shit means."

"This fog feels different, Zee. I think it's protecting us."

The others in the group, just six of the two dozen who had been in the courtyard, gathered around Kate and Zee, whispering anxiously among themselves. "Let's get inside the office, first building on the right, bottom floor, and wait there until we hear the plane," Kate said.

"Link arms," Zee said.

They did and moved onto the property like dancers in a chorus line, except that no one was dancing. Kate was in the lead, Zee took up the rear. As she headed toward the first building, the fog tightened around them, but not in a threatening way. Beyond them, she continued to hear sirens, shouts, the roar of vehicles on Second Street, the noise of the fire consuming everything in its path. The stink of smoke permeated the fog, but the fog was thick and damp and quickly absorbed the worst of the smell.

They reached the first building. The sign on the office door read CLOSED and the place was locked up tight. If they broke the glass, the fog could follow them inside. Even though it hadn't threatened them in any way, all of them had experienced the terror of fog and only wanted to get away from it. So when one of Zee's men said he could jimmy the lock, Kate told him to jimmy away.

While they waited anxiously, the air burst with new sounds—gunfire nearby and helicopters, a lot of them. When she looked up through the fog, she could see the glow of the choppers' searchlights.

"Did your friend summon choppers for us?" Zee asked.

"No. Absolutely not."

"Some feds in hazmat suits came into town in Hummers," Zee said. "These mutants bled them out. So now the feds are coming in choppers. Hurry it up on the door, young man."

The fog climbed higher and drifted over the entire building, a white, thick, protective cocoon. Even the chopper searchlights wouldn't be able to penetrate this stuff, she thought, and hoped that it would cover the entire complex of buildings.

When the door swung open, the group hurried inside the office. Zee shut the door and told his people to spread out and search for water, food, candles, flashlights, weapons, anything, everything. Kate hurried over to the computer, hoping there was still electrical power in the complex. But when she pressed the on button, nothing happened. The complex apparently had gone dark with the rest of the island.

Then she remembered her cell phone. She slipped it out of her jacket pocket and saw two text messages. The first was from Rocky, blunt and short: *Wayra shot and dying on beach near airport.*

Kate read the message twice, emotion hitching in her chest, her heart unraveling. Wayra dying? She refused to believe it.

The second text message, from Delaney, had come in a few minutes later: *Confrontation @ airport, Wayra badly injured.*

"Badly injured" versus "dying." Was this the difference between the perceptions of a teenage boy and an adult man? Or was Delaney simply trying to soften the blow? Kate squeezed the bridge of her nose and forced herself to read the rest.

Can't leave until we can move Wayra. Hold on just a little longer. Stay safe. ♥ D

Several words leaped out at her. "Hold on just a little longer. ♥ D." Maybe she was grasping for substance where none existed. Maybe she had gone around the bend and now read signs in everything. But to her, the heart symbol meant "love you."

"Kate?" Zee came up behind her, set a bottle of water and a lit flashlight on the desk, the beam aimed at the ceiling, and touched her shoulder. "We've found some flashlights and bottled water. You okay?"

She spun around in the chair. "Wayra was shot, they can't move him yet, and Delaney loves me." Then she started to cry—and instantly felt like a foolish idiot.

Zee stood there for a moment, as though he didn't have a clue what she was talking about. He put his arms around her and held her tightly. "Listen," he said gently. "When you were a little girl, your old man told me he knew that someday you would make a huge difference in the world, that you were special, that you had a particular destiny. He didn't know what that destiny was, but he sensed it. So you buck up here, hon, don't go melting down. We need you now more than ever." He bussed her on the cheek, a big sloppy kiss, then turned to the others. "Sit tight. The plane's going to be here soon."

But how soon?

Wayra's consciousness had split down the middle, as neat as a cut apple. Part of him was still on the runway, aware of the warmth and light that Illary's hands sent into his chest, into his heart and lungs. He heard her and Maddie talking, felt the retriever nearby. Another part of him wandered freely through the millennia he had lived, through the dramatic changes he had witnessed and helped bring about in Esperanza. He called for Charlie and Victor, but his voice sounded hollow, unreal, an echo through time.

He suddenly found himself on a high plateau, beneath the light of a blazing sun, surrounded by stone sculptures of animals—tortoises and whales, giant frogs and insects, salamanders and octopuses, creatures that had never lived at this altitude. He saw Egyptian figures, too—Nefertiti, the Sphinx, a pharaoh. He instantly knew this was the place Illary had told him about, the stone forest on a high plateau outside of Esperanza. He struggled to recall what she'd said about the special doorway. It stood between—which two creatures?

He couldn't remember. Despairing, certain he would die if he couldn't recover this particular memory, his knees gave way, and he dropped to the hard stone floor of the plateau.

Help me.

"You're one stubborn shifter, Wayra," said Victor. "Do you have any idea how long it's taken you to ask for help?"

He and Charlie stood there in front of him, arms folded across their chests, and he felt like punching both of them. Charlie was dressed in his usual white attire, but Victor looked like he was auditioning for a part in *Gladiator*. "I've asked for help repeatedly. You two just haven't been around to hear it. And since when is my asking for help a criterion for *getting* help?"

"We're here now," Victor said. "And we're supposed to let you know the council has no use for you in the afterlife right now, Wayra. So you're stuck in physical life for the time being. You have work to do, beginning with Dominica."

"I'm not doing anything about Dominica until you tell me the truth about shifters, Victor. You more than Charlie. He's too young to have rewritten shifter history."

Those words hung in the air between them, a travesty, a promise, a dare. Victor looked deeply troubled, Charlie looked pissed. "What the hell is he talking about, Victor?"

Victor rubbed his old hands over his wrinkled face, and whispered, "The deeper secrets. He's talking about the deeper secrets, known only to a few." Then, in a louder voice: "And it doesn't concern you, Charlie."

"Bullshit," Charlie snapped. "My granddaughter's involved, so it concerns me."

"That's the whole thing with you, Charlie," said Wayra. "You're the only chaser on the council whose roots are still within the physical world. Your wife, daughter, granddaughter. That's why you aren't privy to the knowledge."

"That's got nothing to do with it," Victor said quickly.

Charlie stepped away from his fellow chaser and settled next to Wayra. "I think it's got everything to do with whatever these secrets are, Vic. So come clean. We won't snitch on you, will we, Wayra. We won't go to the council with your transgressions."

Wayra realized Charlie was taunting the other chaser, trying to get a rise out of him. And it worked.

"My transgressions?" Victor burst out.

His gladiator clothing evaporated as quickly as dew on a leaf. He now wore a floor-length robe that dated back to ancient Greece, probably what the intellectual elites wore, Wayra thought.

"I wasn't born in any goddamn Lemurian lab, Victor, and you know it. You've known it all along and just never bothered to tell me the truth. All of you ancient boys on the council know it. My shifter lineage was one of the original seven on this planet, older than you and the council put together. In return for my taking care of Dominica, you'll have to tell me the truth about shifter history. And if you don't, if I sense that you're lying to me, I'll bring her back. And to get rid of her, I'm going to need some help. That's my second condition."

Victor laced his fingers together and turned them out as he stretched his arms in front of him. His clothing changed rapidly now, from the Grecian tunic to plain denim jeans and a blue work shirt, to the armor of a warrior in the time of Genghis Khan. Then to the jeans again, his down-home "I'm your buddy" disguise. "You have my word."

Wayra glanced at Charlie. "Is his word worth a shit?"

Charlie whipped off his Ben Franklin specs and rubbed the lenses with a corner of his spotless white *guayabera* shirt and fitted the glasses on top of his head. Then he brought a cigar from his shirt pocket and his trademark silver Zippo lighter from the pocket of his white slacks and lit the cigar with a dramatic flourish.

"Now *that* is exactly the right question, Wayra." He tilted his head back, blew smoke into the air, and stabbed his cigar toward Victor. "This man was my sponsor, my mentor, and has been my most avid supporter even when I'm breaking all the council regs. They're politicians, Wayra. That's how it works over here. Some are good, some are bad, some are just hypocrites, spiritual assholes. But Victor . . . when he gives you his word, it's better than any written contract."

The recommendation, uttered with such conviction, convinced Wayra it was okay to agree even though it came from manipulative Charlie. "All right. Then we have a deal."

Victor pressed his palms together and rolled his eyes skyward in an exaggerated manner. "Christ Almighty." He sat down so that Wayra was now sandwiched between him and Charlie. "Good thing." He brushed at something on his jeans. "Otherwise we'd have to roll back a whole bunch of years." He rubbed his hands together and Wayra could hear skin rubbing against skin, calluses moving against calluses. "We'd have to roll back centuries. And no telling how long it would take to untangle everything." Then he brought one hand to Wayra's chest and the other to his back . . .

And Wayra gasped and sucked at the air and his eyes popped open.

Pale chocolate against white. Illary's face was the first thing he saw, and they were surrounded by thick, heavy fog. "How . . . long?"

"More than an hour." She leaned over him, her hands moving along the sides of his face, over his hair, tears rolling down her cheeks. "If you . . . I . . ."

"*Mi amor*," he whispered, and cupped her lovely face in his hands. "I felt the light from your hands."

"Are you fully healed?"

He touched his chest, and moved his hands slowly over his ribs, where the bullet had gone in, but didn't feel any wound. He could breathe. His heartbeat sounded strong, steady. Blood rushed through his veins. He was in his human form again. "Healed enough to do what needs to be done with Dominica. As soon as the hostages are on board, we'll find her. In return for dealing with her, Victor has promised to reveal the truth about shifters, what he calls 'the deeper secrets.'"

"Will he keep his word?"

"I told him that if he doesn't, I'll bring Dominica back."

"But something else healed you, too," she said. "It had to." She gestured at the thick fog that covered them and the entire runway. "This is not *brujo* fog. I sense it was generated to buy you time."

He agreed it wasn't *brujo* fog, but Wayra couldn't tell what had generated it. "I went there, Illary. To the place you told me about, the stone forest. Victor and Charlie were there. It's where Victor and I struck a bargain."

"Then let's go fulfill this bargain." She brought her mouth to his, a brief kiss that held an eternity of promise.

$ a n c h e z couldn't find an adjective that described what he felt when he saw Wayra and Illary moving out of the fog toward the plane. She had her arm around his waist and he stumbled a few times, but he was upright and walking and in his human form again.

So was she.

Shapeshifters, the two of them. He had seen some mighty strange things as a viewer—UFOs, aliens, a place with twin suns. Once, he'd even found himself inside a UFO during a viewing. But he'd never seen anything like this, the transformation of a man to a dog or wolf, and now back again, and the transformation of a bird into a woman. But ever since he'd first viewed Maddie that day back in Homestead, his life had become a living testament to the impossible.

Delaney, Rocky, and Maddie ran toward this odd couple, and even Jessie started toward them, then glanced around, saw that Sanchez hadn't moved, and hurried back to him. She whined and pawed at his leg as if to say, *Aw, c'mon, dude, let's greet them.*

So even though Sanchez felt like the outsider, he joined them.

The fog continued to provide a cover and Sanchez worried that it might prevent them from taking off. Delaney was more concerned about the choppers they could all hear somewhere nearby. Once, searchlights swept over the runway, but the fog was still too thick for them to be visible. As the choppers moved away again, they boarded the plane.

They had cleared most of the debris to either side of the runway, but Sanchez fretted about the stuff they couldn't see, pieces of wood, chunks of concrete, bits of bone. He and Delaney put on headphones, and there were two more sets in the cabin that Wayra and Maddie used so they could speak to each other without shouting over the din of the engine. He wondered how they would cram even more people into the cabin and worried about the unforeseen, the unexpected. But the unforeseen and the unexpected were becoming his new norm.

As they took off, the fog fell away behind them, and when Sanchez looked down, all he could see was a white blanket that seemed to cover most of the island. At five hundred feet, out over the gulf, Sanchez's Black-

Berry and his fed cell jingled simultaneously, text messages, both from O'Donnell.

Am assuming you & delaney r in hiding. We lost most of hazmat unit we sent in. Now national guard & fire depts on way & fully armed. They'll help u both get out, just show yr ID. D has questions 2 answer about the escape of kate davis. & you went rogue.

He read the message aloud. Delaney just laughed. "What an asshole. I've got a few questions for *him*. What hazmat unit is he talking about?"

Maddie brought him up to speed. "It was a drill, that's what I think. And it went horribly wrong. They hadn't counted on that. They actually believed there had been a biological terrorist attack, and after the unit was nearly wiped out, I figured they were just going to let everyone die off. But what's happening now changed their game plan."

"That's cynical," Sanchez said.

"Cynical, but likely."

"She may be right," Delaney said. "The feds, the CDC, HSD may have just taken advantage of a situation to see what they could learn from it."

Before Sanchez could say anything, the radio crackled and a male voice was audible in the headphones. "This is the Gainesville tower. To the plane that just took off from Cedar Key airport, we have you on radar. Please identify yourself."

Delaney glanced at Sanchez. "What's your hunch?"

Sanchez thought about it, but not for long. "We can use them to our advantage. I'll talk to them." He adjusted his mike. "This is a blue and red Cessna two-ten, with two federal agents on board." He spat out his badge ID. "The situation on Cedar Key is dire. The island has been under quarantine since March 17, due to a suspected biological weapon. No supplies have come in, people are now rioting in the streets for food, and most of the island is burning. There's no biological weapon here. I repeat, this area was not subjected to a biological terrorist attack. It's all part of a military drill. We are sending videos to CNN's iReport. The residents on the island are desperate."

"We've got video?" Delaney asked.

Sanchez held up his BlackBerry and passed it to Maddie. "Red, send all the video that's on there to CNN. Tell them more is coming."

"You got it. Tell the tower they're getting the video, too." She took the BlackBerry.

"Uh, Cessna two-ten. We copy. Can you get any of these people out?"

"We're going to try. If you can provide an e-mail address, we'll send you the video as well."

"Please switch to a cell phone and call 352-555-7691." He provided an e-mail address and Sanchez repeated it for Maddie.

Sanchez used the fed cell to call the number and the same controller answered on the first ring. "Your badge checked out, Mr. Sanchez. Your video is coming through now. Keep us posted. You'll have priority for landing when you're ready. And by the way, there are six military choppers on radar in your area."

"Thank you. Thank you very much."

Sanchez clicked off, and Delaney said, "Jesus, O'Donnell is going to have a stroke."

He banked steeply to the north, headed back toward the island, and for the first time, Sanchez had a clear view of the fires burning on Cedar Key. It looked as if it had been bombed. The worst fires raged in the downtown area, all the way out to Dock Street. Even though the marina was nothing but asphalt, the streets that led into it were lined with trees on one side and with shops on the other. The park, which was on one of the possible landing sites, didn't have any trees to speak of and the ground was mostly sand and gravel. Even so, the playground items were wood and cheap plastic and if flames reached that area, the seesaws and swings would go up as well.

"Okay, people, listen up." Delaney's voice boomed in the headsets. "The landing is going to be difficult. I'm going to approach First Street from the west and try to land there. My hope is that Kate has spread the word about where the pickup will be. But even if she hasn't, they'll see us. It's not every goddamn day that a plane lands in the marina. Dominica's mutants will see us, too. We're armed, but not well armed. The point is to get as many people on board as possible and get the hell out and hope the additional weight isn't a problem. We've got clearance for Gainesville, but may want to rethink that if the feds move in or if the people we pick up have other ideas."

It didn't sound like much of a plan to Sanchez. And when Maddie leaned toward him and squeezed his hand, he sensed her uncertainty, and knew she felt the same.

Delaney circled around the western tip of the island and turned south, a route that would take them over the cemetery, across the water, then over Goose Cove and the animal rescue center, and then into First Street.

It occurred to Sanchez this might be a suicide mission.

And then he saw the crows.

They came from the west, a black cloud that sprawled for miles and quickly spread out in every direction. On the GPS, it looked like some tremendous extraterrestrial craft as large as a continent. "Jesus God," Delaney murmured. "What the fuck *is* it?"

Wayra's voice streamed through the headphones. "Maintain your course, Delaney. The crows know what to do."

"The GPS just went out," Sanchez said. "And the compass is spinning."

"Maintain your course," Wayra repeated.

"How?" Delaney snapped. "None of my instruments work."

"Instinct," Wayra said.

Now the wave of crows closed in on either side of the plane and Delaney cut back on the power, extended the flaps. The birds stayed away from the propeller and positioned themselves beneath the tips of the wings, around the edges, and along the sides and rear of the plane, guiding it in for a landing.

The wheels touched down, bounced, careened as if across slick patches of pavement. A thick blanket of ash covered the windshield and Delaney flicked on the wipers. The brakes shrieked and squealed but didn't seem to do much to stop the plane. Through the filthy half-moons on the windshield, Sanchez saw the end of the marina and the waters of the gulf racing toward them.

"Shit shit shit," Delaney shouted. "Hold on!"

Seconds before they would plunge over the end of the seawall, Delaney or the crows or both turned the plane sharply to the right and it slammed up over a slight rise and finally came to a halt.

Sanchez couldn't see a damn thing now. The gigantic crows covered the windows, the front windshield. He heard their claws tapping against the top of the plane and then they started cawing, a cacophony that was nearly deafening.

No one spoke. No one moved.

Twenty-five

Kate stood at the front door, peering out through the glass. She could hear the crows, they all could, the incessant din of cawing that was at times so loud she had to press her hands over her ears for relief. But she didn't see them. Only the dense fog was visible, hugging the door. She sensed the fog covered the entire complex now, but couldn't tell for sure; it was still dark outside.

She shone her flashlight through the door and the fog acted like a kind of mirror, reflecting the light back at her. "What is it?" Zee asked, joining her at the door.

"I'm going to take a look."

He rubbed his jaw. "I don't know, Kate. I think we should just stay put."

"It'll be okay. I don't think this fog intends us any harm. And sooner or later, we're going to have to leave this building to get off the island. Maybe that's what the crows are about." She gave his hand a quick, reassuring squeeze, opened the door, and stepped outside.

The fog felt damp and cool against her skin, that was all. She walked slowly into it, keeping her flashlight aimed at the ground so she didn't stumble over anything. When she was far enough away from the building so that Zee and the others couldn't see her, Kate turned off the flashlight, zipped it into the pocket of her jacket, and shifted. She barely noticed the discomfort this time.

She took off through the fog, down the condo driveway. It covered her as far as the playground, then began to thin, and she could see the narrow beach and the pier where her houseboat, lifetimes ago, had been tied. She heard choppers above her, a lot of them, and as the fog thinned a bit more, she could see them, monstrous black choppers that seemed to converge from every part of the island. Their brilliant searchlights swept across the fog and Kate quickly ducked back into the thicker part of it where she wouldn't be seen.

Military? Maybe. Or perhaps these black monsters were the government's janitorial crew, the ones popularized by Hollywood, UFO enthusiasts, and conspiracy buffs. Either way, she didn't intend to be here when these suckers landed. She moved on through the thicker fog until she reached the edge of the marina. It took her a few moments to process what she saw.

A black mountain rose in front of her, impossibly high and wide, covering everything—even the fog. It fluttered and moved, ebbed and flowed like water, yet was much thicker than water, and alive. The longer she looked at it, the more details her shifter vision allowed her to see. The black mountain was actually thousands of gigantic crows arranged in three separate tiers.

The upper tier of crows flew wing to wing, in a perfect formation, creating an impenetrable barrier between sky and ground that shielded her, which would shield all of them, from the choppers. This tier consisted of the greatest number of crows.

A second tier of crows, hundreds of them, occupied trees, rooftops, the dock railing, a backup army. A third tier stood on the ground, black giants that looked to be ten and twenty feet tall, legs as thick and high as the trunks of trees. Their huge heads swiveled one way, then the other. When their wings were folded, they looked like ancient magicians, cloaked and majestic.

The third tier began to move, undulating snakelike across the marina parking lot. Now and then, feathers floated in the currents their movements made. An odor emanated from them—not musty, like birds in a cage at a zoo, but benign, almost pleasant, faintly sweet, like the scent of freshly mown grass on a hot summer day. She watched as the third tier of crows continued to move toward the Old Fennimore Mill, and understood what she should do.

She loped back toward the condo office, the fog moving along with her. She became aware of a presence within it, then of many voices that spoke with one voice. *Shifter, we broke with the* bruja. *We intend you no harm.* The human part of her thought it might be a trick, but her shifter senses told her it was not. That was all she needed to know. Kate shifted again and ran on toward the office and burst through the door. "The plane is here. Let's move out. Fast."

"Where is it?" Zee asked.

"Marina parking lot by First Street."

Zee held the door open while his people hurried out, then they all joined hands and moved quickly into the fog. "This isn't Satan's fog," Zee whispered.

"It's filled with ghosts that broke with Dominica."

"How do you know that, Kate?"

"I just do."

He took her arm. "Listen, I saw what . . . you became in that courtyard. In the old days, I thought this kind of . . . of weirdness was Satan's work. But, truth be told, Kate, my wife came to me after she was dead and I . . . I laid with her. It was real, it happened. So I don't care what . . . I saw. I know your heart. My feelings for you haven't changed. You're still like my daughter."

Kate hugged him quickly. "Thanks, Zee. I appreciate everything you've done for me throughout all these years." And she was grateful he didn't prod her with questions.

Their flashlights were bright enough so that when they reached the undulating line of black crows, Zee stopped, balking. "What the fuck."

"This is how we get safely to the plane on the other side of the lot," she said loudly enough for everyone to hear. "It's safe. These creatures are protecting us—from those choppers you hear and from the *brujos*."

Then the end of the line opened like the gaping maw of some prehistoric fish and Kate went in first, with the others following her rapidly. Once they were all inside, one of the crows opened its wings and the opening vanished. Inside this living tunnel of wings and feathers, the air felt warmer than it did outside and smelled of that same odd sweetness. The caws echoed so loudly it was impossible to speak and be heard.

They moved quickly in a single file, the fog drifting along with them, sometimes slipping like a curious puppy between the crows' gargantuan legs or curling through the feathers of their wings. The beams of their flashlights revealed the crows' tremendous claws, ankle high, as thick as a wrestler's biceps. At one point Zee stumbled into Kate and she caught his arm, holding him upright until he found his balance. He leaned toward her so that she could hear him.

"Can the boots in the choppers see these suckers, Kate?"

"I doubt it. I think that's the point."

"But what's protecting us? And why?"

"The forces of good, Zee."

The cawing suddenly stopped, and in the subsequent silence, Kate heard the choppers again, nearby and flying low. The fog abruptly rolled back away from the marina parking lot and the tunnel of feathers and wings began to shift erratically, breaking apart here and there until bits of light dappled the ground. At first, she thought it was the early light of dawn, but quickly realized it was searchlights from the helicopters, sweeping across the surreal landscape of crows. It was as if the crows had separated briefly so that she and the others could see the choppers.

Kate urged everyone to move back into the thicker fog. There, they waited for the choppers to lift, for the tunnel of crows to re-form so they could make it safely to the plane. Her heart pounded hard against the walls of her chest and she tried not to dwell on all the things that could go terribly wrong.

Their truck whipped right into an alley, a shortcut to the marina where a single-engine plane had landed. "Faster," Dominica shouted.

Whit slammed the truck into fourth gear and it shot through the alley, crashing over cobblestones, clipping a trash can. Then the truck exploded into the street—and Whit slammed on the brakes.

"Holy shit." Whit threw open the door and leaped out.

Dominica got out as well and peered upward. To the east, the sky lightened, and against that dove gray loomed black helicopters, six, eight, ten of them, coming from every direction. They looked ominous, like harbingers of doom and destruction.

"Ignore them," she snapped, and got back inside the truck, slamming the door, fuming that Whit would stop so violently just because some choppers had appeared.

After all, *brujos* could seize those pilots at any moment. Moments ago, half a dozen members of her tribe in their natural forms had been here in the truck with them. She wasn't sure where they were now, but they had to be close, close enough for them to hear her if she issued an order for them to seize the pilots and fly the choppers away from the island. If she issued the command, it would be done.

Her door suddenly flew open and Whit grabbed her arm and jerked her out of the truck and gripped her shoulders. "*Ignore them?* Are you fucking kidding me? These guys conduct the government's dirty work, okay? *We're* the dirty work. These choppers move into politically sensitive areas to clean up a mess. They're a top-secret janitorial crew. They never leave behind a single trace of their existence."

"So what?" She wrenched free of his grip. "All we have to do is seize them. We have power that they don't, Whit."

Whit raked his fingers back through his hair. "Jesus, seize them and then what?"

"With just a single chopper, we can win this battle. Seize the head pilot and he leads the rest of the choppers away from Cedar Key."

He moved in a small, tight circle, shaking his head. "Nica, listen to me. I want an enclave as badly as you do. But this battle is lost. We're too fragmented, the tribe has turned against us, Liam commands the fog, our hostages have escaped, and the entire island is on fire. *We've lost, don't you get it?*"

Tears flooded her eyes, and right then she hated him, hated Whit. He was giving up too easily, surrendering in ways that Ben never would have. "We haven't lost. We—"

The caws of thousands of crows drowned out her voice. They appeared above, these colossal, chaser-conjured birds, their cries preternaturally loud, echoing through the predawn light. This black tide of crows covered Cedar Key completely. The crows formed a dark mantle between the ground and the choppers so that Dominica couldn't even see the helicopters now. She raised her weapon and fired repeatedly at the crows, emptying her clip. Not only did the gunfire fail to affect the creatures, but the bullets rained to the ground.

Furious, Dominica slammed in another clip and started to fire at them again, but Whit pushed her weapon down. "Don't waste your bullets, Nica. We don't have a defense against them. It's just another sign that we don't belong here."

A car screeched to a stop beside them, the doors flew open, and Jill and Joe hurried over, their excitement palpable. "It's a private plane," Joe exclaimed. "Did you hear it? We glimpsed it just before the crows surrounded it. It could get us to Mexico, to the Caribbean. One of us can seize the pilot and all of us can get out."

"*All* of us?" Whit sounded as though he nearly choked on the words, and threw out his arms. "Joe, *all* of us are right here. You, me, Jill, and Dominica. That's it. That's what remains of this tribe. You see anyone else around here? Are there any ghosts here in their natural form? *No.* They've either fled or joined Liam. We don't need to seize the pilot. We need to vacate our hosts and go elsewhere. *We've lost.* That's the bottom line."

Jill slapped the back of her hand against his arm and gave a tight, nervous laugh. "Don't be ridiculous. No battle is lost until it's lost. We're not going to concede. We're just going to . . ." She shrugged and drew her fingers back through her hair. "Find some other place, start smaller, right, Nica?"

A horrifying numbness crept through Dominica. She realized Jill was trying to soften the blow of their monumental loss. How many times would she have to repeat this, building a new tribe in a new place? "Whit, would you want to find a new place, with me?"

"Yes." Unequivocal. He kissed the back of her hand. "And I'll sacrifice my host for the body of the pilot."

"Then let's go check out this private plane," Joe said.

Dominica hesitated a moment beneath the sky filled with crows. She hated the chasers and their tricks and railed silently against them for violating all the rules that had ever existed for chasers and *brujos*. She despaired that none of these ghosts understood why abandoning Cedar Key was so abhorrent to her. They didn't know about the ancient ways, the ancient battles, the ancient enmity between *brujos* and chasers. How could they? In the larger scheme of things, they had been born yesterday and died five minutes ago.

But it was also true that too many events had transpired too quickly for her to handle effectively. It had all worn her down, she had lost control. When she'd lost that, her power had been severely curtailed. Now she was just half a *bruja,* trapped in a kind of netherworld, a twilight zone. Perhaps her only way out was through loving the one she was with. Perhaps that love would set her free. Gypsy knew about this kind of passion; Dominica just hoped it would be true for her.

Love or lust, Nica? She could almost hear Wayra asking her this. The truth was that it didn't matter. For her, they were one and the same.

The four of them piled into the truck.

Maddie moved swiftly through the tunnel of crows, her head aching from the smells, the constant, throbbing *whoop* of the choppers, the proximity of the *brujos,* and the nearly crippling uncertainty of everything. Now and then, a giant feather drifted through the air, supernatural flotsam that reminded her this tunnel was not permanent, that it might break up and come apart at any moment. She moved faster, faster, Wayra and Illary right behind her, the others back by the plane, preparing it for takeoff.

The radio she held crackled with voices from the chopper pilots. Delaney had thrust it into her hand as she'd left the plane and told her to keep it on.

What's with that dark blanket of birds? one pilot asked. *We supposed to shoot birds?*

No, just people, another pilot replied. *Never seen anything like this with birds, though. Spooky.*

Hold positions, said a third pilot.

Then the tunnel of crows snaked to the right, the left, and began thinning, admitting expanding bands of light. The cawing started up again, louder, urgent, intermingled with shrieks and cries. Up and down the tunnel, greater gaps appeared as crows started flying away. The flapping of their tremendous wings whipped the air into a kind of tornadic frenzy filled with sand and sticks and even burning debris from the fires.

Maddie pressed her arm across her forehead, trying to shield her eyes from the ash, and stumbled forward blindly. The wind bit at her arms and legs and cheeks. When she looked again, the crows were above them, still providing some cover, but many of them faded in and out against the lightening sky. Whatever magic this was, it couldn't hold together much longer.

Then the tunnel of crows simply ended and she gazed out across a gaping chasm in the marina parking lot. No crows, no fog, just early light and empty asphalt and a couple of black choppers hovering dangerously low. The hovering choppers seemed to be waiting for that gap to fill with people.

"We need a shield," Maddie said. "Otherwise the choppers are going to mow them down, Wayra."

"We're the shield," he said, and instantly shifted and strolled out into the chasm.

A dog? Is that a dog? one pilot asked. *I'm not shooting any damn dog. Forget it.*

The radio burst with static and half a dozen voices, all of them commenting on the dog and the hawk that appeared behind the dog, and what the hell was this mission about, anyway? Then an authoritative male voice boomed over the radio. *Gentlemen, this is Agent O'Donnell. Your mission is to prevent that plane from taking off. Are we clear on that?*

Yes, sir. Could you, uh, advise about the mammoth crows?

They aren't real, O'Donnell snapped.

Beg to differ, sir. They appear on radar. That makes them real.

I repeat, O'Donnell said, *your mission is to prevent that plane from taking off.*

Two of the choppers peeled away and Maddie dashed across the three hundred yards, her arms tucked in tightly at her sides, and zigzagged to make herself a more difficult target just in case these pilots decided to fire at her. But no one fired. She made it to the other side, where Kate, Zee, and six others waited. Maddie's first thought was, *How would the plane accommodate another eight people?* Even with the seats and nonessential equipment removed, it seemed unlikely that the plane would be able to get off the ground with fourteen people on board. But those logistics belonged to Delaney; she couldn't worry about them. If they had to, they could divide themselves into two groups and Delaney could fly them out separately to Gainesville.

"Maddie," Kate squealed, and threw her arms around her as though they were long-lost friends. Maybe they were.

"Just run. Flat-out run," Maddie said. "The plane is obscured by the fog and the crows. But I don't think it's going to last much longer."

"Will the plane be able to fit all of us?" Zee asked.

Maddie's eyes locked on the old man's face. "I hope so." Around them, the fog shifted, hugging them one moment, thinning the next. Maddie looked frantically around for Wayra and Illary, but they were gone. "Just go. Now. Fast."

And they did.

Maddie watched them, making sure they made it to the other side, then threw out her arms and screamed, *"Charlie, you and your chaser buddies brought us this far. Take us the rest of the way. You hear me?"*

Nothing changed. The chasm remained, a gaping hole through which sunlight poured, and she thought, *What the hell,* and started running.

The two remaining choppers fired on her, bullets pinging to her right and left, forcing her to cut from one side to the other, again and again. And then she plunged into the fog, beneath the protection of the giant crows, and fell to her knees, her body heaving and shuddering, hands pressed to her face, her body rocking forward and back, forward and back.

"C'mon, Red," Sanchez shouted, and yanked her to her feet and pulled her along through the strange, dark tunnel.

Maddie stumbled and lurched, the radio in her hand crackling with static, then voices. Nothing made sense, everything made sense, and making sense of any of it didn't matter. She gripped Sanchez's arm and they raced the last few hundred feet to the plane. She scrambled into the crowded cabin, he barreled in after her and slammed the cabin door. Then he yelled, "Get us out of here, Delaney!"

*   *   *

The fire on Second Street raged so fiercely that they were forced to take an alternate route, backtracking toward the bridge that crossed over to Dock Street. A helicopter was descending at the end of it, a dark forbidding object that looked as if it intended to land in the exact spot where the road curved.

"Go faster," Dominica shouted. "We can beat it and get past it before it lands."

Whit opened the truck's V-6 engine up wide. The truck tore ahead at such an extreme speed that when a hawk and a tremendous white crow swept in front of the windshield, he lost control of the vehicle. It skidded past the entrance to the bridge on its left wheels, slammed into a concrete telephone pole, and plunged into the salt marsh.

Dominica heard shrieking, a horrid, piercing sound, and realized it was coming from her, that she was struggling to unfasten her seat belt so she could pull Whit back into the car. His head was stuck in the broken windshield, jagged edges of glass had nearly severed his neck. His host was dead and he hadn't escaped before the host had died.

Her seat belt popped open and she struggled to climb out the open passenger window. But her right leg didn't work the way it was supposed to. She was distracted by screams from the backseat, Jill or Joe or both of them, she couldn't tell, didn't care. High tide, it was hide tide and water poured into the truck and her right leg was useless, dead to her.

She knew she should vacate her host now, immediately. But Lynn from Key West was all that was left to her. Without her, Dominica would be consciousness without substance again, her senses limited to shades of gray, muted sounds. Even pain was preferable to that prison.

She dragged herself out the window and fell into the water facefirst, with a graceless splash. Her arms flailed, her useless leg weighted her down, she somehow managed to turn onto her back, and there was Wayra, the hawk riding on his shoulder, the shadow of the immense white crow falling over them.

"Help me, Wayra," she gasped, coughing up water, desperately trying to breathe.

"With pleasure," he said, and grasped her shoulders and everything vanished.

Through the window, Kate could now see the choppers, maybe a dozen of them, and just a scattering of crows on rooftops and flying overhead, above them. With their plane fully exposed now, several of the choppers began to descend—one in the parking lot, another midway up First Street, right in the path of what was supposed to be their runway.

A voice Kate recognized boomed from the radio. O'Donnell, the prick who had interrogated her when she was arrested. "Sanchez, Delaney, I'm just saying this once more. Report immediately. You've got sixty seconds before I order the choppers to open fire on the Cessna."

"Tell him to go fuck himself," Delaney barked, and started the engine.

"In two minutes we tell him that. Right now, we tell him what he wants to hear." Sanchez clicked on the mike. "Agent O'Donnell, Nick here. We've got injuries and fatalities. We need clearance out of here. These mutants are still closing in on us. We can land on State Road 24 around Roseland. The road is wide there. If you could have a medevac meet us there, we can get the injured transferred to the trauma center in Gainesville."

"Transfer the injured to one of our choppers. It'll get them to the trauma center faster," O'Donnell said.

"Can't do it. Too risky. The fucks who created this chaos would seize all of us. Tell the chopper to move. Here we come." Sanchez switched off the radio. "Get us out of here, amigo."

"Forget First Street," Delaney said, and made a wide turn and raced through the marina parking lot, past the chopper that had landed next to the pier. Kate watched in horror as the road rushed toward them, as the boat slips vanished from sight, as the children's playground appeared and vanished, as trees and electrical wires glistened in the morning light. Their weight was too great; she didn't think they would be able to reach liftoff. *We're not going to make it.*

Then the plane lifted into the air and everyone on board cheered.

"We're not out of the woods yet," Delaney announced. "O'Donnell may be sending people to Gainesville just to cover his ass. We can be there in twenty minutes. Can you have people there waiting to get you and your group elsewhere, Zee?"

"Absolutely. Give me a cell and we'll all be out before O'Donnell even knows we were there."

Kate started to object that the plan wasn't solid enough, but Rocky slipped his arm around her shoulders and said, "Mom, it'll be okay."

She grasped his hand and held on tightly.

The moment they touched down in Gainesville, Kate pressed her face to the window and saw a trauma chopper flying alongside them. Zee's contacts. She didn't have any idea what kind of strings he had pulled for this one, what kinds of contacts he had, where he and his people were headed. And there was no time to ask. Zee and the others were instantly on their feet, lined up at the door. But he came over to her, and for moments, they simply looked at each other.

Her own history lay embedded within the creases in his forehead, at the corners of his eyes, in the quickness of his anxious smile. "You take care, hon. Drop me an e-mail when you get to wherever. Stradivarius111 at hush-mail dot-com. It's encrypted. It'll ask you a question. The answer is *Anno 1689*."

The year his Stradivarius had been made, inscribed on the back of it. "You, too, Zee. Thank you. For everything."

He leaned forward and hugged her tightly, an old man, the last vestige of her father's generation. She smelled fish in his hair, salt on his skin, and the heart of Cedar Key in his breath. "I'm thanking you, Kate. Me and mine, we owe you and yours." Then he brushed his hands over her cheeks, kissed her forehead, and moved to the front of the plane to hug Rocky good-bye.

"*Go, go,*" Delaney shouted. "Get out of here fast."

Kate threw open the cabin door and Zee's people leaped from the plane to the tarmac, one after the other.

The trauma chopper had landed twenty yards away and they raced toward it in their tattered clothing, several with packs, most with nothing at all, but every single one of them propelled by their odd beliefs that Zee Small had the scoop on the end-time, that he was their miracle worker. Hell, maybe he was.

Kate watched them pile into the chopper, and before it had lifted into the air, she pulled the cabin door shut and Delaney revved the engine. She hurried back to her spot on the floor with Sanchez and Maddie, but the engines suddenly died and Delaney's voice boomed over the PA.

"Uh, people, we're blocked on every side."

Kate peered out the window again. A dozen black helicopters surrounded them, some still in the air, others hovering at their side, four on the ground, with a pair on either side of the Cessna.

"O'Donnell," Delaney said. "Ideas, anyone?"

"Get us out," Rocky yelled from the copilot seat. "They'll put us away in some quarantine hole where we'll never see sunlight."

Maddie quickly stood. "Delaney, Rocky, move back here with Kate and let Sanchez and me sit up front. Then the three of you shift."

"*What?*" Kate said, balking.

"Because they won't be expecting to see four dogs," Maddie replied.

Sanchez piped up: "I'll deal with O'Donnell."

"Maddie's right," Delaney said, and he and Rocky changed places with her and Sanchez.

Kate glanced through the window, where a chopper had landed and belched out men in hazmat suits who marched toward the plane with fierce determination. Maddie was right. Shock and awe. She began to shift and fell back against the floor of the plane.

Only one man entered the cabin, and he wore a hazmat suit. He took a slow look around, shut the cabin door, and locked it. Maddie tried to see the scene the way he did, a growling golden retriever on the floor between the front seats where she and Sanchez sat; a Great Dane sprawled on the cabin floor with a Belgian Tervuren and a greyhound.

The man in the suit removed his helmet. "Fuck. You're hauling *dogs*?"

"Agent O'Donnell," Sanchez said.

O'Donnell dropped his helmet to the floor. A pulse beat hard at his temple, his face turned bright red. "Is this some kind of joke? *Dogs*? Where's that fucking coward Delaney?"

"He didn't make it," Sanchez replied. "He got left back on Cedar Key."

"That's a goddamn lie, Sanchez. I heard him talking on the radio ten minutes ago."

"Oh, you imagined it," Maddie said.

"You'd best shut your mouth, young lady," O'Donnell snapped, and pulled a weapon from his suit and stabbed at the air. "I know who you are. That Livingston woman. You disappeared from Florida a year ago. I don't know how the hell you got into the country, but I'm betting you're traveling under a phony passport. I don't know yet what the hell else you've done, but we can certainly arrest you for that. You and Sanchez are going to be quarantined for—"

"Fat fucking chance of that." Sanchez bolted out of his seat and moved toward O'Donnell.

"Stay back," O'Donnell snapped, waving his weapon wildly. "Just stay the hell back, Sanchez."

Jessie growled more loudly now, the greyhound snarled, the Belgian Tervuren got to his feet, and the Great Dane moved toward O'Donnell, forcing him to back up to the cabin wall. "I'll shoot them, Sanchez, shoot all of them," O'Donnell hissed. "Keep the goddamn dogs in line."

"It may be too late for that," Maddie said, and the three dogs started to shift.

O'Donnell's mouth dropped open, the color drained from his face, his eyes bulged. He looked like a man perched at the edge of madness.

And when Delaney's change was complete, he calmly reached out and took O'Donnell's weapon and passed it to Sanchez, who aimed it at O'Donnell. "Sit down," Sanchez snapped.

"But—"

"Sit. Down." Delaney gripped his shoulder and forced him to the floor. "Here's the deal, Tom. You're going to allow us to fly out of here because if you don't, I'll bite you in the fucking neck and you'll become one of us."

"I—I—" His eyes rolled toward Kate, Rocky, Maddie and Sanchez, Jessie, then back to Delaney. *"How?"* he whispered. "How did this . . . abomination happen?"

"You're the abomination," Maddie shot back. "We should just leave you here on the runway, let the hungry ghosts have you." She didn't mean it, she wouldn't wish that on anyone, but she enjoyed the horror in his expression.

"Please . . . don't . . . I . . . I talked to the hazmat survivors. They described . . . what happened. We . . . I . . . couldn't put it into any reasonable context. I . . . the CDC, DHS, all of them breathing down my neck . . . They didn't want to believe any of it was true. They sent those survivors for a psychiatric evaluation and I . . . I knew they would do the same to me if I . . . I didn't fall into line."

"I told you the truth the day you interrogated me," Kate said. "You thought I was delusional."

"I . . . I don't think that now."

"Clear us for takeoff," Delaney demanded.

O'Donnell's head bobbed as though it had come loose from the tendons and muscles that connected it to his shoulders. "Radio's in my helmet."

Maddie scooped up the helmet, checked the inside of it, then passed it to him. He got on the radio and barked instructions. Someone on the other end apparently argued with him, but O'Donnell seemed to have enough clout to pull it off. Within minutes, the black choppers on the ground lifted away and those hovering around them veered off.

"Nicely done," Maddie said. "If I were you, Mr. O'Donnell, I'd take off that suit. We'll let you off in Miami or somewhere and you can call home from there."

"You may want to put in for retirement," Sanchez said.

O'Donnell looked miserable and angry. "You're all wanted for a variety of crimes. You'll never get away with this."

Rocky laughed. "Watch us."

Maddie pulled her legs up against her chest and rested her hands on her knees, the gun aimed at O'Donnell. "It's really time for you to shut up, O'Donnell." Then she flashed Delaney a thumbs-up, and moments later, the engines revved, the plane sped up the runway, and they were airborne.

Wayra and Illary landed in a vast savannah, beneath a sweep of sky so crisp and perfect, in air so pure, that Wayra felt certain he had hit his approximate target—twelve thousand years back, give or take a few. It was far enough back in time that it might take Dominica the rest of her existence to find her way again to the twenty-first century.

The grass around them was tall and soft, the color of celery. Dominica, still inside her host, lay between him and Illary.

"She's still got a host," Illary said.

"If Dominica releases her, we're obligated to return her host to her own time."

"I know. But her leg's broken. And she'll be crazy."

"She'll go crazy here, too. And this body doesn't belong to Dominica."

He took Illary's hand as Dominica stirred. Her eyes opened, she looked around slowly, eyes widening with horror, and rubbed her hand over her broken leg and cried out. "You . . . you can't leave me here, like this. There's nothing *here*. What have you done to me, Wayra?"

"What I should have done long ago. You'll survive here, among the hunters and gatherers."

"You may even have your own tribe," Illary said.

"Who the—" She stopped. "The hawk. *You were the hawk.*" Then, much more softly, she said, "A *shifter*? You aren't the last of your kind, Wayra? But how can—"

"The how doesn't matter. Release your host, Nica. We need to take her back."

"No." She tried to jump up, but her broken leg crumpled beneath her and she hit the ground. "She's mine. She's staying here with me. She's all that's left."

Wayra's pain was abrupt, unexpected, something from centuries ago, a residue of feeling for Dominica—not love but pity, not concern but compassion, not yearning for the past but an eagerness to put it behind him so that he could embrace the future. He crouched in front of her and put his arms around her. "Nica, Nica," he whispered. "I'm so sorry . . ." *That you moved into the darkness.*

When his arms went around her, her body tightened for a moment, tense and unyielding, then she relaxed and Dominica's essence drifted out of the top of her host's skull. The young woman slumped against Wayra, dead before he set her against the ground. Dominica hadn't bled her out; she'd simply died.

They didn't have any shovels to dig a grave for her, so he and Illary carried her to the shade of one of the few trees in sight. Dominica flitted about, shouting and diving at them as they covered the young woman in leaves.

You can't do this to me, Wayra, Dominica screamed. *You can't leave me out here. How can you be so cruel?*

Wayra ignored her and looked at Illary. "Let's find the others and head home."

"That sounds wonderful, *mi amor.*"

They held hands again. Dominica's screams echoed briefly in the air, rising and falling on a gentle breeze that flitted across the tall savannah grasses. Then even that was gone, the last vestige of his past.

Twenty-six

Five hours after they left Gainesville, the Cessna landed on a strip of grass in the middle of the Everglades. Maddie motioned O'Donnell to his feet and asked for his BlackBerry and wallet. He passed her the items without argument. She tossed the BlackBerry to Sanchez, then removed O'Donnell's federal ID and driver's license and pocketed them.

"You're about fifteen miles from the Seminole Indian reservation," she said. "If you keep walking west, you'll eventually get there."

O'Donnell glanced through windows on either side of the plane, then looked at her, at Sanchez, at Delaney. "What the fuck, man. This is the god-damn Everglades. How the hell am I—"

"You've got two feet," Delaney said. "We figure it will take you about five hours to walk to the reservation and that's if you don't get lost. By then, we'll be out of the country. And since you don't have any ID, it's probably in your best interest not to mention hungry ghosts, shapeshifters, or any of the rest of it unless you don't mind ending up in a psychiatric unit."

"It . . . it'll be dark by then," O'Donnell stammered. "Alligators and shit are out there."

"It won't be dark until six or seven," Sanchez said, and opened the cabin door. "It's not even one P.M. yet. You'll make it before dark." He handed O'Donnell a bottle of water. "You're lucky it's spring. You won't roast out there."

Maddie motioned with the gun. "Out, Mr. O'Donnell."

"Jesus," he murmured, and moved toward the open door. He stood there for a few moments, staring out at the desolation, the utter absence of anything except a dry flatness in every direction and a dome of blue sky. He glanced back, his eyes stricken with terror. "Listen, can't we—"

"No," Sanchez snapped.

"Bye-bye, O'Donnell." She cocked her weapon.

O'Donnell pointed his finger at Maddie, then Sanchez, then Delaney. *"You. And you. And you. You're fucked, all of you."*

Sanchez pressed his hand to O'Donnell's back. "You going to jump or should I push you?"

O'Donnell cast a hateful look at Sanchez, then leaped to the ground and loped away from the plane. Maddie shut the cabin door. "We're good," she called to Delaney, and she and Sanchez stepped back from the door and sat on the floor again.

Sanchez immediately started making calls—to his sister, his father. Maddie borrowed Delaney's cell to call her aunt Tesso in Ecuador.

Forty minutes later, they landed in Homestead. They had less than four hours to get to the Miami airport, where a private jet owned by an Ecuadoran church would take them to Quito. Sanchez's father, Emilio, and his sister would meet them there.

Delaney's car was in the parking lot. He drove them to Sanchez's place and said he would be back in two hours to pick them up.

Maddie, Sanchez, and Jessie got out and stood for a few moments in the driveway, watching Delaney drive away with his fellow shifters. Then Jessie barked and trotted to the front door and they hurried after her.

"What the hell should I take?" Sanchez asked, fumbling with his door keys.

"Your computer," Maddie said. "Clothes. Books. Shit, I don't know, Sanchez, what do you value most?"

"Jessie," he said, and then looked at her. "And you."

They were inside the house at that point and when he said those words, "and you," electricity raced between them, a chemistry so palpable she felt it in the roots of her teeth, the marrow of her bones. He slung an arm around her waist, his mouth met hers, and they stumbled back against the wall.

For long, strange moments, they simply held each other, then his hands moved down her back, through her hair, and his mouth slipped to her throat, her breasts, upward to her nose and eyelids, and fire burned wherever he touched her.

They stumbled back into a couch and fell onto it, kicking the cushions away, tearing at each other's clothes until they were skin to skin, bone to bone, his mouth and fingers and hands everywhere, ubiquitous, igniting such fierce desire in her that she knew it would happen too fast unless he slowed down.

She whispered, "Not so fast," and nibbled at his ear and pressed her hands against his chest, pushing him back, away from her, so she could see his face, explore it, and sink into the dark landscape of his eyes.

But suddenly, everything went haywire, she was in the attic again, when Whit had made love to Dominica, when Sam Dorset had raped her. She wrenched free of Sanchez and bolted upright and covered her face with her hands and struggled not to sob out loud.

"What?" Sanchez whispered, sitting up beside her, his hand sliding from the crown of her head and down her naked back.

"It's not you," she finally managed to say, her voice a harsh whisper. "It's—"

"Whit."

"Yes."

"He's long gone, Red."

Her hands dropped to her thighs, and she stared at them, at these hands connected to her wrists, her arms, and saw that the nails were bitten to the quick, were raw, ugly, the cuticles torn. Once upon a time, before Dominica, her nails had been long and beautiful, her cuticles soft and perfect.

"In my head, Sanchez, he's still there, Whit the fucker, Whit the perv,

Whit who actually loved Dominica in spite of everything, but he could love her only through my body. Do you have *any idea* what that's like? What I'm talking about?"

When she said this, her hand was sandwiched between his hands, and he flinched, then gasped, then doubled over, struggling for breath. "Yes," he whispered. "I get it."

Maddie suddenly understood that he grasped who she was in a way she couldn't comprehend, that she would never fully integrate into her world-view. She realized that when she suffered, so did he. When she grappled for answers, he did, too. His ability enabled him to crawl under her skin, to experience what she had, to suffer as she had suffered. She couldn't stand it, that another human being should be subjected to what had nearly broken her.

Maddie pressed her hand against the back of his head and stretched out against the couch, whispering to him, asking him, "Can you stand this? Can you take it? Do we have any sort of future together?"

When he lifted his head, when he looked at her, she saw the truth in his eyes, then heard the truth in his words: "Give me a chance, Maddie. That's all I'm asking."

A chance. What did that mean, exactly? She didn't know. It didn't matter. She had fallen in love with a man who had found her when she was possessed by Dominica and didn't have any hope of ever escaping the imprisonment within her own body. He had found her, liberated her, and here they were, two people perched at the edge of a precipice.

She drew his head toward hers, kissed him, whispered, "Make love to me, Sanchez," and it began again, her body burning with his touch, their mouths and hands everywhere. She felt him inside her head, beneath her skin, fitting himself into her bones, as if trying her on for size. He brought her to the edge repeatedly, then held her there, her body arched, his hands cupped beneath her, his tongue slipping into her, tasting her.

Shudders swept through her, she cried out and clutched his shoulders, her heart singing, and urged him inside of her. They moved swiftly, effort-lessly, their bodies locked together so tightly she couldn't tell where his skin ended and her own began.

They tumbled over the edge of that precipice together, and then they soared.

Epilogue

Each morning, Kate awakened to sunlight that spilled down the sides of magnificent peaks and spread across the city of Esperanza in dreamlike colors. Delectable scents from the kiosk around the park drifted through the open windows of the house she shared with Delaney and Rocky—freshly baked breads and pastries, cornbread patties stuffed with black beans, rice, chicken, fish, roasting on open grills. An orchestra of sounds played constantly—birdsong, a musician in the park strumming a guitar, the low hum of traffic.

For most of her first several weeks here, she felt as if she were actually inside a dream where history lived and breathed in the ancient, narrow streets, in the parks filled with monkey-puzzle trees, in the magnificent faces of the Quechua people. Some days, she wandered through the city for hours, absorbing shapes and textures, words and images and tastes. She often stopped at the outside kiosks for a tiny cup of coffee and one of the delicious pastries, tried out her paltry Spanish only to discover that the language you spoke was less important than the smile in your eyes.

She, born and raised on an island as flat as Columbus's view of the world, didn't miss the ocean. She took to the mountains like a bird to an open sky. But the altitude demanded stamina and it was weeks before she could breathe without the sensation that she was suffocating. The locals advised her to drink coca tea, but it upset her stomach. Her canine lungs were better suited to the altitude and the chill that persisted even in summer, but she felt weird trotting around town as a greyhound. Eventually, her human body adjusted.

In mid-July, Wayra arrived at the house in Old Town and said he had something to show them. He suggested they wear good hiking boots, warm jackets, and bring basic camping gear. She, Delaney, and Rocky left town with Wayra in an old VW bus. They traveled for three hours on an unpaved, precipitous road without a guardrail that twisted up the side of a mountain. The road emptied into a village at the base of the peak they would ascend. Here, they met up with Illary, Maddie, Jessie, Sanchez, and his father, Emilio, who had horses and additional supplies.

They trekked another thousand feet up the mountain, Jessie leading the way. Kate didn't know what she felt about their destination, the plateau where the stone forest and the mysterious cave were located. The cave, she thought, that supposedly held the living history of Esperanza and of the shifters. A part of her eagerly embraced discovering who and what she was now. But another part of her, perhaps the human part, didn't want to know. Her son didn't share her misgivings, but she knew Delaney did.

The transition to life in Esperanza had been more difficult for him than for any of them. It wasn't the physical aspects of life here that had proven challenging, just everything else—what you sensed and felt, that special something you tasted in the very air of Esperanza. Its history somehow felt immense, *alive*, and as a remote viewer, he sensed it more than she and Rocky.

They reached the stone forest by mid-afternoon, a barren place of rock and sky that was three miles long and a mile wide. They set up camp in the amphitheater, a spot on the plateau shielded on three sides by sheer stone cliffs that protected them from the chill and the wind. They built a fire, brought out food and cooking utensils, and Illary gave them a tour of the huge monuments of stone animals and figures, none of them indigenous to Esperanza or to this part of Ecuador.

"So this is our excursion through shifter history?" Rocky asked. "There's nothing here except rocks and cold wind."

"There's a great deal more than that, Rocky." Illary walked over to a spot between two stone sculptures—one that resembled a huge frog and the other that looked like Moby-Dick. She glanced out at the horizon, where the bright yellow sun was sinking quickly. "In a few minutes, the light will reveal a doorway between these two figures. Inside that door lies the secret of shifter history. You can enter or not, your choice."

Delaney leaned in close to Kate. "It could be anything," he whispered. "Maybe it's stuff we don't want to know."

"Maybe." She noticed that Maddie, Jessie, Sanchez, and his father hung back, that they seemed to understand the cave wasn't intended for them, that they were here to maintain the camp if and when the others went inside. "But maybe it's stuff we *should* know."

Wayra joined them, blowing into his hands to warm them. "This isn't an initiation or anything, Delaney. No one's demanding that you do this."

"Yeah, I know," Delaney said.

Kate slung an arm around Rocky's shoulders. "What do you think?"

"A big yes. We have to know, Mom. Who we are. What we are. What we were. What we may become. The truth."

Then the light hit the space between these two figures and Kate actually saw a door carved into the stone with such precision and intricacy that she went over to it and ran her fingertips around it. She glanced at Wayra, his expression frozen somewhere between belief and abject skepticism. Yet his eyes shone with passion. He had told her about the place he had gone to when he was dying, the place where Victor had healed him. This place.

She felt confident that he would enter the cave.

"Well?" Illary asked. "We have to go in while the light is on it. In another minute or two, the door will be invisible again."

Kate took Delaney's hand. "It's a gift."

"Or a curse."

"Or both."

Wayra and Rocky moved toward the door and Jessie suddenly darted after them despite Sanchez's calls and whistles for the retriever to return. Illary glanced at Kate and Delaney, her brows lifting. *Well, yes or no?*

Delaney rolled his eyes toward the sky, as if to say it was all so foolish. Yes, maybe it was. Maybe the mystery and the promise of magic and insights and wisdom was nothing more than a pipe dream. But hey, Kate thought, what was a bartender if not a purveyor of pipe dreams?

Kate dropped Delaney's hand and whispered, "Yes, absolutely yes."

And when she glanced back at Delaney, he mouthed, *What the hell,* and hurried to catch up with them.